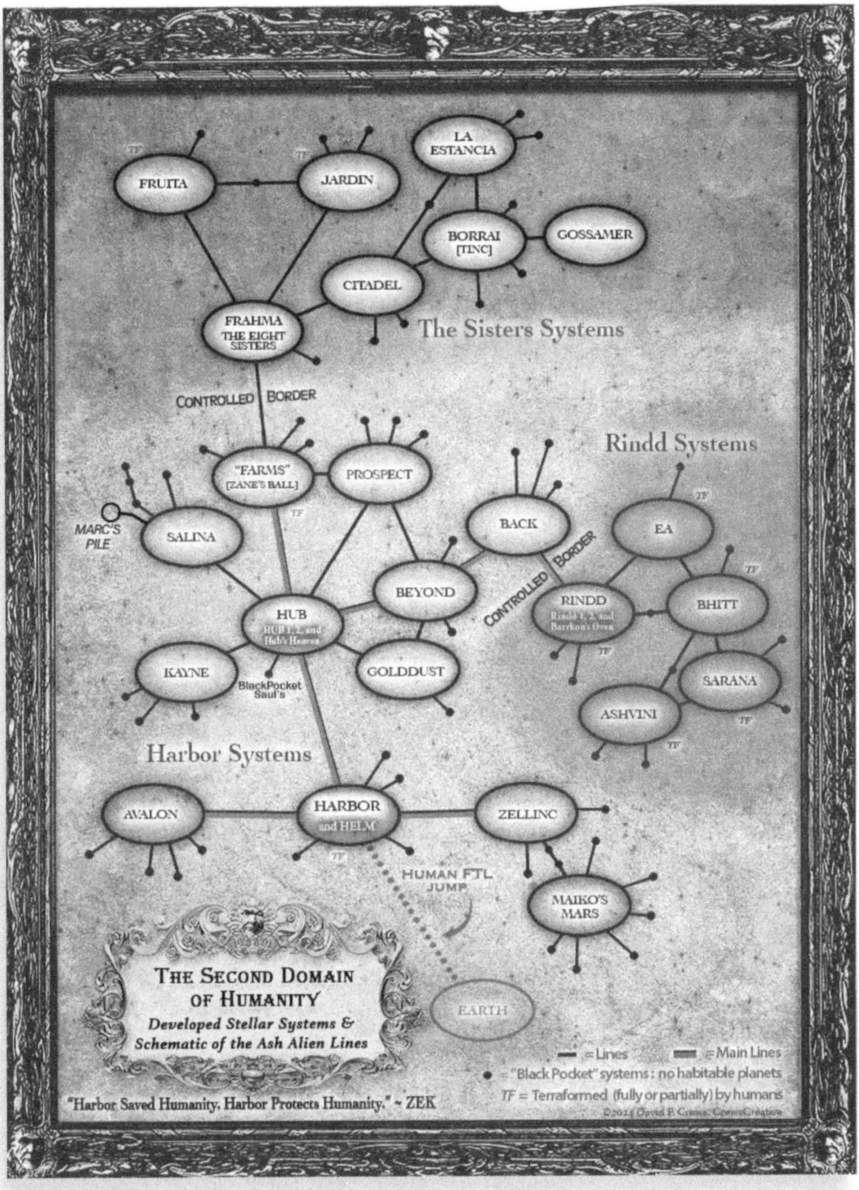

FRUITA — JARDIN — LA ESTANCIA

BORRAI [TINC] — GOSSAMER

CITADEL

FRAHMA
THE EIGHT SISTERS

The Sisters Systems

CONTROLLED BORDER

"FARMS"
[ZANE'S BALL]

PROSPECT

Rindd Systems

MARC'S PILE

SALINA

BACK

EA

CONTROLLED BORDER

BEYOND

RINDD
Rindd 1, 2, and
Barrkon's Own

BHITT

HUB
HUB 1, 2, and
Hub's Heaven

KAYNE

BlackPocket
Saul's

GOLDDUST

ASHVINI

SARANA

Harbor Systems

AVALON

HARBOR
and HELM

ZELLINC

HUMAN FTL
JUMP

MAIKO'S
MARS

EARTH

THE SECOND DOMAIN OF HUMANITY
*Developed Stellar Systems &
Schematic of the Ash Alien Lines*

TF (notations throughout map)

━━ = Lines   ▬▬ = Main Lines
● = "Black Pocket" systems : no habitable planets
TF = Terraformed (fully or partially) by humans

"Harbor Saved Humanity. Harbor Protects Humanity." ~ ZEK

© 2024 David P. Crewe, CreweCreative

Xenoplague

by David P. Crews

JaguarFeather Publishing
Las Cruces, New Mexico, USA

Published by
JaguarFeather Publishing
Las Cruces, New Mexico

www.DavidPCrews.com/author
See the website for a full-color reference Map for the story, and more related content.

ISBN: 978-0-9641859-2-0

Publisher's Cataloging-in-Publication Data:
Crews, David P., author
Xenoplague / by David P. Crews
Description: First trade paperback original edition | JaguarFeather Publishing | Las Cruces, NM, 2024

BISAC: FIC028010   FICTION / Science Fiction / Action & Adventure
       FIC028030   FICTION / Science Fiction / Space Opera
       FIC009050   FICTION / Fantasy / Paranormal

First Edition – Printed in the United States of America

For Mom.
"My imagination really did run away with me this time, didn't it?"
Rest in peace and love.

Xenoplague

Prologue

Harbor Year 1

"Colors! The big ship is displaying colors! Everyone save your data streams. You getting this, Jan?"

Paul Bennett couldn't believe his eyes. He punched in commands as fast as his fingers would go, making sure his own data feeds were recording.

"Yes, streaming to archive," she said. "What's happening, Paul? Ash Alien ships don't generate colors!"

Three days earlier, the immense, gray Ash Alien ship had suddenly appeared in a close, low Earth orbit. Six other, much smaller, standard Harbor Colony military vessels trailed it like a cluster of tiny fish.

"Any word from those Harbor ships?"

He glanced at Jan, seated to his left. Both of them were on the raised rear platform of the central control room inside the lunar farside's Schwarzschild Science Station.

"Nothing yet," she said. "You want me to hail them?"

"No. Let's keep normal comm and data traffic with Earth only. Threats against Earth could become threats against us here on the

Moon. I'd rather not remind them just now that we exist."

He stared at the image screens as the imposing alien ship flashed and rolled through bright primary colors across its normally gray surfaces in an amazing color show. What in the world could it mean? The Ash Aliens were so-named for the *lack* of coloration of their countless metal artifacts and derelict ships. Every single object ever found, from their ships to buildings to power supplies was unrelentingly dull gray. Nothing was painted or colored.

It looked to Paul like these Harbor colonists were eager to take advantage of the recent calamitous environmental upheavals and social unrest on Earth, where a new and hastily cobbled-together world government was nominally in charge. As soon as they had arrived with their massive ship, their Harbor System Exec began issuing direct threats. He claimed the vastly powerful Ash Alien weapon ship was under his control, and they would use it to force Earth's hand. He repeated their old demands: formal independence from Earth, the release of the embargo on Earth's faster-than-light technology, and their relentless petition for new colonists for the more than twenty Harbor colony worlds ranging out along the ancient AA network of habitable star systems–worlds that still needed workers and settlers.

Paul tapped into the Operations Manager's comm.

"Torrie, I want you to suspend all rail launches for now. I don't want any traffic leaving the Moon until we see what these guys are really up to."

The lunar stations were not weaponized, so everyone here and out at the old Mars station as well, could only passively monitor the situation.

The Harborites had probably anticipated immediate compliance in the face of their threatening new ship, but Earth authorities refused to capitulate and flatly told them to go home. The Exec's threats to use their fearsome weapon became more anxious. More and more shrill. Then, with no warning, Earth cut off all communications.

The Exec intensely redoubled the colonist's demands. With

no further reaction from Earth, they had given up their low-orbit position and moved to a higher, geostationary orbit. Now, the alien ship was suddenly producing these vivid colors, glowing in multiple bands–hues that flashed back and forth across its spherical nose and ribbon-like gray rings. It was entirely novel.

Did the swirling colors indicate that they were actually about to back up their threat? Powerful beam weapons and other dangerous tech were certainly associated with the ancient ships, but excepting accidents by the careless or witless, no AA machine or artifact had ever posed an explicit, inherent danger to humans.

"That large front nozzle is glowing red," Jan said.

"Can you get us a closer look? Let's see if we can pick up any data on its energy emissions."

"It's pretty far away from the sat, but I'll try."

This Ash Alien ship was some ten times larger and radically divergent in design from all the many thousands of derelict ships the human colonists of the Harbor Systems had discovered scattered on planets and moons all along the Ash Alien Lines–the long-abandoned network of habitable worlds the aliens had established perhaps millions of years ago. Many such ships were still serviceable and benign enough that the Harbor colonists could hybridize them with human tech, militarize them with the still viable and powerful AA energy beam weapons they discovered, and even fly them here to Earth. They had to use human-made FTL systems for that jump, since Earth was not on the AA Lines network. Six such Harbor hybrid ships were now in orbit here alongside the extraordinary new ship. Five smaller Earth Governmental ships watched them closely.

"This is the max zoom I can get from that orbital cam," Jan said as she adjusted the scan interface.

The new ship had a large AA engine on the aft surrounded by spiked arms of unknown purpose. Its spindle-like midsection was almost hidden by five surrounding hoops of flat metal that seemed not to be physically attached. Its front featured a huge spherical unit with a massive nozzle or exhaust aperture. It certainly *looked* like it meant business. All of it had been the normal plain gray before, but now it was fully engulfed in the spectacular animated color banding.

"Look! The big ship's moving again, rotating," Paul said. "The other Harbor ships are dropping back."

"The big nozzle is heating up fast! It's bright red!" Jan yelped. "It has to be a final bluff. They're not really going to fire the damned thing, are they?"

He could only shake his head and stare at the screens.

He thought he saw the entire ship undulate slightly as the color bands sped past and into each other, encasing the vessel inside a neon cartouche of light. The hues strengthened and flew faster and faster until they blended into a bright flare, so searing white that he and Jan squinted and instinctively looked away from it, even though their view was only on monitor screens. A final pulse warped the ship, then a wide columnar beam of pure energy instantly erupted from the aperture on the prow. It looked like a fire hose nozzle had connected to the interior of a star! The white beam retched out from the Ash Alien craft and struck the Earth directly.

"A hit!" Paul yelled, ". . . west of Ecuador in the Pacific!" Old animations of an asteroid impact and doomed dinosaurs flashed through his mind. He heard Jan suck in her breath.

Everyone in the station's command center was silent. All eyes were transfixed by the dimensional satellite video feeds showing the Earth. Then, their relayed automated mission-support data streams, constantly beamed up from Los Alamos and Guiana, stopped. Multiple screens connected to that data stream flickered in synch, then went black. Murmurs and a few cries came from the thirty or so control crew working the stations in front of him, but Paul was too stunned to move or look away from the view of Earth.

The Harbor colonists' ship comms had been silent since their last broadcast of demands before they moved to the higher orbit. Now, as the awful eruption continued, fragments of distorted, panicked voices came through, ". . . give it to me! . . . it off . . . the star . . . this . . .*what* beam? You foo . . ." Then static. Then silence.

The ship's horrific discharge lanced the Earth below like a white-hot needle, its column obscuring the impact site but illuminating a towering cloud of vapor and debris. Immense shock waves radiated outward across sea and land like ripples from a stone tossed into a lake. Paul couldn't take his eyes off of it.

"Time since impact?" Paul's words sounded flat through his gritted teeth.

"Four minutes, fifteen," a technician replied, his voice strained but quiet.

The Galapagos, just on the sunrise limb, were obscured or consumed. The western half of South America was visibly compressing and undulating. Paul knew those waves would roll on, mercilessly, and collide with themselves somewhere on the other side of the globe, causing more chaos. Nothing would survive this.

Two of Earth's ships were firing their own Ash Alien-derived beam weapons directly onto the attacking ship, but their energies simply disappeared into the colored bands, apparently absorbed by the gigantic vessel.

Fifteen minutes in, someone in the room below uttered a long, moaning expletive. Paul jerked, realizing he had been in a kind of shocked trance. He made himself release his grip on the chair and turned to Jan. Her face was white, a pale and rigid mask.

"The other Harbor ships?" His voice cracked.

Her hands moved automatically to take the scan for him, her eyes flicking down and back up, reluctant to look away from the main screens. "All but two retreated toward the FTL jump zone, off-ecliptic and out-system. No sign of the other three Earth ships that were in pursuit. They may have been destroyed."

"No comms from Earth?" he asked, knowing it was hopeless.

"Nothing, Paul."

One of the support staffers, a man Paul only knew as Jaimes, suddenly ran up the aisle along the right wall, heading for the rear exit. His face was red.

"My son is in Sydney! It's not gone that far yet. I have to warn him!" His voice trailed off as he left the control room.

A cold chill left Paul feeling vacant. He sighed and opened the general comm.

"Everyone stay on your systems. Our lives may depend on these data streams. Good job. Stay with me. I know this is hard, but I need your professionalism now to continue to gather as much information as possible. We don't know how this will play out for us." He paused and surveyed the frightened faces of those of his control crew who had turned to look at him. "Science and services people, stay calm and stay clear of the operations here. Let's do what we can."

The ship's appalling white-hot thread continued to stab the ocean, never varying in strength, nor altering its target spot, some five hundred kilometers west of Quito.

An hour passed and the control room grew oppressive in a pallor of heat, sweat, and fear. Then, without warning, the beam stopped. The earth below it glowed and convulsed in a visible throb. The western continents seemed roughly the same, but strange colors erupted here and there as shimmering fractal movements subtly altered the oceans and landforms. Paul stared at them, fascinated by the strange effects.

João Mendez, one of the lead chem scientists, linked into Paul's side comm.

"What if that thing turns on *us*, Paul? What are we gonna do?"

"I don't know, João. Let's just hope they leave us alone for now. We don't have any warships out here, and I don't think they'd do us any good if we did."

It was hard to keep his focus on the imagery and data while dealing with occasional but continuing outbursts and demands, mostly from civilian workers and science staffers. Everyone wanted to try to contact their families or work groups back on Earth. Entirely futile now, of course, and even they knew it. It was an understandable reaction.

Paul made certain the smaller lunar facilities were monitoring the events and he sent updates to the tiny and now surely doomed Mars station personnel. Then he turned his full attention back to the video feeds of the ruined Earth. He was not just gawking at the destruction, but closely studying the landforms as they changed. There was something odd about them, but he couldn't quite put his finger on it. Maybe it was those gently morphing fractal patterns, showing up now on the African coast, and glinting with strange webworks of colored lights on into the nighttime darkness to the east.

Twenty minutes later, Jan edged up to Paul's seat. "This is nuts!" she said, startling him. He turned to face her.

"What do you mean?"

"Where's the dust and debris? There should have been a vast cloud of it, Paul! That first blast of it settled immediately. It should have been freaking hot and have encased the planet by now. It should last for years–no, centuries! Where is it? How can it all be settling out so rapidly?"

Of course! That was it! That's what was bothering him. He cocked his head to one side.

"You're right! It doesn't make sense. It has to be more of the Ash Alien tech at work. Maybe the Harborites found the old aliens. Maybe they have their help in this. Maybe they don't. Whatever the truth is, Jan, I think that ship is something more than a weapon."

"More than a weapon?" She stared at him with a haggard face, sweat flattening her short blonde hair. "That looks like a pretty goddamn good weapon if you ask me."

"Yes, of course, but your observation is important. There's not enough debris cloud and it *is* clearing far too quickly. Look. I've been watching the coloration. Look at North Africa. See how it's greening now? Maybe those Harbor Military guys requested help from their new ET friends and got a whole lot more than they expected. Maybe it's something else entirely. But, there may be some hope for us yet."

"Hope? We're stuck here on the Moon with six months supplies," Jan said. "I don't think Earth is coming to fetch us or bring us anything ever again, do you?"

"No, not that. The Earth we knew is gone, but there may be a new

Earth to go home to."

"What? You think this is going to settle down enough for us to go back?"

"Yes . . . yes . . . I think there's a chance."

"There's no one and nothing left! All the people, Paul! Billions dead. All of civilization! The plants, the animals, the cities–all gone! What about radiation and atmosphere?"

Paul turned to her, his face veiled in exhaustion. "Jan, the Harbor folks wanted independence from Earth and more colonists to build up their own worlds. Well, this ship–this thing, whatever it is, has certainly given them their independence now, but they've destroyed their entire supply of potential colonists in the process. Idiots! I don't know if they truly found the old aliens or what, but one thing is clear to me now. As cataclysmic as this is, that Ash Alien ship is not a doomsday weapon. Its purpose is not to utterly destroy.

"Everything down there is settling into a new pattern with stunning rapidity, Jan. Think what that might mean."

Jan stared at the monitors again and her face opened up a bit from the strained grimace she had worn since the blast began. He leaned toward the main monitor.

"You see it, don't you? You said so yourself. The skies are clearing artificially fast and the land is not just being broken up. It's reorga-nizing–mutating. Devastated, yes, but not destroyed. Jan, it's being *transformed*."

Part One

The Faces of XEK

Chapter One
Harbor Year 1247

The small cargo ship lurched and rang with a dull reverberation. Alarms wailed. Marc 54Arons sat up sharply against his restraints and jerked his head from screen to screen to see what had happened just as he made their routine exit from the huge, ancient space Gate into the Farms System.

A random rock hit? What?

The shipbot data screens showed that one of his aft cooling arrays had been shattered, but with no environmental breach of the ship so far.

The comms lit up and started making noise. Several tense voices, all with Sisters System accents, were almost overlapping.

"Three ships and closing fast! First one's still firing!"

"That third BlackMil is headed your way!"

"A fourth ship just exited from Sisters. Looks like a cargo."

That would be me, Marc thought.

He quick-scanned for any other ships out here in the system fringe. Kera 17Millies, strapped into the seat next to him, was alert, too. She gave him an alarmed look before laying in a command sequence for the thrusters, correcting for the spin they'd gained from the hit. He felt a quick note of satisfaction at her competence and speed.

It gave him a few seconds to take in their current chaos after emerging from the huge, not quite physical, circular orifice that was the alien Gate connecting into Farms System from the Eight Sisters of Frahma. His scans showed their ship, highlighted and centered on-screen with three of the Sisters ships arrayed around the beaconed horizon of the Gate itself. These Sisters patrols were always stationed as monitors for the controlled border here on the Farms side, maintaining a centuries-long guard on their secretive solar system's only connection to the rest of human space. What was normally a quiet and boring duty was suddenly upset as they scattered in the face of the beam weapon attacks from the other three ships now displayed on-screen: some of ZEK's BlackMils from the human seat of power in the Harbor System.

"Why in ZEK's Faces are Harbor military shooting at Sisters ships?" Kera said as she called up the attack ship's ident tags. "It's crazy! Wait. . . those aren't BlackMil. They're Suite Blue's!"

Marc called up Kera's scan. The largest of the three Blue Guard ships involved in the attack had turned and was heading his way, rapidly blooming on his screens.

"They assume we're Sisters, too, coming in through the Gate," Marc growled. He reached for the ship's external comms. It was time to squeal and move this tub.

"Blue Guards. Blue Guards. Do not fire! I am cargo only. Repeat. Cargo only. Zane's Ball registry–inbound with neutral cargo for Farms. This is Marc 54Arons. Do not fire!"

He put the callout on loop and grabbed his main helm controller. Cargo ships aren't built for tactical maneuvers, but like many other middie pilots, his had a few extra Ash Alien thrusters hidden in the pipes and recesses of its blocky complex, delicacies he had managed to extract from some illegal AA artifacts he'd dug up a few years back.

"Unbelievable. What do they think they're doing!" Kera snapped.

Her short brown bangs bounced once on her forehead as she turned. "One of the Sisters patrol ships is disabled but intact. The other two are heading back into the Gate . . . and gone."

As he maneuvered them "up" from the system's ecliptic, heading zenith vector to try to get out of the fray, Marc felt the g's and the tension settle in his stomach. "At least the Sisters folks on Florinda will know what's happened. Anibale has been agitating out here for the past year, but I didn't think he'd resort to a physical attack! It's harassment. He could have wiped them out. That has to be his ship coming for us now."

Kera shot him a worried look, then turned back to the comms and data screens.

A moment later, a man's scowling visage appeared, confirming Marc's suspicions. The face was handsome in a dark, severe way. He wore a deep blue mantle, piped with golden cording and a silver band formed the margin of his blue velvet cap. The band was embedded with a line of colorful gemstones. His black eyes glared and his long black hair, impractical for space and a flagrant symbol of his position, flowed out of the cap and was tied back to keep it out of the way during flight.

Anibale, Prime Blue–the very embodiment of the Elites class. As the head of Suite Blue, he was probably the strongest competitor to become the next ZEK, the supreme power for all of the many Harbor planetary systems.

Marc frowned. You don't remember me, Elite, but I know you. Not the first time you've come after me and mine.

The man's voice boomed from the comm. "You have very bad timing, middie Marc, pilot of a Harbor cargo vessel. Bad choice of friends, as well. Trading with the Sisters folk? What do you have on board, I wonder? A few *gray* trinkets, perhaps? A Sisters rabble-rouser hiding in one of your bunks? You are moving quite rapidly for a neutral cargo vessel!"

Marc stared at him, stone-faced.

"Standard cargo, Prime. Only myself and my copilot onboard."

Marc signaled Kera to transmit. "We're sending a copy of the manifest. What in ZEK's Faces is going on out here? Why are you attacking these ships?"

Anibale seemed taken aback, then he gave a grim smile. "Not your concern, middie. All you need to know is that you will answer to me for any illegal activities or cargo. For the present, proceed to Farms. I don't have time to deal with you."

With a dismissive gesture, Anibale disappeared as the screen switched to a Suite Blue emblem. The giant cruiser changed thrust and receded toward the Gate.

Marc sighed and made a quick re-evaluation of all the cargo he *was* carrying. Trade with the reclusive Sisters folk was not that unusual and ships like his often made the transit from Farms to the Sisters System and then back, passing through the Sisters Gate here. The Gate itself was just one of a network of these apparently indestructible ancient constructs of the Ash Aliens, now linking twenty-four habitable solar systems containing all the worlds that had become mankind's. These Gates and their connecting Lines leading to the other systems were presumed to be millions of years old–utterly abandoned by their creators. No one had ever met a live Ash Alien and most thought them extinct for a very long time indeed. Marc thought that if he ever met one, he'd thank them for providing the space subway system for all these useful worlds and the means to travel between them with such ease.

Marc started to stand, but immediately realized he could not. Both of his hands were locked to the arms of his seat. He shuddered and looked down at them. During the crisis, they had morphed again, expanding to twice their normal size and glowing a dull red. His Curse. It did not hurt, of course; it never did. In fact, it felt good–powerful, actually–but he hated the way it came when it wanted to and not when he needed it. He hated all the troubles and pains it had caused himself and others in his life, but he tried not to think too much about that. He hated for Kera to see it now, but she did.

"Marc! What's wrong with your hands?"

14

He felt his face redden with exasperation. "It's nothing. I'll be fine in a minute." With an exhaled huff, he relaxed back into the chair and waited for the hands to revert to normal so he could unclinch them.

Kera stared at him, her eyes narrow and her forehead scrunched into lines of worry.

"That's not nothing, pilot. What the hell? You need the medbot?"

"No. Look, it's just something I can do. It's not dangerous." His hands returned to normal and he raised them, gripped them together, and cracked his knuckles. Kera flinched at the sound. "I'll tell you more about it later," he muttered as he wiggled his fingers. "Did we record that exchange with Prime Blue?"

Kera paused, still looking askance at him. "Yeah, I got it."

"Might need it for evidence later. He's plain crazy," Marc said. "What is he thinking, stirring up all the old troubles with the Sisters? ZEK will have his hide for a rug!"

She broke her gaze and glanced at the scan screens. "Well, he's probably thinking about making his moves on ZEK. Suite Blue has been building its fortune for a long time now. He's greedy for the big prize."

"Maybe so, but there's got to be more to this. It's just too radical a move," he said.

"Probably." She looked over as a marker appeared on the displays. "That last disabled Sisters ship has regained power. It just exited back home through the Gate."

"That's a relief. Let's store all our vids here and also feed them down to my secure comps in Tabletown. I need to document what Anibale did and detail the Sisters ships' damages and our own."

She nodded and Marc turned his attention to the process of lining up their injured ship for Farms Station, the geo-synched docking and trade facility above Farms itself, the main planet in this system, and their home.

Marc killed the loop message and started their turn toward Farms when the speakers suddenly came to life with a sound Marc had only heard a very few times.

Xenoplague

"Zzzzzzziiipppppp . . . zzzzpp . . . zzzzz . . . pppp . . . zzz" The thin sounds crackled throughout the ship, almost as if they weren't coming through the speakers at all.

"A Zip ship! Really close!" Kera said. "ZEK's Faces! What next?"

Marc shook his head. "Don't know. What are Zips doing out here? Mixed up in the attack some way?"

"No telling," she said.

Zips were a true mystery; the only live aliens ever encountered. No one had ever seen one, talked to one, or figured out what they are or what they want. Marc's scans couldn't focus very well on them, but that unmistakable "zipping" blasting through all the RF channels always announced their presence. They show up from time to time in vaguely organic-looking ships emitting that typical sound, fly around or through, and then disappear again. They've never done any harm to anyone in all the centuries since the xenoplague, but many fear them and blame them for what happened to old Earth in ancient times. Not too many superstitions left in our modern society these days, Marc thought, but that's one of them.

The sounds faded out and Kera looked at him with one brow lifted over her dark eyes. Marc shrugged and she shook her head, then they got back to their tasks.

After a long and thankfully quiet transit into the interior of Farms System, they arrived at the Station. It was quite large compared to orbital Stations on other worlds because it was designed to handle sizable quantities of outgoing agricultural shipments. Also, due originally to that bulky food cargo, the Station was the upper terminus of a ground-to-orbit cable-based elevator. These days, most of the cargo handling functions had been replaced by ground-based rail launch systems which could handle larger and more frequent loads, but the old elevator was still here and now trafficked personnel more than grains. Marc found it more practical than a lander and he liked riding it. He could see the glint of one of the elevator capsules descending the lower cables to Tabletown as he aligned their ship to Station's approach lanes. Warning lights dotted the elevator's upper utility cables stretching out to an unmanned counterweight as far above the Station as the mostly green planet was below. He and Kera docked their ship out at the Station transfer perimeter and shuttled into the main Station dock.

Marc was surprised to see one of ZEK's large BlackMil warships parked closer in. It set his nerves on edge.

———————————————————

A large group of middies, gathered in the Station's docking zone, stared at the screens and glanced repeatedly at Marc and Kera.

"Did you guys see all that?" Marc said, signing in on the register. "Harassment from Helm is one thing, but shooting!"

Kera was looking the dock crowd over. The in-bound checker, a guy Marc knew, looked back at him and shook his head a bit as if to say, what did you expect? Then, he grinned at the two of them.

"So, what's it like to get shot up by one of the most powerful Suite leaders in Harbor?"

Marc grunted. "At least it *was* an open attack, not like what they usually do to us. All right, Dayl, give me my manifest. I've got to get down to Tabletown and arrange some repairs. Suite Blue's Elites better come up with an interesting reason not to pay for them this time."

"Good luck with that," Dayl said dryly as he keyed in the request. "Weird to hear those Zips out there. Rarely see 'em in Farms System. Their signal bursts messed up our comps for a while."

He leaned closer to them and spoke more quietly, "Better go careful downstairs, Marc. You, too, Kera. A lot more BlackMils have arrived on-world since you left. They've been harassing people right and left, a *lot* more than usual. Some people have gone missing and there've even been some overtly violent incidents around the ground docks."

"Thanks," Marc said, giving him a single nod. "I'll do that."

"Something else you might be interested in, Marc. There are some

Teachers around. A speaking event is on for tonight if you want to attend."

Marc raised a brow as he took his manifest and glanced at Kera. She frowned at Dayl. "May have to check that out. Thanks again."

He started to lead them toward the elevator station, but Kera spotted someone on the other side of the platform, a swarthy, bulky man, who glowered as he made eye contact with her. The guy was a ZELLINC trader she had been dealing contraband goods with for a while. She took a deep breath and Marc watched her expression change from the open, pleasant face he liked to a mask of unease, mixed with distaste.

"Go on down and check your place, Marc. I have to arrange a few transactions up here before I can come."

"Of course. Meet me at Pim's tonight?"

Kera shot him a quick, terse smile, but her eyes lit up. "Sure. I'll see you there around sunset."

Marc tried to relax as the elevator transit took the couple of hours it did to make its way down the cables to Tabletown, the main city of Farms and Marc's home when he got to be at home. It was mid-morning here and the deep greens and yellow-greens of the flat ground below were beautiful in their own pastoral way.

Farms, everyone calls it. Appropriate name for a planet almost perfectly suited for agriculture once the terraforming efforts paid off some eight or nine hundred years ago. They named it Zane's Ball when the first survey expedition found this system with its one larger planet. The world had a couple of shallow seas, but its land mass was mostly covered with soft, pulverized lava flows. The land was so flat and dark that the team teased their leader, Johann Zane, about finding an eight-ball in space, referring to some ancient Earth game, and the name stuck for a while. It was a name not as appropriately descriptive these days with all of the small world's vast green agricultural areas, towns, and the elevator. To everyone now, it was just Farms.

A system news alert on Marc's hand comp interrupted his uneasy reverie. He activated it just as the harsh voice of a Harbor Elite was addressing everyone in Farms System on all channels–a voice he had heard rather recently.

"... these secretive Sisters meddlers are spreading their dangerous ideas and insulting Harbor and ZEK himself with their endless refusals to accept our laws and higher callings for humanity! We will not tolerate their insolence and tricks. Do not be deceived by the Sisters' calm manner. Harbor saved humanity. Lawlessness invites danger to us all! Xenoplague is real and may appear again at any time!

"We have and will continue to stir this out-system pot vigorously and uncover the truth!"

Anibale again, ranting about the old differences between the Harbor and Sisters Systems. The guy was a hard-core traditionalist, for sure. His voice was irritating. This time, though, he might have gone too far for ZEK's liking.

Marc smiled and muttered to the otherwise empty elevator cabin, "And I'll be happy to provide the proof."

The elevator's equatorial ground terminus and trade center were anchored on a low rock plateau overlooking the shallow Sea of Rainbows and the fishing marinas to the east. It was surrounded on its other sides by Tabletown's business and governmental buildings. Marc took the first available tram to his home in the northernmost district called Padd's Docks. There were only a handful of others on the tram with him, all of whom looked either nervous or listless and kept to themselves.

As he passed through the city, Marc was shocked to see how much had changed in the several months since he and Kera had set out on their latest trade run. Dayl was right. ZEK's BlackMil toughs openly roamed the streets with cadres of local PurpleMil militia in tow. Town citizens seemed tense or peeved. Many shops were closed and groups had formed outside when the military was present. He passed one cluster of unlucky middies working under a BlackMil armed guard. They were scrubbing anti-Elite graffiti from a prominent city wall. Another group of about ten or fifteen citizens had been cuffed and were being quick-marched somewhere for reasons he could not imagine. A flash-view down a building-lined street gave him a glimpse of a crowd of people brawling in an intersection.

This increasing disquiet and tension just didn't feel right, here in his own, normally placid, hometown.

Marc's place was an old stand-alone house made of composites with a roof of recycled metal shingles from the nearby industrial docks and cargo launches. It was small and nondescript on the outside, just one of dozens of similar places in this older and more humble residential sector, but it was also discreet and he liked that it wasn't directly connected to anyone else's living space. Ship life made one appreciate such things.

The house was situated just at the edge of the grain fields with a northward view out to a hazy agricultural infinity. He missed the empty and expansive deserts of his youth on Salina and this view, although green, gave him a visual sense of wide open spaces that he could savor when he wasn't flying.

Marc touched the door's bioscanner and heard the alarm beep off as the seal released. A wide shelf lined the entry hallway, holding a few trinkets and mementos from his travels. He passed his hand over a dimensional photograph of his parents, causing them to smile at him. Father tilted his head, eyes crinkling, and Mother's voice said, "I love you, Son." He paused as feelings of longing, regret, and anger washed over him. He touched the image of her face with a finger, making it shimmer, then walked slowly into the rest of the house.

He asked the bedroom window to open and a cool breeze from the fields freshened the close air of the room. He was still in his travel suit, an overall of tight-woven synthetics that also served as his space suit undergarment, but the bed was too tempting. He stretched himself back onto it and brought the extra pillow to his face. It still held a faint trace of Kera's scent from the last time she was here.

They had connected as business colleagues and as friends and had been on enough trade runs together for him to be comfortable with her, but he still couldn't pin down his real feelings. She was smart, attractive, and very competent in her co-piloting work onboard ship as well as in her true forte: the tricky world of selling and making cargo deals, but Marc found himself reluctant to try to deepen their relationship. He told himself he didn't want either of them to get hurt.

Any kind of settled relationship would certainly be tricky. He'd always be flying his ship, yet Kera had talked about wanting to settle on Farms as a legit merchant or in some other role that would provide her security and social status and power–maybe even becoming involved in the political scene. She certainly had ambition and he felt she could likely attain what she was after.

Part of it, too, was that Kera was odd and secretive about her own life and history, but then he knew he was also reluctant to open up about his own secrets, especially about the Curse. He was still dismayed and embarrassed that it had acted up at the Sisters Gate. In certain situations, his hands could suddenly change shape and size, rapidly morphing into energetic, high-strength extremities. They could also give him fits and complications like locking onto his chair.

His Curse had been with him all of his life, and his father had had something of it, too. Hereditary weirdness. Dangerous weirdness. It could be quirky and unreliable, but it had also empowered him to save lives, including his own. At times, it had cost him dearly.

With no expectations of it ever doing so, he wished it would just fade away. He dreaded its random eruption in social settings or in situations where it might prove to be a deadly liability. He kept to himself most of the time because he feared these things. But now, Kera was within the borders of his life and she had witnessed it.

So, how do I explain myself to her?

Lying on his back, he tried to think it through, but fell into a nap instead. His comm woke him up. It was Dayl again.

"Marc. Are you going to the Teacher's meeting tonight?"

"Oh . . . yeah, Dayl. Where's it going to be?"

"Pim's Affliction has that big party room in the warehouse next door. He's supposed to be there just after dark. See you there, maybe?"

"Sure, that's good. I'm meeting Kera at Pim's anyway. I don't think she likes the Sisters Teachers very much, though."

"Well, bring her in if she'll come. She's a middie, too, and we're all suffering this Elite abuse together. Maybe she'll discover a new way to view things."

"Yeah, I'll try. Thanks, Dayl."

Chapter Two

Once the hot Farms sun began to set, Marc sealed the house and headed toward the storage yards. As he crossed a roadway lined with industrial shops and some noisy bars, Kera came out of a side street and strolled confidently up beside him. She was wearing an unusual (for her) brightly colored cloth strap over her short brown hair. He gave her a grin and she flashed her green eyes his way.

"Hey, I fancy a man who takes a shot from Prime Blue!" Kera poked him hard in the rear. "Glad they didn't get you here!"

"Very funny. No, the idiot didn't get my aft, just my aft cooler."

Kera put her hand in his as they walked toward Pim's Affliction, one of their favorite establishments. "Now, is that any way to talk about Prime Blue? He might get touchy about being called an idiot."

"All right, then. Damned idiot."

She looked directly at him. "He kind of spooked you, didn't he?"

Marc smiled a bit. "Well, he did hit us right out of the Gate." He paused. "You were really quick on the response, Kera. I appreciate that."

"Just doing what needed to be done. You really questioned his motives directly, though. It was kind of fun to see his reaction. The big stuffed shirt!"

"It's not the first time we've met."

"Really? Want to tell me?"

Marc looked away. "Maybe. Maybe sometime. Let's just say I have issues with the guy and his bruisers. Hey . . . what about those Zips shooting through there? What do you think they wanted with all that?"

Kera took his arm and steered him toward Pim's entrance.

"ZEK knows, I guess . . . but probably not."

Marc pretended to resist her guidance, then gave in, causing her to laugh. He said, "Let's get something to drink, then I want to hear this Teacher who's supposed to talk tonight."

She let go of his arm. "Sisters Teachers unnerve me."

"I know, but it's just talking. Why not come listen for a bit? You can leave if you want."

It was almost dark when they entered Pim's and the speaker had not shown up yet. A fairly large group of middies were inside. Dock workers mixed with warehouse staffers, agricultural crews, and some more clerical types from the town center, had gathered, spilling through Pim's main door. Marc even noticed a few academics spicing up this particular rough stew tonight. No BlackMils or Purples, thank luck–at least none visible right now. Just a gaggle of middie men and women, all a bit energized and restless.

Middies. The folks in the Sisters reject the term. What would the worlds be like if we weren't all middies or the Elites weren't Elites?

A couple of drinks later, two men approached their table. A mousy-looking man held himself behind an older, bigger one who Marc recognized as Harr Bolsin from Terra Verde, Farm's other main city. Harr was large and had a square jaw. He was known for being quite proud of his looks even though he was a coarse lout.

"Hey-yeh. Kera Sweet," he said. "I was hoping you were back in Tabletown. Those last motors we got were no good. The company

24

can't use 'em. I'm gonna have to get a refund from you."

"Well, Har, as you can see, I'm not working right now, but you did buy those as-is. That's the way it goes with unknown AA items. Might work, might not. Buyer takes the risk, and sometimes gets the big reward, too."

"Yeh, well, my boss doesn't like it when I waste his money, Sweetie, but maybe we can make other arrangements." He leered at her. Kera snorted and turned her chair away from him, but Har put his hand on her arm and turned her back around. The other guy sidled in close behind Har, not saying a word.

Without even thinking about it, Marc reached out with his right hand and gripped Har's extended arm. His hand slightly increased in size, becoming a fat fist. He felt his fingers digging into Har's flesh. Har gave Marc a startled look as if he'd noticed him for the first time.

"Hey-yeh!" he grunted. Kera shook her arm away from him.

"She said she's not working now," Marc said. "Perhaps you've had a little too much to drink already. Let's all talk about this another time, right?"

Marc let go of his arm. Har gave him a venomous look but backed off, stumbling into the smaller man behind him. That one yelped and jumped back.

Har turned to look at Kera again. "You owe me now. I'll be in touch with you." He smirked and pointed a finger at her, then he turned, grabbed his companion's shirtsleeve, and stalked off.

"Creep," Marc said.

Kera smiled at him, but her eyes were tight and troubled. "Just one of my many gracious customers. He's filthy. I get to put up with his kind all the time."

"Unpleasant work. And dangerous."

"Yeah, well, since I had your help, I didn't have to pull my gun. You didn't seem to need one, eh?"

"What do you mean?"

"I saw your hand grip, Marc. We have to talk about this."

Marc felt his face redden. "I know. I'll tell you what I can about it, but it's time to go see about that meeting. They're opening up the big room next door."

She huffed, then said, "All right. Go on in. I have to go make a call. I'll meet you inside."

"Going to threaten his boss?" Marc grinned at her.

She smiled, but her eyes were still stormy. "Something like that."

Marc passed through the double doors into the large room. Others were making their way in, but it was still mostly empty. He passed in front of a comms screen showing a Harbor-wide newsfeed of live proceedings from the Great Seat auditorium on Helm, the center of all governmental and military power throughout Harbor Systems. He stopped to watch it for a while until Kera could catch back up to him.

Helm. The legendary and extravagant metallic moonlet, built to serve as the center of government for all human worlds. It orbited Harbor, humanity's first-found world and home of the Elites. Harbor had been the first planet to be humanly terraformed. Children were taught that Helm was like the helm of a great ship: the ship comprising the Second Domain of Humanity.

Marc had never been there, but he was always astounded when seeing images of ZEK's and the Elite's nexus of power. Storms of ornate designs and exuberant glints and splashes of colors of untold thousands of jewels and gems adorned the walls of the splendid and huge assembly hall that was the Great Seat. Marble and gold filigree panels accented different sections, the decorations clashing in a mad jumble, contending for the viewer's eye.

Vain grandiosity, he thought.

Large custom galleries with sectioned-off areas for each of the Color Suites lined both sides of the room, filled with Elites competing for attention and status wearing jeweled cloaks and hats featuring their affiliation to one or the other of the Colors. In the lowered zone below the galleries, a magnificent marble floor presented all the colors in a swirling galaxy that spiraled in, culminating in a center of blended white underneath the feet of those who were here to speak to or be spoken to by ZEK.

The visual chaos of exquisite ornamentation and bejeweled encrustations covering every wall and column in the Great Seat hall was diminished by only one thing: the Golden Screen, a gigantic artistic construct constituting one entire wall some fifty meters high. Every centimeter of it was covered with golden star shapes, carved curls, appliquéd frames, and multiple sizes and instances of starburst medallions–all done in intricate hammered gold with clear, bright jewels accenting their star tips.

The feed's live camera zoomed into the Golden Screen, focusing on the five huge Faces of ZEK. Centered in what was by far the largest and most intricate starburst frame, the main bio-form golden face of ZEK gazed out with beetling eyes over the seemingly tiny audience as he spoke. His four Lesser Faces were projected onto smaller screens positioned in the four corners surrounding the main one. These independent versions of ZEK's face also glowered, like angry viziers. It was claimed that all of ZEK's faces were a part of him, bio-engineered to be disarticulated from one another, yet forming one human being.

Kera touched Marc's shoulder. "Looks like the Sisters Teacher is here."

"Good," he said, still looking at the screen. "ZEK is talking about our little border incident at the Gate. Let's see what he says."

Marc turned up the volume so he could hear ZEK's voice booming in the Great Seat hall.

". . . unfortunate events are over and the Council of Colors is considering the matter. It is imperative to go about normal business, as all systems and trade Lines are clear. Our intent and purpose is always and forever to protect Harbor from unknown dangers. Harbor Saved Humanity. Harbor Protects Humanity. I am ZEK!" The feed from the Great Seat went dark and the Council of Colors seal was posted.

Marc turned to Kera and they walked on into the center of Pim's party room, which was filling rapidly with a larger crowd than he had expected. People were standing just a bit too close to each other for comfort. Marc assumed that so many had come tonight because they were hoping to hear the Sisters side of what happened earlier at the Gate to Frahma.

A man with close-cropped white hair and wearing a loose light-gray smock appeared and walked up to a makeshift podium at the front of the room. He nodded to a big man who closed the room's side door and stood with his back to it. The speaker took out an unusual style of hand-held and did a spark shock to the room to clear any spyeyes or nanobot recorders. Everyone twitched at the spark, then laughed a little.

Kera looked uncomfortable. She frowned and scanned the crowd, then focused back on the speaker. "This is a little sketchy, Marc."

"I know, but we just got our tail shot off by a Prime and the Black-Mils are pushing violence and abusing people here. I'd really like to hear him. We can leave in a bit if you don't want to stay."

The Sisters Teacher stood calmly until the chatter died down.

"I am Dro. Thank you for coming and hearing," he began. His voice was calm and low. "This latest incident is an important new sign of the increased tensions and techniques Harbor, and especially Suite Blue, is engaged in against all of us who, in the larger view, support them and their exclusive lives. For practical economic reasons, middies and the Elites have been in a fairly stable relationship for centuries. However, you must understand–this is an arrangement based on fear.

"The xenoplague nearly destroyed humanity. Earth and all upon it died. Our ancient home planet is infected with an alien technological plague and therefore, Earth itself is dead and sealed from us forever. These things we know. Harbor Elites and the Council of Colors have forbidden any unauthorized middie handling and dealing of alien artifacts. Who knows if that next artifact will bring a new xenoplague and death to us all? *Fear* is their weapon against you."

His voice was stronger now. The crowd had grown quiet.

"It has been so for over 1,200 years, my friends. We've all seen the old video files of the Ash Alien plague ship that so suddenly appeared and that for no apparent cause utterly destroyed Earth in a matter of a single day. We have never again seen its like in all the centuries since, and through all our generations, no other Ash Alien artifacts, even their useful engines and beam weapons, have ever caused any significant problems or shown any signs of being techno-viral or a doomsday weapon of any kind. Some of you here have–accidentally, I'm sure–handled enough of these artifacts to have realized that yourselves, yes?"

Laughter rippled across the room.

"In the Sisters Systems, just behind us here in Farms, there is a different way of living. We believe in knowledge rather than fear. We strive to provide good lives to all without making some of us persecutors of the rest of us. Fair laws and a common base for opportunity." He paused and looked out over the crowd. The air was close and warm now. "We do not proselytize. We inform so that you can compare and make your own ways.

"We do speak in some haste and alarm now, however, as these incidents against you are increasing in severity and import. We see the real possibility of further rapid escalation. The Old War between Harbor and the Sisters is so long past that we think it can't happen again, but it can, my friends. Such things can start faster than we want to believe."

Kera nudged Marc. He nodded to her as the Sisters Teacher continued.

"Once, the Harbor Elite were necessary to protect the scattered flock of humanity. We were few and there was grave danger. A tiny fraction of humanity survived Earth's destruction and we were sown thinly over twenty-five habitable systems, some just barely habitable. We could have fallen into warring worlds or reverted to separate groups of primitive barbarism. The structures, laws, and powers of

Harbor held us together and protected our birthright of knowledge and society . . . for a time.

Now, we humans are strong and we stretch across the cosmos from the Eight Sisters to Rindd and beyond, but not all is well with our Harbor culture and its leaders–its Elites. They mistake power for the good of all as power to take personal control over others for their own purposes and profits. They assume privilege and they scorn the value of the middies who provide them with all they have, not the least of which is the very food they eat, most of which comes from right here on Farms!"

Several voices made sounds of agreement and there were some exclamations of "That's right!"

"Today, I invite you to realize your *own* power," he continued, "and to consider whether this relationship with the Elites, with the Council of Colors, and with ZEK still serves a good purpose for all of us . . . or whether it does not."

The Speaker gazed calmly as the audience began to murmur amongst themselves. Then he sat down and the meeting quickly turned louder as people began talking over one another.

Kera was fuming inside, but she didn't want Marc to be upset at her discomfort with this Sisters Teacher. She had felt more and more uneasy as the man spoke and as the crowd around her locked into him like his words were casting some powerful spell.

As the speaker finished and sat down, she tugged on Marc's sleeve and whispered intensely, "I'm leaving. You coming?"

Marc gave her a smile and nod and they slipped through the crowd, exiting Pim's Affliction into a warm Farms evening. The air out here seemed cool to her compared to the stuffy party room with too many middies in it.

They walked through gathering dusk along the roadway heading southeast toward the freight port. Kera started to speak when a loud *whuufff* drowned her out. They looked toward the rail yard in time to see a large packet of ag goods being launched down the kilometers-long rail. The up-curve was not visible from here, but after a moment they saw the payload rise and glint as it caught the sunlight, finally diminishing and disappearing over the dark blue horizon. It would be intercepted in orbit and hauled to the Station for distribution. Kera thought it likely Marc would get some of it for his own ship's cargo.

"I *was* going to say," she said, turning back to him, "that it's dangerous to be around that kind of stuff."

"What? Rail-guns are very safe."

He grinned at her and stroked a hand through his short black hair.

"Seriously, Marc. Those Sisters speakers scare me. They're going to stir everyone up and ruin the business systems we've worked so hard to build. He was talking revolution in there! I ought to turn him in."

"Well, that'd be very good of you, but it might turn an unwelcome light on your own sordid affairs."

She couldn't help smirking. "That's why I won't. But, I wish you'd stay away from those guys. We can't be mixed up with that if we want to build a real life for ourselves here. You depend on certain trade routes and routines to be safe and in place, and I depend more and more on the goods you and I find in the different Systems out there. If the Farms middies get worked up over all this nonsense, the BlackMils could make things even harder. We could lose critical access and control."

Marc paused for a moment before replying.

"I think that once a boro beast tastes meat, he just keeps coming back for more. I don't think we can appease the BlackMils by continually yielding to them. It has to come to some form of resistance or the problems won't go away. Look at what's happening right here at home. By now, you've surely seen some of the BlackMil activity in Tabletown. It's happening across all the other Systems, too."

"Yeah, I see it. You know that creep from Station? His boss was arrested today and hauled off-planet. Good for me for the moment, but now he's out of the market and I can't make any new deals with him or his people. Once I landed in town I had to do some track-hiding myself."

She winced at the thought of having to pay her tuber-brained inside guy at town headquarters more than she should have to cover it.

"That's exactly what I mean," Marc said. "The Elites have been in check, but now, they've tasted something they like. I think the Black-Mils and their Elite overseers have passed some critical crosspoint. They're not only asserting their powers within the established legal and civic structures but increasingly as personal entitlements, like that power fever we saw in Anibale yesterday when he attacked the Sisters ships. That attitude is spreading."

Marc unexpectedly took her hand. "I know you want to make a success and find a way to settle and be influential here on Farms. You know I like you, Kera." He paused, "But what we do to make our way is not exactly above-board city government or Elite politics kind of stuff. I have my ship and I know how to be a cargo pilot and trader. I *like* being a pilot. But, you and I wouldn't be doing as good as we are here now if it weren't for some of the contraband goods I find and haul and for your special talents in liquidating them."

"I know," she said, smiling. "You're the Trader of Exotic Space Goods, and I'm the Glamorous Girl who makes deals with Shady Characters." Her grin settled to a thoughtful look. "Sometimes, it's just plain old foodstuffs and plumbing supplies, though." She gave him a wry smile. "I just want it all to work out for us, Marc. I don't want anything or anyone messing things up or taking things out of our control!"

Marc's eyes crinkled. He's better looking than he realizes. Damn it.

"Me, too," he said, and then gave her a quick kiss. "Come back to the ship with me?" She nodded and they entered the ground transport tram for the ride back to the Station's up-cable elevator terminal.

Kera watched Marc as he gazed intently out the tram car's window. She was still trying to figure out her true feelings. Marc seemed so straightforward and good-natured, but she had also seen him reveal a few unexpected traces about things he was otherwise reluctant to share, like his deep past and that bizarre hand problem. She smiled at herself. Marc was attractive and determined, a natural friend. Someone who fit with her life and activities so well and so easily that it seemed almost destined to be that way. If one believed in that kind of thing.

He looked away from the window and his face lit up a bit as he saw her watching him.

"Speaking of exotic cargo . . ." he said slowly. He raised an eyebrow, then waited for her reaction.

She stifled a laugh at his expression.

"*New* exotic cargo?"

"I have a few interesting items I picked up on that last Sisters run. Do you think your Rindd System connections would be interested in some new product?"

She thought about her current connections and the possible market channels.

"Well, it's tough right now with all the troubles and heightened Harbor security off-planet, especially the routes through Hub System. I might be able to route things better through Prospect for now. I'll see what I can do. Is it good stuff?"

"Yeah," he said, "Non-Harbor origin artifacts, a few cases of delicious pimfruit, and some amazing Sisters artwork. Very interesting merchandise. You never know what to expect there at the Frahma System. That was your first run to the Sisters; you probably didn't expect us to dock so far out from their main planet, Florinda, did you?"

"I thought we'd get a better look at them and their home world, yes."

"They only let us dock at that remote Station. Too bad we can't go to some big market or explore their streets for product. They bring their goods up to that controlled trade hall on the Station and you have to deal with what they show you, but it isn't just junk. They do offer some intriguing and valuable items."

They reached the elevator terminal and after exiting the tram, Marc bought them something to eat for the up-cable trip to Farms Station and the ship.

"I do have a surprise to tell you about, though. Later."

"A surprise, hmm? All right then, mister. Take me to your goodies and I'll check them out."

He grinned at her as they entered the transport section of the terminal.

On board the elevator gondola and settled into their nicely padded lift couches, Marc zoned in on an entertainment vid. Kera preferred to look out the windows as they ascended through the thinning atmosphere. Far to the north, she could just make out the enormous old farm where she had grown up mostly without her mother and with only abusive old Gibb for company. He had done his best to keep her locked into that oppressive and prospect-free agrarian life, but she had escaped him and all the other farms and made a very different sort of life for herself–and she still refused to call Gibb father.

As they rose above it, a light mist around Tabletown caused the shallow Sea of Rainbows to live up to its name for a few minutes, and stretching below them, the countless fields of Farms dwindled and became a flattened patchwork of greens, yellows, and browns that slowly took on a haze and a faintly fog-edged curvature against a sky of pure black.

Chapter Three

"In the name of ZEK, you will be boarded. Submit portal lock codes now!"

Marc struggled up from deep slumber and punched his comm. "This is our sleep cycle. Who are you? What's your business?"

Kera frowned as she swung neatly out of bed and grabbed her inner suit and tools.

"You will be boarded. Authority is recorded. Suite Blue demands your compliance."

He cleared their securities as they hurried to the main portal where Kera pulled the hatch. Six visored and armed Blue Guards and one other man briskly entered the vestibule.

Marc looked up at the man in the blue frock and tailored, silver-braided cape. He was a head taller than the guards and his long black hair and brows gave him a fierce look.

"Anibale. Prime Blue," Marc said. "Don't you have more important things to do than harass small-time middie cargo pilots in the middle of the night?"

Anibale's sudden hard grin did nothing to improve his aspect.

At a gesture from him, four of the blue-uniformed guards stepped back and split off down the cross-course alleys. The remaining two raised their handguns. Normally they carried potent AA energy weapons, but these looked different to Marc. More primitive. Anibale's smirk settled into a grim smile.

"There is nothing more important for me to do than to uncover clandestine activities and cleanse the Systems from the dangers they pose. You are Marc 54Arons and you picked a poor time to transit from Sisters. I have reason to believe you have been trafficking in uninspected alien materials. I will find them or you can save us both some time and irritation."

Anibale seemed to notice Kera for the first time. He turned his head and said, "And, who are you?"

"I am Kera." Her expression was set as hard as metal. She looked directly at Anibale.

After a moment, his lip rose. He looked back to Marc. "Well?"

Marc glared at him but did not answer.

"You fools will be the death of us all. What will you do when you bring a plague ship down on Farms, eh? Why do you deal with the Sisters muddlers? They are lawless–dangerous!"

Marc kept his glare, but said, "Have you ever eaten a GreenPlains pimfruit? Nothing else like them in Harbor or Rindd. A valued specialty in Suite Blue, I hear. They are a hybrid, only available from Sisters sources on Fruita. If it weren't for middies like me, you'd never get them. There are many products we provide from the Sisters, a lot of them you aren't aware of."

"Fruit growers don't concern me. Shall we just wait here a bit while my men find what does?" They remained in tableau until footsteps began to reverberate up the corridor.

"Your guards are efficient, I see," Marc said. The returning four emerged from the engine-side alley holding an ungainly bag with gray objects randomly sticking out.

Anibale relaxed his expression, but his eyes did not move. "Here comes your crop of pimfruit now." He turned to view the bag as the guards set it down on the tread track near his blue boots. "Rather tasteless, this batch."

One of the guards said, "Sir. Two long-arm actuators, and several un-IDs."

"Seal those immediately. Yes? What else?"

"They had those stashed in the drive-cowlings. We thought it looked like a plant, so we searched some more and found a secondary stash in their food stores." The guard opened a closed casing he was carrying. "Ash Alien control units of some sort."

Marc started to move toward the guard, but five guns were instantly aimed at his face.

"You need us," he said, "and you need the trade from Sisters and Rindd. Attacking us out here is going to stir up the old troubles and it's all going to be on you–on Suite Blue."

Kera grasped his arm and quietly said, "Let's just cooperate, Marc. They have the artifacts and I don't want you to get hurt."

"A very wise woman," Anibale said. "She is correct. You will surrender these to me now and I will see that you are fined for this egregious deception. As for me, I have my own ways of expressing my annoyance. Do not cross Harbor law again or I will hoist your middie bones to Helm and you can explain yourself to ZEK's Faces in person.

"I bid you a pleasant night." Anibale turned and gave a sign to the guards as he strode out of the hatchway. They turned their mirrored visors toward Marc and Kera and lifted their guns. Marc threw himself in front of Kera as they fired. He instinctively raised his right hand to cover her face and in the instant of that motion, felt his hand change–his skin now tough and leathery. Course webbing stretched between his fingers and tightened. A panic beyond the gunfire flashed in his mind just as a surprising thought expressed itself.

Projectile pistols!

Then, another thought flashed immediately.

The Curse! It came when I needed it!

A round bounced off his hardened hand as several others hit him in the side, chest, and arms. He fell back into Kera.

The guards spun and quickly exited the ship, one of them limping from a ricochet.

"Are you hit?" Marc moaned.

Kera carefully moved herself out from under him. "Only grazed by one, thanks to you." She turned and helped him settle back to the floor, searching his body for wounds. "Non-lethal pellets. He's already in some trouble with the Council and ZEK. This is his way of punishing you without killing you. Deep bruises, but you'll be OK."

Marc surveyed his injuries and answered her with a couple of groans as she helped him up. Kera sealed the hatch and they hobbled back to the cabin.

After settling him into the bedding, she called out the medbot and initiated it to work on him. She picked up his right hand and turned it over and back.

"It happened again, didn't it?"

"Yes."

Kera put his hand down. "You promised to tell me. You'd better do it now."

He looked directly at her and paused for a moment. "It's my Curse."

Kera tilted her head and raised an eyebrow. "Your curse? What are you talking about?"

"I can't explain it. It's something I was born with. It's hereditary, I suppose. Father had it, too. His hands would grow just slightly larger and harden. Mine can grow quite a lot and get really tough, like they did just now. Sometimes they form into organic hooks or tools. Other times they become very energetic."

"What do you mean, energetic?"

"They can get really hot, Kera. Red hot. Hot enough to hurt someone badly. It's an energy that flows through me from somewhere else. It doesn't hurt me. None of it does. It feels good–powerful even."

"So what–you can just turn this effect on whenever you want?" She stared at him intently.

"No. I can't. Sometimes it comes when I need it. Sometimes. I've tried all my life to call it and control it, but it's like it has a mind of its own. I suppose high stress or strong emotions are triggers, but those can lead to problems as well as solutions. The Curse *has* saved my life and the lives of others."

"Like it just did. You were able to make it work here and it protected me from getting shot."

Marc looked up at her and frowned. "But I didn't ask it to. Like I said, I've seen it come when I need it, but I didn't consciously call it."

"Well, there wasn't time to call it anyway," she said.

"Yeah. That's a good point," he said. "The main problem is that it can have unintended consequences. Bad things happened with my parents, Kera. I said I'd interacted with Anibale before. When I was eighteen, he took my folk's mining operation on Salina. We fought him, Father and I. Used our Curse against him and his goons. It was my fault. I couldn't just stand there and do nothing! Anibale was going to take everything we had worked for."

"But, you attacked him and won?"

"Won for the moment. Yes." Marc felt the pain of it again. "Kera, he came back with reinforcements. My parents were killed. I only escaped by a lucky fluke."

"I'm so sorry, Marc." Kera took his hand in both of hers. "But, Anibale . . . he didn't recognize you out at the Farms Gate, right? He's not likely to seek you out for revenge?"

"No. The kid I was then, he believes is dead, along with my parents. There was another boy working there . . ." He pursed his lips as he remembered.

"Well, let's hope we never see him again. I don't know what your so-called curse is, Marc, but it's a remarkable thing. I feel like it could be a powerful tool for you–for us–if you can learn to control its power. Maybe we can do some tests or experiments with it, or something."

"I've *tried*, Kera. It's no use. I hate it! It's just trouble. I want to be normal like everyone else."

"All right." She released his hand. "All right, then. It was just a suggestion."

"Look. It's fine. It's nothing . . ." He exhaled a puff of air. "So, will you still be able to liquidate my Ash Alien artifacts for us?"

She looked askance at him. "You mean all those nice ones they just hauled off to Anibale's ship? That *would* be a good trick."

"What? Those old things?" He managed a wry smile. "I planted those just like he said. Pretty worthless stuff, really. I knew they would find those and they'd look for a secret stash. So . . . I provided that, too."

"And?"

"And, I have the best stuff still nice and secure. Blue Boy just about put his hands on it twice tonight." Kera stared at him with one eyebrow raised. "Secure, inside the outer hatch door," he said.

She shook her head slowly and smiled. "Those are the Sisters items, then?"

"No, actually the Sisters goods were the controllers they found in the galley. Sorry, I had to think quickly and those were more expendable than my *other* items. The door stash finds are truly fresh and unknown AA tech I discovered recently in a new place." He paused, thinking. "Kera, I've found something truly remarkable–an entirely new system. One with artifacts. Lots of artifacts."

Marc liked seeing her face light up.

"A new system? Really, Marc? Where is it?"

"It's behind Salina. I was prospecting for old unknown Lines there a few months back and I found a very subtle one–almost missed it, it was so subtle. Went on through without any problems and found a dim star with a really simple system: a few small rockies and one larger volcanic worldlet. When I went in for a peek, I was shocked. Here, grab that screen and I'll show you."

Kera brought it over to him and Marc keyed in his codes and secure genescan. Images from the survey trip played, showing an almost black planetary surface that obviously had no atmosphere. Scattered in disarray everywhere across an old lava plain were artifacts–Ash Alien for sure. They were in huge piles and conglomerations as if it were the detritus of a battle zone or some long-forgotten alien dumping ground.

"Incredible!" Kera stared at the images and vids as Marc keyed through them. "Marc–this is incredible! There could be whole ships out there. I don't think anyone has ever found such a trove; we could be so rich!"

"Yeah, or dead. Anibale does have a point. There could be some dangerous toys in there," he said. "I did some initial scans and a little bit of survey, but it's a massive and chaotic collection and I didn't want to step on something and blow up the place."

Marc remembered a good friend who had prospected for new system Lines and never showed up again, and a few others he had heard of who found Ash Alien weapons that they only discovered *were* weapons as they accidentally triggered them.

Marc sealed and shut off the display. "We'll have to take the salvage and liquidation process cautiously and slowly so we don't trip ourselves up or give away the system. If we're careful, we could mine this thing for years. At some point, we'll need some of your Rindd contacts to put us in with one of their more advanced engineer types who can advise us on the larger items and help with transporting them out of the system."

"Mmmm. You're right about that, and I can ask around, but before I go in on it, I have to see this place for myself. *Have* to, Marc. This is going to be a major commitment."

"Well, I'd love to take you there, but this might not be a good time with all this business going on." He winced as the medbot completed its duties and withdrew.

"No, Marc, think about it. This is actually an excellent time. Anibale just beat you up, took your goods, and he thinks all will be quiet now that we've been put in our place. Let me see your system while the heat is off. I'll arrange for a cargo run for you to Salina and I'll be co-pilot again."

"Well, OK. Makes sense. There's not too much robust trade with

Salina these days, so I'll do what I did last trip and log that we're going to my parent's old mine. The remains of it that the Elites didn't keep is owned by an old family friend I trust. It would provide some cover story for going that way."

"I'm excited that you found that new Line, but why did you go back out to Salina in the first place? Like you said, you couldn't be making much money trading there."

Marc looked up at the ceiling. "I go back sometimes. I like the solitude. No one to give me any hell. I was born on Farms, but I grew up on Salina, and, of course, my parents are buried there." A frown darkened his face. "I guess I have a strange fondness for the old salt plains and sand."

He did not mention the ghostly voices and vivid images he sometimes heard and saw out in the lonely places in the desert or in the dry folds of the low, parched mountain ranges where he liked to wander.

He also tried not to show how much it hurt to recall the events of that awful time when he lost the two most important people in his life. Father humiliated–Mother with a gun muzzle on her cheek. His own hands flaring red and growing into hard clubs. The smoke coming from the house and the figures in the pit. It had been a hard lesson about what happens when the Elites "needed" something the middies had created.

***

Salina's sun was hot on that bright plain where Father had driven them, out to the dry place where he dug into the ground, but Marc was happy. Father had included him this time. He smiled and held out his little hand, waiting to show Father the treasure he had.

As Father worked just over there in a shallow, rocky spot, Marc had managed to pull one of the meal canisters out of the big bag next to the shade table. It was a snack one–a favorite. He always had to wait for the adults to open the cans, but the trip out here to the ore plain had been long and hot and he was tired and hungry. As he held the can, he touched the seams where Father's metal opener would go and Marc felt his right hand change shape. It rippled a little and two of his fingers thinned and became like little knife points. Curious, he poked the can seam and, to his delight, a puff of air escaped, bringing the wonderful scent of the baked rolls inside. He giggled.

Father, red-faced and sweaty, walked back toward him now, ready to take the lunch break. With a scissoring motion of his sharp fingers, Marc opened the can enough to reach in with his other hand and take one of the rolls. He giggled again and held it up now so Father could see how clever he was.

Father will be proud! I can open the can all by myself!

As Father approached, he felt his hand begin to change shape again–reverting slowly to his normal fingers.

"Marc! No! What are you doing, boy?" Father ran to him.

A sudden wave of guilt and fear came over him. *Father was angry!*

Father reached him and grabbed his hand just as it took its normal shape. Marc dropped the roll into the white dust and gravel below. Ruined. Dismayed, he snapped his eyes back up to Father and tried not to cry as Father pulled on his arm.

"Boy! As I feared–you got this damned Curse! Squelch it, Son! You gotta squelch it!"

Marc did not understand Father, but he could see that he was afraid. This made Marc afraid, too.

"I opened the treats! I did it. I can do it, Father." He felt his lips tremble as he looked into Father's eyes. There was a moment, and then Father's expression changed a little, softening. It made Marc feel a little better, but Father still gripped his hand. He held it up in front of Marc's face.

"Son, this change–this changing. It is dangerous. You must learn to control it. You must not change your hands like that, ever again!" He shook the small hand in front of Marc's eyes. "Understand, me? You must not."

Marc looked into his Father's face and tried to understand. It had felt so good to make his hand open the can. Tears sprang from his eyes.

Father slowly put Marc's hand down and let go. He took the opened can and set it on the table next to the other food items. He shook his head. "It's OK, son. It's not your fault. Father will have to teach you about the Curse and what you must do. Surprised me, that's what." He pulled a rough cloth hanky out of his shirt pocket and dabbed at Marc's eyes. "What will Mother think? We mustn't tell her about this. No. She does not need that worry now. We'll keep this a secret, yes? A *Secret*, Marc. You like secrets, don't you?"

Marc didn't understand all of Father's talking, but he did enjoy games like 'secrets' that other kids would play with him sometimes. At least Father was happier now. Marc smiled up at him, but he thrust his right hand deeply down into his pocket, nestling it under the tail folds of his big brown shirt.

Chapter Four

• The "Spirit Dimension":
An Assessment of Sui Generis Morphological Adaptations
in the Human-Origin Population of Gossamer [3xBack:Frahma]
–by Leenah A. Bordu, SisterSon of Frahma Institute,
Florinda, Eight Sisters of Frahma System

This report follows a two-year field investigation of the remnant human population on the planet Gossamer (Gossamer System). The origin of this population was an isolationist band of religious settlers circa 250 2ndDomain, nearly one thousand years ago.

After establishing on-planet, it was reported that the settlers experienced some type of radical physical transformation causing them to exhibit strange alterations of body and mind. Over many years, these groups retreated further into the ubiquitous and dense jungles of the planet and contact was eventually lost. Envoys to the groups were attacked with an unexplained psychic affliction, leaving them mentally impaired or insane. Some were killed or never re-emerged from the forest. After a decade of continued tragedies, a single broadcast message came from Gossamer's tribal groups. It requested complete isolation of their world due to "Darkness in the Bright. No others should come until the Bright is sustained."

With no prospect of resolution and with the omnipresent danger, the Sisters Elders decided to honor that request and quarantine the planet indefinitely. Other than discreet passive monitoring and the identification of several basic settlements, no outside human traffic has occurred in over 900 years, and the inhabitants of Gossamer made no further attempts to contact the outside systems or to leave their planet.

This held true until 1244 2ndD, 28 Helm Std. Month, when a new message was received from Gossamer requesting a special envoy to come to the planet to work with a particular group or tribe of Gossamer humans. I was selected by the Institute on Florinda to go to Gossamer, where I established communications with this tribe and carried out xenobiological and anthropological studies.

It was time for the ceremony and Leenah was frightened. All her training at the Institute on Florinda could not have prepared her for this. The ceremony would be personal and visceral, an experience simply not to be found in any datastore or book– not that there *were* any data about these people.

Brioleee found her sitting, entering notes into her datapad at the hut at New Camp, and waved her long, sinuous arms in a gesture Leenah knew indicated pleasure and excitement. Even though doing so was part of her anthropological duties here, Leenah truly enjoyed studying her new friend. She was certainly amazing–a remarkable adaptation.

At a casual glance, Brioleee's body still looked human, but the long arms and legs and her elongated head shape spoke of the differences she and her tribes had developed over the centuries here on this small world called Gossamer.

Leenah had no idea why this jungle world would trigger the kinds of adaptations she had seen. Not all of their modifications made sense from a strictly environmental selection view. Certainly, the somewhat lower-than-standard gravity here could affect a more lithe and stretched frame, but these people had abilities she would have considered impossible if she had not witnessed them herself. Apparently telepathic, able to subtly shape-shift their bodies to accommodate practical tasks, and sometimes, incredibly, doing so to the degree of being able to pass themselves through the solid walls of their doorless ceremonial structures.

Yesterday, after watching some of the elders disappear like that, she had jokingly asked Brioleee if they also rode unicorns, but the tall native girl just looked at her strangely with those huge violet eyes.

Of course, she had no clue what I was talking about.

Leenah shook off her qualms and got up to go with Brioleee to the ceremonial complex. It was such an incredible privilege to be here and to be allowed to work with these people. She was the first outsider to set foot on Gossamer in the near millennium of system quarantine, and it was because the Gossamers had requested it! Still, with the initiation ceremony looming, the old tales of induced madness for those who trespassed here haunted the edges of her thoughts and feelings.

Gossamer orbited its small white star three systems–three Lines transits–behind the Eight Sisters System and its yellow sun, Frahma. It was a termination world, the final destination before running into nothing but black pockets–dead ends on that branch of the alien Lines network. It was named for the wispy clouds that trailed and threaded through the verdant jungle tops as seen from orbit. Gossamer was almost entirely enmeshed in that dense forest and its silky webs of vapor. Only scattered freshwater lakes and the drier polar areas showed through.

The original human colony here had quickly disappeared into the primeval maze. When the madness and violence struck those who came afterwards and the Sisters Elders agreed to quarantine the planet, a reputation was established. Gossamer was a cursed world.

When Leenah first arrived just under two years ago, her safety had been assured. Brioleee was her principal liaison with the tribe and had gleefully taken on the job of communicating to her in verbal words, something the Gossamers seemed not to require very much for themselves.

"Come, Leeenahhhh! Come now. Elders are waiting! Come now!" She was almost hopping in her excitement.

Leenah smiled. "I'm coming. All finished here."

A troupe of red zebons went flying and screeching through the tangled dark canopy above them as Brioleee led the way, taking Leenah's hand and tugging her along. Leenah had to trot to keep up with her, but they both laughed as they pushed their way through the crowded green vines and wild vegetation splashed here and there with spots of bright color—reds, bright yellow, vivid blues—all along the narrow and winding path to what Leenah thought of as the pyramid platform temple.

The morning heat increased rapidly as the trail climbed beside a clear stream and then up one of the gentle hills found in this part of equatorial Gossamer. Dense jungle growth covered most of the hill and she could not even see the temple until they stepped into a narrow clearing at its base. Acclimated as she was, she was still puffing after the exertion in this humidity.

The temple formed a square base of about sixty meters on each side. Its stony walls were angled up and inward, pyramid-like, but the top was severely truncated to make a broad platform only five meters above the jungle floor. A strange abstract fractal-like pattern was engraved on all the surfaces of the structure, similar to patterns drawn onto the Gossamer tribe's simple clothing. The angled wall stretched away on each side, its intricate ornamentation silently displayed to the surrounding plants and towering trees. It had no doors or windows.

She was here for what Brioleee told her was a ceremony to "initiate" her into their tribe. She wouldn't explain what was involved.

Many of the tribespeople stood above them on the platform's edge, looking down at the two women. Leenah shaded her eyes and caught the piercing look of the elder man of the tribe, named Tonhaaa. He was dressed in something Leenah had never seen him wear before. It was a long decorated cape and a headdress made of yellow and red fibers and purple feathers from the uuuluh bird. Brioleee referred to him as the Doctor, saying that was the closest word she could find for what he was to them.

The girl scaled the side of the temple in a few deft movements using her wide toes and long fingers that instantly shape-shifted to become more elastic and web-like. Leenah leaned into the wall and tried to use her fingertips and the toes of her sandals to grip the patterns in the angled stone, but even with Gossamer's slightly lower gravity, she slipped back after a meter. Brioleee reached down with one very long leg and indicated she should grab on. With a pull and a twist, Leenah was lifted onto the platform and found herself surrounded by silent, smiling people. A smoky haze drifted from a fire bowl at the far corner. It smelled sweet and strong. Brioleee directed her toward an arrangement of red and green fiber cushions at the platform's center.

Tonhaaa, the "Doctor," remained standing while the others sat down on mats or perched themselves along the edges of the platform's decorated surface. Leenah stood before him, with Brioleee at her side. As before whenever she had dealt with the main tribe, no words were spoken by anyone except Brioleee. As the Doctor smiled at her and then looked serious and tilted his head, she began to speak for him.

"Doctor says. It is dangerous for you to be here. Doctor says. We have lived on this earth for many generations. We had to learn. We had to make decisions. There were many who made wrong decisions. They followed a darker path. Many of us were injured or killed by these other doctors. Some of your tribes who came here also found these people and were harmed.

"Doctor says. We are the people who chose a bright path. We learned how to control the dark energy. We learned how to control ourselves so that the dark would not control us."

Tonhaaa looked very intently into Leenah's eyes.

Brioleee continued the translation, "There are still some on this world who follow the dark. We protect you from them in this earth-place, but where you must walk now, you must be full of care. We will guide you." Brioleee paused.

Leenah turned to her. "May I ask the Doctor a question?"

Tonhaaa nodded. Brioleee said, "Yes, you must ask questions."

"Thank you . . . thank him." She paused a moment to think. "For fear of the madness, and at the request of your ancestors, we have kept other humans from this world for many centuries. Why did you send messages asking for one of us to come here now?"

"Doctor says. Not one of you. You. We called for you to come here now."

Leenah was taken aback. "Me? Me, specifically? I was chosen by the Institute at Frahma for my background in anthropology and xenobiology."

"Doctor says. We saw your skills and knowledge. We saw your *other* skills. We called for you with the bright energy. We knew you would come, and you are here. Doctor says there is a new thing. A danger and a hope for us and for all your tribes. We have seen it here. We will show it to you so that you may also understand and do what must be done. Then, you must go and speak."

Brioleee indicated that Leenah should sit down on one of the cushions. The Doctor's helpers brought the large pot from the corner where it had provided the sweet smoke. They set it down between the Doctor and Leenah, and she saw a greenish liquid inside bubbling slightly, causing some vegetal bits to float around in the convections. She drew in her breath and glanced sharply up at Brioleee, who smiled at her.

For a few moments, everyone else was silently looking at her and Leenah wasn't sure if she was supposed to say or do something, then

Brioleee spoke again. "Doctor says. This is our heart. This is what made us into the Bright People of this world. It is a sacred part of the life. It is named Kaaanlooo. It is the flesh of our life parent. When we first ate, we saw the bright energy and we became ourselves. We could see!" Brioleee smiled broadly at her.

"Doctor says you must also see."

The sweat Leenah felt on her forehead was more than from humidity and late morning sunshine.

Well, I wanted cultural immersion!

Using a wooden hook, one of the tribesmen extracted a segment of the plant stalk out of the brew. He gently placed it on a very beautiful green cloth, embroidered in yellows and browns, into the interlocking fractal patterns. She looked up at him, but he did not move to give it to her.

Abruptly, the entire group shouted out loud, "Yaaaahhh!" and began to sing! The song was simple but lovely. Their voices gathered together and dovetailed in a chorus that became hypnotic. It was bracing and thrilling to suddenly hear the joined human voices of this group of people who had always remained silent in her presence.

Leenah felt her head begin to spin as the smoke from the pot thickened, obscuring the Doctor's face at times. The man who held the plant now reached out and indicated she should take the thing and eat it.

Leenah's hand trembled a bit, but she took the plant. It smelled very sweet. She paused, but then with renewed determination to understand these enigmatic and wonderful people, she placed it in her mouth and ate the Kaaanlooo.

As she finished it, she looked around at the group, not knowing what to expect, but nothing seemed to happen. The others were still singing, the melody broken into separate parts now, each being sung in relation to the others like a fugue. Brioleee sat down beside her and held her hand for a while, then let go as a shiver ran through Leenah's body.

"Ohh!" Leenah heard herself say. It seemed like someone else had spoken it. The temple platform undulated under her, vibrating, then slowing to a soft wave. The geometric patterns in the floor seemed to interlock and move, each one slightly different from the others—all vibrating and dancing in a morphing fractal grid.

The singing continued, louder now, but more inside her head. The singers had risen and stood around the central area of the platform, but even in her now obviously altered state, Leenah was shocked to watch each one of them fold into themselves and disappear into the platform surface, one by one, until all but the Doctor and Brioleee had removed entirely from view. Then, Leenah, too, left the jungle world behind, but in a different way. It was simply replaced by another world entirely.

She could not seem to focus the sensory information she was receiving, but wherever this was, she felt surprisingly good. It was almost completely dark. Blurred colors and shapes flew rapidly by her face, confusing her. Some of the shapes felt cold and threatening, others seemed benevolent and alluring. Part of her thought it rather silly, but there it was. As her eyes adjusted to the dim light, she started to take a step forward but instantly turned a corner instead and found herself in a dusky forest of stately trees and thick mossy underbrush accented with skeins of tiny flowers. Every plant here was tinged with light—an electric force of Life she could feel as well as see. Colors cascaded everywhere and the plants were all singing. They sang the same song the tribe sang, but not in human tones. Life itself was singing of being alive! It was incredibly lovely, yet odd and bewildering. Some part of her cognitive "self" returned to Leenah and she thought to wonder more directly where she was and what she was supposed to do here.

With no answers forthcoming, she began to walk, but as she did so, it seemed that the forest flowed around her instead. Soon, the forest turned dark and foreboding and the singing faded away. Then the trees were gone and she found herself in an expansive and rough barrens under a black sky. There was a presence here. It was off to her left side, tracking her movement. It seemed to call to her, but when she looked, there was only a shimmer in the dim air.

She started to run and suddenly, with a silent crashing, it was *there*, running beside her. Tattered hairlike wisps of black smoke roiled off of a bony, misshapen body. A madly disarranged human face leered at her. Its wild eyes, intent with power, focused on hers. Its legs were like an antelope's and it ran on all fours. She veered away from it, but the thing matched her movements. She could sense its desire for her to join it. It promised ferocious power and terrible beauty. It spoke of deep satisfaction and total freedom, power over danger, and dominance over all who threaten. She cried out and kept running.

Leenah heard singing again and a broad green light bloomed just ahead of her. She headed into it. The forest! Great trees blanketed smooth hills and she heard her pursuer fall behind and stumble. She chanced one glance over her shoulder. The thing flailed its legs and hissed in disappointment, then vanished into the green brush.

After a moment–or was it a day?–she found herself standing in a clearing with a sheer stone cliff face blocking the way ahead. She was still panting.

A huge creature stood there, looking at her. Her mind registered it as a mythical dragon, but then Leenah remembered. It was one of Gossamer's native predators: a moolooo. Normally a rather small animal, with dull gray and green coloration, this one was bright blue with neon yellow stripes. It was also about five times larger than herself. She and the moolooo stood still for a long minute, then the creature spoke into her mind in a clear, deep voice.

"You shall be devoured."

Leenah turned to run again, but as she did, the scene turned with her and she stood again facing it.

"You shall be devoured. You cannot escape."

She sat down on a rock and tried to think what to do. Without intent or understanding, words came to her. She said, "I cannot fight you, therefore I will let you, and then I will escape." The words felt right.

Xenoplague

In a flash, the creature jumped toward her and, in one fierce move, swallowed her up.

Leenah cringed, but there was no pain, nor was she harmed as far as she could tell. She was in a new place. For a moment, she heard more singing. It was Brioleee's voice! But, the clouds–*clouds?*–that now encircled her began to part and reveal the black of space. She floated here, suitless, along with several human intersystem ships above a beautiful blue world. The ships were of a very old style. Something else hovered nearby: a huge Ash Alien vessel.

I know this ship. I've seen it before. I know what's going to happ . . .

Suddenly, a blindingly white energy beam shot out of the alien vessel, striking the blue seas of the planet. The human ships all turned and fled.

Now, a man floated toward her out here in open space. The planet and alien ship had disappeared. Like her, the man was not wearing a suit, but in this dimension, this seemed normal. He held a strange object that looked like a rayed star with multiple rod-like arms ending in orbs. From the fearful expression on his young-looking face, it was certain the man was in trouble. It seemed that he could not let go of the thing as it began to glow and pulse. His hands grew huge and turned red hot, still gripping the object, but he seemed unharmed by it. Their eyes locked as he approached. Leenah reached toward him and he looked at her with longing and tried to speak. As he passed her, his eyes never left hers. She cried out to him and his expression became determined. Leenah felt her heart leap.

In an instant, he was gone and Leenah was looking at another world–no, multiple worlds! Gossamer was here in front of her, and alongside it was Florinda and another dark planet lined with artificial light–*that's Rindd 1!*–all grouped together as they could not possibly be in real life.

Warships were arrayed around the worlds, facing outward toward an attacking force. A fierce melee was taking place. Some ships lit up with beam damage and collapsed in on themselves or broke into countless shards. They were battleships of Sisters design, mixed with non-military, commercial and private middie ships of all sizes and shapes. Now, she could see the vessels who were firing on them: modern Harbor Elite ships. BlackMils. The worlds below her were in grave danger.

She felt a presence, and as she willed herself to turn around, the huge Ash Alien ship that had blasted the blue world rotated into her view. It advanced toward these new targets. "NO!" She heard herself scream at the thing. "Not again! Go back! Noooo!" The giant ship never paused, and without any warning, that dread white beam shot out from it again, engulfing her and the worlds behind her.

When Leenah woke, she was lying on the cushions at the center of the temple platform. The still hot sun was behind the trees and shadows drifted across her face. Some hours must have passed. Brioleee held her hand and looked at her with big violet eyes. The Doctor, sitting on her other side, was humming a slightly different song than before as he gazed at her with concern. Her lips felt numb.

"What happened? Am I all right?"

Brioleee spoke. "Doctor says. You are very all right. You took the bright path. We knew you would, even without our guidance."

"I'm not sure I feel all right."

"You passed the trial and gained its power to see. You will be fine after you rest here a while."

Leenah blinked and sat up. "But, the battle–the alien ship! Did you see it, too? *What's happening?*"

"Doctor says. Time runs different in the spirit dimension. We see things as probabilities and paths that may be chosen by us and by others."

The Doctor looked down at her. "Yes, we see the battles and the great weapon. We called you here to see. You can tell others and we can help from our side, but this must be deflected from its time path.

The man is the nexus."

She suddenly remembered the suitless man. She remembered his determined, fearful face and how her emotions rose when she saw him pass by.

"Who is he?" Leenah asked.

"We do not know him, but we know he has some energies like yours. You must find him. You will know him and help him find the other path. He does not know what he has stirred." The Doctor rose to his feet. "You are one of our people now, Leeenahhhh. You can always speak to us and call for us in the other world. We are there with you. Now, you must return to your place and tell others what you have seen."

As he withdrew from them, Leenah realized with a start that the Doctor had been silently speaking to her without Brioleee's verbal help.

Darkness enveloped the jungle as Brioleee helped her down the wall of the temple platform and they walked slowly through the chirping insects and whispering leaves back to her hut.

Chapter Five

Kera kept her eye on the scanscreens onboard Marc's ship as they began their exit from Farms Station for the run to Salina and beyond. "That Blue Guard ship pushed back from Station pretty close to our own departure," she said. "I don't trust it. That's got to be Anibale or his henchmen."

Marc looked up from his pilot pod and nodded at her. His short hair jounced a bit as their gravity compensation shifted. He fed in the coordinates for the Line.

"Yeah, they'll probably keep an eye on us at least to Salina transit. Then, hopefully, they'll find more interesting people to shoot."

That was one of the things she liked about Marc. He didn't let things rattle him much unless they were truly a threat.

"Don't let him get you down," she said. "He was way out of line with you. His adventures at the Sisters border are going to get him into big trouble back in Helm. He's obviously playing for a power grab. Suite Blue is second tier now behind ZEK's Greens. With Jade, Prime Red, in the running, too, he has his sights on becoming ZEK."

She felt a little thrill of excitement thinking about the political games these famous Suites played with each other, everyone accumulating as much material wealth as they could. It symbolized their competitive status as they vied with each other for positions of power and control over all the worlds. The ultimate prize of any Suite and Suite Prime would be to leverage that wealth influence into becoming ZEK and obtain his alien-enhanced control of the BlackMils.

"Pity us all if he does." Marc glanced at her. "I wish the Color Suites would just eat each other up and leave us alone."

"I know. They do serve a purpose, though. They keep things organized and safe. Even your pals, the BlackMils, do their job policing the Lines and the Gate traffic." She looked to see if he was hearing her. "There aren't any pirates in Harbor Systems."

Marc gave her a wry smile. "Yeah. Some pals. I'd like to give them a little of what they've given me over the years. No, I hear what you're saying, and they do generally make things safer, but at what cost, Kera? Practically speaking, there is no limit to their power over all middies or even over the Elite Suites and all their Guards, but it's us middies who get hurt and abused first. And, it's getting worse all the time.

"See that big load of tubers and meats that just logged out of Farms Station? Half of it was just rerouted to Suite Cyan without any warning or payment. They don't need the food, Kera. It's all about competing with Suite Yellow and political positioning. To us, though, it's an unannounced tax based on someone's whim. We middie traders just have to count our losses and try again."

"I see it happening, too, but even Anibale knows deep down that they need us. They have to keep themselves in check to a point or risk losing their workforce and their privileges."

"Maybe they should. There are other ways to live."

"I care about you, Marc. Be careful who hears you say such things." Then she grinned at him, "Now, let's go get those lovely, illegal artifacts!" And, she thought, find some power of our own.

Back on board Marc's ship and carrying a light cargo of ag tools and foodstuffs rail-gunned up from Farms, they closed in on the system's Gate and its forward (relative to Harbor System) Line to Hub, which would, in turn, lead them through Hub System to the Line back to Salina. Informally, all routes away from Harbor were deemed "back" and going toward it were "forward" since the AA Lines system was mostly serial with only a few cross-links. Hub was Hub because it had direct Lines to six different systems including the ones that led to the separate arms of the Rindd and Sisters groups. Kera watched Marc make the gross course adjustments, and then he just sat back and watched the monitors as they approached the Gate beacons.

Each of the ancient Ash Alien Gates was in orbit around its host star, positioned near the orbits of the most habitable world or worlds of each system, but far enough away to not be a danger to local navigation. If there were more than one Gate, like here in Farms, they orbited in sync with each other along the average ecliptic. Multiple Gates were spaced apart evenly, to great precision, so they always held a mutually stable spatial relationship as they waltzed around the system's star.

The Gate itself was essentially invisible, but human engineers had constructed beacons and in some cases built and positioned a huge but thin physical metal ring–an actual gateway of scaffold-like girders–to mark the location of the orifice itself. There was just such a ring here, since this was one of the major routes in Harbor's linked systems.

Kera thought the ring was rather a pitiable expression of the human ego, crudely glued on, as it were, to the magnificent technology of the ancient ones.

"Are you going to make the final scans?" she said. "Want me to do it?"

Marc seemed not to hear her for a moment. "No, I can get us into the Gate correctly."

"No scans?"

"Don't need them this close. I can feel it."

"That's . . . a little alarming."

He smiled. "No need to worry. Look, we're in!"

Sure enough, the sinking elevator feeling began almost at once, and Kera instinctively held on to her chair arm as the beacons flashed their acknowledge messages and the ship entered the Line to Hub.

These old wormholes (if that was what they were) were very stable. The big ones, like this one, were reinforced and strengthened by use, but some of the more worthless Lines tended to fade away very slowly and some were so faint they could hardly be located. Once in a while, a lucky or talented prospector, like Marc, might find a very faint one and discover a new destination–a treasure trove, perhaps, or more likely just a black pocket. Nothing there at all. Once in a while, he or she would find a hellhole and, perhaps, not return. Those Lines were marked off with warning beacons and added to the maps.

Time always seems funny in these Line transits. It's difficult to say afterwards how long any such passage lasted. Some think it is much longer than the Harbor-standard minute or so it feels like, but the scientists claim it is actually instantaneous, as compared clocks show. Since humans simply can't interpret that inner space/time properly, our brains infer a subjective time span. Permanent comm lines stretched through the Gates have never shown any measurable signal delays.

Doesn't seem to bother Marc, but I always feel like I'm falling down a well.

Once inside the Gate and during the subliminal transit, Marc still held a thoughtful look as he let the Line do its thing with them. After Kera had first encountered him making artifact trades on Farms last year and helped him liquidate his "extra" inventory from several cargo runs, they found themselves spending a lot of time together. She liked his independence and resourcefulness but wondered just how much she didn't know about him yet–like that astonishing and unnerving hand-morphing trick.

Marc was fun and clever, but more and more, she saw him express a deep-seated antagonism toward the government of the Elites. Not that she blamed him. Kera hated the way the Elites were acting, too.

She just worried about Marc's reactions, especially after Anibale's aggression toward him.

Maybe this new trove would prove to be their pass to gain a stable income and set up house on Farms or Hub. Try to make a name for themselves and make the world work for them, for *her*, for a change. Then, she thought, she would never again have to endure the clowns and dangerous bullies who plague her dealmaking and who do their worst to control and take advantage of her.

It was hard to speak during a Line transit, so she watched the monitors, waiting for emergence. It came suddenly, and the comps auto-confirmed arrival as the scans locked on to the large, dim sun of the Hub System. There was no reason to travel down to Hub's worlds or Stations on this trip. With the thrust from their AA tech drives, it would take another couple of hours to make the in-system run to the nearby Gate that would lead them back to the Salina System.

As they emerged from the Gate here, though, Kera watched Marc grimace and quickscan the screens.

A little gun-shy after his last transit emergence. Guess I don't blame him.

"Just empty space and a couple of beacons, sweetie. You can relax."

They passed on through the second Gate at Hub, back to Salina System, and Kera frowned as they approached the dry planet that was once Marc's home, finally docking to the Station, orbiting high above the tan and white sands below. Salina was an out-of-the-way destination and it featured a much older and roughhewn Station with direct grapple-docking, utilizing pressure tubes to access the habitation areas.

Inside, Kera sighed as she checked off the last of the legit cargo to a brisk Station registrar. The woman raised a hand in an official purchase salute and took the manifest receipts back toward the warehouse sector for final deliveries to the world below. Kera turned as Marc approached, exiting from the main corridor. "All off-loaded and ready to go," she said.

He had a perky expression and an impish smile on his face. When he spoke, it was just a little too loud.

"Well, Kera Dear, I think we're finished up here. We need to go take our off-time on board ship, don't you think? I can't imagine what we'll find to amuse ourselves, though." As he grinned at her, she noticed his eyes shift to indicate a shadowy shape in the lee of a support column behind him. Probably a Purple–local Salina police.

She played along. "Well, OK, handsome. This has been *such* an exciting trip, I guess we'll just have to recover with some dinner and a good night's sleep." She winked at him and took his hand as they went the other way toward the Station dock tube leading back to the ship.

Out of range of the Purple, she frowned and whispered, "What are you worried about? He's just routine surveillance."

"Maybe–probably, but I want them to actually see us board the ship, park it out of the traffic zones, and then not leave it for a couple of days."

"Oh, great," she smirked. "When do we get to see your new system?"

"We'll leave tonight, of course!" He smiled, but his eyes still looked nervous.

***

Marc was anxious to get off-station and out of the public scans. They reboarded their own ship and he had Kera command the bots to cast off the gangway tube and service connectors, then Marc took them out of the Station docking area where three other cargo and personal vessels were still umbilicalled. He checked the scans carefully.

No one I recognize. Good.

He slowly taxied out to a parking orbit at the very farthest edge of the public sector. There were no other ships within viewing distance out here, and unless they called attention to themselves, they would only show up as a simple ship icon on most scans.

"Now, we can get the ship ready for departure," he said.

As he turned off the lights and external power systems, Kera watched him.

She's being very patient. I hope she likes this next little dodge.

She finally broke her silence. "OK, I've seen that look on you before, mister cargo guy. What should I be worried about now?"

"Well, first, let's finish shutting down these lights and pretend we're settling in for some wowzie personal time, then follow me down to the storage bays. I've been working with a Rindd engineer I met a while back. Like most of them, kind of a strange fellow and probably about one-third AI biobot, but he was willing to do a special job for me for the right price. I had him make me a pretty balloon."

"A *what?*"

"You'll see. Come on."

Deep in the aft storage bay, Marc activated a workbot to extract a large cargo cart, haul it over to an exterior port, and after cycling through, tug it out into space a couple of ship lengths behind them. Watching from the monitors, they could see the little bot as it opened the cart. An indistinct silver-gray blob began to emerge as it inflated from a gas source. It started to take shape.

"You've got to be putting me on," Kera muttered, smiling. "You made a balloon ship. The whole damn ship."

"Full size and everything, even power and lights for show and comm ID tones, a loop Do Not Disturb message, and stabilizers to keep it in one spot. I've used it a number of times here and in a couple other systems. It lets me go quietly prospecting without competitors spying on me or BlackMils or other Harbor meddlers trying to follow me around."

Kera was almost laughing now, and shaking her head a bit. "That is . . . astounding. And crazy."

"Yeah, but do you like it?"

"I love it. It's just insane enough to work, at least until you get caught."

"Always a chance, but everything is a chance, eh? Well, we need to make sure the real deal is completely dark before I switch the lights and continuity ID signals over to the decoy."

Once that was done, the balloon ship twinkled its run lights and Marc set the black shadow of his own ship into silent slow-motion, away from the commercial zone of Salina Station entirely–a shadow of a half-alien ghost ship whispering toward the system edge.

———————

Anibale, Prime Blue, had moved his flagship and two Blue Guard ships into a wider orbit around Farms System, but still within the orbits of the Gates. He listened impatiently now as the creased face of the BlackMil ship Superior, Tchaldor Lunn, droned on from the comm screen.

"ZEK requires me to deliver his summons directly to you, Prime. He charges you to return at once to Helm to appear before his Faces."

Old Tchaldor was in the largest of the four BlackMil warships trailing Anibale's own group in a close synchronous orbit. BlackMils were always touchy and stiff, being under the psychic influence and sometimes direct control of ZEK through their biological interfaces: the Ash Alien golden armbands that permanently tie them to him. Tchaldor in particular was always a headache to deal with.

"Listen to me, Tchaldor. I am conducting vital surveillance and illegal artifact recovery here. I will return to Harbor when I am finished. Tell ZEK . . ."

"He will be displeased with you, Anibale. You must return."

Anibale felt his face reddening.

"No! I am Prime Blue! Those I am currently monitoring may conceal dangerous people and artifacts! Xenoplague is not a fantasy to be forgotten or ignored simply because it has not recurred within your long lifetime. My duties to protect humanity are more important than a trip back to the Great Seat to endure a sanction or some other chastening from ZEK, as much as I am sure he wishes to bestow such upon me!"

The BlackMil Senior gave him a steely look.

"Xenoplague is certainly a true threat, young Prime, but it has not manifested again in well over a thousand years. I do not believe it will suddenly show up here in Farms tomorrow. ZEK requires your immediate appearance and I shall accompany you in your return to Helm."

"Well, you can accompany me if you like. I go where I need to go. I have things to do, Tchaldor, so go on back to Harbor, or follow me and my Guards quietly and at a respectful distance, or train your weapons on a Suite Prime who is doing what no one else seems willing to do. Do you dare it?"

Tchaldor's face took on a sour expression and he did not answer.

"By the Faces, man. Go home while I complete my work here. I am not some middie renegade. I will return to the splendors and high society of Helm and ZEK soon enough."

Tchaldor cut the connection. A short time later, all but one of the BlackMil ships moved into approach for the Gate to Hub and left Farms through the forward Lines to Harbor. The straggler was to be his BlackMil snoop, then, monitoring his actions for the official record.

Let him tag on like a skulking dog. If the BlackMils interrupt my mission, I might just turn my weapons on them! One day, soon, they will all be mine anyway.

Anibale's helmsman, Captain Bulo, triggered his alert screen.

"The middie cargo is moving, Prime. They're on course for Salina via Hub, listing a standard food cargo and some building supplies."

"We will follow them at a discreet distance and time lag. I don't really care if they see us, but I'd rather they didn't. Why does he make runs to Salina, I wonder? Not much out there but sand and hardship. Not exactly a large clientele for him."

"Wouldn't know that, Prime, but I guess he has to scrape up a

Xenoplague

living somehow."

"Yes, naturally. Keep to it, Captain."

With his own ships moved well off of the main approach lanes, Anibale watched the scans as the little cargo craft bearing Marc and his friend Kera made its transit into the Gate to Hub and beyond. Something about that smart-mouth middie pilot bothered him. A vague bell rang somewhere. Had he met the man before? If so, he couldn't call it up. He searched his memories again, then gave up the effort with a low growl of frustration.

Since the records showed that Marc made semi-regular runs to Frahma, Anibale had initially thought he might be bringing some of those Sisters "Teachers" into Farms and the other Harbor systems. Delbar Seel, his senior staff advisor, believed they were coming directly through on Sisters ships like the ones they had just shot up at the Frahma Gate. Seems he was right this time. Their surprise boarding of the cargo ship had turned up some ordinary illegal AA motors and unimportant trade goods junk, but no stowaways or human cargo.

However they were being transported, the Teachers had to be stopped. Xenoplague technology could appear anywhere, anytime, and the informational black hole of the entire Sisters group of systems was out of Harbor's control. Out of his own control. That was frightening. Eight hundred years they've been a damnable mystery! Plague artifacts could be discovered anywhere out there by Sisters renegades and Harbor wouldn't know until too late!

This guarded border between the Harbor and Sisters systems had been maintained for far too long. It would have to be crossed, and soon. Someone strong had to take the initiative to bring the Sisters brood back into the human mainstream!

The current ZEK and his BlackMils were certainly not going to do it. ZEK was getting old and set in his ways: imposing but passive toward possible xenoplague threats and to the growing influence of the Teachers rabble. The BlackMils themselves were something like ZEK's programmed servants: able to make their own decisions and take action within his set parameters, but subject to ZEK's instant overt control should he wish to assert and take that control. BlackMils were all former middies who jumped at the chance to become something above the Midclass even if it meant losing their autonomy.

Fools. Once you wear ZEK's armband, you are his forever and never your own again.

After an appropriate lag time, Anibale's group of ships followed Marc's path and slipped into Hub System, then through Hub's Gate to Salina, that harsh desert scape of a world out in a rural spur of the Ash Alien Lines. He had been here long ago, working on a mine project before he became Prime. It was not one of his favorite planets.

A voice on the comms broke his thoughts.

"They've offloaded their Salina cargo, Prime," his aide, Praxel, said. "Looks like they are headed to an outer-zone parking orbit. Our Purples on Station think they are going to stay off-line and personal for a while."

Anibale sniffed. "Monitor the cargo ship closely, Praxel. I want to know if they do anything unusual or if they move so much as a meter from where they settle. And, Captain Bulo, keep us well out of range."

"Yes, Prime." Both men's voices combined and collided.

One and a half standard days later, Anibale felt more and more uneasy. The cargo had not moved or changed its beacons or routine feed-outs.

"Enough of this. Send an active bot probe out there and get some data on the ship. They've been quiet for far too long."

A few hours later, Praxel came personally to Anibale's command quarters.

"And?"

"It's very strange, Prime. The bot indicated everything in order until it actually made contact with the ship. It couldn't mag-attach to the hull, Sir."

"What do you mean?"

"As I said, it's strange." Praxel looked unsure of himself. "It bounced."

"Bounced? It bounced? What do you mean?"

"I mean just that, Sir. It approached the side of the vessel and when it tried to attach, it could not. There was no metal there and it simply bounced off the side back into space, but with equivalent velocity. It was entirely unharmed. It must have struck something quite elastic."

Anibale growled. "Nothing metallic and it rebounded, eh?"

"Yes, Sir." He blinked. "It bounced."

Chapter Six

Kera was still amused at Marc's trick, but she also felt a knot of fear growing inside her. This was so chancy and bizarre, that she could see it ending badly in any number of ways.

But, *I know this is who Marc is, and this is how he does some of the things I've seen him do.*

The well-marked mainline Gate from which they had emerged into Salina System was now situated on the far side of Salina's sun from where they were. Marc was taking them into the deep empty zone about as far away from the main trade routes as possible. There were a couple of old black pocket Lines marked out here–rides that would take them to no system at all, just empty space or dead rocks. They seemed to be headed toward one of those, but then Marc vectored off a bit, and she smiled to herself. *Going to go find us his virgin system with lots of goodstuff!*

"That old black pocket Gate is my rough marker. There's a second faint Line off a few degrees this way, but it isn't of any real interest. Just more black pockets. Mine is *very* faint."

Kera settled back into the copilot seat beside him. "I'm excited to see your pile of artifacts. Do you want some help scanning for your Line?"

"You won't find it with the regular scanners."

"How, then? You going to go fishing for it?"

"Something like that. We're getting very close now. Let me concentrate on it and please don't talk to me for a bit."

She was put off for a moment by that, but Marc focused his attention on the screens and held his body very still, his hands hovering above the scan controls. She decided to watch and wait.

It took a long time. Kera was beginning to fidget and started to say something to break Marc's silent meditation when she felt a gentle tug. It was a Line, for sure. The ship seemed to stretch just a little as they approached the faint Gate and the "down elevator" feeling increased. Well, I suppose we stretch right along with it, she thought.

After the vague feeling that some unmeasurable portion of time had passed, a faint smile played on Marc's lips and he opened his eyes. Kera checked the screens. They had emerged from the transit into very dark space–no large star here, just an ember. A brown dwarf, perhaps. Marc was already plotting in the course for his rock, but he had her drop off some fresh temporary beacons so they could easily find the return Line's Gate again.

"Impressive," she said. "How long to get down there?"

Marc looked over and scratched his chin. "Should be under an hour. The mass detectors I added to my ship are from AA artifacts I sourced through the Sisters. The old aliens really had good tech for finding and manipulating masses, even ones like planets. Wish I knew some of how they did it, but I'm happy to use some of their leftovers. Makes things a lot easier. It's detecting 14 different rocks in the system here, only two of them big enough to call a planetoid. None have atmospheres and all of them are dense rock. Our lovely tropical destination is the largest of them."

"The big pile o' artifacts!" Kera grinned. "I think I'm going to name this place 'Marc's Pile.'"

Marc rolled his eyes, then smiled back. "So that's how those crazy place names get started, eh?"

She reached out and touched his arm and asked, "Marc, what really happened back there? You did something that helped you find this Line. I was monitoring the scans and once we passed that other one you said went nowhere, there was *no* sign of any other Line at any time, even when we entered the Gate for it."

He frowned. "I don't actually know, Kera. I have some funny intuitions sometimes about places and things. I seem to sense, to *feel* the presence of the Lines when I'm out here just quietly looking. That black pocket one we bypassed, for instance. It's a rather faint Line, but it has a distinct . . . flavor to it. Does that make any sense? I guess not, but that's how it seems to me when I concentrate and just open my mind to them. That one seems kind of twisty and salty. This one here, now, it feels solid and smooth and narrow, but it is *so* very faint. I don't think it's been used for a long, long time indeed. Maybe not even much by the Ash Aliens after they built it."

"Hmm. I would not have picked you as having paranorm senses," she said. "Do you think it's something to do with your hand thing?"

"No. Maybe . . . I don't really know. My Curse seems to be its own thing, but I guess it could be connected to my ability to sense the Lines. Perhaps we all have that sort of sensitivity, but mine is just stronger."

"Well, your hands might be temperamental, but you were able to control this Line with impressive delicacy and precision, I'd say. I believe there's more to this than you know and you should stop calling it a curse. That's a habit you got from your father. It's a *talent*, Marc–a set of talents. You may be able to control your hands more than you think you can."

Marc had a strange look in his eyes. "I guess I never really thought about it in terms of a talent. But, why me? Why my family? It seems so random."

"I don't know. I wish *I* had some of your talents. I've never tasted a Line, though, so I guess I'm just going to have to stick with you, buddy."

His eyes lit up at that, and after a short wait, the big rock now called "Marc's Pile" blossomed up in the screens as they braked for orbit.

Marc put the ship on botpilot. "That sector there, inside the shallow crater–that's where I looked last trip, but let's go check out the other side of the rock. I saw a huge collection of artifacts littering a plain, but didn't have time to investigate it."

Kera nodded. "I'll get the lander started. Let's go see what we have."

Half an hour later, they had parked it on the hard field. He stared out of the small windows as the fine dust they had stirred slowly settled to reveal a black lava plain. It was rimmed with an almost continuous line of massive gray junk, heaped in great mounds. The piles stretched in every direction and disappeared over the close horizon line of the small world. The system's dim sun glinted–a dying ember suspended in the airless sky.

They suited up and Kera followed him, boots crunching, out onto the basalt plain. His voice sounded hollow to him inside his helmet.

"So, what do you think? Battle debris? Recycling yard?"

"Maybe it's an alien expression of structural art," Kera chuckled. "Whatever it all is, it's truly colossal. I think I'll start looking over that way."

"Let's not get too far apart. This is unknown stuff with a really big capital U. Be careful what you touch and where you put your boots." A memory suddenly flashed of someone he once knew–a young female friend who had been careless in an Ash Alien structure and nearly died in his arms.

"Yeah. You bet I will. Let's check out that collection together then," she said, pointing to one larger gray pile.

Marc increased his speed to keep up with Kera as she hiked toward the artifacts. The group they were headed for was a pasta heap for certain. Tubes and rods, cased machine units, ovoid pods, twisted ramps, and larger enclosures with hatchways–some open, others closed–and more than a few items that could be gun or energy turrets. All of it, every single piece, was the same color: the ubiquitous ash-gray metal. The objects were clumped and dumped in piles with no intentional ordering.

"Found some controllers for you," Kera called. She was a short distance ahead of him at the edge of the main pile. "I'll put locator buttons on them and we can grab them on the way back."

"Great! That'll pay for the trip, at least."

"And, we're just getting started. Where do you think . . . Ohh! What was that?" She straightened up and looked off to the right.

"*ZEK's Faces!* You heard that, too?"

"It sounded like some sort of alarm."

"Maybe," he said. "It's more like I felt it. Like a bell ringing, but not with sound. Wait just a minute, let me listen."

Marc stood where he was and tried to calm his mind enough to do what he did at the mouth of his Line. It seemed right that it should be *felt* for rather than looked or listened for. He quieted his thoughts and projected an awareness into the space here. After a moment, he could sense the strange sound, if sound it was, now like a gentle tone coming from the larger conglomeration to their right. It seemed like an acknowledgment or even an invitation.

He motioned to Kera. "Let's go see. We definitely woke something up, but I think it's safe."

"I'm not so sure, Marc. Be careful. I'm right behind you." Kera had pulled out her gun and Marc realized he ought to pull his, too, but he hesitated.

"It feels safe to me. That big open hatch over there to the right, just past those tumbled beams." He began to slowly make his way through the stuff, clearing a better path for Kera as he went. They reached the hatch and cautiously stepped inside.

It was a ship, or at least part of one. That was certain. Most human ships were hybrids made of human tech (almost entirely from Rindd

Xenoplague

1) interconnected with Ash Alien hulls along with some of the alien's propulsion and other engineering parts like the multi-purpose controllers, gravity assists, and beam weapons. These were parts that had been teased out and understood over the centuries. Marc's own ship was just such a hybrid, but this craft was pristine AA. It was composed of entirely unaltered alien ship parts: hull, corridors, controller units in situ, and more–all consistent with a space-going ship.

Marc noted the wide and tall passageways in here, not yet redesigned for the human form. Original corridors like these had been the only indication of the possible size of the mysterious Ash Aliens themselves. He always thought that if humans had to be a different size, it was better to be smaller than the Ash Aliens. More room for us in their abandoned ships.

Kera was carefully advancing in what seemed to be the direction of the bridge, and sure enough, they entered that larger chamber after ducking some drooping trim rods and panel covers. No one had ever found any chairs or benches in Ash Alien ships, but here, there was a smooth pedestal rising from the center of the room. Situated on it was an artifact, unlike anything Marc had ever seen.

A small gray ovoid, rather egg-shaped and approximately one-third of a meter in diameter, was perched casually on the column. It had sixteen spars extending out from it, each about the same length, another one-third meter, but with some slightly shorter than others. The end of each spar featured another small ovoid shape, about 10 centimeters in diameter. All the spars and smaller orbs were arrayed out in a single plane, so the entire object looked like an artistic representation of a star or sun.

Kera raised an eyebrow at him through her faceplate. Neither of them spoke for a minute.

Marc said, "That's the source. That's where the sound thing came from. It's still singing slightly. Can you hear it?"

"No, no I can't." She paused. "Marc, this could be the real deal. The thing that gets us the kind of wealth that can lead to . . . to what we need to be doing."

"That's for sure, if it doesn't blow us up or something–but, I think it won't. I can feel that it's powerful, but I think it's safe for me to touch it. Can't explain how I know that. Do you trust me on this?"

Kera answered with no hesitation, "Yes. I watched you get us through that Line and it's obvious that you are connected in some way here, to this, but there could still be danger to others. Just be careful. Very careful."

He nodded, then walked up to the artifact and gingerly reached out to it. It did not respond to him in any way, but when he touched the orb, it shifted position slightly. It was not hard-attached to the pedestal, only resting on it. Marc grasped it on two of the opposing spar arms and it lifted easily off its perch. He held it out in front of him so they could both see it better.

"It's not all that heavy. Figured it would be more dense."

Kera touched the gray surface of the central ovoid. "It must be a type of supercontroller or comp system to be in such a prominent place here. I doubt it is purely solid metal."

"Hmmm. Right." He turned, still holding the artifact out in front. "I don't think we need to keep looking around here now. Let's just take it and get out of here. The Rindd engineers I deal with will be extremely interested in this." And, he thought, if it opens up new tech advantages, it could help change the status quo with Harbor in some way. Who knows? The Rindders are none too happy with the way things are, either. With those guys, it's nothing but business, but they've always seen themselves as separate from Harbor, which, of course, they technically are, even if ZEK and Harbor treat them as subjects.

It was a bit awkward to carry the starlike artifact with its spiky arms back through the partially blocked hallways. Once they were outside again, he could lower it and walk more freely. Halfway across the open lava plain between the pile and their lander, Kera came up beside him.

"I'd like to see if I can connect to it like you did. Maybe if I held it for a bit?"

"Sure. Take those arms like I did these."

Kera took the artifact and held onto the spars. She went quiet as she tried to concentrate like he had done. After a minute, the object abruptly started glowing in ghostly blues and greens. It flicked white, and then just as rapidly, the colors were gone. The star was dull gray once again.

"*Oh!*" she said, her exclamation startlingly loud in his helmet speakers.

"*Colors!*" he blurted. "No artifact has shown colors before! Wow! . . . That's simply *amazing!* What did that feel like, Kera? Did you connect with it?"

She took a big breath. "I guess I did! I didn't really feel anything, though. I can't believe it did that. Here, you better take it back."

Kera handed the star artifact back to Marc and they turned toward the lander, but once under his hands, the object suddenly flared colors once again, this time much brighter. Neon blues and greens and yellows fluctuated and rippled along the spars and flickered as sparks off of the terminal ovoids. Then, the loud clang of the sound that was not really a sound rang out again and they turned to look back at the derelict they had just left. It was certain now that this was a complete ship and not just a part of one, for the entire vessel, some parts of it obscured by overlaying detritus, flared up in bright blues, greens, and yellows in response to the artifact in Marc's hands. The ship was huge.

"Oh, Faces! What's going on?" he said.

"That's a real ship, all right. And not so ash gray!"

The alien ship dimmed, its long, circular-banded form disappearing back into its industrial camouflage, but the star artifact continued to glow and pulse in Marc's gloved hands, the bright colors reflecting off of Kera's helmet next to him.

"Come on, Marc. Let's go."

"Kera, I can't let go of it."

She tried to take hold of one of the spars, but her glove slipped on the vibrating, gleaming surface and she couldn't grasp it. "Try to control it, then! Hold on, Marc!"

"Get away from me. In case it blows! Get as far from me and that AA ship as you can!"

Kera looked him in the eye for a half-second and nodded. He watched her lope as fast as her suit and the low gravity would allow, heading across the narrow plain toward the lander, but she stopped before she got there and turned back to see. Marc was still gripping the luminous spars as the bell sound's pitch traveled rapidly up the scale until a loud *whoosh* drowned it out and the world instantly changed.

———————————————

Marc's first thought was one of relief. It felt so good to be home. He opened his eyes and saw that his feelings were misplaced. These surroundings were beautiful, but it was not any place he had ever seen. A lush tropical jungle ran right up to the white sandy beach he was standing on. A greenish-blue sea lapped gentle waves toward him under a cobalt blue sky. The sun was warm and the air smelled organically rich and fresh.

As he stared at the dark green trees and vines, he tried to remember something. He tried to remember . . . to remember . . . who he was? Yes, that was it. He couldn't remember who he was or how he had come to this place.

Something splashed. He turned back to the shoreline just as a fabulous bright blue snake emerged from the waters. It was immense, the size of a transport train, and its neon blue scales shimmered in the sunlight as it shed water. The snake had a curious face: a yellow disc with a man's dark eyes. It's long tongue flicked.

Marc froze as the blue snake slid right up to him and stopped. Then, it spoke into Marc's mind in a deep and rumbling voice.

"To go on, you must overcome me."

Marc tried to speak, but the words would only form in his mind and not emerge from his lips. *Please wait! I mean no harm!*

The snake seemed to have heard him, though. His voice boomed in Marc's mind again.

"To go on, you must overcome me."

Marc felt something in his hand and found he held an energy pistol weapon. A surge of excitement went through him as he realized that some sort of bizarre duel was being proposed here.

"I don't want to fight you. I will die if I fight you. Let me go!"

He looked at the Blue Snake, but it did not speak, nor did it wince in the slightest. Marc felt a spark of anger and raised the weapon to tentatively point it at the creature, but there was something wrong. The world grew dark around him and his hand grew larger and meshed and intertwined together with the gun like some bio-engineered abomination.

A sharp memory flashed in Marc's mind of a cruel man with his hand melted into his gun, while Marc's own hands, glowing red, turned huge as hammers and flailed at him. *Help me, Father! Run away, Mother! Run!* He remembered how the gunman screamed.

Marc looked up as the Blue Snake's tongue flicked again, but there was no sound. He looked back down at his hand, enmeshed in the weapon, but there was no pain–no discomfort. In fact, it felt good, right, and potent. He felt a panic rise in his mind. I could shoot as fast as I think! He looked up at the Blue Snake.

"NO! This is wrong! I don't want to change like that! I don't want to shoot! No, no, no! It's a CURSE."

He tried to pull his hand back out of the gun. Slowly, his real hand began to re-emerge from the machinery of the weapon and Marc put the gun back down to his side. He faced the motionless Blue Snake once more as the air grew brighter again.

"I won't shoot you. It doesn't matter who or what you are. I won't shoot you without need."

Marc dropped the gun into the shimmering white sand.

Very slowly, the Blue Snake began to move, turning itself away from him and revealing the colorful scales on one side of his long body which was still stretched across the sands and tipped into the water. As Marc watched it, an odd notion came to him. Before he thought it through, he strode over to the Snake, took hold of one of the tough blue scales, and quickly climbed up and onto the broad back of the thing.

Marc could feel his heart pounding, but Blue Snake only turned his head slightly and gazed mildly at him. Then, he turned to the front again and began to move.

Well, it looks like I'm going for a ride! Then, Marc remembered what the Blue Snake had said.

I guess I literally *overcame* him.

As they slid along the shoreline, Marc held hard to two of the snake's scales. The beast produced a slow front-to-back wave through its body and suddenly rose, water sheeting off his jewel-tone scales, and flew high over this green and blue world. It was a breathtaking maneuver, but Marc held on without difficulty.

He saw the great forest expanding beneath him, stretching endlessly and unbroken as far as he could see. In his mind's eye, Marc sensed countless millions of infinitesimal creatures at work, all singing some lovely, flowing Song. It filled the world below with life. The growth and the changes, the evolution of the forests and the natural animals–they were all being created and guided by that Song. The flora and fauna grew in response to the music, which now came from one strong voice. It was a woman's voice. He could not see her, but her presence took shape from all the life below him. It was full of joy! She was aware of him! She was smiling at him! He could feel it! She gave him a gift of energy and projected a pure essence of completeness, beauty, health, and deepest wisdom.

Her Great Song reverberated through everything. *"Earth! Earth is Life! Earth is Singing!"*

The energy and emotion of it flowed through Marc like a swift river containing everything that was right and good, washing away all things unwholesome. His heart sang with her Song. Tears flowed freely down his face and the wind of his passage blew them away into a raveling stream behind him.

Xenoplague

The snake was gone. Marc simply floated free above the planet of Life. Was it truly Earth? He had no conception of how long he had been like this. Never before had he known complete Joy. He felt he could fly like this forever, soaring above the verdant greens and oceanic blues, but now some force had tethered him and began to pull him backward, away from that essential, elemental Earth.

"No, WAIT!" he cried out, reaching his hands toward the forests below, but the new force was strong and relentless and the Song diminished as the green-blue planet slowly receded and faded away.

Black space now. Only the stars and a bright nebula to dimly light this void. He was still floating free, and he realized his breathing was normal even though he wore no suit. There were worlds below him now. He recognized them. Farms, Harbor, Hub, and Rindd 1–all situated in an impossible group. A battle was taking place with many Harbor warships firing on a motley collection of non-mils and a line of other warships of Sisters or Rindd designs. They were being slaughtered. Marc wanted to yell, but he could not make any sound.

In one instant, the Harbor Suite Blue and BlackMil warships stopped firing at each other and broke formation. Marc felt compelled to turn around. An Ash Alien ship loomed. It was truly immense, like a small asteroid, and unlike anything he'd ever seen. It had a strange "flavor" in his mind. It tasted of humans and some other alien energies. It seemed artificial in some way and it echoed in his memories as it relentlessly advanced.

A burning sensation caused him to look down at his hands. He held the star artifact again and it was flashing colors. His own cursed hands were expanded and red-hot, locked onto it. Panic rose in him, but just then, another person appeared somewhere between himself and the massive worldlet-sized ship. A woman! Some distance away and approaching him, drifting slowly by on a cross-course, heading toward the planets and the warships.

She also wore no suit, but this all seemed normal somehow. When she was close enough, Marc saw a worried expression on her very beautiful face. She tried to speak, but there was no sound. Then, she reached out to him with both arms and he wanted to go to her but could not let go of the Star. Feelings of desire and frustration flooded him as he saw her turn to look at something beyond him, toward the planets. Silently, she screamed and then passed by him, vanishing.

Marc turned around again, but she was gone. He felt as though he had lost something very important. Now, only one ship was left above the planets. This one looked exactly like the Ash Alien ship he had discovered in his secret system! Its huge rings gleamed in multiple bright colors and its open maw turned red, then white as it turned to face the new moon-sized alien ship, now directly behind him.

"A ship turning colors! I've seen you before! I know you now!"

Blinding white energy roared from it, merging with Marc's scream as he fell into a very black place.

Chapter Seven

"Marc! Marc! Wake up!" Kera's voice sounded funny to him like she was talking in a plastic-padded freight box or something.

Can't she just leave me alone for a little while? This is very comfortable.

Black clouds came, then sunshine again. "Marc! We have to go!"

She's amusing. I'm musing... Ha, ha, ha! I'm funny... huh? what?

"We have to get you back to the ship!" Her voice was clear and loud now.

She jostled his arm, so Marc decided to open his eyes. Kera's face was almost invisible behind the dark helmet visors, but she was leaning directly over him. Some sort of pole was in between them. He was lying on his back, still holding the Star Artifact with a death grip. It was the strut array resting against his own helmet that was in the way. He moved it down so he could see better. The thing appeared to be inactive now–just gray metal once again, and he could easily let go of it. Kera held his shoulders.

"Oh, it's over! You still with me? How do you feel?"

Xenoplague

"Weak. . . OK, I think." He exhaled a body-shaking sob. "Terrible. Terrible weapons and war! But, so much beauty and life! So much at stake. That woman and the Earth . . . It was beautiful! Parts of it–so beautiful!" He fought tears as he rolled over a bit and, with Kera's help, sat up. They were still in the middle of the small lava plain.

"It's fine now," she said, her voice shaking. "We have to get you back on board the ship. Let's see if you can walk." She helped him up but shied away from touching the artifact. Back at the lander's hatch, Marc reluctantly set the Star down so they could cycle in and de-suit, then gently held it again as Kera piloted them back up to the cargo ship, parked in its shallow orbit. The Star's struts felt cool to his bare hands.

In the main cabin, she initiated the medbot. As it worked on him, Marc tried to relate the great vision to her. It was so vivid. He still felt its overwhelming power, emotion, and meaning, but as he spoke, her green eyes searched his. Trying to put it in words, it all began to sound frail and absurd. A frown creased Kera's brow.

"I know it sounds outlandish, but it's important, Kera. This was no fever dream. Something is going to happen and we are already caught up in it. It's . . . I guess I just can't describe it very well in words," Marc trailed off. "I'm OK now. I feel fine." He flinched as the medbot detached and withdrew.

"Let's get out of here," she said.

"Well, at least we got this one artifact. I have to keep it. It's the heart of that ship."

"Means we won't make any money on this run. We'd better hide it."

They moved back into the cargo's bridge, meticulously searching for a place to conceal the Star. Marc pointed to a ledge high above the main screens where ZEK's Face glowered down at them, framed amidst his intricate golden sun rays: the ship's obligatory sculpted icons. He lifted the Star and nestled it in among the decorative spikes and curlicues of the honoraries until it looked like an abstract echo of ZEK himself.

"That's subtle," Kera said.

"Sometimes, there's no better hiding place than in plain view."

Feeling stronger now, Marc prepped the ship for travel and they powered up. Kera watched as the little black world receded in the monitors. She sighed and said under her breath, "So long, Marc's Pile. We'll be back to pilfer more of your riches!"

"Lock us onto those beacons and let's get back home. We've got some work ahead of us. I need someone to do an intense engineering analysis on this Star thing."

"Right," she said. "You'll need a deep Rindd connection."

"I know a Rindder who could probably help. I need to study it, maybe connect with it again. That was no dream battle, Kera. I think it was trying to warn us."

"Warn us? You think it's some kind of AI?"

"That's a possibility that hadn't occurred to me. I don't know, though. It felt more like a special tool or comm, linking me to some other intelligence. Ash Aliens, I suppose, but that doesn't feel quite right, either."

Kera studied him for a moment. "That thing really got to you, didn't it?"

Marc looked up at her.

"I wish you could have connected, too. You'd have no doubt about the power and the overwhelming feeling of intention and purpose I felt."

"Well, I do believe you, or at least I believe *you* believe it. I felt just the edges of that thing's power surge. I don't know if I want to go through that or not."

Marc reached out and took her hand, then pulled her head close to his and just held her for a moment. She relaxed and sighed. Then he frowned as a thought bubbled up from his subconscious.

"What? What is it?" she said, looking up.

"When the ship lit up, did you notice its shape? Did it remind you of anything?"

Kera didn't answer immediately, but pulled up vid from her helmet cam and displayed that moment on the screen. The Ash Alien ship, still buried in its debris piles, glowed from bow to stern. Its massive shape was quite distinctive, from the roughly spherical bridge, down a long bulging mid-section, and ending in a quad nacelle of engines. Several huge hoops of flat metal nested around midships and there was the hint of a larger cylinder under the bridge.

She glanced sharply back at Marc and said quietly, "It looks just like the old vids. The images of the old AA ship that brought the xenoplague. Marc, maybe Anibale is right. This could be another one."

"Yes, I think it is. It's a powerful ship, but I don't think it's a plague ship–not a doomsday weapon. Don't know how to back that up to you. I just know it through the Star." He looked back at Kera and gave a little grimace. "Yeah, we're definitely going to need some help with this one. I'll contact my Rindd connection as soon as we're out."

After a hurried meal, they reached their beacons marking the Gate for the ever-so-faint Line back to Salina. When they emerged, the yellow sun of Salina System was centered on the cross-marks. Marc watched as Kera calculated the course correction to bring them back to the outer sector of Salina Station's commercial zone. Their decoy ship balloon was still presenting its icon and maintenance signals. She made certain that their real ship stayed totally silent and dark.

"Looks like we're still home," she said.

"And well-rested, I'm sure," Marc said with a grin.

"No one around, so let's go for parking . . . Wait! Marc, there's a big ship converging fast from in-system, port side!"

"It's Blue Guard. They're going to attack the decoy!" Marc grabbed the manual control arm and took them off at an angle. "They think we're in there. Gotta get us farther away!"

The big militarized ship did not slow down. Before Marc could move them a few hundred meters, it flashed by their position and receded into the distance. As it passed, the attacker released an energy charge. It struck the balloon. They watched in dismay as it flapped and folded in on itself and then shredded into pieces that began to dance and curl in a chaotic dispersion pattern into the black vacuum.

Kera spoke first. "Can you get us out of here without them seeing us?"

"We can try for it, but full-power will give us away. Here goes best guess."

As soon as he started up the mains, he stopped them again. "No good. They've spotted us."

***

"You have me puzzled, middie Marc," Anibale Prime Blue said. He stood near the cargo ship's main screens. His guards blocked the bridge's exit. "You set up this elaborate and ingenious, if ridiculous deception, you went prospecting to some unknown system you have discovered, and yet, we find an empty cargo vessel. Where are all your alien pimfruits, eh?"

Marc glared. Kera sat in the co-pilot harness next to him, looking tired and stoic.

"Just not too lucky this trip, I guess," he said.

"I believe you must be one of the unluckiest men I've come across in quite some time. That inflated mockery–it must have been expensive? And to think it served you in vain."

"I pay all proper honors and taxes to ZEK. You have no grievance against me. It is not illegal to make a simulated ship. You could have simply held it and taken me to a hearing, but you destroyed it outright, violating my rights, and I intend to make a pleading to Helm for it. You'll find out just how expensive my toy ship was."

"Well, Kera, your friend here has some courage at least. What do you think of his fakery?" His lips smiled, but his eyes did not.

"It worked well enough. Better than you might expect, really."

"Ahh, you think the system he found might be worth something? Yes, I also thought so. We will know very soon. Your nav data was obtained and my helpers are currently investigating, in the Name of ZEK." Anibale activated one of the data screens, which brought up a graphic of the Salina Lines and Gates, including the black pocket ones. "You are a talented pilot, Marc. The Line you found is very faint. Quite faint, indeed."

Kera shot a glance at Marc, but he did not answer.

One of the Blue Guards entered the bridge. "They have returned, Prime. Very faint old Line, difficult to locate its Gate. Leads to a dead system . . . cinder of a star and completely clear–no planets of any kind. A couple of crazy Zips sped by us out there, but no other signs of tech or artificial habitation of the system."

Anibale turned back to Marc and Kera, a real smile playing on his face now. "Well, I guess you are lucky after all. You didn't discover a hellhole and vaporize yourself. But, no nice Ash Alien artifacts either–just a disappointing dead end. A few demented aliens and vast quantities of priceless black space. Rather hard to market that product, though, eh?"

The Blue Guards were grinning at them, too.

Yeah, laugh away. Followed that other old Line, didn't you? Won't find mine.

Marc said, "Well then, you have no reason to hold us or this ship. Let me get back to my cargo runs. I have a lot of profit loss to make up."

"Yes. Yes. You may go back to your scurrying and dealing, but you may wish to remember how Suite Blue has watched over you and kept you from making more mistakes." He leered at them. "Prime Blue will have a golden face one day, and that face will not forget those who have caused him anguish and endless irritation." He made a gesture and his guards relaxed their stances and lowered their guns.

When Marc glanced at Kera, she looked up at the honoraries display where the Star Artifact rested, blending in among the other sun shapes and ornate shields honoring ZEK. She must have looked up there by instinct when he mentioned the golden face.

Stop looking at it! Look down!

To his dismay, Kera continued to stare at the Star without blinking. Anibale caught the edge of their discomfort and paused, studied them a moment, then looked in the direction she was focused. "Ah, Kera. You honor ZEK. This is wise. You should be serving him and not this small-time pilot. You may call upon me, Prime Blue, should you wish to amend your position. I would welcome you into his service."

Kera did not react, nor seem to hear him. Her focus was more intense than before. Then, the Star Artifact began to glow.

Bright blue, then greens cascading over yellows, then a flash of red before turning blue again. All eyes were now riveted on the Star Artifact as it illuminated the entire room with jarring and unexpected hues.

Kera was entrained to it–locked together until, in a moment, it all ended. The room suddenly went dark, and she began to slump. Marc grabbed her and held her.

"What have you two done?" Anibale boomed. "My greatest fear and a danger to us all, and you *desecrate ZEK* with it? This kind of object could bring *plague* down upon us!" He motioned to one of the Blue Guards. "Take it down–with extreme care! Don't look at it!" The guard blanched but did the task, placing the Star on the main console while trying to avert his eyes.

Marc supported Kera's head as Anibale grabbed his suit by the front seam and pulled him up.

"Where?"

Marc just looked at him. All the Blue Guards were crowded into the ship's bridge now, guns aimed. Kera was waking, confusion and pain in her eyes.

"Where did you find it?"

Marc glared back but said nothing.

"You will tell me. I will find it, and I will take what you know from you. Then I'll have your skin for a foot rug! Idiot! . . . Take them. Be careful with her."

They bound Marc and hustled them through the ship's alleys to the main hatch. The Star Artifact was placed inside a protective wrap and gingerly carried by two guards. "Where are you taking us?" he said through gritted teeth.

Anibale did not look back at him. "This is Helm business now. We go to Harbor."

Chapter Eight

From within his specialized control loft behind the huge Golden Screen, and connected through to his five biotech Faces looking out on the other side, ZEK glared down upon the Minister of Culln Lodge. The pudgy man squirmed on the swirled marble floor of the Great Seat hall, directly beneath the Faces. The wretch was wearing one of the ridiculous brown fur suits currently popular with the ZELLINC System's business traders. Their fashions always closely copied each other for fear of any one business lodge gaining some intangible advantage over another. A second man, rounded up at the same time, stood behind him. That one was a rare sight here in Helm. He was obviously from Frahma, the Eight Sisters System, and ZEK's intel indicated he was likely a Sisters "Teacher," one of a growing group sneaking into Harbor's worlds and propagandizing the middies into unrest, undermining ZEK's authority and Harbor's laws–all in the interests of the Sisters, of course.

I'll get to him in a moment. First things first.

ZEK gave his four auxiliary Faces, the two above and two below, positioned at each corner of his main Face, expressions of disgust and disdain. His much larger central main Face scowled as he resumed his grilling of the Lodge Minister.

"My BlackMils are on ZELLINC right now. They have just taken direct control of your lodge's corp center. All of your personnel, all of your records, are confiscated." The Minister started to squeak something, but ZEK cut him off.

"I warned you! Did I not say that ZEK would take whatever steps necessary to prevent Culln Lodge from promoting Suite Yellow behind my back?"

The man shot frantic glances left and right. His body made little unconscious moves, trying to escape the focus of ZEK's scrutiny, but there was nowhere for him to go.

"We did nothing for Yellow! ZEK, you must realize . . ."

"Enough! I have the proof I need. The majority of the Lodges on ZELLINC perform properly within the laws of commerce that have sustained us for centuries, but there is always someone who cheats. You have supplied contraband AA artifacts and gross bribes in the form of cash and jewels to Suite Yellow for the purpose of strengthening that Suite against others and against ZEK. You will forfeit your *self* to me. Your Lodge will be reduced to the base service of the other Lodges on ZELLINC. Your corp center will be emptied and destroyed."

The man had stopped swaying, but his voice was high and nervous. "I offer you a Deal!"

His hands on the podium trembled during the momentary silence. "ZEK Sees you."

ZEK analyzed him using the Faces' strange amplification effect he thought of as the "Other." Whatever the Ash Alien technology was, it gave him insights into whoever stood in front of the Golden Screen with its five Faces. This was especially effective if they stood in the focal spot of the hall where vivid multicolored lines on the smooth granite spiraled into a pure-white center. That the Minister was desperate was obvious, but ZEK analyzed him closely for what he had just said. A Deal? Did the man have the confidence in having something real and new, or was he bluffing? There was nothing there but fear.

ZEK continued to stare at the man without speaking. The Minister's face slowly fell.

"Please! . . . please, ZEK. I will repay you and your Suite! It was all just business, not political. I don't . . . we don't prefer one Color Suite over another! You know that."

"Fool. You have no Deal and you have no standing. All business is political." ZEK grinned at him. "Your Culln shuttle is currently secured down on Harbor, yes? On Suite Yellow's pads, I believe?"

The Minister's expression fell further. He was shaking.

ZEK turned all five of his Faces upward and gazed out over the hall of the Great Seat, scanning the audiences from each of the Color Suites sitting in their assigned sections in the viewing zones on either side and then focused on the jewel-encrusted ceiling and the multi-colored walls at the rear of the hall. The Minister squirmed again and ZEK stifled another smile. He returned his focus to the detestable man.

"You will pay your debt to me now. BlackMil Guards! Take him to the docks. Escort our Minister into an airlock and see to it that as he steps outside, he takes *only* his expensive fur suit as he leaves us here in Helm and *personally* de-orbits to join his Lodge fellows below us on Harbor."

The elite squad of BlackMils moved instantly. The Minister yelled something, but they quickly slapped a gag on him, bound his arms, and dragged him out through the great golden doors at the back of the Great Seat opposite the Faces. It was satisfying to see the crook wiggling like a fish caught on a line. There were only curious stares and silence from the audience.

He looked forward to watching the video replay of the man's ejection later and he would make certain it got posted to all the other Suites and to ZELLINC, of course. Unless they bloat up too much to see, the blue, frosty faces of the recently vacuumed always held a curious expression and ZEK was certain this one would make a nice warning, indeed.

"I am ZEK," his voice boomed through the Great Seat. "The Minister from ZELLINC's Culln Lodge previously standing before me shall be forthwith removed from Helm and Harbor, and so, his crimes shall not recur. His Lodge shall be liquidated and the capital value of it shall come to ZEK, who may distribute some or all of it to other Suites at His own determination and pleasure.

"Bring the other man forward." The older man, standing a few meters off to the side, had remained very still through the Minister's interrogation. A BlackMil guard started to prod him, but he quickly stepped up to the focal point and stopped.

"And you. . . you look like a Sisters man."

It was obvious just from his looks. He had the short gray hair, almost white, cropped in a pilot's cut, plus he wore a long off-white cloak over his plain one-piece work suit.

The man's eyes were calm and focused on ZEK's main Face.

"My name is Silveen and yes, I am from Florinda in the Eight Sisters–the Frahma System.

"You were taken from the Minister's ship. What are you doing here and what business do you have with Culln Lodge?"

"I am a simple traveler. I arranged transport by the Lodge through Rindd space and beyond. I have no part in their business arrangements."

"You are a Sisters Teacher." ZEK watched him closely for his reaction to the accusation.

"I am a Sisters citizen, Sir."

"I say you are one of those Teachers, sent into Harbor Systems to spread lies and stir up trouble!"

"I assure you that I am only a man who travels to learn and to see. I believe we must all work together to improve humanity's prospects into the future. There is much you can teach us, and we also have much to share."

ZEK glared at him with the main Face. The others, he set to eyes closed and aloof.

"Well then, Silveen. You are the first Sisters tourist I've ever met! Other than one lonely trade station, I believe your laws prevent Harborites from ever visiting *your* Frahma System planets, much less seeing any of the numerous Systems beyond Frahma."

"Yes, I must admit that is true. That is why I was traveling with as low a profile as I could possibly manage. Standing here now, I must say it was an ineffective effort in the end."

Soft laughter echoed from the audience. ZEK felt slightly uncomfortable with the cool demeanor of this one. What kind of game was he playing here? Teacher or spy, or both, perhaps?

"ZEK does not accept your claim of passive tourism. You will reveal exactly what you were doing in Rindd space. I have evidence that you were researching into some very old archives. Much of those are classified, but parts of it may be accessible through spurious contacts on Rindd 1 and beyond. Will you now give a willing and full account to my interrogators? You shall not go free otherwise."

The Sisters Teacher gazed up at him without saying anything for a moment.

"You may ask any question you wish, Sir. I have nothing to hide from ZEK, therefore I have nothing to reveal."

The man was infuriating! Didn't he realize he could share the fate of the Minister with no more than the twitch of ZEK's little finger? No, there was some steel in him that even the Other could not penetrate for ZEK. It was unnerving and it called for more serious measures to solve the riddle of this man.

"I don't have time to bandy with a Sisters spook. If you won't tell me what you are truly doing here in Harbor's systems, I'll send you on another tourist trip: back to Rindd. The experts I employ at Barrkon's Oven will convince you to cooperate fully. BlackMils, take him away."

The man went without any resistance as the Great Seat hall filled with a susurrus of murmuring voices, softly reverberating within the huge bejeweled space.

ZEK turned his Faces outward again to the crowd and displayed a coordinated fierce look.

"This session is closed. Harbor saved Humanity. Harbor protects Humanity. I am ZEK."

Chapter Nine

Jindee was driving too fast. The ancient and forbidden field of Ash Alien artifacts lay just beyond the low rounded hills west of Salina's Sidtown settlement. They were now racing toward it with Marc's childhood friend at the controls of the scoopcar. Her hair flew in the dry wind caused by their speed and she grinned at his discomfiture.

"It's off-limits, Jin. You know that. We'll get caught! There's nothing out there but twisted metal anyway."

"Such a spoiler, Marc. Don't you have any curiosity about the artifacts? I'll tell you something. I've been there several times already."

"No, you haven't."

"I have, too! There are still a lot of unknown, undisturbed places where we might find something that will change our luck and get us off this grimy little planet. People are doing artifact mining all over the Domain now and some are getting Elite-rich doing it! We might be next, Marc, but only if you dare to come in with me."

Well, there were some stories about middies getting rich on finds like that. He'd give Jin that point, and it did give him a bit of a thrill thinking of the possibilities. If he could just get back to Farms and go to university there, it would be something. Still . . .

"You've been? There are undisturbed artifacts out there? You're sure, Jin?"

She just nodded at him and made the turn off the main track and onto the trail heading past the westmost dry hill. Marc grunted as she accelerated again and they bumped and flew over the sand ridges and bottomed out in the dried-up seasonal washes that descended out of the hills.

The artifacts were more numerous than Marc had imagined. Most looked really torn up as if this place had been a crash scene or a dumping ground, or both. Jin took them to a more distant wreck that had only one cylindrical gray metal segment showing above the white-streaked sands. She skidded them to a stop and was out of the scoopcar and inspecting the half-buried artifact before Marc could get unstrapped.

"I've never been able to open this main hatch," she said.

"Well, you aren't an Ash Alien, Jin. I wouldn't expect you to be able to open it, you know?"

She tipped her pixie-like face and gave him a sour look. "You're no fun at all. Help me feel for a latch mechanism or something."

He sighed and walked up to the metal hull. There was a line of discoloration that seemed to be a hatchway, all right. He put out his right hand and touched the dull surface. It was completely smooth–no sign of any latches or buttons and he couldn't feel the seam where the hatch presumably was, if it even existed. Jin had moved down to another section of the hull, poking at it, when something as light as a breeze seemed to pull at Marc's fingers. It was very faint, but he relaxed his hand and tried to sense which direction it came from. His hand began to slide up and over, off of the hatch zone, until it was about a half-meter away. Then it stopped. He moved his hand away from the spot and felt the gentle tug leading back to it.

"That's the spot, huh?" he muttered to himself. He let his hand rest there for a minute, then snatched it away when the spot became warm and then rather hot.

"You found something, Marc?" Jinn said as she trotted up to him. Her eyes were shining.

"Don't know. Maybe. Here, hold my hat for a bit so I can focus on this."

He put his hand back on the spot, which began to warm again. He felt his fingers change shape slightly, bringing an immediate feeling of guilt and apprehension. It was the Curse.

The changing showed up every once in a while, but he found it to be more annoying than helpful. It came at seemingly random times and went away before he could do anything useful with it. He had tried, despite his Father's warnings and his own sense of practicality, to call the change–to see if he could use it in some predictable way. It never responded to his requests, pleas, or demands. A few days later, or maybe in a few months, some flicker of morphing would happen, or perhaps his hand would grow and then diminish rapidly in some public situation and he would have to hide himself for fear of being exposed and ridiculed, or worse.

It was a damned nuisance.

Now, it was responding to an alien artifact in a way that sent chills up Marc's spine. He stared at his hand as if it were somehow not a part of him. His fingers seemed to meld together and half-dissolve into the spot on the hull–the spot that was now very slightly glowing in a blurry purple, somewhere in the deep ultraviolet range. Jin let out a little yelp of excitement.

The demarcation line of the hatch zone darkened and then the entire section dropped down about a millimeter as a puff of stale air leaked out around the edges. "Wait, Jin!" Marc yelled, but she had dropped his hat and was already pushing on the panel, causing it to withdraw into the artifact's interior. It was, indeed, a hatch. She aimed her handheld light and stepped quickly into the opening.

The small chamber, filled with pipes, conduits, and odd shapes mounted on the walls, left little room to move around. There were no signs of light or electrical activity. Like all other Ash Alien artifacts, it seemed completely dead, but Marc kept thinking about that UV glow and the feel of the tug on his hand. Jin reached up to investigate a wall box that had some protrusions on it.

"Jin! Stop poking at things! You don't know what you might start up," Marc said, his sense of danger palpable. Jin seemed oblivious, as always, but she glanced back at him and pulled her hand back from the box.

Around a shallow corner, a bulkhead was sealed with another closed hatch. This one, however, had an obvious control box with four studs.

"Hey, look!" Jin said, "Let's see if we can open it! Could lead to the control room for the ship, or maybe even the cargo holds!" She touched one of the buttons before Marc could get a warning out of his throat.

The inner hatch hissed and popped outward, cracking open a gap about a quarter-meter wide before jamming to a stop. All the air around them began rushing into the gap, howling as it pulled Jin in, yanking her right arm sharply into the crack. She turned a shocked face toward Marc as he careened into the hatch next to her. She screamed as her body slipped a little further into the gap.

"Low pressure in there! The door is stuck. Grab my arm! It should equalize quickly."

Jin gripped his extended right arm with her left hand as he held onto the frame above the hatch with only the friction of his left arm and hand against the smooth metal bulkhead to anchor them. They held on tight, her body half bent over the protruding edge of the hatch and her chest wedged in the gap. Her right arm dangled in the space beyond as the fierce wind screamed past them into what had to be a huge dark void inside. Marc was grateful the hatch hadn't opened completely. The sound was deafening and it took longer than Marc thought for the pressures to equalize.

His hand began to slip down the wall and Jin yowled as she shifted another few millimeters in. His fingers transformed again: hardening, sharpening, penetrating the bulkhead like metallic anchors.

The wind finally stuttered and, with a mournful sigh, abruptly stopped. Slowly, Marc withdrew his finger hooks from the bulkhead and looked up at Jin's drained face. "Are you OK? Can you pull your arm back?"

"I, I think so." Her voice was trembling. "Hold on to me–I don't want to get sucked in there!"

"It's OK, Jin. It's equalized. It won't pull you in now."

As he secured her, she rotated her body and began to pull her shoulder and then arm out of the opening, but just as she got past the upper part of her arm, the hatch abruptly slammed shut on her.

Jin screamed and Marc grabbed her around the waist, circling to put his back to the bulkhead and push the hatch open with his feet, but it would not budge.

Blood flowed down Jin's arm.

He rotated back to the front and grabbed the edge of the hatch that was propped open now only by her arm.

"Get it off me, Marc–get it off! Make it let go!" Jin's voice was high-pitched and frantic.

He concentrated on his hands, calling for the Curse to come again and help. Nothing seemed to change. He pulled with every bit of his strength, but the hatch was stuck.

"Stay still. I may have to get help."

"NO! I can't wait for help. Get it off me!"

Just at that moment, Marc felt something. A flow of energy that seemed like it was coming from somewhere far away. His hand was morphing again. No–both hands were changing! He held them up, dumbfounded. They inflated and became claw-like: huge pincers that felt very, very strong to him as he instinctively flexed them. Jin yelped and her eyes widened into red, watery spheres as she saw them.

Marc did not hesitate. He grabbed the hatchway at its edges on either side of Jin's arm and pulled. The metal shrieked as it bent and tore away. Her arm suddenly free of the crushing door, Jin crumpled to the floor and passed out.

Xenoplague

"Damn, Jin, I told you not to touch stuff," he said. In another moment or two, the energy had fled him and his hands returned to normal. He gathered her up and carried her back to the scoopcar. He dug out the car's simple medkit and tried to stanch the bleeding.

She's going into shock. Gotta call Paulo at the hospital and get him to evac us.

In the hospital, Jin's story of Marc's amazing rescue began to spread. He stayed quiet about it, feeling lucky in a guilty sort of way that Jindee was well known by the small community for being rash and a storyteller. Her tale of his magic hands was not really believed by many. There was one, though, who did.

———————— ✳ ————————

"Out there messing around with that damn Ash Alien junk when you *know* it is dangerous, and forbidden *because* it is dangerous! And, you exposed your Curse to outsiders. That is the greater danger, Son. Much harm may come of this." Father's leathery, wrinkled face was compressed into a frowning landscape. His eyes held not anger so much as terror, Marc realized.

"Why do you call it a Curse, Father? It just saved my friend's life today. It came when I needed it to–when I *really* needed it."

"It came at your bidding, did it? Bunch of religious nonsense! You've been listening to that old ball-fruit farmer."

"This has nothing to do with old Zike. It has nothing to do with religion, either. Religion is about beliefs, Father. This is something that *happens*. Yes, it happens on its own terms, but despite what you believe about it, it came today when I needed it most! There is something to this that is not random or purposeless. That's all I'm saying."

"You think it's alive, like someone possessing you? That's religion, boy.

"Son, you know what the Elites will do to us if they find out about the Curse. There are strict laws against propagating cults and

102

religions, and they'd consider this to be just exactly that, even if you don't. There are even worse edicts against messing with Ash Alien damned artifacts! They will haul us all off to labor in their camps and be justified in taking our lands and homes in the process. Is that what you want? You risk it for yourself and for your Mother and me every time you perform these tricks!"

"I was not performing tricks. Would you have me just sit by and let my friend die when I could do something to save her? If a tool comes to your hand, do you refuse it under these circumstances?" Marc paused, somewhat surprised at his own words. "I couldn't, Father. I couldn't."

Father looked into his son's eyes for a long moment, then sighed a low whistling kind of sigh, the kind Marc knew meant he had come to the end of his willingness, or perhaps capacity, to talk things through. After a moment more, he turned and slowly walked back out to the barns. Marc suddenly perceived his father in a new way, as if he had just seen him after a long absence, or perhaps for the first time. A little shock went through him. Yes, that was it—something new. Father looked old. Marc stood there a while longer before he, too, could let go of his thoughts and feelings enough to return to the house.

Chapter Ten

Anibale, Prime Blue, frowned in frustration. "A formal complaint to the Council of Colors, so soon?"

His Suite Board Leader, Chafin, sat across from him, twirling his spotted hand as he revolved the worn knob on top of his ornately decorated gold and ivory walking staff. They were in the elegant private study of the official manor inside Suite Blue's territorial zone located on the prime planet of the Second Domain, Harbor. It was Anibale's first chance for a private conference since he had returned with that dangerous Star device.

"It's Prime Red, of course," Chafin said. "She is making her moves now because of your attack on the Sisters ships at Farms System. You should not be so surprised."

"Jade will not get much from ZEK. He despises her. She will have to make alliances with Cyan or Yellow and I do not think they much like her either!"

"ZEK will only give her what he must. A puny reward for going through the motions of a Complaint and for taking the political risk for doing so. It will be a gain of no consequence for her," Chafin said, "but you should not underestimate her ability to manipulate the other Colors, Anibale."

Anibale looked up at his closest advisor and almost friend. Chafin's expression was not agitated, but serious and even calm. Old fungbeast. Doesn't he ever see the dangers that are all around us? We live in perilous times!

The hot Harbor sun cast muted beams into the embroidered curtains and carefully tooled rare-wood paneling of the chamber, picking up the colors of the skylight mosaics. At a soft tone, a wife appeared, silently offering them food from the Suite kitchens below. Anibale waved her away.

"You advise caution or subterfuge?"

Chafin's lips curled up slightly, then drooped again into his beard. "Some of both, of course. First, though, you must come clean in front of ZEK's own Face and present this new terror you have discovered. It may yet bring the status and leverage you desire, but you must be cautious. This thing could turn and bite you while leaving others in a superior position. Do you truly believe it is plague-related?"

"I saw it come alive in colors–*colors*, Chafin! Like in the old videos of the xenoplague ship. It produced colors when its plague was unleashed onto Earth. I always thought that might have been something added onto the images by an over-enthusiastic archivist a thousand years ago, but then it happened right in front of me! Ash gray for all the other things the aliens left behind but colors for the plague!

"I will know more when my probes return. It is amazing that this middie could find such a faded Line, but his system was empty. Artifacts don't float around in empty space. His Star must have come from another system behind that one. This is exactly the kind of artifact I have feared for years. I will extract its location from his stubborn middie head or find it myself."

After Chafin retired to the back rooms, Anibale stepped through the ornately carved titanium chamber doors and into the hall near his private lift. In a couple of minutes, it would take him down to the transport station for the brief shuttle ride back up to the orbiting governmental moon, Helm. It was time to go check on the two middies who were being examined in his med labs up there.

Before entering the lift, he took a moment, as he always did, to walk out onto the high balcony at the western end of the azure and silver cloth-draped hallway and look out over his home domain here on Harbor: Suite Blue itself, stretching out in a crazy quilt of buildings, roadways, and parks below.

The sun glinted off the waterway that separated the Suite Blue domain from Suite Red's lands just to the west. Territory on this artificially re-made world was never an issue. All had been set equally, long centuries ago. All of this time's battles and games were about the worlds that lay behind Harbor and over the people and resources that could be used and controlled while avoiding ZEK's wrath and the unpleasant interference of his BlackMil forces. This old homestead would always be kept as it is: sacred, if anything could be called that in this essentially profane place. Harbor would always be a safe retreat where each Suite could compare themselves with the others and crow with advantage or cry with misadventure as fate and Elite human wits determine.

All who lived in this part of Harbor were his. They were his wealth and his power. The more wealth he gained, the more people would gravitate to it as to a magnet or be compelled into his service by it, thus building the power. He must continue to gain, and so, his rivals must continue to lose. He would use this newly discovered artifact if he could–use it like a maul to strike his opponents or use it as a wedge to lever them off their feet and into his shadow. One way or the other, but he *must* control it.

Gazing into the hazy distance, Anibale could not see Prime Red's city from here, but he cast his curses to Jade–old dried-up witch! May your riches flee and your lands be emptied!–before turning back to the hall and striding forcefully between the two smartly uniformed men guarding the silver and copper inlaid lift chamber.

Xenoplague

The middie, Marc, was laid out on a lab palette, his head lolling to one side. Anibale frowned as the techs disconnected the chem lines and nanobot ports.

"Well?"

The Suite Blue lead doc, Jantinel, looked up. "He presents an interesting case, Prime. He has memories that are truly buried under a mantra-like image of a faint Line. We cannot get past it."

"He's purposely hiding it from you? Surely you can break through this willful resistance."

"It's not willful. That's the problem." Janitel pulled up a chart on his viewscreen. "He has placed himself in some type of a trance state where he, himself, while in that state, does not know that he is resisting and is as ignorant of the data we seek as we are ourselves."

Anibale smoothed the embroidered cuff of his blue and silver cape. "A subconscious block, then?" he said.

"Something of that sort, but unique in form and much stronger than anything I've ever seen."

"Is he conscious–aware here, now?"

"No. I cannot see any indication of it. He is deep within whatever space he has created to hide in." Jantinel leaned back against the lab cabinets and looked into Marc's puffy face. "We will monitor him, of course. Observe how and when he emerges–if he emerges."

Anibale grunted. "See that he does, doctor. See that he does. There are other ways to deal with him. What of the woman?"

"She is awake and functional. You'll need to ask Binter about her results. Second bay down the hall to the right."

Anibale motioned his two bodyguards to follow him. Hunched over and wearing a lab coat, Binter was going over his data charts in the outer chamber of the med bay. Kera was sitting up on the edge of a palette in the secure, reinforced inner bay just beyond a transparent door.

"She is unharmed? What have you found out?"

Binter looked up with a start, then said, "Yes, she is fine, Prime. She has no hidden strata in her mind and she truly does not know where the Line in question is located, even though she went through it. She claims she simply does not know how Marc–the other middie involved–found the system where the artifact came from.

Binter hesitated as Anibale continued to stare at him without comment. "She has a very strong personality center, but we believe this is a true assessment."

Anibale gestured to his guards to leave him. "I will speak with her–privately." He entered the inner bay and the door sealed behind him.

Kera looked up at him with an open expression on her face. Anibale said, "So. Kera. You have been caught up in events that were more than you planned for, eh?"

"I guess that's one way of putting it."

"You do not know where this Line is located–the Line to the place your Marc found the star-shaped artifact? How could you not know?"

She looked directly at him. "As I told the others, I was just along for the ride. He–Marc–was able to take us into a faint Line he'd found. He's been prospecting out of Salina and other systems for a long time. I thought the one you checked was it. I really don't understand it."

"You were with him when he found the Star?"

"No."

Anibale studied her. She was lying. Remarkable under these circumstances. "The Star activated for you. What did you do? What were you trying to do?"

Kera's face turned a bit white as she remembered. "It was unexpected. I don't know what I did. Marc showed it to me earlier and put it up there on the bridge, in with the honoraries. All of a sudden, it seemed to call me and I just found myself staring at it.

"It *wanted* my attention. I felt like I was being asked to do something–to control something." Her green eyes flicked up to his and stayed. "Is Marc OK? Is he here? What will you do with him, with me?"

Anibale smiled inside. *What will I do with you? The only one who can activate the plague star? Keep you hidden and keep you in my domain! That is what I will do.*

"He is unharmed but uncooperative. We shall continue to encourage him, as I am encouraging you. Your Marc will bear the responsibility for the Star. He will be detained until we can make our assessments and judgments. You, too, must remain here and must help us to understand this artifact. Only *you* have activated it, and this is something no one has ever done since the very beginning of the Second Domain. Do you realize this? Do you understand the significance of it?"

"You think it's plague-related, don't you?" she said. "There was certainly a lot of power in it. I did not feel that it was a weapon or a negative power, but I only got that one glimpse. I could be wrong."

Anibale smiled. "Yes, you could. This is why it is critical that we understand what the Star is. We must–carefully–study it and test it.

"Here is my dilemma. Since you are the only person who has activated the thing, you must stay here in Suite Blue domains on Helm or down on Harbor. I cannot free you for obvious reasons, but I cannot compel you to help in this investigation against your will. It is too dangerous. Therefore, I will offer you a deal.

"You will work for me up here at Helm under the aegis of Suite Blue. I will make it worth your while with a room in the Suite, and everything you may need in terms of food and clothing and so on. I will allow a generous working salary for you as well. In return, you will *willingly* help me explore the Star. We will try to determine its actual nature, how it might be deactivated, and you will report every aspect of your interactions with it."

"That could be very dangerous. You might not have to pay me for very long."

"True," he said.

"What if I refuse?"

"For political and practical reasons, you will be confined indefinitely."

Kera smiled coldly at Anibale and he returned it. "Well then, I accept your kind offer, your honor."

Anibale paused, then reached out and touched her shoulder, his face serious again. "You may help us to save humanity once again." He turned and left the med bay.

———

Kera sat on the palette and thought.

Unbelievable! He's going to put me up in Hotel Blue and have me work for him? What are the possibilities here? He's not stupid, but he is kind of desperate. Anibale is a zealot for plague protection and this Star Artifact is the perfect trigger for him . . . and a huge political tool. If he can control the Star and "save humanity," he'll be ZEK in no time. This is it. This is my chance! I'm going to ride his prissy powder blue coattails as far as I can!

What about Marc, though? I can't help him like I am now. If I can get some control, some power here, I can help Marc and myself at the same time. That's the only way.

Kera's musings were interrupted when the medlab door hissed open and two middie women entered. They were in refined Suite Blue staff dress and both were very beautiful.

"I am Simune. This is Valezah. You are Kera? Well met, then. We have your room prepared."

They led Kera out, away from the utilitarian medical sector, and into an amazingly decorated blue and silver filigreed lift. It suddenly became real to her she was here on fabled Helm itself, surrounded by the wealth of the Elites and the presentation of that wealth at every opportunity by each of the Color Suites as they compete with one another here in this ultimate political arena.

Wonder if I can pry some silver out of that control cover? Banish the thought.

Kera tried to hide her unintended smile.

Her room was not opulent by Helm or Harbor standards, but it was still quite something to a Farms girl, used to ship hammocks and rent rooms. She presumed the Suite builders had attempted to tone things down for the rooms in the worker's area, but their innate compulsion for showy opulence just couldn't be entirely contained. She decided it would do just fine for now. Simune indicated one of the true-leather chairs and showed her how to activate the screens and open out the bed unit. Kera ran her fingertips over the soft, blue silks, thinking how nice it would be to actually sleep on them instead of trading them for crates of ballfruit or AA motors.

"I will escort you to The Commons dining salon in one hour," said Valezah, opening a closet and removing a staff dress outfit. "Please be certain to wear *this* one. I'll explain later. Will you?"

"Yes, of course." Kera admired the details sewn onto the blue gown's hems, then hung it on a silver hook by the mirror. "Valezah, how am I viewed here?"

Valezah studied her face–evaluating her. "You are a valued Suite Blue staff member. Prime Blue has instructed us to give you every courtesy and show you the things you need to know to accomplish his goals and tasks."

"All right. Is that it, though? I assume there are . . . restrictions here."

"We all work under many restrictions. Yes, there are some specific restrictions for you." Valezah leaned closer and spoke softly, "I do not know what your role is, but I do know you are in danger here. Attend me to the salon and I will be able to make things more clear."

"I see. I understand. Thank you, Valezah."

The two women left. Kera waited a while, then tried the door control. It was, of course, locked. Just due diligence.

Kera spent almost the entire hour scanning the info screen for any scraps about Anibale, the artifact, or anything else that might give her a clue about her situation. Nothing. Just standard news feeds and propaganda–music and long-winded speakers. She would need to find more discreet sources. Now, though, it was time to get ready.

Her hands trembled as she tried to fasten the folds and unfamiliar closings of the dress.

She considered her growing excitement.

Frankly, I'm scared. Got hold of a big, hairy, mean boro beast and I'd better hang on for all I'm worth! What have I got to lose, though?

As she thought it through, the dress finally cooperated and Kera took in her reflection in the mirror. She looked good.

Concentrate. This is just another complex trade deal. I can do this. Marc needs me and I need me! OK, girl, we gotta ride and move fast enough to win. Like I have any choice.

The door chimed and Simune and Valezah were there to collect her. Kera turned a bit to show the dress and shrugged. They smiled and took her hands.

The Commons dining salon was designed, they told her, to be a place where off-Helm middies on official business, staff and aides, and also Elites from different Color Suites could interact in an ostensibly neutral zone, here on Helm.

"I have ordered our meal ahead," Simune said. "We like to sit over by that bird mural."

Kera's mouth dropped. The mural was a jewel-encrusted mosaic that covered a recessed wall some twenty meters wide. A fantastic-looking bird creature with a tall tail was depicted in a flashing rainbow of colors, but prominently greens and blues with yellow spots and rings of other iridescent hues.

"Ohh . . . It's beautiful! What is it?"

Valezah glanced at it. "Some imaginary bird. I think they call it a peekok. We like to sit here because it's close to the personal rooms."

It took a moment, and then Kera smiled. Valezah was referring to the women's lavatory.

"Oh, I see."

There were several hundred people in the entire salon, but the place was large and had many recessed wings, so it did not feel crowded. A steady hum of voices was mostly absorbed by the rich wall fabrics and green plants.

The meal was wonderful. Brazed genbull-hinds from the ranges on Beyond, perfectly seasoned corn and spikegreens from Farms, of course, and even a rare pink wine from Maiko's Mars, one of the few Harbor systems Kera had never had a chance to visit.

As they finished the main courses, Valezah whispered and motioned toward the personal room. The three women went together, but once inside, Simune went ahead and Valezah guided Kera to a corner area. No one else was around them. Valezah's expression became very serious and her voice was quiet but stern.

"I said you were in danger here. You did not seem surprised, so I assume you are aware of some of the events that you are involved in, yes?" Kera gave her a nod and she continued.

"Anibale, Prime Blue, is attempting to grab power, but in a way no one has dared in centuries. He is stirring up troubles in the border zones. There is guarded information about a new artifact, possibly a very dangerous one. I don't know how you are involved, but you may be into something deeper than you realize. You are very restricted here. Under Anibale's control, you will be a pawn for him and you will never escape–never return to your old life or world. He will use you without mercy and dispose of you with no regard or regret. You do understand? Yes. I see you do.

"There is someone who would like to help you. If you wish to have options, I can take you to this person. You must decide quickly–there is not much time."

"I don't need time to decide. I'll go, of course."

Valezah stared at her for a moment, then made a quick gesture. Simune reappeared with another woman. Kera did a double take. This person was her clone. Same dress, same size, face, and hair.

"It is a bioactive mask. She will be Kera for a while."

Simune and the alternate Kera returned to the dining salon, presumably to enjoy Kera's dessert, and Valezah took her into a separate area of the personal room where a low table was surrounded by large open closets for guest use. Near the other end of the table, a woman sat with her face hidden inside a large hood. At her gesture, Kera sat down across from her and the woman slid back her hood to reveal a very made-up face with narrow and sharp bird-like features surrounded by wisps of black and graying hair. This was gathered under a bright red skullcap decorated with pearls and tiny red feathers.

Her high-pitched voice startled Kera.

"You know who I am?"

"Of course, your honor. Prime Red."

"You may call me Jade," she said, and her thin face broke into a strained smile.

Chapter Eleven

Marc struggled to wake up. Everything kept coming and going. Real . . . unreal. It was frustrating.

Finally, the bell stopped ringing in his head and he woke into an unpleasant firmness and a quick assessment of where he was. Med cell for sure. Strap restraints on his arms, legs, and torso.

No one here, but they'll certainly be monitoring me.

He tried not to move. The door opened and a medbot trundled in followed by a dull-faced woman with thinning hair. She wore a white smock.

"Ah, awake now. You'll feel better in an hour or so," she said. "You will be positively re-assessed now that we have the location of your new system."

His mind cleared further as he registered what she had just said. Marc searched her unflinching eyes and felt his heart fall. He blinked.

"Did you think we would not find it behind that empty system? How many Lines back was it again?"

Marc relaxed. *She's on a fishing expedition. Anibale must think my system is through that black pocket and behind it on another* faint Line. She doesn't know a thing!

"Seven, I think." He gave her a slack-faced grin.

What little pasted-on pleasant aspect had been on her face fled into a frown and she spun on her heel and left the room. The medbot hummed.

As it extended its probe to inject some renewed psych venom into his right arm, Marc felt a faint energy stirring inside himself. His old primal fear of what his body was doing without his approval rose instantly, but the revulsion and fear of the med-probe and its immanent sting overrode it and he decided not to let the damned thing enter his arm.

Using all his power of intention and determination, he concentrated and thought about leather.

My arm is made of leather, like the steel-hide of a salt-cow on Salina! Yeah, that's right. It's tough! Just try to inject something through that wall, you stupid thing! Leather, leather, leather. Steel, steel, steel!

The other part of Marc's mind, the part that normally observes things, watched in amazement as his arm physically changed. It swiftly grew thicker and a brown calloused texture formed on its surface from his wrist to the shoulder. The medbot lifted the aerosol injector to Marc's arm and activated it. The spray mist bounced off and clouded the air. Marc coughed and quickly turned his head away.

The bot backed off, whirred a moment, then pulled out an old-fashioned metal needle–apparently its backup plan. The needle simply skewed off to one side and broke.

"I'm sorry, Sir," the robotic voice droned. "There has been an unexpected technical problem. Maintenance has been notified. Thank you for your patience."

Marc smiled and watched the medbot retreat to the other side of the small room. When he looked back at his arm, it had returned to normal.

Well, just like that. Now, how did I make that happen? I concentrated–hard. I was determined–angry, even. Intentions and emotions together? Could be. . . So, what else am I angry about?

Marc twisted against the polymer restraints holding him to the table. "I just HATE these!" he said.

This time, the Curse worked so fast that he rolled off the gurney when the bands snapped. He grabbed its rail to stay upright against the sudden blood-rush dizziness. The medbot was in standby mode, and he quickly disabled it.

Others would return soon. Escape was the only thing now. He gingerly pressed his hand against the door control and focused on the word "OPEN," softly repeating the word out loud. Something happened. It felt like a filament leaving his hand and moving into the door's circuitry. The door suddenly slid aside. Still agitated, Marc spared no thought for where he might go.

In the outer room, the woman in the smock snapped her head and yelped as Marc crossed the space between them and struck her viewscreen, shattering the plastics. His grab was too late as she ducked under his arm and ran for the outer door. She got it open and spun herself out into the hallway. Before it closed completely, Marc's re-hardened hand blocked it and, after a moment, he forced it to reopen.

A quick look outside. A long hallway stretched to his left, eventually curving away. The nurse was just disappearing around the bend. The same sort of hallway to his right had the additional feature of a purple-caped guard sprinting toward him from about twenty meters. Marc ran at him and they met with a rough crash. Marc's hard right hand struck the guard's weapon away as he tried to raise it, then made a mess of his face.

Marc's hands throbbed as he pulled the Purple's limp form back into the outer room of the medlab. He stripped off the guy's robe and coms helmet and put them on, thanking his luck that they weren't too small for him. Outside, no one else seemed to be coming, so he grabbed up the short energy gun the guard had lost and headed down the right-hand hallway, walking briskly but not running. His head was still spinning and he tried to calm his breathing down to a more steady rhythm.

No alarms. I guess their medlab zone security is not designed to cope with someone with my kind of curse.

There were other medlabs on the right side along the hallway, and he quickly checked each one to see if Kera was there. All were empty.

If she's still down here, she'll be up the other way. Too many guards and med staff there. Must try to find a place to blend and hide for a while until I can think.

On the left side, a little further down the corridor, a hatch stood open. It was the Purple's guard station.

Marc slipped quickly into a small room filled with monitors. A master viewscreen with "Entry Alert" superimposed over a red background glowed at the center of the array. Marc closed the room's hatch, pulled the shaded visor from the guard's helmet down over his face, and stepped up to the consoles. The collage of keys and buttons was confusing at first, but he soon found a standard set of menus.

Ahh, there's the one: *Cancel Alert*. I believe I shall.

OK, maybe I've bought some time. Now where do I go?

This was Anibale's designated zone here in Helm. He'd have to find his way into a more neutral sector. The other Suites would not likely turn him over to Suite Blue out of hand. They would want to hold him for their own reasons, however, so the critical thing was to remain undiscovered. Then he had to find a way to find Kera and regain the Star.

Marc searched the comp for Helm building plans and, after a moment, some general public-style maps appeared. He was apparently deep into Suite Blue's interior levels. Rather than a natural planetoid with things arranged on the outside, Helm was a construct—an artificial hollow moon with the main habitation areas, including the Great Seat auditorium, the Council of Colors' legendary White Hall, and the governmental areas, all situated near the more accessible surface. Spaced evenly around the moonlet and going down toward the center were each of the Color Suites' designated and separated zones, arranged like pimfruit wedges. The deepest central interior sphere was off-limits and unmapped except to show general icons for huge water tanks.

This artificial world was massive enough to exhibit some minor gravity, but not nearly a standard one-g, so it had been built by the Harbor ancestors like an old-style station with added AA artificial gravity units in the lower regions to supplement. They had also placed those huge water reservoirs near the core to help provide and normalize standard gravity. The water could be redistributed as needed to optimize Helm's mass apportionment and rotational physics.

Marc added "schematics" to the search and got something more interesting: maintenance maps showing what appeared to be access hatches to the work areas.

That's better. OK, that one should do. If I can get deep enough, I might find a way to cross over into another Color or government-neutral zone and make my way back up without being detected.

The hatch was close by. Marc straightened his visor and brushed down the robe with his hands before stepping back out into the hallway. As he emerged, two Blue Guards sprinted his way, weapons in hand and heading toward the medlab.

"Out of the way, fool!" one yelled as they blew past him. Marc backed up to the wall, grinning to himself, and immediately walked the other way.

Once he was safely through the other metal maintenance hatch into the work area, he felt rather at home. It was an extended area of pipes and conduits, control meshes, and circuitry nodes–almost like being in the bowels of his own ship. Most of the stuff was a mystery, but he got a general sense of what some of the substructures around him were by studying them for a minute.

He made sure the hatch was back in place and displayed no signs of having been opened, then headed through the dim, yellow light to a descending ladder.

Marc climbed down a couple of levels and exited onto a metallic grid walkway that led past large machinery giving off a nearly subsonic hum. Two mechanics in gray suits were making adjustments to a control mesh when they saw him approach. The larger man thrust his chin up.

"What do you want? What are you doing in here?"

Marc came right up to them. "There's been an escape by someone in the medlab. Suite Blue wants all of you to secure your upside hatches and hold anyone suspicious."

The other man said, "Damn. Just when we're getting this thing to cooperate. They won't like it if the coremass gets off-balance again. You sure about this?"

"Those are the orders, straight from the Prime. Don't blame me, I'm just the delivery boy."

The bigger man looked sour, but the other one smirked. "OK, but we'll blame it on you Purples when they ask why the dinnerware is falling off their fancy silver tables."

"Any more of you guys down this sector?" Marc asked.

"None from my crew," the big one said. "Nobody down there 'cept a few ugly BogBiters near the reservoirs. You best stay clear of them rascals." He laughed.

"All right. I have to make a quick check, though. You two better go on up and deal with those hatches."

The two men nodded and trudged to the ladder. Marc walked the other way into the darkness beyond the machinery.

He reached the bottom of another section and paused to catch his breath, thinking about how lucky he was so far and how that was surely changing right now. The unrobed real Purple Guard would be discovered quickly, along with that drab nurse's report and his own disappearance. Then, those two mechs would report seeing a Purple down here.

A beam of light slashed somewhere off to his left. He heard voices faintly reverberating. There was no time to lose.

Marc turned to his right and immediately a big, black shape appeared around the corner. Marc jolted to a stop and then tried to take a step back. Another worker was holding a heavy metal ratchet tool in one hand. The man slapped the tool against his open hand a couple of times, then he leered and grinned, exposing misshapen teeth. He was one of the ugliest human beings Marc had ever seen. His huge head was distorted like a twisted and lumpy earthpotato, and his arms and legs were thick columns covered in dense black hair.

"Take it easy, friend. I'm . . ."

"*I don't like Purples,*" he interrupted—his voice a rough rumble. "You're not s'posed to be down here." His contorted smile widened and he stepped forward, raising his ratchet over his head. "This is my place."

"Wait—I'm not a Purple! I'm trying to get away from them!"

"Can't fool me." His words slid into a guttural laugh. The man's tree-like arm came down with the massive tool. Marc's arms flew up and his hands instantly grew to twice their size and hardened. The heavy ratchet bounced off of them and flew out of the guy's hand just as Marc's big right fist found his repugnant face. The tool clanged loudly as it ricocheted off the tight maze of metal pipes.

With a *humphh*, the man went cross-eyed and slumped to the floor grating—out cold. He was too large to move, so Marc jumped over his bulky torso and scampered down the dark metallic corridor where the brute had appeared. The noise would soon bring others to his location. Must find another option.

He slid down a ramp and a short metal ladder then stopped to investigate another kind of light that caught his eye: a small and dim splash of multiple colors that came from a dirty backlit sign mounted above an old-style round portal hatch. The sign frame and hatch were both made of a yellow metal, causing it to stand out from the otherwise rusty wall. Like its sign, the hatch was covered with dust, but it featured a highly sophisticated electronic genescan lock, lit with one steady red lamp.

That's the old-fashioned rainbow pattern, the sigil of the Council of Colors! Whatever is behind here is tightly secured, but that also makes it an unlikely place for anyone to look for me. An effective barrier to others if I can access it.

He felt renewed panic as another swipe of light flickered on the walls and piping beside him, much closer this time. He was reluctant to mess with the hatch controls directly. That would likely set off an alarm. But he remembered how he had been able to manipulate the medlab door. It was time to call the Curse on purpose again and see if it would respond.

He extended his right hand to the hatch's seam and concentrated. His hand felt like it dissolved into sand, but when he looked, it was unchanged. There was something, though. He *felt* the portal. Not just the outside surface, but inside as well. He felt the edges of the seam between the door and frame as if it were a widening metal canyon. He touched something. Was it a bar? Yes, a short bar with fine gear teeth and wires. Circuits and sensors. Electrons flowing through those wires like water in a microscopic straw. He reached for the wires and *touched* them while his hand still gripped the outside seam. His fingers, if they still were fingers, felt the data flow–felt the information itself expressed in that digital lock. Then he detected a change and he relaxed his fingers.

He gave the geared bar a final nudge and removed his hand. With a small puff of air, the hatch popped open.

Marc glanced once at the smudged rainbow sign glowing above it. The colors were flashing now. As another, brighter light beam swept over the pipes and machinery behind him, he quickly stepped inside the hatch and pulled it closed.

It was dim in this new zone and quiet. A strange odor, like old mold mixed with slightly sour chemicals permeated the air. This region was less crowded with piping and wiring, but walled with much larger tank structures. Presumably some of the water reservoirs for the mass adjustments, but perhaps serving as part of Helm's drinking water supply, too.

A black shape skittered and rushed by Marc's boots, making him jump.

A BogBiter, I suppose. Must be those water reservoirs I'm smelling.

I wonder what the Council of Colors has to do with this lower zone. At least I'm technically out of Suite Blue's territory.

Moving along the ramp down here was easier. The Ash Alien artificial gravity was diminishing this close to the center sectors of the planetoid. It would be zero-g at the bottom.

Suddenly, his head hurt. A silent, yet very loud bell reverberated–that same distant ringing that took him back to a black lava plain and a jumble of artifacts. In his mind, he saw himself holding the Star with both hands, powerless to let go.

A gleam of colored light dimly reflected off the side of the large tank next to him. It flickered up through numerous layers of metal mesh walkways arrayed along the depths beneath his feet. As the painful sound increased, he watched, transfixed, as the flaring hues changed from blue to red to green.

Something far below him was glowing.

As the sound increased to a crescendo, Marc held his hands over his ears and fainted.

When he came to, the bell sound was gone and the gloom of the reservoir chamber had returned. He was on his left side, sprawled across the walkway where he had fallen. The colors and bell sound must have been an alarm he had triggered, because a bright beam of pure white light now passed over him, then shone directly in his face. He squinted–trying to see the form behind the lamp.

"Intruder. Stand up and show your hands." The voice was firm and sounded slightly unnatural–robotic, perhaps? Marc slowly stood up and held out his hands. The light moved off of his face and down onto them, allowing Marc to see. A very old and strange-looking man stood there. He had curly white hair closely matted on his leathery head. Both of his eyes were biotech modifications: artificial lenses that shifted shape rapidly as he focused them on different things. He wore a worn-out uniform in an old style he didn't recognize. He held the lamp in his gnarled left hand; his right one gripped an energy pistol, aimed directly at Marc.

"You are detained. Turn around."

"Sorry," Marc said. "Can't let you detain me. I have to rescue someone." He concentrated on his hands and they immediately began to expand. He raised them and *intended* them to heat up. They glowed red in response and he stepped forward, brandishing them. It was a gamble. Maybe the man would be intimidated. If not, Marc was ready to use them like he did on the last worker.

The man did not fire his weapon. Instead, he deliberately put it away and hooked the lamp onto his belt. There was an odd look on his wrinkled face as he turned back and extended his own two hands. They began to expand like Marc's! He reached out and gripped Marc's red-hot fists, covering them completely with his own large and solid hands. Panicking, Marc tried to keep them energized–concentrating on them, *determining* them to break free–but he felt the heat being siphoned away with an audible hiss as his own hands rapidly returned to their normal size.

The man cocked his head to one side. "That was interesting. I am curious about your ability. Never met another who could do what Jonas did. How did you develop it?"

Marc was nonplussed. He glanced down at his hands, immobilized in the man's unyielding grip, then back to the man's face.

"I . . . I don't know what you mean. Let go of me."

The man stared at him with the mech eyes until one of them made a little buzz as a lens focused.

"You cannot escape from the Bottom. If I release your hands, you will not run or attack me again. You must tell me about your biological abilities. Do you agree?"

Marc nodded at him and the man released his grip, his furrowed hands returning to normal size. Marc's hands throbbed but were not damaged. He examined them and lowered them to his sides, then looked back at the man.

"My name is Marc."

"I know," the man said.

"You *know?*" Marc squinted at him. "How do you know my name? Who are you?"

The man's eyes whirred again. He made a stiff shrug and touched a faded name patch on his old uniform.

"Elder Chau Bai calls me Old Jonas. I know your name as I know everyone's name who comes to Helm. It is a talent I inherited from Jonas."

Stunned at this unusual sidetrack, Marc sat on the handrail and leaned back against the water tank wall.

"This Jonas was your father?"

"No, I was Jonas long ago. He and I were joined as one. I was designed by EEA engineers and activated with Jonas, but he eventually died."

Marc suddenly understood. "You're an AI, then? You were merged with a human named Jonas?"

"Correct. There is an old Earth term: I was a cyborg of Jonas. Now, I am Old Jonas."

"That's . . . interesting. So, how do you know everyone's name?"

"I sense all the people on Helm. You are Marc. You are the one with the Secret Place. You seek your friend, Kera, and an artifact you call the Star. The knowledge comes from the talents Jonas has. He can sense things in the other way."

A remarkable reveal, he thought, and quite alarming that this AI should know so much.

"I thought you said Jonas was dead?"

"Human Jonas was very old when his biology stopped in H207."

"Wait, H207? You've been functioning for over one thousand years? That's incredible!" The EEA reference and his strange uniform suddenly made sense. The old Executive Earth Authority preceded and eventually became the Rindd people and culture.

"Ash Alien technology is millions of years old, yet it functions well," he said. "I have maintained Jonas's form. We blended for most of his lifetime and we are still blended in the other realm. I can call on him and his talents. That is how I know things. It is my ability." He paused. "You have similar abilities. I am curious. Have you had them all your life?"

"Well, yes, I guess. I've had my Curse–the ability to change my hands–since I was a child. It always caused problems, but I can call it and almost control it now–enough to fight with."

"Or to get into sealed places."

"Yes, that too." Marc thought for a moment. Maybe he could talk the old AI into helping.

"Old Jonas, I've never met anyone who could do what you did to my hands. You and I are tapped into some special energy that allows it to happen. I recently experienced a powerful Vision that vitally connected me to that energy. I'm still learning what it is and what I can do with it. . . Look, I need to get that Star artifact back. It will let me control an important Ash Alien ship and bring desperately needed changes to Harbor. It might even prevent war. I know you won't believe me, but I'm destined to do this, and I need to find and free my friend Kera to help me."

"I believe you. I am constrained to do some things and to not do others. I guard many things. I maintain and protect the Bottom for Elder Chau Bai and the Council of Colors." Old Jonas paused and his irises hummed as they refocused. "Jonas says you are correct. I cannot help you to leave the Bottom, but I can help you to contact Kera."

"Right. . ." Marc tried to keep any sign of disbelief out of his voice and just go with whatever Old Jonas was proposing. "All right, how can I contact her?"

"Jonas says to remember your Vision. Tune your intention through that kind of place and I will help you to find it. Once you find the path this time, you will recognize it and you will be able to use it again whenever you need to. Are you ready?"

"Yes, of course! What do I do?"

"I will touch your hands again. It will help. I can send energy and direction. Construct the image of Kera in your mind. Close your eyes and open them in the other place."

It all sounded crazy to Marc, but he put out his hands and Old Jonas placed his rough ones over them again, this time without any expansion or heat. He closed his eyes and thought about Kera.

At first, he heard confused, mingled voices. They sounded like the ghostly intonations he often heard back on Salina's deserts when he was a kid. As they slowly faded away, Marc discovered he could, in fact, open his inner eyes in this new place in his mind. It felt like a window had opened and he could look through it. An abrupt sense of presence jolted him.

Kera was lying on a bed with blue silk spreads. She was reading something on a portable comm. Marc didn't know what else to do, so he called her name. She flinched and rapidly looked around her room, then put the comm down.

"No, Kera. Close your eyes and listen for me."

"Who's there!" She strained to hear something.

"Close your eyes, Kera. It's me, Marc."

"Marc? Where are you? I don't understand!"

"I can't explain now. You have to help me keep this open. Close your eyes and concentrate on my voice. . . Yes, that's better." Kera had shut her eyes and the *signal* seemed to strengthen.

"It's some form of telepathy, I guess. Just speak to me in your mind. Call it paranorm nonsense if you want, but I'm able to reach you this way right now. I broke out of Anibale's medlabs. I'm down near the center of Helm, trying to break free and get back to you and the Star! I don't know if I can, but I'm trying. Where are you, and are you all right?"

It took a moment, but then Kera relaxed and her voice came more confidently. "I'm in Suite Blue's sector. I'm all right, yes. I'm . . . Anibale wants to use me to his advantage, so he's put me up in one of his suites. I'm trying to play him against one of the other Primes. It's complicated."

"I'll come for you as soon as I can get out of this. If you can, find a way to approach the Star. You can light it up, Kera! Use it if you have to!"

"It's too dangerous. No. . . . No, Marc. Listen! *Don't* come for me," she said. She shook her head. "You'll be caught and it . . . it would mess up what I'm doing. Go find the Star yourself. That's the most important lever we have and you are the one who can interface with it the best. If you can't get to it and I can, then I'll try to activate it."

"I can't just leave you in Anibale's cage!"

"Yes. Yes, you can. I *am* contained, but it's not a bad cage. I can't pull out now. I've made a contact that I can use. This is an incredible opportunity, Marc, and I can't waste it. Listen, I've been in far more dicey situations more often than you know. I'm nimble and resourceful, and I have to see this through! You got me?"

Marc felt exasperated and let out a whoosh of pent-up breath. "Yeah, I hear you. You're sure? I feel like I should. . ."

"Don't get chivalrous on me! I can take care of myself. You take care of *you* and try to find that Star without getting caught yourself! Are you all right where you are?"

"I think so. I'm being assisted by a thousand-year-old cyborg."

"Uhh, . . . right. That's very strange, but I'll take your word on it. Hell, this whole thing is strange. We can fill each other in on details later. So, you can talk with me like this anytime now?"

Marc felt the window begin to close within that other place and the presence of Old Jonas, still touching his hands, came back to mind.

"I don't know. I've been told I can, but it may be difficult. I can't explain right now. I'll try, Kera. I'll try."

He opened his eyes.

Old Jonas removed his hands from Marc's and stared at him.

"Your talent to connect to the other realm is stronger than I expected. That is interesting. It is good to use our talents. Jonas is pleased. You must ask Elder Chau Bai to allow you to come here again. I would like to examine your gifts more closely."

Marc felt a chill go through him. "Old Jonas, why did you help me just now? Can you help me get out of here and find the Star?"

"Other than Elder Chau Bai, I have not seen another human in seventy-nine years and thirteen days. You are interesting."

Marc heard a noise, like a hatch opening.

"You will leave the Bottom now. I serve Elder Chau Bai. He is here to escort you."

Marc fought the instinct to run. It would be hopeless in this place with Old Jonas able to constrain him and the Council Elder himself right here, right now. A tall figure in a white robe appeared behind Old Jonas.

Elder Bai was bald, his face humorless and stern. His otherwise pure white robe had multicolored highlights woven and braided through the hems. A large rope belt was tied around his waist. Each strand of the belt was of a different bright primary color. The gun he pointed at Marc's face was only one color–gray.

Chapter Twelve

"The central observation of this report is the demonstrated ability of the Gossamer tribespeople to operate in two different "modes" of physical existence. The first mode is our everyday physical reality consisting of Newtonian, Einsteinian, Ash Alien, and even quantum, physics. This "mode" is referred to by the Gossamers (in best translation) as the touching or "Tangible Dimension."

It is problematic to describe the second mode in their own terms, as it is likely to be misclassified by many as a religious concept. The Gossamer term literally translates as "place you cannot touch." I believe this mode is, however, best translated by the complementary term: "Spirit Dimension." The Gossamers do not see this as a religious or magical/mystical concept. They are very practical about their definitions of and uses of this "mode."

After working with them for two years, I have come to understand that this Spirit Dimension is something like, or actually is, a parallel dimension of reality–a dimension we cannot normally "tune into" or detect in any known empirical manner. The Gossamers have acquired this ability, which is, literally, second nature to them.

Xenoplague

The closest experience non-Gossamer humans have to this other dimensional physic is the use we make of the Ash Alien Gates and Lines in transiting from one system to another. Most scholars and investigators agree that each of our Second Domain's solar systems individually exist in a different so-called "parallel" physical universe from any of the other systems. This is why there have never been any mapping correlations between the stars seen from one system to those seen from another, and presumably why there is no relativistic time shifting between systems. The Ash Aliens seem to have carefully arranged this to make the systems usefully linkable in terms of space and time.

The Ash Alien Lines, then, must operate as wormholes in an inter-dimensional manner. They are of an *alternate dimension*–one that we use every day. The Gossamers' explanation of accessing other "dimensions" is, therefore, not entirely fantastical. It becomes especially plausible or believable when the remarkable physical evidence they display is taken into consideration.

For the purposes of this assessment and report, and as a suggestion to further establish working terminology, I will use the abbreviations TD, to refer to our everyday "tangible dimension," and SD, to refer to the secondary "spiritual dimension" accessed and used by Gossamer.

The Gossamer humans have developed what I will refer to as *dimensional bi-modality*, the ability to operate in both the everyday TD, in which they are rooted as we are, and in the SD realm or dimension. Their ability to display and use SD differences to assist their normal TD tasks may represent an evolutionary advantage and development vector for the human species.

A prime example of this is their remarkable ability to dissociate their physical bodies from our TD long enough to pass through the walls of their ceremonial structures, eliminating the need for undesirable or vulnerable doorways. Rather than perceive this process as one of "magic" or, conversely, of involving some unknown and highly unlikely TD physical process of mass decomposition and reassembly, we can think of this as using an invisible trans-dimensional doorway. The Gossamers may simply transit through to the SD realm entirely for a moment, move "over" a small distance in the SD dimension, and then transit back into the TD, where they would now be positioned inside the closed structure. This might be analogized as a very localized Line transit on a personal, human scale.

Other examples of practical shape-shifting have been observed and documented, such as appendages becoming morphologically modified to accommodate a task such as lifting a large load or operating a tool more effectively."

– Leenah A. Bordu, SisterSon of Frahma Institute,
Florinda, Eight Sisters of Frahma System

The air in here always smelled musty to Anibale. Likely, he thought, from all the old, decayed politics and politicians that have had to wait and sweat in this little room.

Chafin stood between him and the sealed door that led from the exclusive Suite Blue antechamber into the Great Seat hall itself. "You take a chance showing him the artifact."

"Perhaps, but he does not know its nature. I can use it and turn the wedge against Jade."

Chafin twirled his staff's knob and then sighed. "As you wish, but ZEK is no fool. I remember how he was when he was *merely* Prime Green. He did not get to be ZEK by accident."

"Yes, we all knew him, but our protocols and traditions are not disrupted without great cause. The Star Artifact rightfully belongs to Blue, and I'll use it to win time and status today. Then I will study it and find its secrets and origins. There may be danger, but also opportunity out there for us today, Chafin."

"You'd better go in, then. The signal is flashing."

Anibale nodded and Chafin stepped back to let him pass. At his coded command, the silver and gold striped door slid silently into its recess and the reverberant sounds of the Great Seat chamber flooded in.

Colors bombarded him as he entered the hall at the floor level. For a moment, he shivered, thinking of how the Star had erupted into colors on the middie's bridge. Here, though, the hues were coming from the monumental walls and columns of the Great Seat chamber: polychrome sets of jewels and precious metals vying madly for the eye, encrusted and overlain in complex geometric patterns on every wall surface and across the ornate ceiling. Each addition had been a gift from one of the Color Suites, demonstrating their status and strengths over time. Only the floor seemed plain in comparison, although anywhere else, it would have been an amazing artistic display on its own. It was glassy smooth, a translucent marble with induced hues, swirls of the main colors of all the Color Suites merging in a frothy central nebula of pure white near the foot of the massive Golden Screen of ZEK. It was in that spot that one stood when being addressed by him. A trim and evenly-spaced line of ten of ZEK's formal BlackMil guards, armed with energy rifles and pistols, stood at stoic attention below the Golden Screen.

Anibale quickly scanned the viewing sector boxes. Other than his retinue in Blue's area, only Suite Cyan and Suite Yellow were represented today. He saw no one from Red. So, Jade was playing an "I'm noble" card, not wanting to appear to be publicly gloating at him over her charges.

Attendance of Suite Green's staff was compulsory but irrelevant, as they held the office of ZEK. *For now!* He smiled to himself and walked boldly up to the center of the color swirl near the base of the Golden Screen.

ZEK was already online to his Faces. The large main Face looked out glumly over the golden hall and its inhabitants. His black eyes gleamed under puffy lids, which were dyed a faint green. The four smaller auxiliary Faces were quiet, their eyes closed for the moment.

Anibale waited impatiently for the formalities.

ZEK's huge voice abruptly boomed out into the Great Seat, "Harbor Saved Humanity. Harbor Protects Humanity. I am ZEK."

Murmurs of ritual approval echoed off the golden frames and con-glomerations of gems, then grew silent. Anibale made a perfunctory bow to the great golden Face above him. "I am Anibale vin Andres Alderson Samul, Prime, Suite Blue. I serve Humanity and ZEK."

ZEK's four subsidiary Faces opened their eyes. The two upper ones looked away at the top and sides of the hall as if bored. The lower two focused intently on Anibale and the main Face glowered down at him.

"Anibale, Prime Blue. I have concerns. You have been stirring troubles along the Sisters System border, upsetting centuries-long understandings between them and Harbor."

Anibale shifted his weight behind a small podium made from deeply carved aromatic wood. It had risen for him from the edge of the color swirl. He looked directly into ZEK's main face to answer him.

"I have long been a fervent protector of Harbor and Humanity. I seek only to prevent avoidable dangers to us and to our way of life. I have been vigilant in this pursuit."

"Vigilant, yes," ZEK's massive lips curled. "Honorable until it slips into unilateral *vigilante* actions. You were not directly provoked, yet you pursued them and even fired upon them. How is it that you actually fired your weapons upon Sisters ships without Council's approval, much less mine? I have a report that you even shot the tail off of one of our own cargo ships."

"That was unintended. He was emerging from the Line at that moment."

"Ahh, so you admit these actions? Not that you could deny them." The top two Faces looked down their noses now, giving Anibale the full weight of ZEK's visual attention. "There is a Complaint."

Anibale smirked. "Well. Shall I postulate the origin of that Complaint? Who would cast such a burden upon me? Who would have an interest?" He looked pointedly at the viewing area for Suite Red, where only a few expressionless staff members were sitting. "And, how is it that the complainer is not here to claim the Complaint, eh?"

Xenoplague

ZEK's main Face turned dark and his forehead furrowed under the edges of the golden starburst frame. "When the Complaint is made to me, it becomes my Complaint, and in this instance, I agree with it. Your actions were uncalled for, provocative, and dangerous.

"You shall be fined and restricted. Suite Blue will record a seven percent reduction in Elite status, and I trust this will discourage further adventures."

Anibale paused before delivering his prepared response. "I offer valuable and mitigating information to offset your unreasonable sanctions and devaluations." Anibale raised his head high to look directly into the Faces.

"You have a Deal to offer us?"

"I have an artifact. I have acquired and now own a highly unusual Ash Alien artifact that may prove to be key in understanding the remaining dangers we face from xenoplague or other unknown alien hazards. It may also present great technological value to Harbor and Helm. Unlike Red and others who waste time and resources with empty *complaints* rather than taking bold actions when necessary, I personally, along with all of Suite Blue, have been unrelenting in my pursuit of such black market materials. The distribution of untested and unreleased alien technology through clandestine channels is inherently dangerous! I fear that some uncritical and careless middie will activate something he or she does not understand, to the ruin of us all! ZEK and the Council should fear it as well!

"I offer to cease my border activities and turn my Suite resources to research the item. I will stake status on its worth, one way or the other. This should satisfy ZEK and the Council of Colors and must be regarded as far more than a counter value to the issues raised in this Complaint by Jade Red." Anibale pronounced her name with a sarcastic tone.

"ZEK Sees you." ZEK's Faces went neutral and the top two closed their eyes. Anibale felt a chill run down his spine as the Faces of ZEK analyzed him in some alien manner that no one but ZEK could do. Most of ZEK's human-alien hybrid technology was kept secret, even from the Primes–perhaps especially from them. He stood there, growing more uncomfortable under that scrutiny until, finally, ZEK's Faces all opened again and stared at him.

"You speak accurately of your prize, but that is not all. Your greed and subterfuge are also obvious. However, I shall consider this artifact and its value. You may present it to me."

Anibale relaxed just a bit as things moved back toward his plan.

"I will gladly display it to ZEK and to Helm. It is here now." Anibale turned and motioned to Chafin who was waiting at the open portal to their antechamber. The shock case with the artifact was brought in. Anibale opened it to reveal the dull gray orb with its extending rays and small end orbs. "I refer to it as the Star Artifact, for obvious reasons." He raised it and rotated it, showing it to ZEK and the audience in the Great Seat.

"Where did you obtain this object?"

"A middie prospector has found a new system with artifacts, from where he brought this. He refuses to reveal its location. I am interrogating him now and I *will* find out." Anibale smiled grimly at the Faces.

ZEK paused for a moment, then said, "Very well, Prime Blue. This artifact along with your task, spoken here, to test and evaluate it and to determine the location information of this new system, I will consider as mitigation for the Complaint for now. I require regular reports on your progress and I . . . What?"

ZEK's small Faces suddenly went to sleep and his main Face looked out into the hall as if not seeing anything. A moment later, the Faces returned to their former animations. "I have spoken to the Council Elder. The Council of Colors has a formal concern and is interested in your artifact. The Council requests the favor of a passive examination of it for the span of one orbital day."

Anibale was silent for a moment, then he flitted his eyes from one to another of ZEK's faces. "You wish me to loan the Star to you? This is outside of protocol. This is not usual. It is in Blue's possession! I don't know if . . ."

"Anibale." ZEK cut him short. "Be satisfied with your Deal and let us see it. This is my decision and it should be your wisdom to accept it. Do you agree?"

Anibale closed his mouth on the words he was going to use and simply nodded. "Yes, I agree. One orbital day, but the technical analysis is Suite Blue's!"

"Yes, yes. You will get your chance. This matter is ended. Present the artifact to the Screen Guards. This event is closed. I am ZEK."

Anibale slowly handed the Star Artifact over to the guard nearest the doorway leading to the backstage areas and watched with chagrin as possibly his most potent political lever disappeared into the exclusive sanctuary of the Council of Colors behind the glimmering Golden Screen. As he looked up at it, his teeth still clenched, the Faces of ZEK slowly closed their eyes.

Chapter Thirteen

Kera had his food ready on the table and Gibb's old stained plastic mug filled with his dark ale. He'd been working in the fields all day and she tensed as she heard him clanking around in the shed, putting tools away and deactivating the bots. He'd shuffle in for his supper in a while.

She thought she might as well watch the vid since she had to anyway.

At least the vid lessons were *something*. A distraction from the isolation and loneliness. They could even be interesting. She was pretty much stuck here in their dirty, dented old dome house amid an endless field of green, one of many on a planet that was, itself, basically one big agricultural field.

She poked at the comm screen and it lit up with the obligatory Harbor Lesson from ZEK. She sighed. It was the First Lesson in the old "History of the Second Domain" series again, starting with the "Destruction of Old Earth and the Xenoplague: the Birth of Second Domain of Humanity," the crucial event of their history that occurred over a thousand years in the past. She had viewed it far too many times throughout her sixteen years, but then everybody else had, as well.

With life moving so slowly for her here on Farms, Kera found it difficult to come to grips with the vast number of years that had elapsed since these old scenes were recorded. Watching them seemed like time travel–a magic window into the far past. Who could ever really imagine twelve centuries?

The dramatic music started up as the vid showed a group of old human Ash Alien hybrid ships lined up in orbit together above the strangely beautiful, if unbelievable, planet Earth below them. Could there truly ever have been such a blue-green world? A world that was our origin and where every human in existence once lived only in that one single place, all scrunched up together? It boggled her imagination.

ZEK's sonorous voice began a narration.

"This is our true history–the history of humanity. We must always remember it. It tells of bravery, glory, sacrifice, and grave dangers: dangers we all still face today.

"Harbor's ancient and chronicled history tells us that as our people expanded into Harbor and all of the many useful worlds beyond, we were restrained more and more and threatened by those who were still on Earth. Our legendary home planet was itself in crisis, descending into chaos from overpopulation, wars, and sudden environmental disasters. Our first ZEK and his Council Elder repeatedly went to Earth System to negotiate for colonists, technology, supplies, and to demand the independence of Harbor, but they were continually rebuffed.

"At the time of the final attempt to gain Earth's support, the first ZEK and first Council Elder arrived in Earth orbit.

"Suddenly, Zips flew through Earth's system. Then, with no warning, a huge Ash Alien ship appeared. This ship was unlike any other Ash Alien ship ever encountered. Its purpose was unknown and there were no communications from it. Its appearance was that of a large and fearsome weapon. As wild Zips flew about, our

ZEK and the Council Elder watched in horror as, without warning, the Ash Alien ship turned toward Earth and fired its great and evil weapon upon it!

"ZEK commanded our Harbor ships to fire upon the Alien craft, but it was to no avail. The terrible thing was a doomsday weapon designed to kill entire worlds and it was at that moment unleashed upon the Earth, causing total devastation."

ZEK's voice paused as ominous music played. Kera studied the old, familiar images of the AA ship with its hoops and the ugly cannon mouth thing. She watched as it aimed itself toward the Earth and let loose its horrifying beam weapon. It was a blinding white light at first. Then, she saw the close-up images of the destruction wave expanding upon the Earth's continents and incredibly blue and huge oceans. Blurred streaks lit up across Earth's near space: Zips flying in wild and nonsensical patterns as the comms shrieked with their crazy sounds. Views of the ZEK and others inside their Harbor ships showed them reacting with dread.

After seeing it so many times, the scenes were like some old overly familiar entertainment vid. Kera knew these things had truly happened, but it just seemed so unreal, so unlikely, and so very, very ancient. Still, the images sent cold freezes down her spine.

"The evil beam destroyed all the landforms and all the cities and works of mankind. In one day, all of Earth's humanity was lost. But that was not all. To make certain Earth's total ruin, it also spread a terrible Xenoplague–an artificial radioactive and highly poisonous bio-technical virus. This pestilence rendered the surface of our ancient homeland permanently uninhabitable. No human can ever again set foot on Earth.

"The Zips had departed the scene of this devastation, but ZEK and Elder Bhat did *not* flee Earth or the Alien ship. Realizing the grave danger it posed to Harbor, they heroically challenged the doomsday ship again, but it would not respond to them. After the planet's destruction was complete, the Alien ship appeared to shut down completely."

The images changed to show the original ZEK and his Council Elder standing in their funny clothing and looking shocked and then angrily determined. The music swelled as ZEK's voice continued.

"As deadly as it was, our Harbor forces valiantly approached the immense ship! They were able to board it and determine that it was indeed robotic and now inactive. They knew the danger for themselves: that it might reactivate and cause more harm. If it could appear at Earth, it could appear in Harbor systems. *What happened to Earth could happen to us!* They knew they must protect Harbor at all costs, and so before returning home, ZEK and Elder Bhat attached engines to the dangerous Ash Alien ship and pushed it to utter destruction, letting it fall into Earth's sun! They completely sealed off the Earth System, leaving the Xenoplague quarantined behind them." The music swelled. "With their foresight and their brave actions, Harbor and the remnant of humanity scattered across its many new worlds were protected from utter destruction."

Kera put the video on pause as Gibb 17Millies stomped into the kitchen where she was sitting. She looked up and watched him. He wore that surly expression again. A sour waft of the vegetable field's air came in with him and slowly faded as he shuffled papers off their plain brown table and took a short swig of the ale. He did not look up when he spoke.

"Why don't you go see that Jol Brindel over in their section? He's going to have a lot of farm soon, you know."

He swiped his hand across his rough forehead even though the dome house was cool now–a long-ingrained habit. No greetings or anything. That was not Gibb's way. Just jump right into whatever he was thinking about. Lately, that meant thinking about her and how he might arrange her prospects for unioning and, more to the point, position her out of his pockets and concerns.

When Mom died two years ago–has it been that long, really?–he seemed to be surprised to be suddenly responsible for her. You'd think the man had never considered the possibility before. There were only the two of them out here now, well if you don't count the ag bots out plowing the veg fields. At least some of the bots had friendly and engaging personality interfaces. Kera smiled grimly at the lame joke.

"Jol Brindel is about as homely as the back end of a snagbird, and he thinks way too much of himself. He farms *tubers*, Gibb. Some by *hand*, in case you didn't notice."

Gibb gave her a one-eyed glance. "That's not a very useful way to look at things, girl. Root crops are important and Jol is already a good farm manager for his family. They'll turn it to him in the next few years. Don't ignore what's next to us that could be yours one day soon."

"Useful?" She snorted as she remembered the last time she saw Jol. "He could inherit half of Section 59 for all I care. He's still gross. I don't want to be stuck out here, Gibb. I want to find something bigger. More. I'm alone and bored and I don't want to swap one green field of nothing for another!"

"Stuck, is it?" His face turned red. "You should be grateful to be here instead of having no prospects and getting yourself into bad trouble down in Tabletown. Hard work and *discipline* keeps you from making a ruin of your life! You're sixteen years now and it's time for me to make some serious plans for your future, girl."

Kera remembered the last time he'd hit her. The bruises on her face were only just now fading some. She felt the frustrations well up in her. "It's time for YOU to make plans for me? What about ME making plans for me? I don't share your dreams for me being a farmer girl forever, tending bots and babies in my muddy boots until I become fertilizer for the veggies myself!"

"Hold yourself, girl."

"Stop calling me that! You never call me by my name. I am not *girl*. I am KERA. And I *won't* hold myself. You don't understand. I'll die if I have to stay out here with nothing but a cracked dome, a bunch of dumb bots, and a so-called father who wants to control me and make a few coins, forcing me into unioning with a stupider version of YOU!"

She involuntarily cringed at her own outburst, but at least he looked directly at her now. "I said *hold* yourself. I know you're upset. You are young. Jol is not the only option, but he is a good one and he is available and interested. I talked to his folks last week. If you do not choose him, I don't see another who can offer as much. That's just the facts and the reality, and you have to accept it."

Jol interested? That was shocking to hear. It was even more shocking to learn Gibb had approached them about her.

"You spoke to the Brindels about me?" She felt her face heat up again. "All you care about is getting me out of your way," she growled. "You don't really love me. You never have, and . . . and you don't own me. Nobody will ever OWN me, you hear? Especially not Jol Tubers Brindel!" She paused, surprised again by her anger. "I'll make my own way. You watch and see!"

"You little ingrate. You need to learn your place and your lessons."

Gibb stood up from the table and she involuntarily winced as he approached her with his hand up in a fist. He gave her the most intense, dead-eyed glare she had ever seen. His whole body shook for a moment, but then he slowly put his hand down, turned, and trudged stiffly back out to the sheds.

As she sighed and sat down, her own hands trembling, a vision suddenly came to Kera's mind–a strong memory of her Mom looking at her with doe-eyes and a sweet half-smile.

Poor Mom. You were my only friend growing up. Why did you have to leave me with this selfish robot? I miss you so much.

Gibb stayed out, so Kera ate the dinner she had prepared and turned the video back on, more to distract her from her thoughts than to listen to the lecture. ZEK continued to speak as the images now showed the first ZEK and Elder emerging from the plague ship with some of their odd-looking military men. Then, it showed scenes of Harbor as it was all those ages ago before the terraforming. That brought home again how much time had passed since these ancient events. Helm, the governmental satellite world, had not even been constructed yet! The celebrated and notorious Color Suites had not yet been established down on the world of Harbor itself.

She laid her chin on her folded hands on the kitchen table as she watched it play out and tried not to think anymore, but visions of the panoply of history and all the great worlds beyond Farms kept circling in her head.

Grand music ended ZEK's presentation. "With the destruction of Earth and all its populations, Harbor became the true center of all people. With the first brave ZEK at the head, our second home world now took on its role of Capital and center of government for all post-Earth systems. The Second Domain of Humanity was established, and after a long and challenging struggle to recover, repopulate, and rebuild, it has remained stable and prosperous under ZEK, the Council of Colors, the Elite Suites, and the important Midclass, for over a millennium.

"We remember our history! In response to the very realistic fear of unleashing another xenoplague, one that might this time destroy Harbor, our other worlds, or even annihilate all of humanity, all unauthorized alien artifacts are deemed *forbidden* by Harbor. No experimentation is allowed without proper approvals and oversight. Tools and hybridized ships will be provided by Harbor and Rindd authorized suppliers to those approved. Any and all discoveries of Ash Alien artifacts of any size or form are required of every citizen to be reported to the nearest Harbor authorities. Our ultimate safety relies on the vigilance and compliance of every citizen of Harbor, Rindd, and Sisters Systems. This is your solemn duty."

The official Seal of ZEK, surrounding his huge golden Face appeared on the screen.

"Harbor Saved Humanity. Harbor Protects Humanity. I am ZEK."

Chapter Fourteen

Even after many decades of being ZEK, he still got a secret thrill when he was invited to a conclave with the Council of Colors in their own secluded hall. This was the ultimate private club, almost a secret society, and the only way into it outside of being a Council Elder or Council Senior was to become ZEK.

So, that's what I did, of course. As ZEK, I'm more inside than the Seniors, and they sometimes forget that.

These thoughts made him smile, something that came a bit easier now that he was unplugged and off-line from his Faces and stood beside his chair here in the Council's White Hall with only his own quite human face to manipulate. He purposely didn't circulate much outside of his own Helm offices and the Great Seat, preferring the general public to retain the idea of him as a more-than-human, even alien, being. He enjoyed being mysterious and intimidating to others.

Although it was a smaller room compared to other important spaces in Helm, the White Hall was imposing. It did not need to be huge, only large enough for the eight major players here: ZEK himself, the Six Seniors of the Council, and, of course, the Council

Elder. Tired from his just concluded Faces session, ZEK took his seat as Council staff and support team members scurried here and there preparing the room for this hastily called meeting, but they were soon shooed out as the Seniors arrived. They took their accustomed seats, padded white true-leather chairs arranged in an oval around a large, intricately textured rug. The hall had its own feel of high energy but tempered with a calmness after the color-filled cacophony of the Great Seat.

The White Hall was truly all white except for soft multi-colored bands of light crossing the textured ceiling and culminating in a globe where the hues mixed in swirls to blend into a bright and smooth glass lamp chandelier of the purest white, suspended like a planet or a sun over their heads.

Elder Bai arrived, and the White Hall was emptied of all outsiders and made secure.

So, now, only the important people are here! ZEK smiled and settled more comfortably into his chair.

Senior Apenlade spoke first, "Well, Elder Bai, this meeting was called so quickly, that I could not finish my meal with Senior Iridia and her staff members. What is so urgent this fine day?" A light chuckle spread through the group as all knew of Apenlade's fondness for Senior Iridia and his patient acceptance of her gentle but never-ending rebuffs. Iridia's eyes crinkled as she tried to hide her smile.

Elder Bai raised his hand. "I apologize, Senior Apenlade. I do. This is important, though, and I ask for your forgiveness and your attention. I ask it of all of you. I say again, this is important in the extreme."

All the chatter stopped and everyone's eyes were on Elder Bai. He stood up slowly and looked around at each of the familiar faces, studying each one for a moment. The light from the suspended lamp seemed to collect around his bare head, giving him something like an aura. ZEK suppressed a snort.

Bai has that Star artifact in its case there at his feet. I wonder what he's discovered? Nearly lost my shunts when Anibale revealed it and

Bai yelped in my ear.

He watched Bai unconsciously shy away from the thing as he started to speak.

"For all my life, this Council has been for all practical purposes a body politic. Today, we are shaken hard into remembering who we are and *why* we exist–our true purpose here in Harbor. That purpose is not to serve the Elite only, nor to serve ZEK only, nor even to serve our own needs and goals only. These things are what we do each day, but it is not why we exist. Most of the time, we forget and our true purpose is rarely engaged. Today it is so engaged. Today, we shall remember."

The casual manners and smiles were all gone now. ZEK leaned forward in his seat. Everyone was listening with full attention.

"We serve Humanity. We serve to protect ourselves from *any* threat to our existence. What greater threat could there be than that which caused the utter devastation of humanity's original home, Earth? We all know that story and believe we know it intimately, but allow me to briefly summarize it to give perspective on what else I have to share with you.

"The terrible xenoplague that destroyed that once beautiful and rich world, came in one fell blast from a unique Ash Alien ship, the likes of which we have never seen before or since. It arrived without warning and fired its weapon with no preamble. The impact site was instantly destroyed and the biological and nanotech virus agents spread–literally disassembling all the constructions, all the cities, all the great and wondrous works of humankind. And, of course," Bai touched both hands to his breast, "life, itself, was not spared. No plant, animal, or human being survived. Total annihilation. Earth was devastated and remains ruined and contaminated."

ZEK fidgeted. Yes, yes, yes. We know this, Bai. What about the artifact?

"Many of our citizens have forgotten that Earth does not lie on the Ash Alien Lines. Humans originally jumped to Harbor using our own, human-designed FTL technology. The Ash Alien tech was yet to be discovered upon their arrival here. To this day, the Council has protected and kept in reserve all human-design FTL technology, and therefore we control all access to Earth. It is technology neither needed nor used since the destruction.

"We do not know how or why the Ash Alien xenoplague ship appeared at Earth. It did *not* do so using the AA Lines and Gates. After it did its terrible work, the original members of the Harbor Fleet, who were there to peacefully conduct business in Earth space, bravely attacked the alien ship. They hoped to prevent any further devastations, and most importantly, keep it from following our human FTL ships back to Harbor Systems space. If it should pass into the established Ash Alien Lines network, we could all have been quickly doomed.

"Strangely, they found no resistance. They boarded it and found no aliens of any kind within."

ZEK had often wondered if the Ash Aliens had set their ship to attack remotely or if, perhaps, an unknown AI onboard was responsible for the deed. His own pet theory was that it had been an automated weapon, programmed to follow FTL Lines not constructed by themselves.

"All of us have spent time with the old data and there have been many discussions and studies." Elder Bai paused and indicated the case at his feet. "Today, something appeared that raised my highest alarms."

Now, he's getting to it.

"You must all see this thing and then I will have more to say about it."

Senior Torr's gnarled hand emerged from his soft white robe sleeve. He gestured to the case. "The Council hears, Elder. Show us what has disturbed you so."

Elder Bai paused a moment, then bent down to open the case. Carefully, he removed the Star Artifact and held it in front of his chest. He slowly pivoted so all could see it.

ZEK thought it looked like some fancy sunburst thing–just *artistic*

Ash Alien junk. The Council members muttered, scrutinizing the artifact and each other's faces.

"This object . . ." Bai spoke clearly to regain their attention. "This object was found by a middie in an unknown system, a place he has not revealed and which is still unknown to us," Elder Bai said. "It was presented by Anibale, Prime Blue, just a short while ago in the Great Seat as a bargaining chip in a Deal with ZEK. I intercepted the object with a formal request that the Council of Colors be allowed to examine it for one day before returning it to Suite Blue. Unprecedented? Yes. Here is why I requested that."

He stepped to a viewscreen that rose from the floor.

"For generations, we have all viewed the ancient historical video recordings of the xenoplague incident. Every schoolchild knows it by heart, but few indeed have seen it in its entirety. Some parts of the data from that event have been kept secret for security reasons. Yes, even secret from the Council." Murmurs swelled from the Seniors. "It has become necessary to show you *this* portion of those recordings."

ZEK sat up straighter. Secret from the Council and secret from me–from ZEK? What is this nonsense?

The screen began to play the old, familiar vids showing the white blast of xenoplague destruction emerging from the Ash Alien ship girdled by its five huge multi-colored metal hoops. Then came the images of the little group on Earth's Moon calling out their distress messages, the one close shot showing a long-nosed Moon official as he tried to contact the Harbor ships on a clunky-looking comm and speaking in the odd-sounding old AmerEnglish dialect. Finally, the screen showed the Harbor Fleet converging on the Ash Alien xenoplague ship after the destruction event was over.

ZEK was amused by the Harborites' clothing–so funny looking! There they went, into the weird ship, finding only empty chambers and a bridge room. Then, when the familiar images finished, a new scene appeared.

What's this? ZEK leaned forward and a shiver went through his spine. Here were new shots of the officials coming back *out* through the passageways of the huge craft, and a man with gray hair and an unusual insignia on his tunic was carrying something. The video cut to a closeup of it.

Gasps and muttering from the Seniors broke the tense silence. It was an artifact exactly like the one now before them.

"My fellow Council members and friends," Elder Bai said, "this is not the first time we have encountered a Star Artifact, if I may use Anibale's term for it. The Fleet officers at the time of the destruction were able to remove this object from the bridge of the Ash Alien xenoplague ship. They determined and we believe it to be the master controller for the ship and the vital part that controls the plague weapon itself."

Senior Gromr stood up. "But, that means there is another plague ship!"

"Unless this is the same controller we just saw on the vid from the original plague ship?" said Senior Smyth. He and Apenlade were shaking their heads.

Elder Bai raised his arms to regain quiet. "I can assure you all that this is *not* the original Star Controller." All went quiet again. "You know that the plague ship was destroyed–manually de-orbited to its total annihilation in Earth's own Sun."

He walked over to a wall panel and touched a sequence of metal protrusions. "One thing was kept in order to study it and hopefully prevent another such unannounced attack."

The panel opened revealing a perfect duplicate of the Star Artifact, sitting on a simple cloth and resting at an angle against the sides of the recess. It looked gray, metallic, and dull. It had the same number of radial arms with the exact same egg-like pods on the ends of each one. Elder Bai carefully took it out of the panel niche and brought it over to his seat. He placed them side by side.

"You've held this inside your wall here for over a thousand years, Bai?" ZEK said.

No wonder you yelped. Cunning old rogue. You're going to have to explain to me later why ZEK has been kept in the dark about all this!

Elder Bai looked at ZEK and each of the Seniors in turn.

"This is the original Star Artifact, in the Council's solemn protection, yes, for twelve hundred years. It should be obvious why this has become necessary–the revealing to this group of one of our most guarded secrets. You must see these sitting together here and understand the danger we are now in."

"So, there *is* another plague ship," said Senior Dorring. She walked up to the two objects and touched one of the gray arms. She looked up sharply at Elder Bai. "Who was this middie who found it, and what are we doing to determine where this ship is?"

"That is what we are working on, all of us, starting right now. This is obviously an emergency situation. You, the Council, must be informed at the outset, but that means we have not yet begun our search and assessments.

"*We!*" Elder Bai's voice was suddenly sharp. "This is outside everyone's comforts. ZEK and I will begin with the middie himself, whom I understand is being held in Suite Blue's med section. I ask for your ideas and suggestions as we begin the most important work of our lives."

The other Council members rose from their white seats and approached the new Star, gesturing at it and talking to each other. At Bai's suggestion, Senior Gromr interrupted their musings and led them to a separate conference chamber to begin sorting out their thoughts and plans. ZEK stayed behind as Bai returned the original Star to its secured niche, closing the wall over it.

"Well, Elder. The new images, the original plague ship controller! What other surprises do you have for us, I wonder?"

"None like that, I can assure you," he said.

ZEK stared at him. "This new Star must not go back into Anibale's hands. We have to find the ship that goes with *this* controller." Elder Bai glanced up, his blue-gray eyes giving silent agreement. ZEK huffed. "I will go down there now and take the middie into my direct custody. You will, of course, keep this new one secure here?"

Bai did not answer him, but turned back to the wall and opened a second niche. He gingerly placed the new Star into it and sealed that up as well. He turned to ZEK and started to speak when a stern-looking staff member came into the hall and strode quickly up. "Pardon Sirs. Elder, there has been a breach of the Bottom Zone–a callout for you from Old Jonas. It appears to be a single person down in one of the lowest-central levels."

"What did you say? That's impossible! A single person? No, no. Those portals cannot be breached! Show me the alert and scan."

ZEK watched Bai stride out, his white robe and colored belt flying. After he was gone, he found himself standing alone under the bright white lamp of the now-silent White Hall. He stared at the blank wall where two Star Artifacts now rested in their secret niches and he let out a soft whistle.

Seems to be the day for impossible things. Well, I have my own way of dealing with it. One thing is certain, Anibale has lost his toy.

Kera studied the smiling face before her for a moment, then remembered to say something. "Thank you, uh . . . Jade."

The woman's pasted smile did not change until she spoke again. "We must talk quickly here, but I wanted to meet you. I have heard much about a certain event, a certain artifact that you have been involved with recently, yes?"

"The Star Artifact. Well, that's what we called it."

"Many odd artifacts show up all the time, but this one did something I've never heard of. It turned colors when it was activated! And you, my dear, did the trick!"

"How do you know about that?"

"I have my ways. In this case, someone I can trust in the Blue Guard–someone who was there when Anibale, Prime Blue, confiscated the Star Artifact, as you call it, from you and your pilot friend."

Kera felt the political ground shifting under her like a swarm of minor earthquakes.

"I see. Well, that makes sense, I guess. Yes, I activated the thing. It was not intentional, but it did come to life for a bit. Why does this matter to Prime Red?"

"I have many fears, my dear. I fear for my people and myself, of course, but I fear most for Harbor. Prime Blue is engaging in dangerous activities! Anibale is grasping and grabbing for power. He wants to be ZEK, of course, and he will do anything to get it. I am not averse to gaining power myself, naturally, but I would never do what he is doing! Surely you've heard, he's actually attacked Sisters ships out on the border at Farms–shot one of our own ships, too, I hear. This is outrageous! He will reopen the old wounds and start a fight between us and our neighbors, all just so he can bully his way into the ultimate position of power here in Harbor! He must be stopped! I want only to protect Harbor and all of humanity from his foolishness."

Jade reached over and patted Kera's hand. "Kera, my dear, you are in a special position to help me in this. Anibale wants to use this new artifact to impress ZEK and gain prestige and points over Red and the other Suites. We can disrupt him."

"I don't know." Kera pulled her hand back. "I'm caught up in some pretty big things here and I'm just a Farms girl myself. Prime Blue has offered me some work and a place to live here on Helm."

Jade narrowed her black eyes and her powdered cheeks stiffened. "He will never let you go. You will never be free again in Suite Blue. Anibale will use you and then he will dispose of you for knowing too much. Do not be naive! You are not a guest in Suite Blue, Kera. You are a prisoner!

"Work with me. Help me stall his actions! If you agree, I will offer you something you can count on: a status position in my Suite. This means you will be a legitimate employee and protected by the full strength of Suite Red. Anibale won't be able to touch you. Afterwards, we will find suitable work and accommodations for you, whatever you want to do." Jade's stiff smile reappeared.

"Will you help me in this important mission, Kera?"

"Well, that is a comforting offer. What do you want me to do, exactly?"

"I want to introduce you to ZEK. I want you to tell him how you activated this Star thing and how dangerous it may be if it is left in Anibale's hands. I will try to get him to confiscate the thing and then you can activate it in front of him! That will surely take the matter out of Anibale's control and diminish him. You and I will emerge looking like the heroes we truly are, helping humanity and Harbor avoid a dangerous situation and a dangerous man! What do you say?"

I say you are a rather dull-witted woman to be a Suite Prime if you think that is all this artifact is worth. You bet I'll play along! You against Anibale . . . Anibale against you, and ZEK, too! Who knows where else it may lead.

She let out a held breath. "Yes, Jade. I will help you. Truth be told, I don't trust Anibale and I despise him for what he did to me and to Marc and his ship. I do think I can activate the Star Artifact and I'll do it for ZEK himself if that's what you want, but I have to be in contact with it. You'll have to make sure he can produce it for us when the time comes."

Jade's smile increased to a broad curve and she reached out and patted Kera's hand again.

"You have no worries about that. That is a very good decision, my dear! I am pleased, and I thank you for your help. Return to your Suite Blue quarters now and I will have Valezah tell you when to move and where. Perhaps working together, we can even keep war at bay and preserve the lives and livelihoods of all the Elites of Harbor, and all the middies, too, yes?"

Yeah, thanks for including us as an afterthought, you old bird.

"Yes, of course, Jade," she said.

Chapter Fifteen

ZEK sank into his large and ornate green chair, relaxing behind the desk he once used at Suite Green down on Harbor. He touched his left wrist, gently stroking the smooth surface of the wide golden band that tightly circled it, then poured himself some Maiko Pink. All those years ago, when he had defeated and replaced Young Amber, becoming the eleventh ZEK, he'd insisted on having his personal Prime Green furniture installed in his receiving offices here on Helm. They were comfortable, he was used to them, and their presence served to remind others which Suite was in power.

He scratched the tiny hairs on his round, almost bald head. Whenever he finished a Faces session in the Great Seat, his scalp always itched afterwards. His puffy face stared back at him from the mirrored wall panel next to the desk. He was allowing himself to get too fat in his old age, but some things just can't be helped. As ZEK for life, he decided that at this point, he really didn't care too much about keeping his body in top military shape. Besides, he had a martial asset no other person could claim: the entire BlackMil Corps. It was preeminent power to have them all under his direct command.

Xenoplague

Something in the transfer of the Faces to whoever was to become a new ZEK also gave him or her a kind of spooky control over those who take the vows and don the uniform and AA arm-band of the BlackMils. The Suite Primes covet that ultimate source of power, of course. With the BlackMils, ZEK can police the populace in general and assert his laws and judgments upon the various Color Suite's Guards and even the Primes themselves. Only the Council of Colors and especially their Elder could exert any countering power to ZEK should he wish to assert himself militarily. Today's meeting made ZEK wonder, though, how much secret power old Bai might have. He thought about the surprising and disturbing presentation Bai had given, revealing critical and undisclosed information and, perhaps more to the point, revealing there *was* that kind of information being concealed, even from him.

Council Elder, Chau Bai. Now, there was a truly unusual man.

The eighth ZEK, known as "Red Dog" (and the last Suite Red ZEK), was only 29 when he seized that office. Years later, he tried to take complete control, attempting to set himself up as an emperor using BlackMils even against the Elder and the Council. It was Chau Bai who personally killed Red Dog in H989. That was 258 years ago and by all accounts, Bai was not a young man even then.

It was rarely spoken of, but everyone in the Elite ranks of Harbor knew that the Elder was unnaturally ancient. It gave him a mysterious air and made most people uncomfortable in his presence. ZEK wondered if the Elder had access to a more potent rejuvenation technology than what was available to the rest of humanity. If so, it would surely be a far more closely guarded secret than those he had so recently revealed.

What would it take, I wonder, to wrest some of that from him?

ZEK closed the mirrored panel so he wouldn't have to keep staring at his reflection. He was appreciative that the biological tech revolution of the final five hundred years on old Earth had brought enhanced longevity treatments to humanity in time to serve the Second Domain. Had it come much later, it might have been lost in the xenoplague destruction. Now, most Elites lived to about 180, occasionally reaching the 200-year mark. A rapid decline and senescence sets in starting around 160 years. Most of the middie ranks could not afford the best enhancements and lived naturally to around 120 or so. He did not envy them. They were interchangeable and replaceable.

But, Bai now. He outlives everyone else, but that means his condition naturally grows more and more out of balance. Can he protect his advantage?

Just at that moment, a message arrived from the Elder himself requesting a meeting in one hour. Something important about the intruder he found in the Bottom. ZEK entered a quick acknowledgment, then shifted his weight, leaning over the old desk, and on a whim, invoked a secured high-level search for the oldest image of Bai. There were many pictures and vid files of him, of course, but they petered out back at about the time of Red Dog's reign. The earliest one he could find was from H860 during the seventh ZEK's years (a Suite Blue ZEK) with the Elder looking quite the striking young man nearly four hundred years ago. Four hundred years! If there were more of Bai's personal statistics and any earlier imagery, it was all secured behind truly imposing Council of Colors datawalls.

ZEK dismissed the search just as movement on the monitor showing his outer office caught his eye.

Jade Red. Just what I needed.

She had only now arrived accompanied by a staff woman. Time for a last sip of Maiko Pink before he had to deal with the Red Lady.

One sip only, then the staff comm chimed. He gave the access and the door opened. ZEK turned the chair to face her.

"Jade. I suppose this is about your Complaint."

She looked confused for half a second, then said, "Complaint? Oh, yes. I heard that Anibale leveraged his way out of it earlier."

"He offered a valid compensation. An artifact of unusual design and possibilities."

"Yes, that is actually what I came to see you about."

"You know something about it?"

"I do, indeed. Something that you need to know, as well. Whatever Anibale has told you about it, he has not told you everything. This Star Artifact thing is not just some ordinary Ash Alien relic."

"Yes, I said it was unusual."

"I don't mean the way it looks, ZEK. I mean it could be powerful or even dangerous, especially if it falls into the wrong hands!"

He huffed, "Like Anibale's, you mean."

"Yes! Like Anibale–the fool who just went blundering off to Farms System to attack Sisters ships for no reason! The fool who would do anything to gain power over you, even if it brings disasters on everyone!"

"I know he's hot-headed, but I also know he is dedicated to protecting Harbor from any threats. What is your interest in this artifact, Jade?"

She gave him a strange look. "What if your Star Artifact was not passive? What if it could be *activated?* Not as some mundane control unit or comm device. Not as a propulsion engine or even a weapon." Jade put both hands on his desk and leaned forward. "What if it were something much more powerful?"

ZEK turned to face her straight on and dropped any pretense of a neutral expression as she continued.

"I have a woman who was with the pilot who found this thing. My people witnessed her *activating* this artifact while in its presence on board the pilot's cargo ship. ZEK, it lit up! It turned *colors!* That has never happened before with any alien artifacts. It must be–could be very powerful."

He sat up straighter and tapped his fingernails on the desk's green marble. "Or very dangerous."

"Oh, yes. It could be dangerous, ZEK."

Is this day going to continue to spout surprises? If her woman can truly activate the Star, she might be able to control it–control what it controls, eh? This could change everything. Those old Harborites couldn't operate their controller. That's why old Bai and his predecessors kept the damn thing for study. Now, some middie woman can turn it on, just like that?

"Well then, I must meet this person. Is it the one who came with you today?"

"Yes. Shall I call her in?"

ZEK spoke a word to his comm and then gestured to the door with his hand. It opened and the woman walked in slowly. He had seen this before: middies or lower-level Elite workers coming into the presence of ZEK for the first time, shy, unsure, almost cowering. It made him smile.

She walked up to the desk and stood near Jade.

"What is your name?"

"I am Kera, Sir."

"You look a bit confused, Kera. Yes, this is my natural form. The Faces are for public and official presentation. Many middies who do not come to Helm sometimes think of me only as the Faces of the Great Seat. You may be at ease in front of me."

Kera blinked but did not move.

"Jade, Prime Red, has been telling me of the amazing find your pilot friend made. That Star Artifact. Where did he find it?"

Kera looked straight at him now, her green eyes unwavering. "We found it together on a hard vac planetoid. It was on a new Line that Marc found recently."

"Oh, you were with him, then? What is this thing, do you know?"

"Some sort of controller, presumably."

"Yes, presumably. But, where exactly was this artifact? On some shipwreck, perhaps?"

She nodded. "Yes, it was on a ship. We did not have time to explore it. We took the Star and left rather quickly. The Star alone was enough to make us a good profit."

ZEK saw Jade's expression change–surprise, then desire blossoming in her pasted face. The old thing can't hide it–that's one of her weaknesses.

"Ah, afraid to poke around too much, eh? Well. That was probably wise. Jade tells me you discovered a special talent in regard to this artifact."

"It just happened, Sir. I had no intentions to do so, but I activated it. It seemed to call to me, to attract me, and I entered a trance. It responded to me. It lit up in beautiful colors for a short time, then it stopped and I fell out of the trance state."

Jade shifted her position and said, "That concurs precisely with my informant's eye-witness report."

"So, Kera, do you think this thing is the controller for that ship you found?"

"I don't know how I know it, Sir, but yes, I do."

He nodded. "Do you believe you could activate it again?"

"Yes, I'm sure of it. It made a connection with me somehow." She paused and looked directly into his eyes. "If it would serve you, Sir, I could try it so you can see it for yourself. I would have to be near the Star to do it, though. I'd probably have to touch it."

"I know you and the Council are holding it, ZEK," Jade said, "Why don't you bring it in here, and let's see if she can do it? If she can, you'll have very strong leverage against Anibale for you to keep it permanently and, more importantly, to take it out of his dangerous hands."

Something is going on here that I can't quite pin down. This is too simple. Jade is too eager. The woman, Kera, is too compliant. No, this is far too dangerous. I need to confer with Bai and maybe twist Anibale's neck until I know where this ship is to be found.

"You said you were with this pilot when you found the ship. Do you know where this system is? On a new Line, you say?"

"Sir, my friend, Marc, is very unusual. He is more sensitive to Lines than anyone I know. He found that Line, out behind Salina, and it led us to that planetoid, but I have no clue how to get back on that particular Line. Prime Blue's men tried to follow up on us after we were boarded by him, but they couldn't find it either. I truly do not know where it is."

"I see. Well, then. I *will* ask you to demonstrate this amazing ability, Kera, but we must wait now until I can speak with Anibale. I must find out what this man, Marc, can tell us about your mystery ship.

"Sir, does Prime Blue still hold Marc? Is he all right?"

ZEK looked at her through half-lidded eyes. "He is safely under our control until this investigation is completed. Have no worries for your friend. You go on with Jade now. She will protect you until we can meet again. Jade?"

She was frowning. "Yes, ZEK, I will protect her, but we must move fast. Anibale is not napping or counting his blue jewels down on Harbor."

ZEK smiled again. "Yes, Jade. We shall hurry."

"I don't care about Purple's police complaints. That guard was already half-dead after the middie attacked him. No one lets *my* prisoners escape–and especially not on HELM!"

Anibale paced a short pattern behind the workstation in his Helm office. The man on the screen looked scared but he did not back down. "They are claiming you killed him yourself, Sir, with your hand weapon. They say they will file a Complaint."

"Let them. ZEK himself will back my right for serving an execution when a Purple guard fails to hold one restrained, medicated man in a secure medlab! Not to mention that they still can't FIND HIM."

He broke the connection with his fist.

Serves them right and it makes a good example!

All of his security and military staff had scrambled to find Marc, but other than the brain-dead disrobed Purple he'd finished off, nothing had been found–not a clue as to where the worthless middie might have gone. Just vanished? More likely a kidnap operation by someone who saw a game piece to be taken. Jade. It has to be Jade.

His comm lit up again. "Prime Cyan, Sir. On the secured line."

"Damn–not now!" He took a deep breath, ". . . all right. Put him through."

Old Pas-Guin took over the screen, his gaudy light-blue headband almost more repulsive than his nervous, superficial smile. No strength in that Suite. Cyan had never produced a ZEK, but they had just recently pulled ahead of Yellow's Elite status, and that was no small victory. Sometimes, the old sneak had something useful to say. Sometimes.

"Prime Cyan–I'm a little busy right now."

"I know, I know. Got yourself in a tizzy, so now you're busy! Hee hee hee!" His high-pitched laugh trailed off into a stupid smile.

Trickster.

"All right. What is it Pas?"

"Oh, nothing. Just that you are looking for one lost sheep and while you've been dancing a jig, there's another one that got swiped. Just thought you'd like to know. Just trying to be helpful."

Anibale felt his blood rising to his head. "What other one? What are you saying, Pas?"

"Oh, now Anibale. You are not as careful as you used to be. This is Helm, not Harbor. We all live together here in a cozy little ball where everyone knows what's new.

"She was seen being guided and handled by someone we know is in Jade's clutches. And, I know how much you like our Prime Red with her ridiculous green name! Hee hee!"

"Yeah, funny, Pas. She loves me, too. OK, what's your angle? You're no altruist."

"Why, Anibale, I'm hurt!" he said as he grinned broadly, but Anibale saw he was sweating some under that headband. "You'd do the same for me, I know!"

"Yes, you got that right. I certainly would. Anything to help, eh?"

"That's the spirit! Well, I have to go now. We'll see you at the general session!"

"Pas! What general session? Where did you . . . Damn him!" The screen cut to a vivid light blue banner with the Seal of Suite Cyan, self-styled as "The Color of the Ancient Sky of Earth."

What a bunch of boro dung. He just wishes he were the REAL blue, deep and dark and with power behind it.

Anibale turned it off and stood there in the sudden quiet for a moment. "Kera," he muttered to himself. At his swipe, the door opened and he stormed out into the corridor.

Kera's door opened as easily to his command, and he found her at the room's comm screen, sitting in a sleeping gown, her green eyes suddenly turned to him.

"OH! . . . Prime, Sir. You, you startled me!"

"I meant to. You have been here all day?"

"Most of it." The surprise drained away from her face and she looked at him thoughtfully. "I went out earlier to eat with Simune and Valezah when they came to get me."

"Where did you go with them?"

She blinked. "To the Commons, I think it's called. The dining hall? There was a wonderful bird mosaic on the wall."

"Did you come into contact with others there?"

"No, some other people were eating, but it's a large place and we three ate together. Is something wrong?"

"That's to be determined. I will check the monitors. There are many currents here, Kera. This is Helm and there are many who would use someone like you as a tool. Do you understand? That is why I have sequestered you here. I would not have you harmed, nor have someone use you to harm me."

"I understand."

"These are strange and treacherous times. I need your complete cooperation. It is for your own safety."

Kera looked at him for a time, then bowed her head a little and motioned to the room's other chair. "If you will, please sit. There are obvious trust issues in play here and I see that I should give you what I have that you need to know."

Anibale did not move for a moment, but her expression was completely serious and calm. He stepped over to the chair and sat down. "I am listening."

"What I told you and your people was true. I do not know where the Line to Marc's system is located. It is somewhere near the one you followed to that empty system. I *can* tell you that the Line is extraordinarily faint."

Anibale raised an eyebrow. "We scanned that sector thoroughly, Kera. There were no more Lines."

"I know. You'll never find it. I don't think anyone else could, either. I did a scan myself when we left, but Marc did find it. He has a special talent for finding the Lines. I don't want to call it paranormal, but it sure felt like it watching him do his thing."

"His thing?"

"It was scary, really. I thought we were just drifting out of zone, but he kept reassuring me. He just went very quiet and focused for a long time. Then, I felt the pull of the Line–very gentle! . . . and then we fell in. I put up beacons on the other side so we could get back to it. Then we went exploring.

"Your suspicions were correct. We did find a ship."

Anibale closed his fist. "I knew it. A complete ship?"

"I think so, but I'm not sure. We both saw it light up in colors when Marc activated the Star Artifact."

"Wait, *Marc* activated the Star?"

Kera had been looking down, but now raised her eyes to his. "Yes, Marc. I actually activated it first, but only for a moment. We had just left the wreck, carrying the Star back to our ship. I held it for a moment and the whole Star lit up in colors! It was amazing! But it scared me and I gave it back to Marc to carry. Then, *he* activated it, but this time it was *much* stronger! There was a bell-ringing sound in our heads. We turned back to look at the alien ship and the entire thing lit up with changing colors, too! It was breathtaking! I think it was a complete ship's form lying under a lot of other debris, but I only got that one short glimpse."

"What else happened, Kera? Did you just leave and not investigate further?"

"Probably would have explored it more if Marc hadn't been incapacitated by it."

He paused to take that in. Kera was looking directly at him with no appearance of nervousness.

"Go on."

"When Marc activated the Star and the ship, his hands became locked to the Star's arms and he went into a deep trance state. He stood there for several minutes with the Star glowing and casting colored light even over Marc's suit and helmet. I was beside myself with worry, but then it stopped, and Marc just fell over flat on his back, still holding the Star.

"I thought he was dead. I really did. He started to groan and move, though, and I encouraged him to get up so we could get on out of there before something blew up or worse. That's why we didn't investigate it anymore."

"And, Marc was hurt? He seemed fine when we caught up with you at Salina."

"No, he wasn't hurt. He said he'd had a great vision. Something about a very beautiful planet and a war in space that was coming soon. He got very emotional about it."

Fool middie pilot nearly got himself killed. But war? I must find that plague ship! Humanity needs us–needs me to take the lead. Kera is the key. If I can use her to open the ship to me, I could neutralize it and save humanity again before we were ever actually threatened. This could make me ZEK!

Kera looked exhausted. Anibale leaned toward her.

"Kera, why are you telling me this now?"

She gave him a wan smile. "It's like I said. There are trust issues here on Helm. My old life is gone. I know that. I would like to live a better life here on Helm or Harbor, with Suite Blue. You have been honest with me and helped me land safely here. I know you think that ship is plague-related. It may be. I appreciate your desire to prevent another disaster and I want to help you. I may be able to control the thing for you if we get the chance to go there again, and I hope I can, but I can be helpful in many other ways, Anibale."

His heart stirred unexpectedly when she called him by the familiar name.

"The truth is," she continued, "if the Star Artifact and that ship are what we think they are, and if I can function as the controller of it, then I would gain some status and even some power in Suite Blue. I could rise to heights I could never imagine before–just a middie trader girl from Farms.

"Now, I desire what I can see. I am a strong-willed Farms girl and I can make my own way. I *will* help you if you will help me, Anibale."

He paused a moment to take all that in, then he reached out and took Kera's hands. She smiled.

Chapter Sixteen

Leenah sighed and looked up from her notescreen. Julyan approached a workstation beside hers in the small side room off the main library. This particular parlor in the Institute always attracted her like a magnet. It had padded hide chairs, the best Rindd and Sisters tech comps, and screens for data analysis, and it smelled richly of old leather and the faint vanilla scent of paper. She thought it was probably the only place in the Second Domain that could boast that particular combination of attributes.

"Still editing your Gossamer report?" Julyan asked.

"Just about finished, I think. Have we heard anything more about Sil?"

His face dropped into a frown. "Nothing more than you've already heard or read. After several months of doing updates and training with the Teachers on Farms and Hub, he was off on one of his own missions–you know how he is. He was working under an assumed ID in Rindd space, trying to sniff out information about their possible FTL work. We were able to track him through his nanotracers just fine until seven weeks ago. That's while you were still on Gossamer.

Then, he just vanished off our streams."

The older man swiped on his data screen, then pulled out several true-books and printed maps from a large brown leather satchel. He slowly spread them out across the ornately carved wooden desk.

Leenah paused before asking the next question.

"You think he was taken by the Rindders for Harbor–for ZEK?"

Julyan sat down at the desk and raised tired eyes to her. "I hate to think so, but I can't come up with any better scenario. Sorry, Leenah. I know he's like a father to you."

She sighed. "He's important to everyone in the Sisters. Of course, I'm worried, but in his own serene way, Sil is courageous and re- sourceful. He's always pushing the limits and surprising me. I just hope he surprises us again by showing up soon and unharmed."

"You know we will keep turning our sources over to find out where he is."

"Of course. Thank you, J."

She still couldn't quite picture Silveen as missing. It hurt her to think of him in real trouble or worse. He was the man who had mentored her and given her an opportunity to learn and specialize here in the SisterSon of Frahma Institute on Florinda. It was a position she had worked hard for, especially after moving here from her home on Felice where she had grown up among the sublime and majestic trees of that larger world. After her parents died in an accident, she came to Florinda hoping to pursue biology and sociology at the Institute, but she never dreamed she'd become attached to the man who started it all, much less have the opportunity to become his friend and supporter. Sil was, well, special and unique. Julyan was right. Leenah had loved her parents and greatly mourned their loss, but Sil was like an unexpected new father figure in her life.

That evening, Leenah was alone under the emerging stars of the Florindan sky. She had brought the big, soft uuuluh bird feather cushion she had made on Gossamer and sat on the iron bench in the Institute's extensive garden, surrounded by the fragrances of thousands of exotic flowers. It was her preferred method to get away from distractions and other people so she could concentrate deeply on one idea or problem at a time. This night, though, her thoughts were only on Sil and their inability to contact him. She thought about her recent encounters with the Gossamers and remembered the strength of the SD telepathic communication she had experienced and the Doctor's pledge to help her. He had promised they could hear her when she needed them.

Well, I need them now. I have to know if Sil is all right and where he is. It's important to the Gossamers, too.

Sil's role as the unspoken leader of the Sister's great middie project was critical, and it's those efforts that might trigger the very repercussions to the Second Domain that the Doctor was worried about.

She focused her thoughts.

Help me, Brioleee. Help me, Doctor. If you can sense my mind, if you can hear me here, please help me know what to do. I need Sil and he is lost!

She stayed there until an hour after twilight, sending her pleas into the voids of space and those of her own spirit, but no new thoughts or communications or visions came to her. Her mind was racing too fast, perhaps, getting in the way of any more subtle communications. She would have to relax, using some of the meditation techniques Brioleee had taught her.

Back in her own room, she did those patterns, calming her mind and body, and in a while, she lay down and drifted off to sleep. She woke without opening her eyes because she was hot. It felt like she was out under a harsh sun and there was no air to breathe. She tried to move, but a weight pushed her down, immobilizing her arms and legs. She felt panic coming, but the scene instantly changed and Leenah realized she was not awake, but dreaming. Her new surroundings were in a cave. It was gritty and dim, its walls scored with gouges and rough stone. Piles of loose rock covered the ground. Two men sat here, crouched on the dirty floor near one scarred wall, but she couldn't make them out. One was older and the other younger. *Sil!* The older man was Sil! That was suddenly clear to her.

Xenoplague

The younger man sitting beside him was doing something with his hands. Suddenly, they glowed green, and bright sparks filled the cavern. She saw Sil's face. He was smiling and singing at the same time! The other man turned. A quick shock of recognition passed through her. It was *him*—the same man she had seen in her Vision on Gossamer! Her heart leaped. The two men were together in that strange place, seemingly unharmed, doing something (she somehow knew) to break free and come home to the Sisters. Music and green sparks flowed together, slowly hiding the men's forms completely, and then the dream scene faded and became something else.

When Leenah woke the next morning, she stretched and automatically started to check her bedside comm, but instantly stopped with the sudden recall of her dream. Sil and the man! Sil was alive and unhurt! He was coming home to Florinda, coming back to her! She remembered looking at the other man, the one from her Vision, but inside the dream, she had not focused on his eyes. Now, within her mind, they shone at her. They had power and energy in them. Bright power.

She realized then, that her requests to the Gossamer folk had been heard and answered.

She sent a Thank You, and an image of Tonhaaa, the Doctor, glimmered, alive in her mind's eye.

Before she got out of bed, Leenah let out a long and heartfelt sigh, freshened up, and logged into her Institute comps, ready to face her new day.

Chapter Seventeen

ZEK was already positioned in his control halter in the Great Seat's command loft. It was a small, but tall room directly behind the Golden Screen outfitted with his padded chair and an array of backup screens showing what each Face was seeing. Those were mainly for his assistants since he would be seeing directly through the Faces themselves. Doing that was second nature now, but it had taken a lot of practice at first to process and manipulate the multiple simultaneous streams of perception.

Elder Bai stared at him as the assisting engineer hooked up the neural shunts connecting him to the five Faces. Those went to the back of ZEK's head. He extended his left arm a bit so he could see the exquisite golden Band of ZEK adorning his wrist. It was the heart of whatever Ash Alien technologies there were that gave him his ability to work the Faces through the shunts. The band was directly integrated into his skin and nerves via millions of invisible nanothreads, binding to him permanently. Forced removal would kill him as instantly as losing his head. He would never remove it. It was through this golden band that his technical authorization to be

ZEK was manifested. It also gave him that unexplained control over the BlackMil forces, all of whom wear another version of the band.

He assumed it was some sort of spooky AA receiver tech, but not even the most brilliant Rindd engineers, working on the puzzle for centuries, could figure out how it actually worked. The mechanical parts of it didn't seem complex enough to cause the effects that they obviously do.

A nuisance, all this tech interfacing, but he wouldn't trade it away for anything. To *be* ZEK inside those faces–that was palpable power.

"You have him here and ready, yes Bai?"

"He is here. At your signal."

When ZEK was integrated into those five Faces, he connected directly with the mysterious ancient Ash Alien technology that underlay the Golden Screen. Now, as each of the shunts became active, he was immediately aware of an ineffable data feed, one that responded to his mental requests as if it were alive. Perhaps it was an alien comp or AI, but it had never been traced to any of the AA components of the Screen's equipment. It was not overt; it never "spoke" to him, but it was there, active, and responsive to his need for information. It was the "Other."

It was especially adept at reading and analyzing minute details of whoever was in the Great Seat before the Screen. If a person were the subject of ZEK's scrutiny, and were positioned near the focal point below the Faces, the Other could provide instant feedback of micro-expressions and measure exact temperatures in multiple bodily locations. It gave him the subtle analysis he needed to determine if that person was lying, truly confused, or was someone prone to instant violence while trying to hide it. A very useful and powerful tool that seemed like magic to his subjects. All who appeared in person to the Faces feared being *Seen* by ZEK.

"Any last progress with him?" ZEK asked Bai. "How did your medscans go?"

Elder Bai stepped up to the backside of the Screen so he could look back into ZEK's human face. "No, no progress. He is still a blank about the Line or the ship. It appears his companion was truthful to you. The pilot has some disturbingly strange talents. He seems to be able to dissociate and block off parts of his mind in a way I've never seen."

"Hides out in in there somewhere, eh?" ZEK grimaced as the last shunt went on.

"Something like that."

"Barrkon's Oven will take care of that."

"Are you certain you can trust the Rindders for such a sensitive case? We must know what he knows, but they must not harm him or lose him, or gain his information exclusively for themselves, ZEK. He escaped from a Helm medlab and intruded past my genescan level securities *into the Bottom*. That has never happened before."

"I understand your concerns and I share them. Anibale underestimated our pilot. His lab security team was inadequate and careless. We apparently can't break through his unusual blocks ourselves without killing the man. Rindd has far more experience with these situations. They will do the job and they will succeed. Helm is too fragile a prison for this middie. He may have gotten into the Bottom here, but no one has ever escaped Barrkon's Oven and, given its realities, no one ever will.

"No one here at Helm, not Anibale, not even you, Bai, has been able to dent the man at all. We must find that Line!"

Elder Bai did not look very happy, but he nodded and moved back out of his line of view as ZEK turned to begin his session inside the Golden Screen of Helm.

ZEK's Faces looked down into the Great Seat hall. The general session was about to begin and the representatives of the Color Suites were in their sectors. Anibale was not in the Suite Blue group since he had been called to the floor first. Jade was in place in the Red sector and Pas-Guin looked nervously cheery in his Cyan section. Yellow's Corrinda was present, looking noble (but her passive expression always did look noble), and his own Greens were represented in the neutral sector closest to the Screen.

Something caught his eye in Suite Blue's zone. The woman in the front. Was it the pilot's friend, Kera? Yes! Sitting with the rest of the staff members and dressed in Blue's colors! What sort of political twist was this? He scanned back to Jade amidst her Reds, but she did not seem upset or nervous at all. The game's afoot, then. We shall see what turns up at the end of it. Time to get this business started.

"Harbor Saved Humanity. Harbor Protects Humanity. I am ZEK."

As his voice boomed out into the chamber, the murmuring voices of the onlookers went quiet and ZEK focused his large, main Face toward the front of the resplendent hall. The subsidiary Faces were eyes-closed for now.

"This is a special general session, requested by Elder Bai of the Council of Colors. I require Prime Blue. Attend me now."

There was a short pause before the door at the base of the Suite Blue sector opened and Anibale stepped out.

Well, here's someone who does not look so happy today!

He waited until Anibale approached the Screen and gave his formal name, then he said, "At your last appearance before me, you stated that your artifact was found by a middie pilot, whom you were interrogating for the location of his find. It has become necessary for ZEK and the Council of Colors to see this person and make assessments of our own. You may produce this pilot for us now. We will wait for your staff to retrieve him."

Anibale's face turned purple and his eyes flashed, then relaxed again. "I regret to inform you that I no longer have custody of the middie."

ZEK's main Face frowned. "You no longer have custody? What does this mean?"

"The fool has escaped."

There were audible gasps from the audience.

ZEK opened all four of the smaller Faces and glared at him. "You let this man escape? The man who found the Star Artifact and refuses to tell us where? How could Suite Blue allow such an egregious error to happen? You stir up border troubles and then this!"

Anibale started to speak, but only a stifled growl emerged.

ZEK took his upper Faces to a haughty look and made the lower ones sneer. The main Face was stern but more aloof. "Your incompetence is striking and appalling, Prime Blue. However," ZEK paused for effect. "You may turn to the Council and to ZEK for a solution to your situation." Anibale looked up with suspicion in his eyes as ZEK sent the signal to Elder Bai. The Screen Warden in the hall below opened the door situated under and to the audience's right of his main Face and brought Marc into the Great Seat. He was cuffed and accompanied by two BlackMil guards. The one directly behind him had a drawn energy pistol aimed at his back. The other carried a large shoulder rifle.

Anibale struck his podium with a closed fist, its amplified boom startling most of the audience. "I should have known. You take my property and now you steal my prisoner!"

"Your *prisoner?* An escapee cannot be stolen when he is already lost!" ZEK had his main Face and the two uppers leer at Anibale while the lower two glowered sternly.

"In any case," ZEK continued, "he is now found again. I bring him here so we can tie some things together and then tie them up."

Suddenly, Marc cried out, "Kera!" and tried to take a step toward where she was sitting in Blue's sector above the well of the hall. The first guard instantly poked the muzzle of his pistol into Marc's back and he stopped. ZEK saw that Kera had half risen in shock. She was visibly upset, shaking her head slowly but not speaking. She sat back down.

"Middie Marc 54Arons." ZEK turned all his Faces to the pilot, who was still looking up at Kera. "Attend ZEK. Now." The man relaxed somewhat and slowly turned to face him. Anger in this one, and strength. He is fearful, but not intimidated standing in front of ZEK.

ZEK glanced at Anibale, still standing at his podium but looking like he'd eaten a sour pud. His eyes flashed with his anger.

He turned his attention back to Marc. "You have discovered a new system–a new Line, behind Salina. Will you tell me where it is, now, in front of all the Suites and the Council of Colors?" The man glared at him but made no move to comply. "No? You do not speak. That is your trouble and you will greatly suffer for it.

"Primes and Suites, I called this general session for you to witness an important and dangerous object. There are two such items. One is the object you witnessed before when Prime Blue displayed it here. Warden!"

The Screen Warden brought out the Star Artifact, uncased it, and set it on a small table under ZEK's main face.

"This artifact was found by this middie pilot. It is claimed by Prime Blue. The Council Elder and myself have examined it and we have determined it to be directly related to *xenoplauge*." ZEK let that word echo around the hall. "This is a contraband artifact of the highest order, unlike any we have encountered in the history of the Second Domain."

Murmurs and shuffling sounds came from the assembly. Good. That got their attention.

"If any see another artifact like this, you shall leave it in place, quarantined, and notify the BlackMils or my staff members immediately. Do not handle the artifact or try to move it. This Star Artifact before you is under control, but it is too dangerous and important to be left in the hands of any of the Suites." ZEK had all his faces glare at Anibale. "Especially Prime Blue, after your incredible negligence in losing the person who found it!"

Anibale grabbed his podium and yelled, "It is MINE! This is my property and my right! You will not take it from me. Suite Blue tracked this artifact down and presented it to you and even to the Council with due and proper respect, not to mention TRUST! I have the technology to study it and the methods to learn where this fool found it!"

"Your methods have failed, Anibale. You even lost the pilot. No! This artifact will be kept under the highest security. The Council itself will investigate it and the pilot will be dealt with in other ways. ZEK himself will compensate your loss with a reimbursement in jewels.

"The second dangerous object here is, in fact, this middie standing before us. He is dangerous because he knows where this object came from–and he refuses to tell us." He snapped all five Faces down at Marc. "You realize this is *xenoplague material!* You would put all of us, all of humanity, in danger! Well?"

Marc's chin came up. "I do not believe it is dangerous."

"NOT dangerous? And what gives you such confidence?"

"When I activated the Star Artifact, it gave me a powerful vision of great beauty. It sang of life and renewal! There is an intelligence in it. I know it is not a weapon nor is it a threat to us. It warned me about a war! It spoke to me." Marc took a quick glance up at Kera in the Blue sector to his left. ZEK glanced, too, and saw her more agitated now. Squirming, even! Laughter trickled through the crowd and he saw Anibale smirking despite himself. ZEK looked for Jade and found her with an expression of dismay on her powder-white face. Most pleasant! Whatever her plans were, they aren't turning out so well!

ZEK turned back to Marc. "You said when YOU activated the Star? What do you mean?"

"I told you, it spoke to me. It sings, it speaks, it gives information. It is some sort of AI or something else we don't have a name for. I carried it and it lit up in colors. Then it gave me the great Vision of Life. I am . . . tuned to it."

ZEK focused his intention for the Other to analyze Marc. The pilot was not positioned in the most sensitive spot for its work since Anibale was still in that place, radiating hatred and deep frustration that took no alien analysis to determine. The answer came to him, however. The Other showed him that Marc was not lying, not making a bluff, or playing a trick. The Other assured him that the man standing there before him truly believes the drivel he had just spouted. The pilot is a crazed zealot, then! Enough.

"You are a naive and dangerous fool! You have dealt in unauthorized and hazardous alien materials. You have placed Harbor and Humanity in grave danger! You have cost us resources and revenue. You will forfeit your ship, your person, and your labor to ZEK!"

Marc raised his voice, "You need me! I offer you a Deal!"

The audience gave a low noise of surprise. ZEK glared down at him.

"You have no standing for a Deal."

"I do have standing! I will activate the Star for you. I will be the interpreter and ambassador to what it is trying to tell us all. It may be our only hope of avoiding war and another terrible destruction!"

A verbal came to ZEK's earpiece. Bai.

"Let him try, ZEK. If he can, indeed, operate it, we will need him to pilot the new plague ship once we obtain it."

ZEK replied through the line, "Dangerous, Bai. You take the responsibility?"

Elder Bai did not answer him, but a moment later, ZEK saw the familiar old form in his sweeping white cape emerge below into the Great Seat chamber, something no one here had ever seen before. A gasp went up from the assembly, then quiet.

Marc and Anibale stared at him. Elder Bai gazed over the crowd, then turned to Marc.

His soft but intent voice carried throughout the hall. "We have met once before. I am Chau Bai, Council Elder of the Council of Colors. The Council has agreed that we need proof of this claim. We must know if you can, indeed, activate or operate this artifact, young man. I have a talent for reading people. It is a burden sometimes. I believe that you believe what you have told us here. I authorize you to show us. Now, please."

"I would need to touch it, Sir."

"Slowly, then. Slowly, Marc. Your life is at stake, and maybe ours as well."

Marc nodded once, then walked to the Star Artifact, the first guard now pressing the energy pistol to the back of his head. ZEK held the two BlackMil guards under his special direct control so they would not actually shoot the invaluable middie, but Marc wouldn't know that, of course.

At ZEK's silent cue, the second BlackMil unfastened Marc's hands. The pilot glanced once again at Kera in the box above. She looked terrified. He rubbed his wrists, then reached slowly out to touch two of the arms of the Star. He gently laid his fingertips on the gray metal and stopped, seeming to meditate. ZEK concentrated on the scene with his large central Face.

Minutes passed. No one spoke; no noises from the crowd. Every eye was intently focused on Marc. Then an "Ahhh!" resonated as the Star Artifact lit up in an eerie blue glow. It faded out, then glowed again in green and then yellow and back to blue. Marc was motionless–a statue still just barely touching the metal arms. Then the Star abruptly burst forth in a blinding white flash that receded to a brilliant red. It physically jumped up from the table and slammed into Marc's chest, causing him to grab it tightly. The guard with the pistol was pushed back for a moment, but immediately re-aimed his weapon. The second one hoisted his rifle.

The crowd screamed and a few rose up, starting for the exits, but ZEK saw Anibale standing firm. Jade was still looking. Kera had her hands stretched out toward the Star and Marc, her entire body straining forward.

Marc looked up at the ceiling now, but his eyes were closed. The Star rolled through a color set, displaying vibrant coruscating bands of the purest hues, almost too bright to look at. Bai still stood there, watching, but he had a look of stark fear on his face. *Enough of this!*

"STOP! STOP NOW! Let go of the Star!" ZEK heard his voice boom around the chamber, but the Star seemed to drown him out, even though it made no noise.

Xenoplague

"GUARDS! ATTEND ME!"

The two BlackMil guards seemed entranced by the Star and did not respond.

Inside the booth, ZEK reached out with his left arm and focused on them. As he had used the Other's enhancing perception, now he used his power as ZEK to cut through the chaos and command them directly with his mind and overpowering will.

DO NOT SHOOT him! Strike him! STRIKE HIM!

Both men jerked awake and the one with the pistol tried to hit Marc over the head with it, but the weapon bounced off his glowing skull as the energy coming from the Star flowed around Marc and propelled the man backward onto the marble floor. The second guard glanced up at ZEK's Faces. All five Faces were open-eyed in instinctive fear. A blinding bright flash erupted from the Star. The BlackMil cringed, then reversed his rifle and swung the butt end of it toward Marc's head.

"NO!" screamed Kera from the seats just above.

The glowing artifact seemed to push back at the gun with a wave of crackling light. The guard staggered and tried to hold on while averting his eyes from the glare, then he took another grip on the weapon and swung it much harder. This time the heavy end of it forced its way through the beam and struck Marc squarely on the side of his head. Marc flew back and fell onto his left side, the connection to the Star broken. The Star dropped straight to the floor, landing with a solid metallic thud, and dimmed immediately, fading out to dull gray.

The Great Seat had reflected so much of the Star's light from all the jewels and precious metal surfaces that the room seemed unnaturally dark now that the Star's colors were gone. ZEK shivered in his harness and tried to focus on the scene below. His eyes were still giving him afterimages of that final white blast.

Elder Bai had stayed back, but now walked up to Marc's prone body and looked down at him. Under a purplish bruise, a trickle of blood ran off Marc's ear and down the marble floor, mixing its red with the other colors swirling in the stone. As staff members came to help, the Elder backed off and slipped into the Council area behind the Screen.

Kera bent over her hands, crying. Anibale had also backed away from the central podium and now turned and stalked out of the hall. ZEK spoke again, "Attend to the pilot. Guards, secure that thing–carefully! Use the remote bots, but put it back in its case now! This meeting is over. You have all seen the dangers. You've seen it first hand and I repeat my warnings! Go on back to your Suites while we clean this up. I am *ZEK*."

Bai was standing at his side when he climbed out of the harness.

"Dangerous, indeed," the older man said, his eyes blazing, "but we learned much today, ZEK."

He glared at Bai. "Learned how little control we have over this situation, you mean?"

"Well, yes. We also know that this thing can be activated by a human and that it is, indeed, the real live item: a controller like the one we saved from the original ship. That surely means that the ship Marc found out there is another such ship. *A true xenoplague ship*, ZEK! We have to have it and we must be able to *control* it when we do have it. This man is the key. I just hope he recovers from that blow."

"The medics are reporting now. He will survive. We can't take any more chances, Bai. That pilot is going straight to Barrkon's Oven and through them, we will find his Line and the damn plague ship, too."

"I still don't trust them, ZEK. They are Rindd, not truly Harbor."

ZEK huffed as he motioned for the helpers to come in and disconnect him from the Faces shunts.

"Rindd will do their job thoroughly, just like they always do. Trust is not an issue with them." ZEK glowered at the Elder. "All they ever want is to be paid–full price."

Part Two

Barrkon's Oven

Chapter Eighteen

The sinking sensation of a Line transit woke Marc up. It made him feel a bit nauseous, but then it passed and he thought about opening his eyes. He was inside a small cabin, sitting on a modified transit couch–one of those designed for passengers on paid transport carriers. Definitely an atmospheric lander. He was bound and shackled and there was a bandage around part of his head. He wanted to reach up to feel it.

Two men sat in front with their backs to him, one to each side behind a small bridge control panel and a view outside through a transparent window–an *actual window* in this thing! The man on his right was a BlackMil, grimacing as he stared out that front viewport. Obviously a guard. His energy pistol glinted above the brighter gleam of his gold armband.

The one on the left, concentrating on his readouts, was certainly a Rindd pilot, which explained the window. Only Rindders or maybe some of the Sisters people would take the time and engineering effort to build an actual viewport into one of their hybrid alien/human ship bridges. The Rindders would do it to give themselves a practical backup to screens. The Sisters folk would probably do it just because they liked it.

Marc kept his eyelids low and watched what was going on. They seemed to be in a final orbital maneuver for a planet. As they rotated the ship, the world swam into view for a minute. The sudden brightness of the land mass made him flinch. A stark white desert landscape spread out below. Several strong glints came in an even, rapid sequence of five, then seven, then three. Something man-made was catching the sun down there. It was too bright to make it out. The ship rotated past the view of the planet, then the sun of this system entered the window, which automatically blacked itself, turning the star's image into a dim circle. It was huge. They were very close to this star. Marc began to suspect which system he was in. As his memory cleared, a name came to mind. A sharp jolt of adrenaline, mixed with anger and a flush of despair, made him groan softly.

The BlackMil looked back. "Awake, finally. Might as well go back to sleep, middie." His expression was hard to read–or maybe just hard. Marc tilted his head, trying to feel the weight of the bandaging. He could not move his arms or legs, so he stared at BlackMil and said, "We're at Rindd 1."

"Close, middie. Right system, wrong planet." the BlackMil grinned.

The Rindd pilot turned his head and Marc saw he had a bioengineered vision mod for his left eye. "We are on entry to Barrkon's Oven."

Marc was afraid he was going to say that. Great.

"You'll survive your wounds, middie," the BlackMil said, "but doubtless, you'll acquire a few new ones by the time they get through with you here."

Marc's heart fell. Barrkon's Oven. A place Harbor used to handle inconvenient prisoners and wilders–those who dare to directly challenge the Harbor Elites or those too crazy to follow the laws and protocols. Not for minor crimes, mind you, just for the special cases–like mine.

This was a valuable mining world or it would not otherwise be inhabited. Rindd 1 was much larger, farther out, and far more comfortable for humans, but Barrkon's Oven was very close in to Rindd System's actually rather small sun, and its rock was barren and dense with minerals. Marc reviewed its other endearing features. Surface gravity about one and a half standard–a heavy world to walk on.

Let's see. What else? Rotational lock with one hot side always facing the sun. Minimal atmosphere. Habitats pressurized to be livable. . . Paradise.

Marc turned his stare back to the guard. "I won't be here that long. I have a few scores to settle."

The guard gave him a twisted grin. "Yeah, you look like you're ready to take off running. You want me to open the back hatch and let you out?"

"Sure, just give me a suit and transport. At least I wouldn't have to keep looking at your ugly BlackMil face." Marc enjoyed seeing the guard tense in anger.

"Why don't you just shut up and go back to your coma, middie."

"Why don't you tell me what happened in Helm? We have a lot of time before we land."

"You got your bead smashed when you tried to attack ZEK, that's what I heard. Not real smart."

Marc tried to crack a sneer, but it hurt. "Ahh, it's too bad I don't remember it."

The guard glowered. Marc looked at the pilot, who was calmly flying the ship and had given no reaction to them.

"You Rindders still making a fortune renting out this garden to the Elites?"

"Rindd has a long-standing agreement with Harbor," the pilot said. "Barrkon's Oven provides their required containment zone for detentions outside of Harbor Systems, and they buy our metals and gemstones. It is an honorable agreement."

"I guess so, as long as what you get in return is worth it in the long run, eh?"

The pilot's bioeye glimmered as he glanced back at Marc, but he did not answer. BlackMil frowned again.

"I said shut up."

Vibrations indicated the start of aerobraking into flight mode and the approach to landing. As they touched down, Marc's view was limited to the plumes and billows of yellow-white dust that rose around them into the thin, blue-black skies of Barrkon's Oven.

The view was better from the ground transport vehicle, but the feeling of a crushing weight on his body was not an improvement. The BlackMil was not taking the gravity here very well, either. His face was drawn, lips pursed, eyes narrowed underneath his sweating forehead. The Rindd pilot seemed not to take any notice at all.

Stark desert filled the transport's windows. A thin band of purple-blue atmosphere on the horizon quickly faded to black above. Marc was glad of the transport's roof over their heads, masking the fierce glare of the sun from its permanent position almost directly above. The dusty plains, stretching to a distant rill of low hills, were dotted with tractor-like vehicles combing the soil, leaving a matrix of deep trenches like some giant's plowed fields.

"Titanium ore is mined outside," the pilot ventured. "Emeel Barrkon's deposits."

BlackMil grunted. "Lucky prisoners get to drive those trucks all day, middie. Maybe they'll let you drive one. All day lasts a long time here." His chuckle sounded more like a gurgle.

Marc wondered what the famous old miner would think of his world now. Barrkon had spent years prospecting this searing side of the planet. Everyone said he was foolish to try to work here. He was just an eccentric hermit with a fixation on discomfort and pain. He'd find nothing in the burning dust and either burn himself up or die of gravity stress, but Barrkon proved them wrong. He found the richest known deposits of titanium and several other precious and useful metals, including gemstone-rich ore, right here in the substellar point on the hottest side of the heaviest planet used by humans in all the Lines systems. And, he lived to 167, several decades longer than most men of his era. They called him a "tough old budgie," whatever that was. Indeed.

Marc stared out of the side windows as they rattled along. The gravity combined with his restraints made him feel like his eyes were the only thing he could move. Plumes of white dust receded into the distance, marking the locations of several of the tractor units, scraping away at their trenches and filling their huge hoppers with soil. He winced when something caught the sun and reflected a bright glare over them. They approached a large circular field, its surface made of shiny metal, just slightly domed.

"Alpha-seven Pit Mine," the pilot announced. "We will be in the containment zone momentarily."

The transport entered an air-locked portal and descended a ramp, then turned onto a narrow gravel shelf road hugging the perimeter of a deep vertical shaft, perhaps 100 meters across. Narrow terraces, exposed girders, and a scattering of mining machines lined the pit at various levels as far down as Marc could see. The harsh sunlight filtered through the domed roof cap, casting wan yellow beams that flickered in the suspended dust but dimmed rapidly as they tried to pierce the darkness of the well. Below that, only pinpricks of work lights along the wall and the mouths of cross-shafts marked the depths.

As the transport slowly rolled alongside the unprotected precipice, Marc stared into the abyss beside him. He felt a sudden pang of terror. A memory of a narrow dirt road high in the Salina mountains near home hung in his mind. Jin had been driving.

Slow down, Jin! We're too close to the edge!

Tires had locked, scrubbing the ground as dirt clods sprayed up into their faces. The old scoopcar stopped, perched right on the rim. He couldn't see the road underneath them–only yawning space and an ancient bed of tortured black lava five hundred empty meters below.

Marc cleared his head of the memory and turned his eyes away from the view of the mine pit. He decided to watch the pilot instead. Fortunately, the man seemed unperturbed and after a few minutes, they left the pit's edge, entered a garage, and came to a silent stop.

When the hatch opened, several Rindder men and women entered the cabin. Two assisted the BlackMil guard as he attempted to stand on shaky legs. One gave the pilot a hand, but he seemed to be all right without further assistance. They slid Marc onto a gurney, much to his relief.

Minutes later, they deposited him onto a padded bench in a white-walled room. Marc steeled himself for the med probes and interrogation that would surely follow. Sure enough, a lab-frocked Rindd woman came in with something in her hand. She greeted Marc with a nod and deftly pressed the object to his neck. Then she withdrew from the room as quickly as she had arrived.

ZEK's Face . . . here it comes.

Nothing? . . . No psych drugs–no . . .

The door opened again, and a round-headed man wearing a Rindder-style business suit and a bland expression walked in.

"Marc 54Arons. Welcome to Rindd System. This is Barrkon's Oven, as I am certain you are aware. Harbor, under special requests from ZEK, has remanded you here for analysis and containment. The containment is to this facility in Alpha-seven Pit Mine and other areas to be determined; in practical terms, it is to Barrkon's Oven itself, which by its nature is extremely restrictive. The analysis has begun. We have introduced proprietary nanogenetic engines and comps into your system. You will be neuron-mapped and gene-analyzed for our reports to ZEK and Helm."

"You can't take from me what I don't know or have. How long will you keep these damn wires around me?" Marc tried to sound more cavalier than he actually felt.

"There are many things your conscious mind does not know about the rest of you, Mr. Arons. We shall discover these things. As for your Helmer bindings, those may come off now. There is no reason for you to be tied up here on Barrkon's. There is no place for you to go and the gravity does much to restrain us all naturally, as you see. We will quickly determine if you are violence-prone, requiring more specialized restraint."

It was obvious that the woman had given him the nanobots, and . . . that was it? He was free from restraints? He tried to think it through quickly, but something else hooked his attention–the man had called him "Mr. Arons." What a strange antiquated phrase! No one had ever called him that before, especially not cutting off the surname number group that designated his middie clan.

"You will adjust to the excess weight. You will be immediately assigned to a work area for the duration of your stay here. We must all do our work here to maintain the habitats and economy."

"What determines when I get to leave this hellhole?"

"That will depend on our analysis and the needs and requirements of ZEK."

"So, how much are those thieves paying you to hold me here? What am I worth?"

"We never disclose or discuss our business arrangements, Mr. Arons."

Marc thought a minute, then said, "What if I can double their offer? I have access to a special trove of alien artifacts, Mr. Rindd."

"You may call me Chief Karms. Are you willing to tell me where your new system is, then?"

"Not a chance. You'll sell me twice over to ZEK and Anibale. If you want the goods, though, there may be a way we can reach a deal."

"I will consider that, Mr. Arons, but not until after our analysis is complete. After all, it is most likely that we will not need to create a new deal with you." Chief Karms nodded once, then turned and exited the small room, leaving Marc to an aide who removed his bindings and shackles and very carefully assisted him to stand up for the first time.

Marc's head swam and his legs felt rubbery after being restrained for so long. It was all he could do to make one foot go in front of the other one. The scalp laceration was healing fast, but the impact site ached and his head itched under the bandages. The aide led him through a hatch, into a metallic hallway, then into a utility-style lift. The sudden descent felt delicious for a moment as the gravity of Barrkon's Oven was offset by a few tenths of a g. Then they paid for it. He groaned with the deceleration at the bottom. The hatch slid open and Marc was led out into what appeared to be a crude dormitory hall with steel-framed plank beds and rough, raw rock walls. Actinic light from a few grilled lamps cast a bluish hue to the room.

"You may select any unused partition, Mr. Arons. Someone will be along to instruct you further in your work duties."

The aide left him and disappeared back into the lift. Marc stood there, hunched over and trying not to fall on his face. The dull eyes of about 25 others in the dorm stared at the new arrival. Mostly men, but a few women as well, all sitting or lying on their simple bunks. No one spoke or offered to help.

Marc stumbled over to an empty palette and sat down hard, causing the heavy metal frame to creak a little.

"Got to learn to hold on to something and settle down slowly," said a youngish man in the next bunk. "It's damn hard at first, then you get more used to it."

"It's damn hard later, too," someone over a bunk or two said. A muted chuckle spread around the group. The young man spoke up again, "We are just off an ore shift and everybody's exhausted. You look like you could use some sleep yourself, Mister."

"Probably could at that," Marc said, "but, what do you people do here?"

The young man just looked at him through heavy eyelids and Marc noticed how dirty he was–how dirty they all were. Another man, brawny and thick-limbed, spoke up. He wore a green thinshirt and stared at Marc with a hard look of revulsion.

"You're no observer, Mister. You mean what do *we* do here? If we're lucky enough to find some in the seams, we dig the gems out of the damn pit walls. We sort 'em and grade 'em. Then they go off to be some Elite Suite's newest baubles. It's fun work. You'll enjoy it." Another chuckle went through, but then Greenshirt turned away and settled heavily on his bunk. Silence fell as they all lay back into their palettes for sleep. One older man with short white hair kept staring at him for a minute, then he, too, lay back in his place.

When he woke again from a strained sleep, Marc had to repress a feeling of panic as even simple breathing was difficult here. The dorm was unchanged–dimly lit with all the miners either still asleep or just waking, making minimal movements to prepare themselves for whatever lay ahead.

A large door at the other end of the dorm abruptly opened with a loud bang, and a brawny guard strode confidently into the room. She wore a Helm-style Purple Guard's uniform. She had a sidearm, and her lower torso featured a Rindd exoskeleton that hissed as it worked against the high gravity.

"UP NOW. This is work session 73 and you have 15 minutes for your meal. Arons–new miner–see me NOW."

The other prisoners shambled out of the dorm room as Marc struggled to get up out of the palette and take heavy steps toward the guard. She looked at him with disgust, then strode briskly to him. "You are a part of the Alpha-seven Pit Mine work crew now, Arons. The work is simple. Learn from the others and don't make any trouble for me. I don't care who you are, who you were, why you're here, or what you want. Got it? Good. You screw up and I'll personally kick your ears in. Looks like someone else tried that recently, yes? Good. Any questions?"

"Yeah. What are you Helm types doing in charge here in Rindd space? I didn't think Rindders could tolerate you."

Her metal-knobbed glove was a blur as she struck the unwounded side of Marc's head. "That's not your concern." She raised her chin, stretching her thick neck as she smirked. "The Rindders find us most useful here in the mines. We keep *order* for them and do the services

197

that ZEK requires. They can stay out of it and leave all of this to the experts. . . and I *am* an expert, middie."

She shoved him through the door and into a smaller room with stand-up shelves where all the others were eating something from small metal plates. He found a space with a food plate and tried the stuff. It tasted like false-lettuce and basic protein rice.

"Huh. You enjoy that, now, middie. You have eight minutes to savor the flavor." The woman grinned at him, then strode out of the room–her exoskeleton emitting a rasping sound.

Eight minutes later, Marc trailed the others as they struggled onto one of the shelf roads surrounding the deep pit. He glanced up at the bright dome cap, three or four hundred meters above, and then down into the drop below. His foot slipped on a bit of gravel, and, heart racing, he shied away from the unprotected edge. Finally, they all shuffled into a horizontal passage that smelled of dust, burnt electronics, and the sharp residue of explosives.

No one had looked at Marc. No one had spoken.

Jade's face was splotchy with rouge-red and pale-white patches, her agitation making it worse.

"Damn Anibale. Damn ZEK! You said the *woman* was the control agent for the Star device! Now, ZEK hauls that pilot in and he nearly takes down the Great Seat itself with it!"

Valezah looked properly cowed as she stood stiffly in front of Jade's gold braided acceleration chair. The Suite Red Prime's ship had been scrambled as soon as Jade could get back to her Helm command post after the debacle in the Great Seat. She and her staff had transferred to it immediately, even as the ship was starting its low-powered troll out of system center.

"My guard was there, Prime. He saw her do it. The man did nothing at that time. It seems they can both control the thing."

"Control it? Or, trigger it, more likely. I wonder." Jade slapped her chair arm. "What did you find out about Kera?"

"It is unknown if she is still favorable toward you. She is out of our reach now. Anibale pulled her into his inner circle when they left the Great Seat."

"Hmm. Make sure Simune keeps her eyes open for any opportunity to intercept her. She could be the key to success if we can't get the pilot. It's obvious now that they can both operate the Star Artifact, but he did more than just turn it on. That thing was pulling in energy from somewhere and bonding with him like a parasite. That was the most dangerous display I have ever witnessed." She slapped the chair arm again. "I must have that pilot and we must find his nasty ship!"

Valezah lifted her eyes to look Jade in the face. "Won't Anibale also be in pursuit?"

"Anibale? Of course, he'll be in pursuit of the middie. Frantic pursuit, indeed, if I know him. And, I do know him pretty well, sad to say. That's why we must be first and be the smartest. Go check the pilots and make sure we are set for Rindd 1 . . . and arrange our normal cover stories and decoys! I don't want Anibale or ZEK or any of the others to know *we* are in frantic pursuit ourselves!

"Well? Don't just give me a face, girl. GO!"

Chapter Nineteen

Marc stared at his dirty hands and then strained to lift them up to the ore pile again. The constant gravity load made him feel listless and depressed. The rough face of the mine wall was surprisingly rich with gem deposits. Sometimes Sweet Pea (his private name for the guard woman) would come around and make the workers hack at the face with manual tools just to see them struggle, but then she'd buzz away, making a show of her ease of walking in that stupid, humming exoskeleton. Then, the small black digger-bots would come and pry off another layer of ore into piles.

At first, Marc just sat and refused to do the work, but Sweet Pea threatened him with no food and longer hours in the mine shafts. There was also the sheer drop off into that big pit down at the end of the passage and as she said, "Accidents do happen around dangerous places like this. Wouldn't want one of our guests to get hurt."

The gems were tough to identify in the ore matrix, but once in a while, he dug out a large colored crystal. Most of it was embedded in ore that had to be separated and gone through carefully with machine filters and simple hand work. Seems the human eye with attached brain was still the best method for this type of discriminating task.

Still, it was heavy, dirty grunt work and meant to be so.

At the end of the first day, the older white-haired man and Green-shirt worked at the ore piles next to Marc. The bots had just scraped off another layer and with newcomer's luck, Marc pulled out a large beauty of a crystal, half encased in rubble matrix. Suddenly, a huge wrinkled hand grabbed Marc's. Greenshirt grunted as he tried to wrest the stone away from him, now using both hands.

"Give it, middie boy. That one's mine!"

Marc really didn't care one way or another, but something in him rebelled at this crude giant just taking something–anything–from him. He clamped his hand down harder on the gem, but Greenshirt's huge hands, gripping his, were very strong. He felt his own knuckles compressing and the stone slipping away. He almost gave in just because the huge man smelled so bad.

"Give it, I said!"

Marc gave a determined huff and concentrated. His hand began to *fill up*–change–and a greenish-white glow escaped from between Greenshirt's fingers. It grew brighter and then the man's hammy hand was forced to spread its grip. Marc's hand was extraordinarily enlarged now and Greenshirt could no longer keep his hold. As he let go with a yelp, Marc felt an arc of energy pass through to him. The man lurched back on suddenly crossed legs and sat down hard and unceremoniously, kicking up some of the dusty fines into the gallery's heavy air. His bark-like face went through an amazing and rapid transformation from dead-on mean, to shock and surprise, and finally to raw fear. Marc coolly watched him, massaging his hand now as it returned to normal. He held the gemstone up, turning and looking purposefully at it, just to goad Greenshirt a little more. A few feet away, the white-haired man watched both of them with a curious expression on his face.

From then on, Greenshirt took care to never come near him.

The Rindder medics had come to Marc twice since he first arrived.

They removed their batch of nanoagents and injected a new one, or that's what he supposed they were doing. The fact that it was taking more than one try and quite a long time, gave him hope that they were not finding what they wanted.

They can't find my new System in my system! Ha.

Why not, though? I can remember the Line and Marc's Pile just fine, but when they try to get the information from me it feels like a cloud or something rises up to protect it—no, to defend it! Weird, but wonderful!

Several more days passed and the work was hard, but Marc noticed that he was being treated differently from most of the other prisoner-miners. Sweet Pea moved the white-haired man to the same wall with Marc and they had the use of the digger-bots, but all the others were forced into tough manual picking on the walls. As they passed each other in the dorm or meal room, they glared at Marc. Greenshirt kept his distance, but once threatened him in front of the others, accusing him of giving the guard sexual favors for better treatment.

No one else had the energy to talk or share information after the work days. In any case, there was no new information to share.

Sleeping was hard, too, and Marc suffered recurring nightmares of the battle scene from his vision, his parents on Salina, and the giant golden Faces of ZEK glowering down at him. He'd wake up in a sweat, the gravity making him feel like an insect, pinned down to his hard bed plank.

Marc sat on the rocky floor of the mine, sifting ore through his dusty, scabbed fingers. The white-haired man was near him, working on his own pile. Marc stretched his neck to see a sudden commotion down the gallery.

It was Greenshirt, yelling something and flailing his hands in the air. Sweet Pea was down there, too, and she began to yell back at him.

Xenoplague

From his position, Marc could not see the details, but Greenshirt made a lunge toward Sweet Pea, then turned and ran–ran!–down the gallery toward Marc, his huge legs and feet hammering the ground. As Marc painfully scrambled over his pile to get out of the way, Greenshirt let out a wild yelp. He stopped and grabbed a few large ore rocks and hurled them back toward the approaching guard, but the gravity brought them down far short. His harsh voice grated off the walls, "You will NOT force me to the surface, you BlackBot! You rot face mockery! You're less human than these crawlers!" Greenshirt leaned down and grabbed one of the hapless mine bots and hurled it–its little articulation arms swinging frantically–with all his considerable might right at Sweet Pea's quickly approaching face. "Just LEAVE ME ALONE!"

The bot struck her hard–hard enough to momentarily stop her run. Greenshirt, eyes wild, charged her. She drew her gun and Marc could feel the sting of the shock wave himself when the beam's bolt hit the man, who was now only a couple of meters away from him. Its crackle hurt Marc's ears. The thud when he hit the gallery floor caused another shock, then all was quiet.

Sweet Pea put her weapon down and said, "Huh. Stupid Wilder." She glared over at Marc for a moment, then rotated her exoskeleton with a loud *whish*, and marched back the way she came. Greenshirt's blank, gray eyes were open, and seemed to stare accusingly at Marc.

A few minutes later, two large utility bots rolled in to scoop up the hapless hulk and carry it away as Marc slowly clambered his way back to the spot where he'd been working.

On the sixth day, the white-haired man sat next to him again at the mine wall. He was tall and his bright white ruff was very short-cropped. He wondered how he kept it trimmed down here. His own was a tangled mess.

He was an older man, and having an obviously harder time with the gravity. Today, they were near each other and farther away from the other workers. Sweet Pea seemed a little less zealous after the incident with Greenshirt, and only came around to harass them a couple of times a day. She had just made her second inspection tour and was off to enjoy her afternoon, however Purple guards do that on Barrkon's Oven.

The older man glanced at Marc and almost smiled, but his hands kept busy with the dirt and gravel he was sorting through. He began to hum a melodic tune. It was repetitive and simple, and after a while, Marc found himself being caught up in it and moving his own hands to the pace of the song. It seemed to make the work go easier.

He reached into his own pile of raw ore and pulled out another larger clear crystal that was surprisingly clean. He held it out in front of him for a moment, even though the relentless gravity pulled at his tired arms. The man's song seemed to reverberate in Marc's mind and he focused his attention on his hands, still gripping the stone. Suddenly, Marc's face felt hot and he thought he might faint. He tried to lower the gemstone, but his hands and arms would not obey him. More heat came up through his body and he could feel it coursing through his veins toward his outstretched arms. His hands began to glow.

The stone, too, began to glow as bright specks and sparks flowed out through Marc's hands into the crystal. The man's song had hesitated for a moment, but now he sang it stronger and slightly faster. Marc could not look at him, only at the specular flow of light from his own limbs into the now brightly glistering gemstone. Then, it stopped flowing and all the light was inside the gem. Marc's arms instantly released the long-held load and the stone dropped to the rocky floor and shattered. Green and white sparks shot out of it and raced away in every direction, like some demented firework, until the sparks died out and the gloom of the mine returned as if nothing had happened.

The man stopped his tune. "Well, that got rid of the little buggers, eh?"

"The little buggers?" Marc said. He slowly turned his head to look at the man's face.

"Buggers. The nanobots they filled you with. Never saw someone do *that* before!" He smiled at Marc and set his stones down on his pile. "Very impressive!"

"I didn't know that was what I was doing, but that sounds about right. Yeah, that does sound right. I'm Marc."

"And I am Silveen, but please call me Sil."

"What is that song you've been singing? It may have helped me do whatever I just did."

"Oh, that? Just an old folk tune from my people on Florinda. It helps pass the time, yes?"

"Sister's System. You look a bit like a guy I saw on Farms not too long ago. Are you a Sisters Teacher?"

"Oh, yes. I've been a Teacher for many years. There are quite a few of us making the rounds in Harbor space these days. Things are changing–becoming more dangerous."

"Yeah, I guess it *was* dangerous for you. I assume you're not mining here for wages."

Sil smiled wanly. "No, indeed. Yes, times are certainly hazardous for me, but I really meant that things are dangerous for everyone–for all of us humans, middie and Elite alike. Everything in Harbor Space has grown more and more polarized."

Sil's soft, fluid voice carried a pleasant but distinct Sister's accent. "Others may label it as they will, but you and I are obviously enslaved here. The thing is, all the mid-class is also enslaved, but they don't quite realize it because, for a very long time, most of them have been given just enough in goods, wealth, and power by the Elites to keep them satisfied. That was a wise technique for the Elites to use, but real power has been pooling at the top for centuries and corrupt attitudes have solidified. The top folk have begun to forget the middies and now resort to suppressing them. They have begun to forget that they need middies and all the cultural and commercial under-structure that supports them."

"Yeah, I have a lot of friends on Farms who can attest to that. It's especially problematic if you get on the bad side of one of the Elites like I did."

Sil nodded at him, then a bot pulled down another layer of rocks. The older man turned back to his ore pile and began to sort listlessly through the debris. Marc thought he'd better make a show of it also in case Sweet Pea came by unexpectedly. When he checked the corridor, there was someone standing at the cross-passage at the far end, but it was not Sweet Pea. A male Rindder stood there–tall and wearing a med jacket and half-helmet with bio-enhancers. He must have been monitoring on vids.

Sil said, "You seem to have an admirer."

"Well, that episode surprised me, so I guess it was out of the box for them, too. Should have known they'd check it out."

Oddly, though, the Rindder did not come further. After standing there a while, the man turned and disappeared. Marc's back was hurting again, so he copied what Sil was doing now by laying down as much as he could, reclining while still positioned to reach into his pile of rocks and dirt.

Like some ancient Earth Roman, feasting from his couch. Right.

Anibale was impatient to get his ship off Helm. The Lines from Harbor through Hub System would make for a tense and long transit haul, but he was determined to take back what was rightfully his!

Blue Senior Agar and Tactical Pilot Tommit were with him in the data and guidance chamber of Suite Blue's principal ship. Agar said, "No question. They're taking him straight to Rindd and Barrkon's Oven."

Anibale's mind was still reeling from the betrayal at the Great Seat. After the fiasco with the pilot, the Color Council's guards had bandaged and bound Marc and shuttled him into one of their ships incredibly fast. As Anibale rushed to get his own vessel away and into hidden pursuit, his men monitored that Council ship, watching as it took the back-bound Line to Hub. Its pilot then took a standard course for the main Line on to the Beyond System, as Anibale had expected.

"Yes, they would choose their deepest lair for him. You have triggered the alert for my special guards to join us at Beyond, in the system outer fringe?"

"They will be there, Prime. We will leave the envoy ship at Hub and take your fast flier to Golddust first, then on to Beyond. They will meet us far enough away from the system center to avoid unusual notice."

"Tommit–you are coming as the pilot on this?"

"Yes, Prime. I know the route to Rindd intimately. We will need to skirt the main traffic and pick our times carefully if you don't want the Rindders to anticipate you too much. That's also the reason for the Golddust detour."

"Of course, but we waste no time now. Launch in five minutes. Report to me then. I'll be in my cabin." The air of his fast stride down the ship's carpeted hallway lifted Anibale's embroidered blue cape out behind him like wings.

They passed with no complications through the very large and busy Hub System, center of the biggest assortment of useable Lines. Then, a short transit in Hub space to the far less trafficked Line to Golddust System. A main Line would have taken them from Hub to Beyond in one step. That was certainly the Council ship's route. A detour here to Golddust would help defer prying eyes from other Suites and from ZEK and Council's spies. He needed to fly quickly through this backwater system and emerge at Beyond's less trafficked zone to meet up with his own clandestine support ships.

It took several hours to transit Golddust's space. They would not pass anywhere near the system's small sun or its planets, of course, but fly along the orbit of the Gates, making as short a run to the Beyond Gate as possible. There was not much to do in between.

Golddust did have one amazing claim to fame. Anibale felt a little ridiculous and self-conscious, but he could not pass through Golddust without seeing the unique spectacle that gave it its name.

He left his control cabin and, after making certain no one was monitoring him, climbed up-ship to an engineering area that provided a small utility operations nodule extending out onto the ship's outside surface. It was designed for direct observation of bots and suited personnel when they were working on the ship and had the unusual feature of an actual transparent dome. He unsealed the iris hatch that led to it and entered the dark bubble.

He uttered a growl of appreciation as he rose to the window dome. Hundreds of thousands of specks of yellow and gold and a few red ones spread like sand in all directions–suns of the globular cluster they were inside of. The starry lights pooled and thinned here and there in wave-like fractal patterns determined by gravity and cold math. The bright dust of them was achingly beautiful, but they also made him feel small and helpless against such numbers and size and distance. After quietly staring for a few long minutes, the transparent dome seemed to disappear to his senses, leaving him apparently floating, forgotten, and alone, in the black void inside the vast halo of radiant golden dust.

Anibale could never be truly alone in his roles and life as Prime Blue. Whenever he came here, he could feel and even relish this absolute aloneness as something of a counterpoint to the rest of his existence. And, sometimes, once in a while, he could loosen his senses even more. He felt it now–something in the very back recesses of his mind. It sounded like a voice. Was it his own voice reflecting back to him?

It rolled and fluttered in his head, seeming to make no sense, but then faintly, like a word echoing in a vast cavern, he could make out a pattern emerging from a rush of "rrrrr" sounds. "Power," it seemed to say. Then "uuuuuu" reflected in his thoughts and, "True," reverberated into his mind. Was it the voice of another? Electricity ran up his spine. Terror and excitement mixed incongruently with the overwhelming sense of isolation he felt, suspended in this tiny droplet in deepest inhuman space.

A shiver ran through him.

He withdrew, closed the iris, and made his way back to his cabin–back to the world where he was in control. They drifted on, cross-system to the Line to Beyond, and quietly fell into it.

The Beyond System was a complete contrast. Black space. Only the faintest smear of stars in one direction. They were on the very outer edge of this galaxy, wherever it really was. The three Beyond planets hugged close to their lonely and singular yellow star. Not much else here to speak of except for plenty of darkness.

A good place to hide ships full of my own troops.

BlueMils. He wished he could call them that openly. But, that time is coming. Perhaps now.

For the first time as a single force, his hand-picked and long-groomed Blue guards and fighters would be gathered here. It was a tribute to his own rigorous planning that it happened so fast, with all of his clandestine, embedded ZEK personnel activating their decoy mission scenarios where they were normally stationed, then rushing full-speed to meet him here in the black zone of the Beyond System.

Anibale turned the problem over this way and that, consolidating his certainty that this was the right time to show his hand. There was truly no question–no higher priority he could think of. There was no time to intercept the Council ship carrying the valuable pilot. It had taken the direct route at express speed and Marc would already be inside the Barrkon's Oven prison facilities. He had to get that irksome lout out of there before Jade or someone else does. ZEK's and Council's ties with the Rindd System government were tight, to be sure, but the Rindders were practical business people first and foremost. They would at least listen to him. He would make them a very good offer. If they don't choose to take it . . . well, that's why his BlueMil militia will be waiting in the outer orbits beyond Rindd 2.

The route from Golddust placed them into the fringes of the Beyond System, well off the main trade Line route from Hub. After passing the Gate monitors, Anibale's ship altered course toward the system's outer zones and silently and rapidly rendezvoused with four of his BlueMil ships which had been altered to appear as commercial transports.

Three hours after getting underway as a group, a single ship appeared on scan, heading toward them on a distant fly-by vector.

"It's a Rindd, Prime. They must be keeping some regular patrols out here."

"Looking us over, eh, Tommit? Maintain course and speed. Let them see; let them wonder. Watch him carefully and let me know if he alters course."

Closest approach was under an hour later. The Rindd ship had not changed its route, but just as it passed and began to recede, alarms lit up the bridge controls. Tommit was on comm instantly. "Unknown ship or ships incoming–above the system plane! Initial evasives and report in!"

He started to say something else when a startling sound broke into their audio feeds. "Zzzzzziiiiippppppp . . . zzzzpp . . . zzz . . . ppppppp . . . zzziiippppppp"

"Four–no, five Zips incoming. NOT on collision vector. Hold steady." Tommit leaned over to see the nav displays. Anibale studied the larger plotting screen above. It clearly showed the Zip ships as dots with trails recording their known path so far and yellow lines showing projected paths. Their course would take them close to that Rindd ship.

"Damn ghosts! What are they doing out here?"

"They're just a nuisance, Sir. They never really do any harm."

"They are a nuisance at a very sensitive time and place. Somebody needs to confront them and make them *stop it!*"

Tommit and the other staffers gave Anibale an instinctive glance at that. Anibale huffed. "I know. I know. Damn ghosts. Can't even talk to them, much less shoot them. Might as well try to swat those fast-flies on Hub's Heaven." That got him a few grins. Most of these officers had probably experienced the heaven dance there: lots of arm swinging and never a dead insect to show for it.

The Zip sounds sputtered out to silence and their strange ships blinked away as fast as they had come. Tommit was still watching the nav screen. "The Rindder is gone, Prime."

"Mmm. That was fast. Did he change course?"

"No, Sir. He's just not there. All routes ahead to the Line Gate are clear."

Anibale allowed himself to relax a bit. His men and women were here–ready to follow him on to Rindd, two systems behind Beyond. They would all transit the next system together, a system the ancients had naturally named "Back." Thus, the old joke, "Question: what's back of Beyond? Answer: Yes."

Idiots.

Chapter Twenty

Rass-Ruuk Biniun was already heading that way when he received the summons data in his out-level neural stream. Karms wanted to see him in person in his office near the top of the pit mine. Bureaucrats were always interrupting his official medical work, but RR knew that was just how the system worked and he did not particularly begrudge it. No doubt, Chief Karms had just read his last report.

Well, I would have called me in, too.

He arrived at the sparsely appointed chamber Karms kept here, and his aide ushered him in as she scanned his readits and idents. Karms studied a monitor at his console, then looked up at RR and nodded for him to take the one reinforced guest chair. RR sat down carefully and gratefully. His internal mesh supports helped in this awful gravity, but he was still not as at ease here as Karms always seemed to be.

The older man raised his brows a bit and said, "Unprecedented. Are you certain of your tests, RR? This seems like a system error or data distortion."

"Yes, Chief, I know it sounds that way, but we thoroughly checked and filtered everything. Rechecked and even took a second sample from him. The third sequence of nanogenetics were simply gone from his body–as if they'd never been there."

"Well, what happened to them? You have solid data on their injection and internal dispersion. Where did they go?"

"I don't know yet, Chief. I suspect . . ." he paused.

Karms leaned forward. "Yes? What do you suspect, Doctor?"

RR sent an intention download to Karms's console. "Watch this monitor vid. The cam was not close enough to where he was working to see the details, but . . ."

The video ran in both men's internal virtual space. The scene inside the mine was dim, but they saw two shirtless men sitting next to two of the rough ore piles, their backs toward the source camera. The man on the right–the pilot, Marc Arons–was holding his arms out in front of him. Whatever he was holding gave off a green glow. The older, white-headed man was singing something. Suddenly, there was a snap sound and the rock hall lit up for an instant in bright green light, followed by darkness again and green and white sparks flying off in different directions.

RR said, "I suspect he got rid of them himself–somehow."

"Strange, indeed. You think the pilot expelled them? Absorbed them? What?"

"Again, I don't know until we test further. I was instantly alerted to the anomaly when the data stream cut off. I headed over there and walked in enough to see them just after the event, but nothing else happened and I didn't want to alarm him until we saw clearly what he was doing. Now, I will actively observe him with more plentiful and focused surveillance. Let's give him another nanogenetic sequence and watch him to see what happens."

"All right, RR. I certainly approve that. We must understand what's happening before making any further plans. This man was already problematic. None of the previous tests have produced the information we seek. Your report is clear. His DNA sequence is distinctly unusual in some of the noncoding areas. There are mutations we have not seen at this scale and complexity. This new ability, if that's what it is, may be connected. You saw the reports of his abilities with the alien control device at Helm, yes? He may be of interest to us at a deeper level.

"We need to keep him in our domain–delay Harbor's plans for him and keep him here where we can study him. You must help me with this, but remember, RR, this one is ZEK and Council Elder Bai's very special toy. More and more, I see why they think so. Proceed with enhanced caution."

"Yes, Chief."

Only an hour later, the med staff had re-injected Marc with the new batch and RR had set up his viewer bots and connected to them in virtual so that he felt like he was sitting right next to the man.

———

Jade checked her face in a tiny mirror she always kept hidden in a pocket in her red cowl. Her official reason for visiting Rindd 1 was to shop for new gems and arrange for cutting and art settings for them. All Suite Primes did business with Rindd, as most of Harbor's gem-quality stones and workmanship came from here. Sometimes the Primes themselves got involved in the selections, hoping to find that one special piece that could give them an edge over a competitor or curry political favor with ZEK. They did not often go so far as Barrkon's Oven itself, though, and she needed to keep a very low profile except when necessary. Nasty place, this, in more ways than one.

Valezah arranged a temporary office at the pit mine under the story of Jade Prime being dissatisfied with the recent purchase of amethyst crystals. The mine would be required to allow a Suite Red technical staff on-site to evaluate the new stones as they were produced from the mine. Under her regular disguise and alt-ident,

Jade came down with the crew. The next person who would see her, however, needed the full Suite Red treatment.

The female Purple Guard was ushered into her temporary audience room, which her staff had done their best to decorate with Suite Red paraphernalia and colors. Behind her small console, Jade sat on a stiff, square pillow to ease her from the extra weight, but also to raise her smaller frame to a height she could use to her advantage. The muscular guard woman was talking to Valezah as she was walking in.

". . . still don't know why you need me. I just guard the miners. I don't get involved with the mine or its business, that's all handled by . . . Oh! . . . What's this?" The woman looked suitably disconcerted. Jade smiled to herself and then forced her game smile onto her face.

"Prime Red, here?" The guard straightened up in her uniform and stared.

"It's all right, my dear. Yes, I am here."

"Madame Prime! I . . . it's not often we have a Suite Prime come to Barrkon's."

"Yes, I dare say, it may be a first! But then, I am often driven to take risks and create opportunities for my people, you know. Please be at ease. You are Paris 63Cranz, special operations Purple on Barrkon's Oven, assigned by Helm and ZEK to the pit mine crew here, is that correct, my dear?"

The woman gulped. "Yes, Madame."

"Paris–named for such a lovely, legendary old city, yes? The ancient Earth metropolis with its wonderful old metal spike."

Paris looked confused. "Sorry, Madame? I don't know what you're talking about."

"Ahh. Well. Don't worry then. So, Paris, I wanted to ask you a few questions. First, I know it's different and exciting for you to have a Prime here, but I must ask for your complete confidence. I have to oversee some important things here at the mines and I can't have my presence publicized in any way. I'm sure I can count on you. Do you understand? Yes? Good, then.

"There is one miner here who has something that belongs to me. No, it's not a jewel or anything like that. It's some specific information that I need him to give to me. You understand? Good. It would not do for me to wander around Barrkon's Oven or these depressing and dangerous mine shafts myself–surely you do understand?–but I must have a conversation with this man. I'd like for you to arrange it! That's all. It would need to be here at this office so that I can stay incognito, of course. Will you help me to do that?"

Paris was still staring at her, but she was clearly thinking now. "What man is it, Prime?"

"A recent arrival named Marc 54Arons who I understand is in the group you oversee."

A troubled look came over Paris's face, then she lifted her chin some. "That particular person is a special case, Madame. He is under a direct mandate from the offices of ZEK and the Council of Colors. He is also under the medical staff's direct control. I don't believe he could be withdrawn from the control areas."

Jade gave her her best all-knowing and understanding look. "Yes, this is what I, too, understand of his situation. That is why I am seeking *your* help, my dear. As I said, this Marc person has information I require. Information about something important that he took from me."

Or, rather, that I shall take from him! She thought about how pleasant that would be once she had him in her Suite Red labs down on Harbor.

"You are charged with overseeing him, therefore, you have access and control over what it is that I need for my suite, for Suite Red, and even for all of our people. If you will help me with this, I will make your life much more pleasant, Paris. There are many excellent places to work and live that are not on Barrkon's Oven! There is much wealth in my Suite. You would be taken care of."

"Madame. I could never do something that would cross the orders of ZEK! It wouldn't be worth my career or my life for that matter. I'd like to help you, but . . ."

Jade gave her the stern and commanding look. "Yes, I understand and admire your practical political assessments, however, this situation is beyond the ordinary. This man may be the key to some very dangerous and worlds-changing events." She paused for effect. "Did you know that ZEK is quite old? ZEK doesn't live forever, Paris. Others are positioning themselves to their advantage for when that seat becomes vacant. It would have been years from now, but this middie, Marc, may change things. His information and his very existence may bring things to a point *very quickly*. I am here in order to position myself. Do you understand what I'm telling you?" Paris was gaping at her now. *Good.*

"You have a unique opportunity, Paris. You happen to be in a place of great leverage. I do not forget those who have helped me. Suite Red will wear the gold, perhaps sooner than you can imagine."

Jade glared at her now. "I also do not forget those who are too timid to take bold actions when the circumstances call out for them—actions like I myself have taken, and do take now."

Paris stiffened even more and a bead or two of sweat appeared on her forehead under her fabric cap. She paused for a long time while she thought. Jade knew just to wait for it. Finally, she said, "Madame, I'm stuck here for a two-year term. Politics got me here–you can look up my record and see how I got blamed for something I didn't do–so, maybe politics will get me out and improve my prospects, too. I really don't know how I can get that guy out of there for you, but I'll try to think of something."

Jade gave her the smile again. "Yes. That's good, Paris. Remember that you have an important advantage. The Rindders and ZEK's people have no clue that you might take some action in this way. Use that advantage, but remember it is only good once. I will give you some time to think about this, but we must move quickly. Return here in the morning and let me know what you have come up with. Valezah here will prepare a cover story for your visits."

"Yes, Madame."

"You may call me Jade," she said and gave her one of her sweetest

218

smiles.

———————

Of course, they would shoot him up again. Marc thought he could almost feel the nanoagents in his bloodstream this time, but that was probably just an illusion.

I wonder what they said about that missing batch. 'There seems to have been a malfunction, Sir!'

Marc smiled as he lifted his pick and, brushing aside one of the digger bots, began fiercely assaulting the most recent ore face, pushing through the weight and pain of it and making sparks fly with each animated strike.

I just wish I knew how I did whatever it was that I did.

Sil looked up at all the noise he was creating. They had managed to stay next to each other since the expulsion incident.

"You trying to dig your way out of here, Marc?"

"In a way." He grinned at Sil. "I have to build up my strength in this heavy grav so I will be ready to leave when the opportunity comes. Leave *forcefully*, if I need to, which I probably will. You want to join me, Sil?"

"Well, I'm too old to do what you're doing, but I still might be able to help."

"All right, then. You can be my coach."

Sil put down the rocks he was holding. "Just what I was thinking. I would be honored, Marc. Here's the first thing, then. Keep doing the physical strengthening–that's important, too–but, let me help you focus that other energy you have. Remember, your nanos expulsion happened while we were both mentally entrained to the song. You have some unusual talents, my friend. I've seen some of this before in others, but not to the level you seem to possess."

"Energy, huh? It's some kind of damned energy, that's for certain." Marc put down the pick, "but, Sil, I'm afraid of it! I've had to call on it several times recently, and it's helped me, but having these abilities is unsettling and sometimes it backfires. It goes back to when I was a kid on Salina. I used to experience some weird bodily changes that happened for no reason. My hands would change. Sometimes, the new shapes were ghostly and immaterial, but other times it was truly there. I couldn't control it and I couldn't call it up on purpose.

"My Father called it the Curse, and he was right. In the end, it cost us our home and our livelihood, and the end result was that they lost their lives. Thanks to me."

Sil said, "I am sorry for that. Do you still think it is a curse?"

"That's a hard question to answer. The changing has served me many times–usually when I needed it most. It's saved my life and others, too, but it is fickle and frustrating. When I figured out that I couldn't just call up my magic hand when and how I wanted, I did think it was a kind of curse. There were times growing up when I could sense the presence of people and hear vague voices–people who weren't there. I thought I was crazy and I hid that from my parents. Hid it from myself, even. All I wanted was to be normal–just another regular guy, you know?"

Sil said, "But, the energy and the effects didn't go away, did they? They got stronger."

"Yes, they did. They helped me escape in Helm and peaked with that incident with ZEK there in the Great Seat when it combined with the added energy of the Star Artifact. And, well, you've seen it here with the nanoagents thing. Even now, I just want it to go away–let me be what I am."

"Perhaps that is just what is happening, Marc. I know it is disconcerting, but perhaps this new thing *is* who and what you are. If I am to coach you, my first instruction is this: I say you must face and learn to expand and control these strange effects and abilities. Make the decision to work *with* these talents and develop them into something that will serve you rather than frighten and upset you–for they are talents, not curses. Let's work with it together. It may be the one thing that sets us free so we can help others."

"How do you know about these things, Sil, and, how did you end up here, anyway?"

"Well, I'm a bit of a knowledge-seeker. I like to prowl about the universes and learn new things, then subject the really interesting things to more detailed testing and analysis. Sometimes I find very useful things, but other times that process gets me into trouble. As I mentioned, I've seen your kind of phenomenon before in certain people. I've even had reports of an entire isolated human population that exhibits it more strongly than can quite be believed."

"Hmm," Marc sat down at the pile to relieve his aching leg muscles. "You believe it, though?"

"Yes, I can vouch for the researcher who reported it, and I have other sources that back it up. Your energy seems to affect mostly your hands. These people can manipulate their entire bodies." Sil looked up at Marc and gave him a sly look. "You can, too."

"Oh, I don't know, Sil. It seems to take all my concentration and effort to call the energy for the hand changes, even when that works."

"Those Rindder nanoagents were well distributed, were they not? You directed them out via your hands, but they were everywhere inside your body, yes?"

"Well, yes . . . they were. Good point." Marc picked up a small dirty green gemstone and studied it for a moment, then tossed it back onto his pile. "Sil, I've already told you my story about what happened at Helm and why ZEK wants to hold me here, but what about you? These super paranormal people–are they the reason you got sent to this lovely resort?"

"No, not really. I said I like to explore information and knowledge–two different things, of course–and sometimes that means digging into areas that are forbidden." The older man settled further down next to the ore pile. "I was pursuing stories about the old human-designed FTL drive that first brought us from Earth to Harbor. Most people have either forgotten about it or just don't think about it, since Earth is off-limits and that was the only system jump that required, and still requires, our own old human trans-lightspeed technology.

"It seems that some of the Rinnd folk here are experimenting, clandestinely of course, with that technology, trying to revive it and see if there are other uses for it. The original information has been locked up for centuries by the Council of Colors on Helm or Harbor, and no one these days presumably still understands that technology, much less knows how to actually construct a new device. It is quietly rumored that they keep a human-only designed ship with the old human engines intact–after 1,200 years!–in case there is ever a need to re-access the Earth System. Who knows?"

"So, what do you think the Rindders really want to do with old human FTL tech?"

"Oh, I imagine that they hope to eventually find some new systems to colonize into–systems that are *not* on the Ash Alien Lines. I think most of them have had quite enough of Harbor and its class controls and the ever-present threats to them as a people. They would like to retreat to a more secure and separate region with Rindd as a well-secured border. It serves them as a Gate now, protecting their collection of strictly off-limits Rindder worlds on the Lines behind it, but it is a fragile barricade. Harbor is too close and too dangerous, and becoming more dangerous to them all the time. Also, using human FTL, the gateway barriers to their newer worlds would likely be one of time as well as space, since relativistic effects would apply. We fly the Lines almost casually and tend to forget that they were amazingly designed by the Ash Aliens to work as an integrated system–one that presents no relativistic time issues. They knew that no destination system could be from the same universe as any other destination or there would be problems with relativity between the two. They must have done a tremendous search to find each useful destination, carefully selected from a unique parallel universe for its presumably accidental chronological correlation with the other star systems on the Lines. The black pockets are just systems they found that match our time flow but happen to be barren of useful planets or other resources."

Marc said, "That makes sense. So, you're saying it would be impossible to place a Line from here to another star in this Rindd System's universe without time problems. It snaps the mind thinking how the AA's did what they did. I never really thought about it before, but I guess that means there's a time differential between Harbor and Earth since they are in the same universe and were linked only by the original human FTL."

"Yes, indeed. I do not know what the ratio is, though." Sil made some small piles out of his big ore piles as he spoke, but neither of them were really looking for gemstones now. "Earth is a special interest of mine."

Marc said, "I always thought of Rinnders as being happy to work with and for the Elites–happy to take their money, anyway, or mine for that matter. I've had some business dealings with them. They don't strike me as being either fearful or particularly ethical."

"Oh yes, they are a practical people. In their situation, maintaining one's security while also transferring wealth from one's oppressor is, I think, a rather practical and wise plan. One might even say ingenious except for its fragility. That's not to say that many of them have not become corrupt themselves. The Rinnders I was interfacing with are using all that commerce structure along with their carefully crafted persona as a shield for their secret research and manufacturing efforts into human FTL. Probably into a lot of other projects I'm not aware of, too. I wanted to learn more about their work, so I connected with some of them and learned much. When I left Rindd 2 a few helm-standard months ago, however, one of the BlackMil ships that I believe was under Suite Blue's influence intercepted me and discovered some partial engineering schematics for the new Rindd reconstruction designs. I claimed it was my own research. They placed me here until Helm *evaluates my situation*–and you know what that means. At least they didn't fill me full of nanobots like they did you."

"Yeah, I'm special. I nearly blew up the Great Seat along with ZEK and the Primes, too, or so they think."

Sil raised one white eyebrow. "But, you don't."

"No. That artifact is not the weapon they think it is."

"It could be a control for a weapon, though?"

"It's the control for a ship. I was on board it, Sil. It was not a doomsday weapon."

"Are you saying it wasn't another xenoplague ship?"

"It may be the same kind as the old xenoplague one, but I don't believe it is meant to destroy us. The Star Artifact gave me a Vision."

Through his virtuals, RR listened to Marc's account of the vision to Sil. All he had heard of their conversation up to now had been a revelation to him. How could Silveen be so connected to RR's covert working group without him knowing about it? The fact that Sil had, and still contains in his mind, any of the plans for the human FTL project, was extraordinarily dangerous. Neither of these men could be allowed to remain in the control of ZEK or Harbor Group in any way. Something had to be done, and RR was the only one in a position to take the necessary action.

Marc's bio-morphological abilities were stunning, and Sil's report of the other humans with vastly larger capabilities was almost too good. His own group members had observed a few cases of limited bio-morph in some Rindd people, but nothing like this. As for RR's personal experiences with the phenomena–that, he kept to himself.

The idea of a new xenoplague ship and the ability of this man to possibly control it–well, now I know why he's here and why we've been trying so hard to get that system location from him. These two men are an important nexus of power and knowledge. They might be just what Rindd needs to break Harbor's status quo and help institute a more benign neighbor.

RR gene-locked the recordings he had made and when he returned his attention to the mote feeds, he smiled at what the two were doing now. "This is what I was waiting for," he muttered to himself.

Silveen was singing his song again–repetitive, tuneful phrases in a language unknown to RR. Marc was squatting down, concentrating on a fist-sized clear gemstone he held with both hands. He watched in amazement as Marc's hands began to grow larger and give off a glow. Light trails and sparks flowed down his arms into the glowing fingers and into the stone until it was filled with green-white light. Sil kept singing and RR noticed that Marc was singing, too. Then, Marc dropped the sparkling crystal. It hit the mine floor and burst. *And that type is not a stone easily shattered!* Green and white animated sparks fountained out of the stone and flew in all directions, each particle finally decaying to darkness after a few searingly bright seconds.

Wow. There goes another expensive batch of agents. Got it all recorded, though. Simply amazing. Karms won't be seeing this feed!

Time to go talk to these guys.

Chapter Twenty-one

Marc realized he was still holding his hands out in front of him even though the sparks had been extinguished for a few minutes. He was shaking a little, so he put them down. Sil looked at him with one brow raised under his sweat-matted hair. "That seemed a little more controlled. How did it feel for you?"

"Better, I think. Yes, a bit more controlled or 'willed', I guess. I could really feel the nanos being attracted to the fingers like in a magnetic force field."

"Yes, but certainly not magnetism as we know it."

"You've encountered it before. What do you think it is, Sil? What's your guess?"

The older man didn't answer for a moment. "Most people would dismiss this as paranormal nonsense. It's paranormal, all right, but real; in your case, observable and almost certainly measurable, at least in its effects on normal matter. I have spent a lot of time studying old Earth documents and archives, Marc, and there are some of the ancients who believed that humans once had such abilities and lost them in an evolutionary diversion or branching. We may be seeing another such branching and the re-development of certain . . . cross-dimensional effects, shall we say?"

"You think this comes from another dimension? That's pretty speculative, but I guess it's as good an answer as any."

"It may not be an answer–yet. But I think it is a path worth more research."

A noise from down-gallery made both men look up. A Rindder in a gray suit approached them.

He wore an eye-bot on his left eye and had a med insignia on the suit's chest plate.

Without looking back at Marc, Sil said, "Well, that didn't take long. He's probably getting annoyed at your little trick."

The man reached their wall sector and stood in front of the ore piles.

Marc thought that he didn't really look angry. Can't ever read these Rindder guys, though.

The man studied them a moment, then unfastened his data glove and held out his bare right hand, pointing at them with his first and second fingers. "I want to show you something," he said. "I've never shown this to any other person."

He stood there for a moment, concentrating, and then the two fingers began to gently glow with a white aura. Then, they merged together into one fat double finger as the glow brightened a bit. No one said anything. The effect held a moment more, and then the man's fingers slowly returned to normal. He quickly shoved his hand into his suit pocket where he'd put the glove.

The Rindder looked a little sheepish. "It interferes with my data streams and virtuals when I do that. I've never been able to understand why exactly, or what the phenomena really is."

Marc nodded. "And you saw what I did to your nanos, and you'd like to know how I did it."

"Yes." The man looked relieved.

Interesting.

"Well, with Sil's help, here, I believe I expelled all your agents into a crystal." Marc gave him an ironic smile. "Sorry for your loss."

"Losses. But thank you. I don't really care about them. I'm interested in the phenomena–and in you two. You are Marc Arons and you are Silveen Donn. My name is Rass-Ruuk Biniun, but those who know me just call me RR."

"Call me Sil. You're med, aren't you?"

"Yes, I'm in charge of the medical staff and programs here on Barrkon's. I'm charged with your interrogation, not with your confinement or labor here."

Marc said, "Sweet Pea does the labor thing. You just do the internal rape."

RR looked back to Marc. "That is true. It is not a distortion to put it that way. You have ample reason to distrust and dislike me, but I hope you will listen to me. Things are happening here that you don't know about. I believe we can be of some use to each other." He swung his optical off to the side of his face revealing a puzzled look. "Who is Sweet Pea?"

Sil said, "I wouldn't advise calling her that to her face, RR. It's Marc's pet name for our Purple Guard here."

"Oh, you mean Paris. Yes, she's a special case, isn't she? Sweet Pea!" Marc watched as the man actually began to smile, then chuckle. After a moment, both he and Sil couldn't help but join in.

"Speaking of whom," Sil said.

Sure enough, here she came, rapidly whir-sliding along. She looked surprised to see RR with them.

"You trying to get these lazies to work harder, Doctor? You're wasting your time. They just sit around all day until time to go dine and sleep in their luxury suites, right middies? And, it's time for them to go NOW."

RR stared at her with almost no expression (a Rindder specialty) and said, "You'll have to leave them here for a while. I need to interview them further for Karms."

"Huh. You say? Well, who's going to corral them back to the dorm?

I have a lot to do, you know."

"I'll handle that. This is Rindd business. Go take care of the others and I'll bring these two to you in a while."

Sweet Pea looked dubious, but she shook her head and huffed off toward the other inmates farther down the gallery.

RR turned back to Sil and Marc. "Look, I know you have no reason to trust me for anything, but this is an unusual moment in an unusual circumstance. You've been through a lot recently, Marc, but I don't know if you realize what a pivotal situation you are really in now–what a central position of power you hold."

Marc laughed. "Power? You'll excuse me if I don't exercise it right now. I have some Elite baubles to dig out of this pile of crap. Look. Doctor–RR–I'm pretty much nothing right now. I've lost my ship and livelihood, my home, my girl, and almost my life, *and* I'm vacationing in this lovely place for who knows how long."

"I know. I know it. But again, you don't see the larger picture. I do. This system you discovered and the ship and artifact, whatever they may be: this makes you the most desired prize in human space right now. Yes, you are here in what must seem like literally the lowest pit in the universe, but as we speak, Marc, there are forces lining up to fight over you–forces coming from different directions, each with their own interests and agendas. This situation will not stay stable for long."

Sil said, "So, RR, you are also one of those forces, yes? What is your interest in Marc's information?"

RR looked at Sil and nodded. "Yes, I am. I represent Rindd, of course, but not the main line government. Karms is from that group. I am a member of another."

RR did something to alter his suit support system, then carefully sat down on the floor with them. "We call ourselves Suite Gray. We desire Rindd independence from Harbor."

"Ah yes, Suite Gray," Sil said. "Independence? But you have that already, do you not?"

"Technically, on file, yes. Our business relationships with Harbor, and the Sisters Systems, too, Sil, have allowed us to maintain a practical independence ever since the Old War, but Harbor is becoming dangerously top-heavy. The Elites have been dishonoring commercial deals with us in a manner that indicates they simply don't care anymore. We have become just another of their subjects–and they assume they can take what they want simply because they are the Elite. This situation has accelerated in the last few decades. Some of our proprietary research has been threatened by their cavalier assumptions of control. They show up unexpectedly and demand to see our facilities or actually confiscate some of our technologies. At first, it was just harassment, but it's getting more serious every year. We cannot, must not, let it continue."

Marc had copied Sil now, lying down on the floor in the Roman Dinner pose to even out the weight load on his body. He said, "You need something to change the power equation with Harbor."

"Yes. Obviously, the Ash Alien artifacts you have found may be that kind of lever. I don't expect you to just give me what is so valuable to you and to your own survival, but I may be able to compensate you in several ways. For starters, I could get you guys out of here."

Sil said, "Do you mean out of this mine, or off Barrkon's Oven? And, not to critique a gift, but why am I included in this offer?"

"I mean off Barrkon's entirely. Suite Gray has a research facility that Harbor is not aware of. My father and I established it a long time ago. It is very secure. As for my interest in you, Sil, you are wise to heed the old saying, 'A gift from an Elite must be carefully weighed.' I am no Elite, but my interest in you is practical. First, I watched you and Marc work together to bring out and enhance his bio-morph talents–phenomena that are obviously of the same general sort as my own. I don't understand what either of you are doing, and I would very much like to. Second, you've already heard of Suite Gray, haven't you, Sil?

"Yes, I have. You certainly know now of my interest in your group's work with the old FTL tech."

RR nodded. "It surprised me. I was not in the loop on your involvement, but I've been isolated for a while here as the med tech on Barrkon's. Those considerations alone are compelling enough to include you, but the main reason, as I see it, is that the Sisters have a strong coordinating interest in what Suite Gray is trying to accomplish, yes?"

Sil was smiling, now. "Oh yes, indeed. We are more isolated from Harbor than you Rindders, but we also feel the rise of their pride and assumptions of power. Even aggression, now. Prime Blue went so far as to attack us at the border at Farms recently."

"I saw the reports."

"Yeah, well I was there," Marc said. "Got my tail shot off by Anibale. That's what got this mess all started."

RR looked a little surprised. "You were there? Interesting. That makes sense. Well, you certainly have an interest in these things in terms of your personal situation and properties, but it's much more than that. All the middie class is at risk, just as Rindd and Sisters are."

Marc said, "Yeah, you have that right. I'd love to see Anibale spend a little time here digging his own jewelry out of the dirt. I do have my personal grudges with him." Marc grimaced at the memory. "But I've been thinking for years about ways to help myself and other middies. It's daunting when you're just one guy up against Harbor's Elites and military. The clandestine artifacts trade is about the only thing any of us can really get away with."

"Yes, you are just one man, Marc, but now you have a powerful tool–a lever that can be used only by you. I don't know whether your artifact truly exists or will turn out to be actually important. However that develops, your real tool right now is the *perception* by ZEK, the Elites, the Council, and anyone else who is tracking this, that you have sole access to a thing of great power and, perhaps, grave danger–plus the perception that only *you* can possibly activate or control it. As I said, you are the prize, and at least for now, that gives you more power than millions of middies rallying together against these injustices."

Marc stared and blinked.

"You certainly can't stay here in the control of ZEK and his proxies on Barrkon's Oven. They *will* eventually get what they want and they'll tear you apart. You can't do anything until you are out of their grasp entirely. When you are, and are working with myself and the others in Suite Gray, we can examine your shape change phenomena to see if it gives us any leverage over Harbor. Then we can talk about your Ash Alien find and whether it, too, gives us the leverage we hope for.

"I will promise this: I will only gain that information from you if you willingly give it to me because you believe it will help our situation and our cause against Harbor and the Elites."

"No more nano agents, eh?" Marc said.

"I promise that. Once you're out of Harbor's grasp, you may be able to change everything. I can help. I know you would help him in this also, Sil. Am I correct?"

"Yes, of course. This is the work I and my Teachers friends have been trying to accomplish for so many years."

RR's bare hand had been out of his suit pocket for a while and he absent-mindedly looked at it now and then as he spoke. "So, here's what I'm offering. Let me arrange a way out of here–an escape. I can't just take you straight out. My work and freedom here serve Suite Gray and that would be compromised. I will have a functional plan for us, though. Once we are out, I'll take you to our out-system facility. You and Sil agree to explain your hand and body morphology phenomena the best you can and let us experiment, with your help, to see if we can learn more." He looked up at Marc. "Then we can decide what to do next."

Sil said, "Beats hi-grav manual mining all to crap."

RR noticed his hand and shoved it back into the pocket. Sil smiled softly and had a twinkle in his eye. Both of them looked at Marc.

Marc shook his head a couple of times as he felt a stupid grin coming on.

"Well, hell, RR. Sounds like fun. Let's do it!"

Xenoplague

The terror and implications of what had happened two days ago haunted Marc as he stalled and wavered out here in the desolate sands of the Ghost Hills. He needed time to think it all through and make some plans. His actions on that day had cost nearly everything, but he could not see any way he could have avoided it. Not only had their pride and basic dignity been at stake, but their livelihood and home as well.

One of the young migrant workers from Kayne System, named Seffy, had come to Salina this season to help Father with the fieldwork, so after the arguments and the fight, Marc had taken his old modified ore cart and headed out to the sand hills that nestled at the base of the scabrous peaks west of the family mining operation. Ghost Hills, they were called by most people around here, not that there *were* very many people around here. Ghosts, maybe. It was an appropriate name. Marc had often thought he heard voices and felt other things that should not be heard or felt when he was out here alone. Other than that, he liked being in the desert, and, especially when troubled, he always sought this particular spot where the largest dune met the low rock cliffs. Sand is a good acoustic insulator and it made this the quietest place he knew. Dead quiet.

The day before yesterday, three Elite BlackMil goons had come out to the mine looking to cause trouble. It was plain-face obvious that their company leader wanted the mine for himself and this was how he knew to do it. Come out here with a couple of his best toughs and intimidate the newly successful middie family into selling out for nothing. If that didn't work, well, there was always intimidation and force. His memories still stung. Mother with a gun to her head. Father not able or willing to do anything about it.

Seffy was off in the work fields and Marc and his parents had been taking a break under the big canopy tent that served as a porch and protection from the relentless sun when the Elite cadre arrived and marched in like they already owned the place.

"You seem reluctant, 54Arons. Your mine is needed for Harbor and the Elites and you will sell it to me right now. I'm not going to steal from you, fool! But I will take possession of it one way . . . or another!" The dark haired Elite with the sharp nose and blue tunic laughed at Father. The man's two guards had drawn their energy pistols. Mother looked petrified and Marc had stood at the side of the big tent, seething and clenching his fists. The leader's grin suddenly shut off like a valve had been flipped.

"Sign this now, old man. You won't live long enough to work this place on out anyway. My bots and my contacts will make it worth more than you could ever dream of. I need the minerals for Suite Blue's purposes and you need to retire. Now!"

A hot wind blasted through the open sides and the Elites all blinked with the sand sting.

Marc grew more and more restless. Anger surged in him at the injustice of it all. Father had farmed all his life on Farms and then moved them to Salina where he bought this land to start the mine. It was his and Mother's and Marc's own successful hard work that was so attractive to this dirt clod now. The Elites were all mineral and gem crazy, ready to feed their greed whenever they wanted to.

Marc's mouth was in motion before he realized it. "This is our sweat and blood–*our home*, Mister." Marc spat the words out at him.

"Marc!" Father barked. "Be quiet son."

Marc just glared at the leader who turned a calculating look on him.

"You should listen to your dried-up sire and obey him like you will obey me. I am Anibale, a rising member of the Suite Blue Elite staff. Yes, you remember that name, *son*. I'm in charge and I plan to be in charge of much more than *this* piss-forsaken world in short order." He gave a feral smirk.

Yeah, Marc would remember. He would never forget. He was galled at Father's shame and impotence and Mother's fear in front of these goons. He couldn't stand silent and not try to protect what was theirs.

The guard next to Anibale grabbed Mother and shoved his pistol into her cheek, grinning at Marc. Father winced and then shot a hard look at Marc and said, "NO!"

Anibale took that as a refusal, but Father wasn't addressing the Elite. Marc had felt his hands growing and glowing hot and Father had anticipated it. Was warning him. Too late.

Marc's hands glared red now and he jumped faster than a sand flea, grabbing the two guards' guns, one gun in each of his now huge hands. The guns melted into radiant metal bars and the first guard yelped, dropping his and letting go of Mother. The other one's hand was caught up in the glowing mess of his gun. He screamed. Marc released the gun and flailed his morphed hands at the guard's tortured face. Father came at Anibale with his own hands changed into rock hammers, not glowing hot like his son's but still very imposing. He struck the man in his midriff, doubling him over. Marc heard the breath whoosh out of his lungs. Father backed off a step or two.

Angry, confused, and hurt, the three Elites turned and scrambled, feet and arms tangling, making a chaotic exit as fast as they could go.

Marc had rehashed the events over and over again after retreating here to the dunes, wrestling with what had taken place and why he had acted out. After the fight, Father had been right to be angry, but Marc had stood his ground–again. He truly felt he had had no other choice. He was sorry Father had to join in with him, but it was straight-up self-defense! They had to protect their own and each other, didn't they? Father said the end results might not be worth the momentary victory. He was likely right, but what else could they have done?

He spent the rest of the afternoon at the base of the dunes and cliff arguing it over to himself and eventually passed into a fitful sleep, napping on the soft sand. Voices troubled his dream. A strange old man with big dark eyes and leathery skin was looking at him from in between lush green leaves. A woman's suit-gloved hand touched his arm. The great ZEK's golden Face loomed over him and laughed. A beam weapon struck a planet. He jerked awake.

An alert light was flashing on his hand comm. No message, just a red blink bar. Marc called home without getting a response, then he jumped up, ran back to his open cart, and gunned it.

He topped the rise where he could first see the mine and their house and skidded to a stop. The tent canopy was torn to shreds, flapping wildly in the wind, and the main house was on fire. He squatted down in front of his cart to watch without revealing himself further. That wind was kicking up a lot of dust. A group of about twenty Elite BlackMil guards were at work putting up marker wands around the property for a beam barrier to keep outsiders out. Then he saw Anibale and three of his guards emerge from the tool house and walk over to a shallow pit they had blasted into the hard ground of the utility yard.

Three elongated shapes lay there, smoking. Anibale nodded to his men, then happened to look up in his direction. Marc ducked down instinctively as a gust threw up sand and grit. The Suite Blue Elite stared out in his direction for quite a while and Marc thought he had been spotted, but Anibale finally turned and went back inside.

With his heart in his throat, Marc carefully looked once more to be certain of the situation, then he slid back down into the sand and put his head down onto his cursed hands. It felt like he was melting into them, but they did not change shape again.

"You were right, Father. You were right! I'm so sorry. Father . . . Mother. My Curse brought this."

He wanted to scream and run his old cart right into the compound and strike them all down! Instead, he sat up behind the dune and shook himself sharply. A colder resolve set in. There was no time to mourn his losses, only time to get out of here, and fast. He'd grieve later and, by all the imaginary gods, he'd get satisfaction from that Bluenose, Anibale.

They obviously mistook poor Seffy for me, so for now, they don't know I exist. Best keep it that way. I have to get to town and withdraw the mine's cash accounts before they think to take it themselves. Old

Zike will help me hide the transaction.

It was a tense journey into town, but Zike did help him extract the family funds through his name. The Elite didn't care about the money. He just wanted the mine and its possible mineral wealth and the status associated with possessing it.

Zike also offered to help him buy a clunky old cargo ship so he could start working the trade Lines. That might be the best thing for now. Get off Salina, stay mobile, and build some wealth of his own. At nineteen, Marc was already a good rough-and-ready pilot. Maybe he would run into Anibale again someday and find a way to exact revenge! Dangerous thought, that. Better to stay low and covert for a long time and just see how things go.

Chapter Twenty-two

As the newly arrived group from Suite Blue entered the reception suite, RR stood off to one side of the room, trying to remain still and not attract the outsider's attention. At first, he studied Karms and his advisor, Luinn. To any outsider, they looked as Rindder-calm as always, but RR could tell that Karms was uncomfortable with this visit. Anibale and five of his blue-suited strongmen strode heavily into the room, assisted by their lower torso exoskeleton rigs. Old models from a few years ago. They should pay us for the newer ones, but I guess they don't really need them anywhere except here on Barrkon's Oven.

RR unthinkingly ran a hand down his own smooth, titanium leg brace. As Anibale greeted Karms, the other Blues formed an arc behind their blue silk-robed leader.

Karms sat back down on his chair, which was raised on a platform behind the room's long, narrow marble table. There were no chairs for the visitors.

"What brings you to Barrkon's Oven, Prime Blue? You should not subject yourself to the conditions here. There is no need. We can service your needs from orbit, or even from Harbor."

Anibale's facial muscles were strained as he glared at Karms.

"There is something here that belongs to me. Something that was stolen. I intend to retrieve it."

Karms put on an expression of surprise. "Stolen, you say? That is serious, Prime. How may we assist you in this situation? What is this item?"

"The item is a man—a meddling middie you have in your mines. The one ZEK and the Council arranged to have you interrogate. The pilot, Marc 54Arons."

RR suppressed a smile as he watched Karms drop his expression to one of cautious concern.

"Prime, this is surely a matter between you and ZEK and the Council. I have no authority to release the man to you. There is a contract."

"Your contract means nothing to me. This man is mine. He is dangerous! Not just to me, but to everyone, including you Rindders. You know what he means. Your contract is to find out what he knows! *That* is my property, and I demand you turn over the man himself and anything you have learned from him."

"My contract is a Polychrome Bond directly from ZEK and Elder Bai himself. Contracts with the Elite do not get any more important, protected, or confidential. I can assure you, Sir, regardless of your claims or your urgencies, that Rindd will in no way release the individual or any information concerning him. I say again, you must take this issue up with ZEK."

Anibale took two steps toward Karms, their eyes level with one another. "I will have this man and I will not be dealing with ZEK. Do you understand? This is too important. I am here now, and I intend to leave with him one way or another."

"Prime Blue. How dare you threaten me here in Rindd. We have long-established relationships with Harbor and they do not include breaking treaty with the office of ZEK or the Council of Colors just to accommodate one citizen's wishes, even if he is a Prime. You and your men need to return to your ships. Consider what effect your demands and your actions will cause. I cannot help you."

"My actions are my business, Rindder. You people have been playing at being better than the rest of humanity for too long." Anibale, visibly vibrating now, leaned toward Karms, but after a moment, the tension broke and he straightened up again. "For now, I will return to my ship. I will give you some time to think about my demands. Then, I shall require them."

Karms was a study in implacability. RR was impressed. Not getting a response from him, Anibale and his blue-suits noisily turned and whirred their way out of the room.

Once they were gone, Karms turned to RR and said, "Let's put some extra security around our special guest, RR. Will you see to it?"

"Of course, sir. I'm going to do some analysis work now anyway. I'll take care of it."

RR quickly exited the room and hurried down the office area hallways. He had to reach them before they got to the dock and their lander.

He quickly realized he shouldn't have worried. The blue-clad crew and their leader were ponderously making their way to the transfer docks and he caught up to them as they passed some of the empty sorting rooms and equipment storage areas. He spoke loudly, but calmly. "Prime Blue."

The cadre turned heads and stopped, ungracefully, in the hallway. Anibale's expression was hard and angry.

It was like poking a stick at a hungry, wounded swampcat. Not happy.

"You were in the room with Karms. Who are you?"

"RR. I'm the head of medicine and in charge of your man."

Anibale's expression changed from seething to suspicion. He said, "What do you want, Rindder? Did Karms send you to make sure we leave your pretty little hole here?"

"He does not know. I may be able to help you with your request."

A pause, then, "Truly? And what would compel you to do that–R . . R?"

"Marc Arons has successfully evaded our interrogations. Completely evaded them. This is unheard of. As head of medicine and medical analysis, I am responsible for it."

"Ahh, your Rindder head is on the line, eh?"

"You could say that, yes. I have followed your career, Sir, and it is obvious to me that you are a man of action. It is also obvious that you have no intention of staying on your ship. You're planning a raid.

"I need a way out of here that will protect me and my own interests. Allow me to 'assist' you in your plans. My help can be critical in putting you in the right place at the right time. In return, I must escape with you to Harbor, but it must appear that I have gone *unwillingly*, you see. That will protect others here on Barrkon's and on Rindd 1, and will give me options for myself in the future."

Anibale stared at him. "Now, let me understand this. You want to help me, but only if I agree to kidnap you?"

RR smiled at him. "That's about it."

Anibale shook his head and a grim smile broke out on his face, as well. "Very well, Doctor. I am listening."

"Here, let's talk in this sorting room."

Anibale paused a moment, then nodded to two of his BlueMils. They took up guard positions outside the room hatch as the rest entered. Anibale stepped right up to RR and looked down at him. "This should do. Speak, RR."

"If you come in with your troops without help, the Rindd militia will be on you very quickly. Robotic countermeasures are everywhere. You would not be successful, Sir, not even with your special military. This is ZEK and Council business and we take it most seriously. The Rindd militia have ZEK's own personal authorization to take whatever measures necessary to protect his interests here.

"I can prepare a pathway that is deactivated and leads you to the pilot. It will have to be done at a specific time. I can also misdirect the Rindd militia long enough to give you your opportunity. When you take the pilot, I will make some type of resistance–something that will be documented–and your men can take me prisoner in order to evacuate me with you."

"How soon can this be arranged?"

"A day or two. I'll send a secure detailed message with the instructions."

"And, how shall I trust you . . . RR?"

"You'll have to trust your own judgment. My situation is plain enough, Sir. Otherwise, I can only offer you my word. I, too, am a man of action."

Anibale nodded once. "Very well, Rindder Doctor. I will wait. That is something I hate, and there are other forces afoot, so do not delay your instructions. You have one day." He turned and gestured to his BlueMils, and they exited the room, resuming their slow march to the transfer dock and their lander. RR stood there a while amidst the leftover tools and loose rocks strewn about the long metal work tables, looking at them but not seeing them.

Sure hope this works.

———————

Marc kept going over what they learned in their remarkable encounter with RR. Since then, Sil had been very quiet. He looked tired. Marc tried doing some of his physical training exercises, but just as they settled down into their spots, he noticed Sil looking back down the gallery. RR approached them around the curve of the hall. He sat down next to the pair and flipped his optical out of the way.

Sil said, "You have some plans for us, RR?"

"Yes. Things are happening and we will need to make our move quickly. Prime Blue–Anibale–is here. He has a thinly disguised militia with him. He wants you, Marc. He wants you badly enough to challenge not only Karms, but also the Rindd treaty and ZEK and the Council of Colors, as well! I was there in the meeting and it was shocking. I've seen plenty of egotistical Elites before, but this guy is taking some big chances."

Marc leaned back on the ore pile. "Why didn't he just come down here and take me?"

"Karms won't have it. Stood up to him and the Fierce One actually backed off! Wish you could have seen it. In any case, I caught up to him afterward and made an arrangement."

Sil looked up sharply. "You made an arrangement with Anibale?"

RR gave him a small smile. "Yes. Look, to get you two out, I have to get *me* out without compromising my status in Rindd. I have to appear to be under the direct control of others, against my will. As far as Anibale knows, I sold you out and I'll happily lead him to you if he will make it look like he's forcing me to do it–and then takes me with him."

Marc said, "Errr, that sounds terrible."

"Yes, but here's what we really do. Tomorrow at a set time, I'll bring them down the gallery. You two prepare one of your glow sessions and be ready to expel some nanoagents I'll give you now. These are benign, but they have some extra stored energy in them. Hopefully, when you get rid of them, they'll cause a much bigger set of sparks!" RR leaned over to give Marc the nanos injection. "I'll make excuse to come close to you two, then I've arranged a particularly spectacular pyro eruption that will separate us from Anibale and his men. It will create a lingering fire zone, but we'll still need to move as quickly as possible."

Sil said, "You expect us to *run?*"

"No, there is an open bot-cart–just a flat tray with wheels. I'll have it park itself just beyond your ore piles, out of view. That will give us the speed we need to get away. Remember, Anibale and his people are not used to the grav here and I've seen them struggling with it. Once we are out of the gallery narrows, I'll take us to a ship I've prepared and we'll clear Barrkon's."

"We're placing a lot of trust in you, RR," Marc said, squinting. "For all I know, you could just turn us over to Anibale."

"I am not Harbor's friend. I could do that, but I won't. Here–let me give you something as a token of my sincerity."

RR reached into his med-robe and extracted three hand-held energy guns. "You'll need these, and I may ask you to point them at me at times, so it looks like I'm your prisoner. The third one is for me, so hold onto it for me until the time comes." He grinned. "You might want to put those right away, though, for now."

Sil took his and the extra one and pocketed them without a blink. Marc gripped the other one. It felt really good. He held it a moment, looked up at RR, then hid it in the folds of his dirty work smock. RR nodded once, then gave them the exact time for the operation.

Marc had both hands outstretched as he crouched near his ore pile the next day. Sil was singing his songs, sometimes briskly and other times smoothly entrancing, and the energy built up and up until, now, the greenish glow was strong. Marc could feel the nanoparticles coalescing and pooling–ready to leap out of his fingers at any moment. They felt more jittery than the previous batches. The extra spark content RR mentioned, he supposed. Now though, he felt like he had some new level of control over the process. Sil brought his song to a hum, then paused just long enough to ask him.

"Managing them OK, Marc?"

"Yeah, so far. They're feisty, though," he said through his teeth.

"You won't have to hold much longer. Here they come." He nodded toward the hallway and Marc glanced up just long enough to confirm an image of Anibale and the blue-clad guards working their way toward them. RR was in front. The Blues had their guns out and pointed at his back.

Sil brought his voice back to full volume in the song pattern, and as if it were a magnetic pull, Marc couldn't help but join in now. His hands were almost completely invisible, buried in the engulfment of the glow. He snapped his head up to look at Anibale. The Harbor

Elite looked decidedly nervous.

"Pilot!–Stop this now!" Anibale called out.

RR turned his head back to him and said, "I've seen this ritual before. Let me talk to them."

Anibale gave him a look and then a single nod. RR slowly walked over to Marc and Sil.

"Here, what are you two doing? I've warned you against this! You must stop it now."

Anibale called out, "Rindder–have a care! What he is doing is dangerous!" He and all the BlueMils pointed their guns nervously at the scene.

RR, with his back still to Anibale and the guards, sidled more toward Sil, taking himself out of Marc's direct line of nanobot fire. Sil, still singing loudly, reached into his smock, pulled out the third gun, and quickly handed it to RR.

RR turned to look at Marc and gave him a silent, mouthed "*NOW!*"

Marc felt his voice locking into one major tone and the energy inside his body was at its peak of power. With the cue from RR, it seemed to take a motivation of its own. All Marc had to do was aim. He made his move quickly–a snap of his arms to point the expulsion directly at Anibale, Prime Blue of Harbor and Helm.

Eat this, you murdering thug!

The bolt of light was tremendous. Marc wasn't sure what form it would take since he was not holding a target crystal. It ballooned out, leaving puffs of lesser light and color behind, but the main energy pulse flashed across the chamber and struck Anibale directly on his face. Anibale's gun fired as it flew out of his hand, sending a much smaller, yet still deadly, energy pulse charge bouncing off the rocky ceiling. Anibale fell back hard into his BlueMils, but before they could get their shots off, RR keyed his pyro and the entire chamber lit up in white and red with a terrific bang followed by an angry roar.

Sil jumped behind the nearest ore pile, and Marc flattened himself where he was sitting. RR spun partway around as a shot clipped him from one of the BlueMils, who fired blindly through the wall of flames and smoke of the pyro. He yelped and flopped down between Marc and Sil, but pulled out his gun and started firing back at the guards and Anibale. Marc and Sil added their gunfire to the assault.

RR's voice was strained but strong, "I'm OK, just touched my left arm. Let's go NOW."

Marc realized with a moment of surprise that he had not been hit during the exchange. He stood up and put an arm around RR's good side while Sil emerged from the pile. His head was spinning, but they hobbled and heavy-stepped away from the firewall, down the gallery in the direction of the exit to the main shaft. It couldn't have taken long, but it seemed like forever to reach the promised bot-cart. It was just a flat shelf on wheels like RR had said, and they quickly hauled him and themselves flat down onto its scarred metal surface. It rolled them slowly away from the scene as alarms began to sound. Two fire control bots passed them going in, but RR said, "No worries . . . chemical supplies for them removed . . . and they're reprogrammed not to be aware of it."

"That was bigger and hotter than I expected, RR," Marc said, "so how did we not get burned?"

"The pyro charges were shaped: aimed away from us and toward them. It was close, though."

"You OK, Sil?" Marc called.

"Yes, I'm fine, but where is this thing taking us, RR?"

"We have to get out of this gallery at the main shaft. Then we can slip into a few back tunnels that I and my Suite Gray associates have kept cleared and secret. That will get us to an equally unsuspected dock where our ship awaits. Once we get there, my people will help us directly."

Marc felt the air change as the cart with its odd payload got closer to the exit of the gallery at the mine's main vertical open shaft. From that direction, a large group of Rindd militia came around the curve of the gallery and slowed as they saw the moving cart. RR sat up and raised his hand, pointing back toward the fire scene. The leader of the Rindder group recognized him and motioned his men and women to keep moving. They flowed around the trio on each side, and the rocky hallway cleared again. Marc could see the portal to the main shaft just ahead.

For a moment, Marc felt an irrational fear that the cart would just continue to roll them forward and right off of that ominous ledge to fall heavily and quickly to their doom some hundreds of meters below. The other two men were not afflicted with this terror, apparently, and the bot did begin to slow them as they came to the actual opening.

Then, they were out of the gallery and the cart turned them to the left on the ledge circling the inside of that huge cylindrical borehole in Barrkon's crust. Even though their low platform was moving smoothly, Marc was still edgy next to the drop off and he was staring at it when the cart suddenly jolted to a halt. He turned to look as the other two men slowly stood and started to raise their weapons. Sweet Pea was standing on the ledge pathway just ahead of them. She had a large energy weapon aimed at them.

"Nope. Put 'em down. I just want Marc." Sil and RR put their weapons back down.

"Toss 'em over the side. NOW." After a moment of hesitation, they complied. All three guns disappeared over the unprotected edge. In part of his mind, Marc wondered if he'd hear them hit bottom, but there was no sound.

All three men worked their way off the cart and, with difficulty, stood up next to it. Perversely, the cart bot must have assumed they were through with it and it took off back the way they had come.

"You're my ticket off this rock, middie!"

Marc stared at her. "What are you talking about, Paris?"

"Oh, so you know my name, do you? Well, a lot of other people are going to know it, too, once I get out of here! Important people! That's who I'm helping. I'm on the path back to Harbor and some prestige, by ZEK!"

Sil said softly, "Who are you working for, Paris?"

"Jade Red wants your friend, Sisters man. That's right, she asked me to call her Jade!" Paris' face flashed pink in her excitement.

RR made a slow, wide gesture with his arms. "She will betray you, Paris. They all will. You should know this from your history and experience."

"She's going to be ZEK, and I've helped her. Do you know what that will do for me?"

"It will get you killed. The Primes do not do real favors for people like us, Paris. Every single thing they do is calculated for their own advancement," RR said. "If you are working for Jade Red, you are her pawn, that's all."

Her face reddened, but she did not immediately answer him.

Marc suddenly had a thought. "Paris, come with us. We're leaving Barrkon's Oven and we're working to change the way things are with Harbor. Come with us and help us. We'll give you honorable work and a chance to really make a difference."

Sil and RR turned to look at Marc. RR seemed surprised. Sil was smiling. Paris seemed nonplussed for a moment, but said, "No tricks! I'm helping JADE PRIME, damn it. And I'll take you to her now!"

There was movement behind Paris as four people emerged from a side hatch onto the ledge.

"No need, dear Paris. I've come myself," Jade said. "You've well captured them, I see! Excellent work, if a little late in the game." Paris gave a quick look back, then turned again with a sneer on her face.

The Prime Red and another woman, presumably her aide, were with two of her Red Guards. Jade was seated on a mobile chair. All but Jade bore weapons trained on them. She motioned the guards to take the three men, then the entire group headed back through the hatchway and on toward wherever and whatever Jade had planned for them. RR looked down at his boots. Sil was somber, and Marc felt sick to his stomach. Close. So close. Dammit!

As they were slow-marched into an access hallway, Sil edged over to Marc and muttered, "Remember your song. Look for an opportunity. I will assist."

One of the Red Guards poked Sil in the back with his weapon.

There wouldn't be another chance to talk for a while.

When they finally stopped the high-grav heavy march, Marc's legs trembled and ached. Jade had taken them directly to the mine's transfer docks and her own shuttle ship. It was secured within the huge but otherwise empty hangar, and a basic metal service ramp angled up to the ship's personnel hatch.

The guards held the men at the bottom of the ramp as Jade's aide went up and opened the hatch, then came back to assist the Prime as she stepped carefully off her chair. They ascended slowly with Paris following eagerly behind them. At the hatch, Jade turned around and gave Paris a stony look. "No. You must stay here and clean up the mess you made."

Paris' voice cracked. "What? Stay here? . . . No! You promised! I have to go with you. They'll kill me if I stay here!"

"You have served my needs. My needs are ZEK's needs. They are vastly more important than you, dearie." Jade crooked her head at one of the two guards holding Marc and the others down at the base of the ramp. That guard ascended with his weapon aimed at Paris and then forced her to retreat off the ramp, passing where Marc, Sil, and RR were standing with the remaining guard. She was trembling in some tart combination of fear and anger.

"Don't try to run back up, dearie!" Jade was cackling now. "We'll just have to put you off the hard way!"

The remaining Red Guard behind Marc poked him with his gun and motioned for them to go on up the ramp. Just as they started to move, Sil let out a loud hum in one solid note. Marc felt his internal energy surge as it had earlier. He hummed the note, too, and as they started up the ramp, he made a quick stop and dip as if he were stumbling due to the gravity. In that moment, he put his right hand out and steadied himself on a strut of the ship–a strut made of Ash Alien metals, part of the original AA ship that had been hybridized, probably here in Rindd, many years earlier.

Panting, and with the guard trying to prod him on, Marc gripped the strut strongly and increased the volume of his hum. Sil and even

RR hummed it now, and Marc's hand glowed. The guard grabbed his arm, but immediately yelped and was jolted strongly backward, like some puppet on a string. He was out of Marc's restricted sight range, but he heard the guard's gun clatter below on the hangar's metal floor.

The aide next to Jade yelled something and Jade herself was gesticulating. A groaning sound came from the strut, which itself glowed blue now. Marc glanced over at the other two just in time to see Sil pull a large, clear crystal out of his filthy smock. Part of Marc's mind supposed that one single gemstone would probably purchase Jade's ship and half of another. Sil had a different way of valuing it, however. He expertly threw the stone at Jade, striking her in the head. Her red robes with their white trim seemed to collapse into nothing as the older woman simply folded to the floor of the hatchway at the top of the ramp. Her aide dropped into defense posture at her side and fired her weapon at Sil, but he had also dropped to the floor and rapidly skittered sideways in a manner Marc had never seen him do. It almost looked unreal. RR had circled to get behind Marc.

In those couple of moments, the strut had begun to soften under Marc's hand. Then, the entire back half of the ship–the Ash Alien parts–came to life in dazzling colors. Marc heard an energy weapons discharge and looked up to see the aide fall, wounded or dead onto the hatchway floor. Then, still holding the strut and wondering, he turned the other way and saw Paris holding the gun she had just fired–a grimace of hate twisting her mouth and eyes. Her own Red Guard seemed to have been taken by surprise by his fellow guard's knockdown followed by the light show on the ship and now, Paris had his weapon. He rotated back and tried to grab her, but she was quicker to move in this high-grav environment she'd been living in for a long time. Her second shot took out the last standing Red Guard.

A commotion was happening somewhere beyond the entry to the hangar area, but Marc could not turn that far while holding the strut, so he let go of it. The ship returned quickly to its normal gray and

Marc's hand also stopped glowing almost the instant he let go of it. RR said, "Rindd militia."

Paris looked wild-eyed at Marc and at his hand, her gun swinging this way and that. A crunching sound came from the strut area of the ship. Marc said, "It's like RR said, Paris. The Primes will use you up and kill you if you cross them. Come with us! Rindd has documented you working with Jade. You have no choices here, Paris."

Sil spoke, "Help us all escape this place, young one. We will help you, too. It is a true promise."

A different look came over her face then, and she shuddered. Then she lowered the gun.

"All right. I'll help you." She let out a long breath, then said, "You'd better have a good plan, RR. You're in this mess now, too."

Jade could be heard moaning and cursing up on the hatchway. The Red Guard who had grabbed Marc's arm was mewling a few meters away on the deck next to the ramp but had managed to get to his hand and knees. Paris stood over him with her weapon beaded on his head. "Don't move, slimewash. Your master's scheme has blown up in her face."

Sil had returned to RR and Marc's side, seemingly unharmed.

"They're coming on in now," said RR. Marc looked back to the entry area of the hangar and saw the Rindd force headed their way. "They held off because of Jade's normal exclusivity privileges. Follow my lead now and don't mind the gun I'm going to point at you guys."

The initial Rindd force was about thirty-strong. When the leader came up to RR, his head scanned all the various parts of the tableaux before him. "Sir, what is going on in here? There was a major fire in the mine two levels below, but I had an emergency call from Karms to check on Prime Red's sector."

"It's been a crazy situation, Balli. Prime Red tried to grab these prisoners and Paris and I got caught up in it. The Prime is up there, hit and hurt, but alive as you can hear. She's the one who caused that fire to be set if I had to guess."

"You've been hit. You OK?"

"Yes, we're all right for now, but Paris and I have to return these men to a safe sector immediately. Balli, this is a *major* political situation. Sensitive, because of the Primes. Prime Blue is here on Barrkon's, too, and he and Red are both vying hard for these prisoners, but these two are extraordinarily special to ZEK personally and to the Council itself, understand?"

The man lifted his chin. "Yes, Sir!"

"There's one dead guard and this one who is wounded. Prime Red's female aide is also up there. I don't know her condition. Please have your men assess and secure this area while I get these two to a more protected zone. Also, 'ware that strut area there. It was hit in the crossfire and is likely unstable."

"I understand. We'll take care of this."

Marc and Sil slowly began their walk out in front of RR and Paris, who followed with weapons aimed at the two men's backs. Paris was shaking her head as she walked. The hangar entry gate was not that far away, but it seemed to take an age to get there. As they reached it, they heard a louder crunching sound. Marc turned back just long enough to see Jade's ship slowly lean over as the strut he had held gave way with a final sharp snap. Balli's men were back far enough that none of them were in danger.

At last, they were through the hangar gate and RR led them a short distance further before stopping at a nondescript maintenance hatch which opened at his touch.

"Let's get out of here, shall we?" he said.

Chapter Twenty-three

The burns on Anibale's face were beginning to hurt, now that the shock was wearing off. His sight had returned about three hours ago, but everything was still fuzzy around the edges. The medbots still hummed and clicked somewhere next to him. This was the single thing that was good about being here in Rindd–their medical systems were the best.

"Praxel, where are you?"

"I'm here, Anibale. Is your head more clear?"

"Yes, damn everything! I have to know what's going on. What happened to the pilot and the other scum?"

"Apparently, the Rindd man, RR, was caught by the pilot and his Sister's friend on the other side of that blast. They were gone, once our men could get through there."

Anibale saw his aide's face now as he leaned over the medbot's shell bed. The man looked bad and his cloth cowl still smelled of the smoke and volatiles from the explosion. He could tell from his reflection in the shell bed that he had those facial burns across his right cheek and a patch of hair missing on the left side.

"Where is this med station? Are we secure here?"

"It's in the Rindd sector next to the dock. It's secure, but not by us. The Rindd militia is in control. They await your minimal improvement, then they insist we embark and leave Rindd space."

"They insist?"

"At gunpoint, Sir."

Anibale emitted a deep and long growl.

Praxel raised a small vid screen into Anibale's view. "There is this of possible interest. A skirmish and trouble in another of the main docks. One of our techs grabbed it off the Rindd internal feeds before it was censored."

The vid was not of good quality, but Anibale could see some militia working around a ship that seemed to be leaning oddly. One man was helping lift someone near the gangway to the craft. A flicker of bright red caught the light before the people entered the ship.

Anibale growled again, sharper this time. "I should have known. Jade is here."

"Jade? . . . you think she set this up?"

"I think she is an old, sly opportunist. That's what I think. I do *not* think the pilot or his Sisters friend would allow themselves to be captured by her, and look! Jade and her cronies do seem to be in some distress." His smile was grim. "It appears they had a problematic encounter, eh? I don't think it was with our Rindder hosts. She may have tangled with a fiercer beast than she thought. Serves her right to get burned like me. What have you found on that Sisters fool?"

Praxel said, "His name is Silveen Donn. He's listed as from Florinda. He was detained for dealing in restricted tech, but we don't have any details on that. He and Marc, the pilot, have been seen together here in the mines for the last couple of weeks at least."

"Well, that's perfect. The *Sisters* man has gained access and control over the one person who could lead them to a weapon of vast power over us. They are planning to escape to the Sisters System, Praxel. We must keep the tightest scan possible on this rock. Watch Jade's ship! I want to know if *any* kind of ship leaves the surface of Barrkon's Oven or departs the Station. I don't care if it's an ore scow driven by Emeel Barrkon's ghost!"

"Yes, Sir."

"And, we must be ready to move *instantly!* Especially if Jade makes any signs of launching."

"Indeed."

When the medbots finished with him an hour later, Anibale no longer felt most of the pain of the burns and abrasions, but the scars would have to be corrected later–and at great expense, damn that pilot! Three more hours and a shuttle transfer took him back inside his own ship docked at Barrkon Station orbiting the small planet. Two of his other four ships were already away and patrolling. He would remain on station until it became clear which of the remaining docked or hidden ships might carry his very expensive prize.

RR led Marc, Sil, and Paris through some maintenance areas, crowded with conduits and wiring of the mine infrastructure. Marc and Paris had to duck a few times and he helped Sil when the gravity caused the older man's step to falter. They were all bone tired, but RR was not rushing them through now. Marc thought this must be his own secure territory, then.

The group came to a stop when two men dressed in gray smocks and hoods blocked the path next to a hatchway. RR gave a kind of weary salute and the two stepped forward to grasp his hands.

The man on the right said, "We watched the feed from Prime Red's bay. Bold moves and a fortunate outcome, RR. Let's get you and your friends on inside the facility. You look terrible."

"Thanks, Pall." RR turned to the others and said, "This is Pall and Merkeen–Barrkon's Oven chapter of Suite Gray, and, though you were unaware of it, Marc, they are two with whom you have had previous dealings here in Rindd."

Paris still looked shell-shocked, but Sil gave a little bow and Marc nodded to the two Grays. "Greetings. Which dealings?"

"You'll see," RR said with a slight smile.

They were escorted through the hatch and into some offices and hallways filled with other men and women working at comps or, in a larger room, doing some sort of hand work on materials and large forms. After a few hundred meters and several zig-zags, they reached a large hatch leading into the docking hangar. Marc stopped short in amazement. The ship inside was far too large for the available space, but even more shocking: it was the front end of his very own cargo ship.

RR was grinning now and waiting for Marc to say something.

"My ship? What in ZEK's beard is it doing here? And, where's the rest of it? Wait a minute. . ."

"That's right. It is another inflatable of your ship, just like the one we made for you a few years ago. Only the front end would fit in here, but I wanted you to see it before we deploy the full version as a decoy."

Sil said, "An inflatable? That's remarkable, RR." Paris let out a snort. Sil continued, "This is a realistic likeness of your ship then, Marc?"

"Oh, yes. I had them make it to size and with enough comm and other indentifiables on board to fool all but close inspections. So, it was your Suite Grays who I dealt with, eh?"

RR said, "Yes, Merkeen is the lead engineer on it. We kept your ship's plans, of course, for future business or, in this case, another use altogether. A fortunate coincidence, is it not?"

"Perhaps, though there are often strange alignments that show up in life," Sil said.

RR gave him a look without comment. Marc asked, "So, what's the plan here? You're going to send this thing out and hope Anibale and Jade take the bait, yes?"

"They will certainly take the bait."

Sil said, "What happens when they discover the ruse?"

"We shall be well on our way out of system. I have a small ship, almost a pod. It is the most discreet ship we have available right now, and it will do fine for the final escape sequence I've arranged. It's impossible now to go to our research facility as I had originally hoped. You three need to leave Harbor space entirely.

"Pall and some of the others have been working on a very unique and special communications project for years. Thanks to their amazing work, I can offer you a quick and safe ride to Frahma System. How would you like to go home to the Sisters, Sil?"

"That would be extraordinary, RR. But, I don't understand. What kind of communications project? Does this involve your human FTL research?"

RR had a strange look on his face. "Only in a tangential way. I'd rather not say more right now. You'll see soon enough."

"What kind of crap is that, RR?" Paris said. She had been so quiet, that Marc had almost forgotten about her. "I'm supposed to trust you on some crazy blind plan?"

"Yes. I'm afraid you must, Paris. You cannot stay in Rindd now, and you can't hide in Harbor space forever as some renegade Wilder. Your game piece has been thrown and your future lies in Sisters System or beyond. Marc is a critical fulcrum of these important events. I will not let anything happen to him; I will get him to safety. Your very best chances are to be in his company. Help me protect him and Sil, and I believe you may find your new role and life very satisfactory in the long run."

"Huh," she said, but Marc saw she was taking that in.

"Once I get you three to the podship, Marc, take it out of the system plane–zenith vector. You'll go out in a cloud of other ships right after the Primes make their move, then hit the fastest speed you can. I'll keep you linked to what the Primes are doing so you can make the best run."

Marc said, "Aren't you coming with us?"

"I'd love nothing better, but I need to hold Rindd's interests first, plus I have to do some preparations for what will come after. I will meet up with you in Sisters space a little later, once we see what plays out with the Elites here now and over the next few months."

"I see. So, once I take your podship up to Rindd System's ceiling, what happens? They'll figure it out either quickly or really damn quickly and be right on my tail. Do I have an FTL engine? What kind of evasive capabilities in that little ship?"

"No–no direct FTL. No evasives. It's better if you just do it. You won't need to coordinate anything else. Just take the ship up anywhere in that direction and stay ahead of your pursuers! I trust your piloting skills, Marc, but perhaps not your normal reactions to something outside of your experience." RR paused and a funny look crossed his face. "My associates will intercept you out there. You won't have to do a thing. Just go for the ride."

Sil looked at RR with a curious expression. Paris said, "I don't know, RR. You sound crazier than Jade." RR started to answer, but she interrupted, "No . . . it's all right. I know I need to go. I did say I wanted out of this damned system."

Marc said, "Well, and *I* said it sounded like fun. Blind trust, eh? All right, RR, you've gotten us this far." He looked over at Sil and saw an almost amused smile. "So, where's this podship of yours?"

RR led them out of the hangar containing Marc's faux ship nose and back through the rooms and halls of the facility. Eventually, they came to a much smaller bay with a standard Rindd podship shuttle inside.

"Take the shuttle up to Station. It's already scheduled and data logged. There will be some others making the normal rounds and no one will question it that far. Dock it for an hour, then go wait in a stand-off parking spot until we release the decoys and the Primes go scampering after your cargo ship. You'll know the right moment to fly up and out of Barrkon's Oven and eventually the rest of Rindd System."

"Normal traffic, Sir. A few landers coming and going. All of them registered and no unusual moves." Praxel ported Anibale some of the chart files. "The lander Jade was using was damaged in that fracas we saw in the video. She abandoned it in situ and we presume she found another way to get herself up here to the Station."

Anibale frowned at the readouts. "She is here. There is no doubt. Stay on it, Praxel."

His operations aide gave a chest salute and left Anibale's cabin. He watched the blue silk curtain flow slowly back down to hide the hatch as the man left.

She was certainly here, on one of the docked ships, ready to pursue their target just as he was. He was slightly less sure of the Pilot and the Sisters fool. They could be here, but taking what form? Big ships were hard to hide, and small ones were plentiful and generic. Perhaps they are lying quiet, hoping we'll go away. If so, Anibale thought, he does not know me nearly well enough.

The burns no longer hurt, but it hurt in another way to see himself disfigured. His men, however, seemed to be slightly more respectful since the explosion, so maybe his more fearsome look wasn't entirely a bad thing.

Two hours later, he was dozing in the big chair when the comm popped to life, causing him to jerk awake. He scowled and gestured the thing to connect. "What?"

"To the bridge now, Sir. The pilot's ship just emerged from a Station portal and is fleeing fast."

"His ship? The Pilot? Well, don't wait! Go now! I'm coming, but watch for Jade!"

"We're watching. The pilot is running full-speed toward the main Gate to Back System. . . . Wait, what? . . . Yes. Another ship is off Station now, Sir. In pursuit."

Jade. "Get us gone NOW, mister!"

"Sir!"

At the bridge, Anibale settled carefully into his console chair. The medbots had done a good job on the burns but hadn't completely ameliorated all the muscle pains from his fall in the mine. "Tommit, you have not caught up with him yet."

His pilot took a quick look back at Anibale, who gave a grim sneer at the man's discomfiture. Tommit nodded, still unsure, and said, "His ship must have been fitted with some special propulsion, Sir. Its speed is far more than that ship should be able to do."

"How in ZEK's faces did they get his ship over here to Rindd and do the retrofit so quickly? This conspiracy is much larger and more sophisticated than I had dreamed," Anibale said. "The Rindders are in it up to their rotten, technical necks!"

"Sir."

Jade's ship was ahead of them, but they were quickly catching up to her. Hers was not true military, just an upscale transport she'd commandeered from somewhere. Looked like an older ZELLINC corporate ship to him.

"Prime!" Praxel called out. "A swarm of activity back at Station. Twenty–no, maybe thirty small ships are off and scattering!"

"A distraction," Anibale said. "We stay on target."

Anibale could not see how Jade was calculating her odds. He activated his private Suite comm hoping she might be online. He spoke quietly, "Jade. What do you think you are doing out here?"

There was silence for a while, and he thought she must not be on, but then came a spitting, popping sound. It was not interference, but rather her unsettling cackle, far too close to his ears.

"You shouldn't bother yourself with this one, old Blue! Let me have him and you go on with your friends and find another poor middie to torture."

"You know he is mine, Jade. You will only get yourself hurt out here in that little scow of a ship. Go home. I should not like to take the time and effort to force you."

"Anibale, Anibale . . . You are the one in danger out here. This fellow has you all undone! You're losing your signature calm focus!"

She laughed, and then her voice turned cold. "I know what you did at Barrkon's Oven, you fool. I have it all documented and I won't hesitate to reveal it to ZEK. You have no authority to commandeer the Rindder facility or to take ZEK and Bai's prize prisoner! You've forfeited all your power and status on this now! Give him to me. I'll find his little secrets. When we return to Helm, I'll back you up in front of ZEK and the Council."

"You think I was too rash here, Jade?" Anibale growled. "I have only begun to set things right. This idiot may destroy us all! I *will* take him, and as for you–you may take your sly old carcass back to Harbor and stay out of my way!"

"You cannot have him, Anibale. You are too dangerous yourself. If I can't take him, I will not let you have –"

His lip twitched as he cut off the comm. He glared at the display of her ship on his screens. They were both finally catching up with the pilot's cargo ship. "Monitor our defenses. If she moves toward us . . ."

Tommit spoke up. "The target is not changing course or speed, Sir. Prime Red's ship is accelerating."

Praxel was at the scans. "She's firing! Energy weapon directly at the cargo ship!"

Anibale jumped up from his seat. "NO! Muddling crone! We must have that man's information!"

"That was a low-energy shot. She must be trying to disable it!" Praxel said.

Anibale watched the cargo ship's image on the screen. It seemed to absorb the energy beam, glow brightly for a second, then–implode. It vanished off their scans and screens. He felt a sinking feeling in his gut.

"It's . . . gone, Sir! There's no debris. I don't understand," Praxel said.

"I do," Anibale hissed. "He's made a fool of me twice with that cheap trick. The Rindders will answer to ME for this." All eyes on the bridge were looking at him, most still confused, but some with a look of dark anger–the men who were with him at Salina. "It was a decoy,

263

you fools. Same as he did before: an inflated impostor of a ship. Jade just popped a damned balloon."

Tommit said, "He's probably made some other plans, Sir?"

Anibale grunted acknowledgment, "Yes–at least someone is thinking on this ship! That scattershot launch back at Station. We're scanning them, yes?"

Bilner said, "Prime, Sir. We are tracking thirty-four ships outbound in all directions. Three are further out than the others. Seven have braked into looping orbits around Barrkon's."

"Ignore the others. Vectors and speeds on those first three?"

"All are at top speed for the types of in-system podcraft they are. Two are heading for the two Line Gates. The third one is probably a rogue distractor, Sir. It's heading zenith right up and out of the system plane. If there's anyone on board, they are probably not going to be able to return to Rindd."

Tommit said, "Which Gate do you want us to head for, Sir?"

"Neither. He's in the zenith ship."

"Sir?"

"They're in that ship and they have a way out of this that we haven't thought of. Gunner! Fire a single shot at the Prime Red ship. Disable her only! I don't care if she is stranded for a year, but don't destroy the ship! Clear?"

"Yes, Sir!"

"Well, do it now! One BlueMil ship stays here to make sure she does not recover and follow us. Tommit, get us turned and pursue that pod with all the speed this thing can make–and then some!"

"Sir."

Marc watched the passive system feed intently. It was almost funny to see Anibale and Jade take off after his ship like that.

Funny since I'm not in it this time!

He turned his attention back to their own launch. The outer hatches were open now and Sil watched the screens. He spoke out as the data streams lit up.

"Here comes the mass launch, Marc. Let's go!"

"Just a little pause, Sil. Let's be part of the middle of the group. Less noticeable, perhaps."

Paris said, "That vector will call attention on its own, eventually."

"That's what I'm worried about. We just have to hope RR has the answers for us lined up the way he promised. OK, let's get this bucket out of here now."

They launched in the midst of the crowd of some thirty or more ships—all breaking out in random directions. Marc activated the comp nav for a zenith trajectory, away from the plane of the Rindd System and out where no Lines or anything else awaited them except capture by Anibale or Jade. Unless, of course, RR has his people ready out there with some pretty good capabilities for rescuing them and some way to repel two angry Suite Primes.

As they accelerated, the g-forces built up, reminding Marc of the weight he so recently shed on Barrkon's Oven. It was good to see that fiery cinder of a planet receding into a white dot as they left it and its Station behind. Just being in Station for that short time was like heaven. He and the others had all luxuriated in the weightless areas of the facility before boarding the podship.

Now, the plan was irrevocably in motion and it would certainly not be long until they found out how Anibale and Jade would react to the fake cargo ship.

"What do you think RR has for us out here, Sil?"

"Must be some of his Suite Grays, but I can't imagine what ships they could have that might get us and them out of Anibale's grasp." Sil kept his eyes on the screens as he spoke.

Marc said, "I'm leaning toward some of their human FTL tech, maybe?"

Paris monitored the comms originating from Station. "There. Found another feed. Here's the scene from one of the system remotes.

Looks like Jade fired on your ship, Marc."

Marc watched it for a moment, then said, "They're turning. I bet he's furious now. If RR doesn't get us out of here, we're going to be nothing but a shimmer of redshift radiation."

"You're forgetting how valuable you are, Marc," Sil said. "He'll do anything to take you alive."

"Well, in any case, their new vectors are all zenith. Won't be long now."

He meant that in relative terms, of course. Even with the most powerful of AA engines, Marc knew it would take some hours for them to change course that radically and pursue them. In any case, they were sitting targets. He looked back at Paris. She was nervous–sweating some even though the cabin was almost cold. Sil looked calm like always, but Marc had known him long enough now to tell he was tense. He decided he'd better spend the time looking diligently for any source of possible rescue out in this remote zone. He wished he could be out here under other circumstances.

Bet I could find some more Lines.

As time passed, Anibale's ship closed on them steadily. Amazingly, the feeds showed that he'd fired on Jade's ship and left her stranded. *No love lost there!* There was no comm traffic from him. Marc supposed he had little reason to want to talk.

There was also no sign whatsoever of anyone else out this way. No ships on scan, no secretive Stations appearing out of the dark, no Suite Grays with instructions forthcoming on what to do next. As Anibale's ship bloomed larger in the screens, Marc began to despair.

Paris muttered, "Damn Rindder doc. He's set us out here for his own purposes. We're gonna get caught, simple as that."

"Maybe so," Marc said, "but let's just play it out his way. Not that we can do much of anything else anyway."

Sil pointed to his screen. "He's turning on his close-in scan and lighting us up."

Marc looked at the data and frowned. "That's about it, then. We just have to remain calm and don't give him any reason to fire on us."

"He may still be unsure we are really in here," Sil said.

"Might give us a few seconds of something, I guess–if RR does come through for . . ."

As he spoke, the speakers came alive with an unexpected squeal. "Zzzzzzz . . . zzzz . . . zzZipppp. ZIPppppppppppppp · · · ppppp"

They were instantly surrounded by several unusual shapes. Zip ships appearing out of . . . where? Nowhere. Marc yelled, "Zips! Stay alert guys!"

"What in the worlds are they doing?" Sil said. "RR can't have made arrangements with *ZIPS*, could he?"

Paris said, "Could be a diversion or something! Maybe they're mad at Anibale? Maybe they'll attack him!"

As Marc watched his screens, though, the Zips did nothing like that. They swarmed around their small podcraft. Marc had never seen Zip ships so close before! Strange, organic-looking cocoons, like some sort of hairy bean pods. Green and brown with spots of something shiny scattered here and there on most of the surfaces. The colors seemed to fluctuate, slightly iridescent with each small movement. Four of the Zips came closer to them and surrounded their relatively tiny ship in a pyramidal formation with the podcraft at the center.

"Looks like we have our rendezvous, boys and girls," Marc said. "Rindd has learned to communicate with Zips. *Astounding!*"

"What a view of them!" Sil crowed as he hovered over the external scan cam controls. "So close and such detail for so long! Paris, make sure those backside cameras are recording all this! Anything on comm?"

Marc was actively monitoring it. "No. Nothing. These guys are definitely taking us in though. Look at the colors shifting on these closest ships."

The four Zips marking the points of the tetrahedral zone were closing together just slightly and the nearest sections of their "skins" began altering color dramatically now, forming a highly iridescent blue and purple patch closest to the center of the pyramid–closest to the human ship.

The colors intensified until a kind of netting, seemingly made of the blue light itself, streamed out and blossomed into a web formation that enclosed the podship. All their screens were nearly overwhelmed with bright blue light and they could feel a slight bump and a skewing motion as the podship was entangled in it. Marc looked back at the single screen that was still showing Anibale's ship.

"He's firing at the Zips!"

Sil looked up, startled. "What? Firing at them?" He snapped around to see the screen view.

They watched as the energy beam struck the largest of the Zip ships, trailing the pyramid group. The skin of that ship turned a bright green, then yellow, and then there was a single blinding flash. When the screen recovered the view, the Zip ship was still there, looking no worse for wear, but Anibale's ship was in obvious distress, falling off its course and rotating slowly.

Then, a soft "zzzzzzippppppppp" sound started building into a louder buzz, and the blue-light web they were caught up in brightened considerably. It began to affect the metals and hybrid substances forming the structure and walls of their human/Ash Alien podship. Inside the bridge, the three of them watched in wonder as the room around them began to glow in an entrancing, ghostly light. One patch of the bulkhead glowed and pulsed brighter in blues that were so high into the edges of ultraviolet that it hurt to look directly at it.

Marc unlatched himself and approached the patch. There was something about it. Then, he noticed his hands now glowing, pulsating slightly along with the blue light.

Sil and Paris turned to watch him as he put his now brightly glowing right hand to it. It seemed to sink in and Marc closed his eyes and tilted his head in intense concentration. After a few minutes, he spoke without looking back at them. "There's something here–something about the light. I can feel it. It's like I can reach across to the other ships and put my fingers on some kind of control surface. I think I'm supposed to do something."

"Careful, Marc. This is not our game," Sil said quietly. "We don't know what these beings want or what they'll do."

Marc nodded, holding very still.

"Or you could trust what RR said and just push the damn button, Pilot," Paris said.

Marc turned quickly to look at her without removing his hand. She stared at him with one eyebrow up. Suddenly, he grinned at her and Sil. "I do believe you are right, Sweet Pea!"

He pushed the button or whatever it was and everything fell into a hole.

Chapter Twenty-four

Paul Bennett was working on the data archives in the cool darkness of the comm shed when Jan burst in, out of the heat. Their granddaughter, Penny, a bright shadow constantly a step or two behind her, was excited, hopping from one small foot to the other.

"Something you need to see, Paul," Jan said, almost out of breath.

"It's a THING," Penny said.

Many decades had passed since he and the other survivors had constructed the shed from the remains of one of the makeshift reentry capsules. It seemed like yesterday to him, though: Jan and the others hastily cobbling together those capsules to attempt the return to Earth. They had survived in this one where so many of the others had perished in that attempt. Their symbolic graves stood at the outskirts of the little settlement he had named New Anchorage.

Shelter and farming had been their first priority once they landed on the still-morphing landscape of this newly terraformed planet–for terraformed it certainly was. It had been reshaped in breathtaking rapidity into something like a clean slate biosphere, but a planned and structured one with only the basic shapes of the oceans and old continents of Earth remaining from before. The new lands were alive with flora and fauna, all unknown before, but familiar and compatible with their bodies. New plants, new animals, new mild climatic conditions. It was truly, as his wife always put it, a new Eden for the tiny remnant of mankind left here to cultivate and settle. The Ash Aliens' terraform technology was little short of magic and still sent shivers down Paul's spine when he considered what they had all witnessed and lived through.

The survivors of the lunar colony had grown into a number of scattered communities and several thousand in population over the years. In a few generations, perhaps they would even prosper. He was beginning to feel the effects of his own 139 years as he slowly worked through his middle age and into an inevitable decline that would start at about age 160.

For now, however, there were still many challenges and dangers in this place, and he was the one in charge, by default if nothing else.

"What have we got, then, ladies?"

"A visitor. You'd best come look," she said, her face tense. Paul raised a brow, then put down the data files he had been restoring and stood to go with her. Penny had already popped back out of the doorway. The sun was certainly warm on this blue-sky day and Paul wiped his forehead as Jan led them at a fast walk through the nearest field of newgrain. At the next clearing, a town plaza of sorts had been set all those years ago. It bore a well-worn lived-in look, he thought. Six community structures faced the wide central plot of gravel and grass and several of his neighbor's roofs could be seen along the pathways leading into the fields behind. Three or four citizens had gathered around something on the ground. It was about a meter long and looked at first glance like a robotic spider.

"What've we got, Rob?"

The older man, his eyes shining through a face streaked with dirt, looked up at Paul as they approached. "Looks like Harbor has finally come back and found us. It homed in on the RF beacon for sure."

"Hell you say. Let's take a look." They had all made a wide circle around the mechanical intruder. It was partly AA tech, with gray components, but had plainly been hybridized with human parts as well. It made a hissing noise mixed with little snaps like it was cooling.

Jan said, "It landed here about fifteen minutes ago. Penny saw it first as it flew in. It hasn't moved or done anything since, right Rob?"

"Not a thing. I asked Jan to get you right away."

Paul stepped closer to inspect it. There was a comm screen on the outer shell, but of a design he had never seen. Jan and Rob leaned over his shoulders to stare at it.

"Even after all this time, I can't say I'm truly surprised to see this," Paul said. "A hundred and eight years now, but that's well over a thousand years in Harbor. If they haven't torn themselves apart in all that time, someone may have finally wondered what happened to Earth and sent this to communicate or at least assess our situation."

"Yes, but why now?" Jan said. "I've always wondered if the Harbor folk thought Earth was dead and they just didn't monitor it anymore, but that never felt right to me."

"Yeah, it's not like the planet disappeared. I'd be curious, wouldn't you?" Rob said.

Paul looked up at them. "They may have had cause to avoid us."

Jan said, "I was beginning to think *they* were all wiped out somehow, like what happened here."

Paul looked at the small craft, itself a stark confirmation that the rest of humanity still existed. He reached out and carefully touched the small screen. It beeped and an image appeared. The face of an older man wearing some type of optical lens over his right eye appeared. The image was streaked through with some interference lines for a moment, then smoothed. The man's lilting voice came clearly from the start.

"Greetings. Do you receive me? Do you understand me?" He gave them a questioning stare.

Paul leaned in and said, "We receive you. There is an accent, but

273

yes, I understand you. Who are you?"

The man's expression changed to one of relief, and Paul noted the silver-gray cloak sitting over his shoulders and a streak of white in his hair.

"I am Sal-Soren Biniun of Rindd. Forgive me if I am blunt in my speech and questions. I may not have much time to speak with you. Who are you people, and what has happened here on Earth?"

Paul took a second to process this. "Sal Soren," he said slowly, trying the name. "I am Paul Bennett, an elder member and the common Director of our settlement here. We call our home New Anchorage. We farm, we hunt, we work on building and rebuilding our technology. We live."

Paul squinted at the man in the screen. "Are you Harbor, then? There has been no contact from Harbor since the great disaster and terraform. We know nothing of you or your history, which has been a very long time for you since then, yes?"

Sal-Soren nodded and seemed to grow excited as he listened to Paul's words.

"Call me Sal. Very long, indeed, Paul. Over a millennia has passed on our side. I cannot tell you all things now, but no, I am not Harbor. My people are descended from what was once the EEA–the old Executive Earth Authority group. We are semi-independent from Harbor and seek our own path and our own knowledge. You have had no contact because Earth is entirely quarantined. No one is allowed to come to Earth."

"And, why would that be?" Paul said.

"Human FTL technology–technology we Rindders once helped control and restrict–has been hoarded and held in deepest restriction by ZEK and the Council on Harbor. I and my fellows from Rindd have formed a clandestine research group to put together what scraps of information we had and to recreate our FTL tech, quite illegally and dangerously, on our own. That is why there is no time to come to the surface ourselves or to speak with you at length as I would dearly wish. We are stationed at the old Earth-Harbor transfer zone, ready to retreat if we are caught here. Harbor has many bot spies and other policing protocols in system here as well as on the Harbor side.

"It is obvious that there has been misinformation and misdirection concerning Earth. I wish to understand the reasons and motivations for that," Sal said.

All the others, plus some coming in from the fields now, had crowded around Paul and the little screen on the bot probe, and Paul sat down in the dirt facing Sal-Soren's image. "We don't understand either, Sal. I witnessed–many here witnessed–the terrible destruction of our home. The planet surface was certainly blasted clean and replaced with amazing speed. The Ash Alien terraform tech is nothing short of magical. But, our New Earth is beautiful now! It is open and it is completely safe to the best of our ability to measure it. We can't imagine why no one from Harbor has seen this and thought to make contact. Frankly, we could use a lot of human resources and technology from Harbor. You say there has been a quarantine? Again, why?"

Sal raised a black brow from behind the eye with the lens.

"You are quarantined and no one has come because you live on a forbidden planet that is completely overrun with a bio-tech 'xeno-plague' that was delivered in anger by aliens for alien reasons. It is a plague that causes dematerialization and radiation. Earth, you see, is a burned-out, hellish world and to come here would be to experience horrors and a gruesome death."

The group around Paul all laughed. Paul was smiling, too.

"Well, Sal. That's quite a story. I don't think I've encountered any horrors lately, short of someone getting too much sun working in the newgrain fields or not being able to get my old circuits and comps to cooperate as I try to rebuild our data from the lunar colony. That's where we were, by the way, on Earth's moon. We constructed some basic reentry vehicles and we, or at least some of us, made it back down here after the terraform pass was complete. The Harborites who were here in-system must have thought the AA terraform effects represented permanent damage before they went back home. They

275

should have stayed."

Sal leaned into his camera. "There are mysteries here, Paul. Mysteries that I want to understand. Unraveling them may help us to break down the absolute control of Harbor and ZEK, who are taking great advantages over their fellow humans, both within Harbor Systems and in our Rindd Systems along with one other outlier group based in the Sisters. They have become rich off the backs of others and they believe now that they are truly superior and deserve anything they want. They keep us under their golden toes."

"I'm not sure who your 'zek' is, but I get the picture. You are taking a considerable risk coming here, then. Our situation is simple, Sal. We made our landing here. We settled with the resources we brought and with the new resources we found on the reborn Earth. We are still struggling and limited, but we are generally well and beginning to thrive.

"Many of the things I witnessed on that terrible day have bothered me greatly over the years. I just can't figure why that unique AA ship appeared alongside the Harbor fleet and just decided to fire its energy beams at the Earth. It was clearly meant to terraform, not to be a doomsday weapon, but the effects on Earth's civilization were the same as if it were. I don't believe it was meant as a weapon at all. Why would they bother to terraform what they wanted to destroy? Why didn't they appear or return to Earth to harvest their terraformed world? Was it all some kind of robotic malfunction? I don't know, but I've tried for decades to figure it out.

"I've retained some of our data of some of what happened. Actual data feeds from the Moon at the time, media feeds, and private comm streams. All these years later, I'm still trying to reconstruct the parts I missed or that were damaged, but I don't have all the tech tools here to do a proper job of it. What I do have is suggestive. Your information today has confirmed much in my mind."

Sal was intent. "You have *actual data* and you have your own personal perspectives. These could change the Second Domain of Humanity forever. This is beyond my wildest hopes, Paul. Would you be willing to share it with us? We could open up your New Earth with the resources you need and gift you with over a thousand years' worth of our knowledge and technologies."

Jan grasped Paul's arm. "Before we commit to this, we need to know so much more."

"Yes, I agree, but I think we can at least start by sharing some of the basic data that all here have access to. We need their help, too." He turned back to Sal on the screen. "We will do that if you are willing."

Sal looked excited. "Yes! Anything you are willing to provide! Let's move quickly now. Can you interface with this bot's system? We can devise a transfer protocol if you need us to . . . "

The screen went dark.

"Sal? Can you hear me?"

They waited, but it did not restart. Paul pressed on the screen again. Nothing.

After a while, most of the others went back to their fields or homes as Paul and Jan still watched the bot and screen. Penny played around the plaza with one of the pets and eventually got hungry. Jan took her home, and then brought Paul something to eat as the sky turned red and pink. He had not left the bot and was trying to learn and work the screen's inert controls.

Jan watched him for a while as he absent-mindedly ate the sandwich, then shook her head. "Set up a watcher bot of your own, Dear Old Man, and come back home."

Paul did that thing, but no new message ever came on the little Rindd craft that had brought them so much news and hope. He made sure the New Anchorage permanent RF beacon was in good working order.

Chapter Twenty-five

Marc nursed his still-aching arm and hand while Sil peered at the main screen with a most intense and happy look on his face. Marc grinned.

Why, he's almost beaming!

They were approaching a beautiful planet, two-thirds lit from this angle and glowing with blue and green and salmon colors. Wisps and curls of cloud formations draped it and lights appeared on the bit of night side below.

"This is your home, Sil?" Paris asked.

"Yes. Welcome to Florinda, my friends. Moreover, welcome to the Eight Sisters of Frahma! Only five are on this side of their orbits now. Here, let me move the scans around and show you what the first discovery mission saw."

As he arranged his display, Marc was still trying to cope with the weirdness of the Zip encounter and his own involvement in whatever had just happened. That hole they dropped into was like a wild, makeshift Line. It seemed to abruptly deviate directions and alter its shape as they made the transit. How they did that, and where that Line came from or went back to, only the Zips know. The podship popped out here like a float on a fish pond, clean as you please, and they found themselves placed (certainly not by accident) on a perfect course to intercept Florinda's Station orbital zones. The Zips were gone. No waves goodbye or invoice presented. No smiling images to remember them by. Nothing.

"Like a suite of true jewels set on a cosmic string," Sil said. "By some amazing fluke, when Owen Nimm's group first transited the Line from Farms, they saw the major planets almost perfectly lined up in their orbits. Someone in his discovery group (we don't know who it was for certain) said they looked like eight lovely sisters all gathered together, gracefully attending their star mother."

Marc looked over Paris's shoulder at the display. The Eight Sisters–bright and dim dots arrayed in a cluster that was almost a straight line, with their home star Frahma sitting golden at one end. It was impressive in this reconstruction. It must have been stunning to see it in reality.

"Here they are. I'm not displaying the three little hard-vac rockies, Ipa, Ika, and Ina, because they are tiny and close to the star. We call those The Fires. Then the Sisters begin with desert Flamina, then Fleta, Fria, Felice with its great trees, Ferne, Florinda (our home world), and smaller Faith and Fia. Our two giant gas planets, Oba and Osa, circle much farther out."

Sil took the controls now and steered their little ship toward the Florinda Station. Having come so many times to the official Trade Station, which was situated much further out near the Farms Gate, Marc was glad to have this unexpected chance to see the inner worlds here. Who would ever have thought that a middie pilot from Farms would get the chance to visit the forbidden Sisters System? He wondered what surprises were in store for them on the beautiful planet spinning below.

He looked at Paris, who was gaping at the image of Florinda. She looked back at him and shook her head as they grinned at each other.

S ometimes the thing was like a huge metallic spider. Sometimes, it spoke in low rumbling words that could not quite be understood. Other times, it changed into a thing more like a web of wires that sang and pulsed with energy. When it did that, Kera felt like she could put her hands into that mesh of possibilities and begin to shape it like some unimaginable tool. She felt its power. This was one of those times.

The dream always began with the Star Artifact perched on its pedestal inside the alien ship and faintly glowing. She was drawn to it–compelled to reach out to it, to take it and use it, but something kept her from it. The Star seemed to react to her frustration. It flashed in angry colors and started changing its shape. It could be a mouthless predator that pounced upon her and broke her from the dream. Or, it could become that intriguing web of energy, like it was doing now.

It called to her and she strained to reach out her hand, but someone had bound her arms to her sides and she wanted to scream at her hindrance. The lattice had a different texture now: more organic like molecular skeins of neurons all busy with potent traffic–instructions being sent and received by something or someone, to and from somewhere unknown. She ached to tap into that stream, to guide and control it herself. She strove against her constraints with all her main force and gave a guttural yell that resounded in her mind as it escaped her sleeping lips and woke her up sharply.

Kera sat up in her blue-sheeted bed. It was still dark and she was alone. She had sweated through her gown.

After the fiasco with Marc in the Great Seat up on Helm, Anibale's staff had transported her downworld to Harbor, to Suite Blue's home and headquarters before the Prime himself left on some new mission. As luxurious as his Elite estates here were, it was frustrating to be stuck here for days and days, and to be so much further removed from the Star Artifact orbiting back up on Helm. Anibale had suddenly returned home a few days ago, but Kera had not seen him, and no one was giving her any information, sequestered as she still was within his domain.

She admired the man's single-minded determination and raw power, but she was repelled by the idea of ever actually merging into his world.

He will control everyone he can. He's too obsessed–too ardent and fanatical–too foolishly dangerous for this girl to get tangled up with. He's a tool and I just need to find a way to wield him.

So far, adopting the helpful and admiring middie girl approach seemed to have worked. He'd taken her in and made her one of his personal group of women, but also kept her well contained and isolated. She had to devise a way to get back into physical proximity of the Star, and that strange object seemed to want her to find *it* again, or so the compelling dreams implied.

A soft chime from the carved wooden double doors to her chamber alerted her to the attendants. She called out "Open" to the voice lock and two younger girls entered. The two women she had dealt with before up on Helm had abandoned their pretense of employment with Suite Blue and retreated to Jade's domains–apparently a rather common phenomenon or tactic in these Elite circles. It made her shake her head, half in consternation and half in amusement.

These two seemed innocent enough but looks could plainly deceive, so Kera remained careful and noncommittal around them.

"Prime Blue wishes us to gather up and prepare to lift to Helm, HandFriend," the one with darker hair said. It was hard to tell these two apart.

"How long?"

"Right away, HandFriend. We will help you with your things," the other one said. They began to gather up her Suite clothing, about the only possessions she had now other than her compromised personal comm. Someday, she swore to herself, she would go back to Farms and collect her few family treasures and bring them to her new home somewhere here in Harbor Space proper–some place of her own making where she was in control and where no one could ever control or threaten *her* again.

As she boarded the shuttle with her attendants, the route display showed they would be required to make a couple of orbits of Harbor to line up for docking at Helm. It would be a wait, then. Anibale was already on board and as he passed her, he silently motioned for her to follow him. When they were inside his private cabin, she saw that he was pale and preoccupied, staring out the small viewscreen window and not speaking. He seemed to have some bruising on his face and part of his hair was shorter than she remembered. She sat still and watched him until his eye and attention landed on her again.

"You're caught up in something. Planning. This is something really big, isn't it?"

Anibale stared for a moment. Then he said, "It's big. Perhaps the biggest thing to happen in Harbor for centuries, and I am tasked to carry it out."

"Tasked by whom? Yourself?"

He jerked his head up some and stared hard at her. "You are forward. Do not take your situation too casually, Kera." Then, his expression relaxed somewhat. "But, yes, I task myself in this. No one else will do what needs to be done. I will. It is that simple. There is danger and my tasks are a burden that I gladly bear."

"Whatever you are planning, it has to do with Marc, doesn't it," she said quietly.

Again, that stare from him. Its coldness made her quail inside. "You still have feelings for your old boyfriend, do you?"

"Marc is a good friend, yes, but he challenged ZEK and clearly lost. He is no longer a part of my life, Anibale. I require a strong person to guide me and provide opportunities to improve myself and my station." He returned his stare to the viewscreen as, within it, Helm grew in apparent size as they slowly approached.

She decided to venture another question. "Why are you taking me back to Helm?"

"Our plans were disrupted by the circus with your pilot. I want you to begin working with Chafin, my head of board on Helm. We cannot conduct direct experiments with the Star, unfortunately, as it has been so boldly stolen by ZEK and the Council, but I can have you begin a detailed analysis of what you did experience with it and make ourselves as ready as possible for when it returns to our possession. I want you to be able to use it, Kera! Use it to take the fangs out of whatever that plague ship has. There is no question the ship will be found now. Your pilot is in the hands of our enemy."

She must have made a look of surprise. He said, "Yes, the Sisters have him, and with his abilities available to them, they will surely grasp for the power of that ship."

The Sisters are our enemy? This guy is really trying to stir things up!

Anibale turned back to the screen again and said, "Kera, did you and Marc ever have any interactions with any Zips?" He returned his gaze to her.

The question took her by surprise and she thought for a second before replying. "Zips? . . . No, we never saw any of them when I was with him. No, wait–there were some Zips that flew past when we were caught up in that skirmish with you at the Farms Gate."

"No other Zip encounters?"

"No. What happened with Zips and Marc?"

Anibale turned away and would not answer her. She thought she heard him mutter, "Damn ghosts," but she wasn't sure.

They docked at Helm an hour later and she was led securely to the Suite Blue sector where she'd be handed over to this Chafin and lots more tedious questioning, she was sure.

ZEK had put off court duties and sequestered himself in his private suite on Helm for the past day. He had to find a way to mitigate the damage of losing the middie. 'This man is the key,' old

Bai had said about the pilot. But, Bai doesn't know about the woman, Kera, and how she can also connect with the Star.

The incredible reports of what happened on Barrkon's Oven had stunned him. The Rindders were always secure and thorough. This kind of thing simply did not happen. It was unthinkable! The early reports revealed some rumors of a secretive faction within Rindd that may have been responsible for the incidents, but after hearing Marc's story and seeing the raw power he demonstrated right here in the Great Seat, he was not so sure the escape wasn't something the pilot himself had managed.

He was frustrated not being able to take immediate action, but ZEK had learned to cultivate patience in these situations. Something will change. An opening, an opportunity, will present itself. Perhaps one will manifest as a result of his earlier planning and work to get old Pas-Guin elected into the Council of Colors. He had been only too happy to sponsor the old fool. Suite Cyan was making some modicum of progress under the direction of Pas-Guin's son Dor-Guin, but they were still weak and the Council saw the current Prime Cyan as a safe candidate to bring into that most elite of groups. ZEK had made certain to *impress* upon Pas how he had made it possible for him to attain that position–the influence of ZEK and all that. Pas-Guin was a jittery man and he feared ZEK's power and position even though he tried to hide it under a skin of nervous humor.

Gets on my nerves, he does. But, the old goat may be most useful to me, and right soon.

The hatch chime interrupted his meditations.

"Do you understand the word *uninterruptible?*" he growled into his comm.

His suite manager answered in a calm manner, well-trained as he was to deal with ZEK and his various moods and tenses. "Yes, ZEK, with the exception of a direct request for audience from a Prime."

"And?"

"Prime Red, Sir. She would like a word."

Jade and her flaming tail that got shot off by Anibale. He should have known she'd get back here fast and want to stir up as much dirt and revenge as possible. He sighed. "Let her enter."

After a moment, the hatch slid open and Jade came with staccato steps toward him.

"ZEK. You know what happened in Rindd space. Anibale is out of control! He shot us up. Disabled my ship. MY ship! On purpose! He could have killed me!"

ZEK stared down his nose at her for a moment. "Well, Jade, I suppose he could have, but I imagine he has more sense and better aim than you may be willing to ascribe to him."

"Don't you laugh at me, ZEK. What he did is unheard of and unacceptable! I want you to sanction him and sanction him *hard*."

"I will take appropriate actions at the right time. If you want revenge on Anibale, you know how to go about it. Don't come whining to me."

"Whining!" Jade stopped a moment and made a sound like a growl. "You are ZEK. You were not always ZEK. You certainly will not always *be* ZEK. Anibale wants power and he's going about getting it in ways that you would be wise to pay attention to. He's still intent on getting that pilot and his powerful ship artifact. He has the *girl* and has brought her back to Helm. I don't want to have to make my pleas to *him* once *you* are gone." She had turned a hard glare on him–eyes like two black stones.

The girl, back here? That is interesting, indeed. Could be just the change I needed.

He said, "You are bold. I understand you are frustrated, but there is little I can do about him without more data and evidence. He needs to be monitored, covertly of course. I assign you the task. You have the motivation, yes?"

That broke her glare. "Well, yes. What do you want me to do?"

"I want you to watch him, that's all. Record his activities and travels. He's good at deception, so you'll have to be better. I wouldn't get caught by him or his own forces if I were you." He flashed a smile at her.

"You're a tough worm."

He smiled more broadly. "Of course. That's how I became ZEK."

"I'll do it, but not for you. I'll do it to find a way to bring Suite Blue down a notch or three and harm Anibale like he has *me!*"

"That's the spirit, Jade. Now, if you don't mind, I was uninterruptible for a reason."

———————————————

Kera was back in the same suite she had occupied when she was first taken by Anibale. He had been even more preoccupied since their arrival at Helm, and then he suddenly left on another mysterious mission without so much as a word to her. The work with Chafin's people was rather boring. Just questions and probes. She had little to hide, so there was not much to it except to endure it.

Coming at such a late hour, a chime at her door surprised her.

As it opened, a man in a tech robe and cowl came quickly inside. His face was masked with a tech's comm and data shield. Kera started to move back involuntarily, but the man raised his hands and indicated she should close the door. She nodded the command cue and it closed.

"I am sorry to alarm you, Kera. There is no danger from me." He removed the cowl and data shield. She took in her breath as she realized who was standing here in her room.

"ZEK? It *is* you. What are you doing here?"

"I must sometimes act carefully and covertly to accomplish my goals. Surely you understand, someone in my position cannot just go places without everyone knowing each move and turn, especially on Helm. I want to talk with you and see if you would be interested in helping me with a little project?"

"Help you on a project? What kind of project? . . . Sir."

He smiled at her. "One I think you will be keen to participate in if what you said is true. You *can* interact with the artifact, yes?"

A thrill ran up Kera's spine. "Oh, yes. Yes, I can. You have a way for me to try it?"

"Let's just say, I believe there is a way. I must know for certain that you can do this thing. It will determine which of several future paths I and we may take. You will work with me, then?"

"Yes, of course! But, I'm not free to leave this sector. How will we go?"

"There are some privileges to being ZEK that even the Primes do not know, my dear. Just come with me and we shall go where we must. Oh, and Kera? This is secret–*most* secret. You understand?"

"Yes, ZEK, I understand. Completely."

"Good. Very good. Follow alongside me, then," he said as he replaced the tech items onto his face and donned the cowl once more.

He led her out into the corridor, where none of her clandestine "guards" were evident. It seemed that ZEK had already taken care of that little obstacle. She had no doubt he'd taken care of any others along the way to wherever they were destined.

The walking journey ended in one of the fancier sectors of Helm. Lots of fine stonework lintels and jewel-encrusted handrails and such. It all looked a bit silly to a Farms gal, but any one or two of those sparkly gewgaws would probably buy her a nice cargo ship. That made her think of Marc and she wondered where he was this night.

They came to a hatch outlined in copper and silver and covered with embossed leather. ZEK held up some small object to a hidden scanner before it silently opened for them. He led her into a small room where another man was nervously pacing. As they came fully inside, the man stopped short and looked at ZEK, then at her, and then back at ZEK.

"You did not say you were bringing someone! ZEK, this is sketchy enough allowing only you inside like this!"

"Calm down, Pas. I have my reasons for it and they are important to the System itself. May I present Kera 17Millies, formerly serving Suite Blue and now serving ZEK. She may be the most important person here this night, my old friend. Kera, this is Prime Cyan,

Pas-Guin, newly elected to the Council of Colors."

"Prime Cyan." She gave him a formal respect-nod. "I thought a Prime could not be in the Council?"

"Yes, yes. That is true, young woman . . . Kera." He began fidgeting again. "I have begun the transfer of Prime to my son, but the Council has allowed me to begin my service to them anon. Thanks to you, ZEK. Yes . . . yes," he trailed off.

"All right, Pas. You have secured the room?"

"Yes. I disarmed the monitoring and deterred the night staff for a while, but we must hurry."

"We will hurry, Pas. It won't take long." He turned to Kera and said, "I once told you I would ask you to demonstrate your ability with this Star object. We are going into the White Hall now. Do you know that you are the first middie woman to ever enter it? I will ask you to keep entirely quiet and do what needs to be done as rapidly as possible."

"I will do my best, Sir." She felt the back of her neck prickle as it sunk in just where it was that she was now standing.

ZEK nodded to Pas-Guin and the older man hesitated only a moment before leading them to an opposing hatch, which opened at his touch. They entered a darkened room–only one dim white light coming from a large globe above. She was in the legendary White Hall! It was such an unbelievable idea, it didn't seem real to her. Toward the dim sides, she made out several chairs arranged in a partial circle. Here, the Council of Colors met under the Council Elder. ZEK took her elbow and guided her on to follow Pas-Guin toward one wall. The newest Council member was whispering, but so loudly he might as well have spoken to them.

"They placed the Star in a secure niche over here, ZEK."

"Yes. Open it, Pas."

"I don't know if I can take it out of the niche."

"It may not matter. Just open it, Pas."

Kera and ZEK had reached the curved side wall of the Hall now and Pas-Guin fiddled with something on his personal comm. After a moment, a panel silently slid up and out of sight, revealing the Star Artifact sitting on a small cloth and leaning against the back of the niche. A thrill ran through her as she saw the gray metal controller again.

"You always were the tech master Pas," ZEK said. He turned back to her and said, "*Now*, Kera. Try it now. We don't want to be here very long."

She tried. Closing her eyes, Kera recalled that strange hypnotic state she remembered from when she accidentally activated it in the cargo ship. Nothing happened. Pas-Guin made a soft, nervous hum under his breath. Something appeared in Kera's mind–a pair of yellow eyes, narrow and set in blackness. She twitched as something brushed her with the feel of cold scales. Whatever it was, it was trying to lure her into a deeper place. She heard a huff from ZEK that prompted her to open her eyes again. The Star glowed very faintly. A purple halo, almost beyond human range. The glow brightened to a deep red for just a moment, spiked into a fast and bright white, and then faded back to dull gray metal.

Pas-Guin was almost whimpering now, "Please, please. . . let's go! This is too much! Too much!"

"Be calm, Pas. I've seen what I needed to see. Shut the panel and let's go. Are you all right, Kera?"

"Just a little dizzy. Take my arm again, please."

So, there she was, she mused. The supreme leader of all Harbor and Humanity gently guiding *her* with his hand on her arm as they walked back through the fabled White Hall of the Council of Colors. The most powerful people and legendary places in all the galaxies and yet, she felt like she was a natural part of what was happening here. It was frustrating to be this close to the Star and to make contact with it, but not to be able to go further. ZEK was rightly careful with it and with her, but just being here and making that contact opened up many new possibilities. She had felt the incredible power latent in the Star. It seemed somehow to be aware of her and waiting, just waiting for the right moment. *Patience. My chance will come.*

"I will take you back to your Suite Blue quarters for now, Kera, but if you get in trouble or need me to meet you, use this alerter. You can speak a message into it or just press if you need instant help." ZEK placed an insertion device on her left arm and it injected the tiny alerter under her skin, then he led her out of the White Hall. Pas-Guin was still making worried sounds and staring at the Star, but ZEK simply ignored him and they walked into the outer hall as the beautiful doors closed silently behind them.

Chapter Twenty-six

Anibale had one hand on his chin and absently tapped his rock crystal desk with the other hand's fingers. Delbar Seel, sitting across from him, maintained a determined look on his normally somber but unreadable face.

"You asked for my thoughts. Damn it, Anibale, I'm your Senior Staff Advisor. It's my duty to alert you to possible boundaries issues as well as procedural tactics, and that's why I'm telling you this. Wait. See how things settle out now. You've already agitated ZEK, the Council of Colors, and Faces knows who else with that business on Rindd. Further adventuring could bring everything you've worked for down in a flash."

Anibale's fingers stopped drumming. "Or, it could be the bold move that is needed to defend Harbor and all of us from another terrible plague." He looked up. "It could be the move that puts Harbor solidly in my hands, Del. I know the risks. That's why I'm in this position–I can and will make the decision to take those risks when I believe the rewards are worth it."

"Are they? Now? Right now with so much uncertainty about this possible plague ship and its whereabouts? Look, the pilot has escaped off to the Sisters, we *think*. He could have been just looped up by those Zips and taken off to Zip Land for all we really know."

Anibale huffed and said, "I hope they made a good meal."

"And, you assume the Sisters are complacent and unprepared for any kind of military action against them."

"They are sheep, Del. I've been patrolling the Gate at Farms for years. I've consulted with my on-site experts about the trade with Sisters. I've captured and *interviewed* some of the cargo people like this Marc. The Sisters have been sitting in their idealistic isolation for far too long, siphoning off our food and materials resources in trade for their useless artwork and baubles. They have no need of a military presence – just a few police and border ships to keep the Harbor pilots to their restricted trade zone. You've seen what kind of merchandise they produce! A few tools and tech items–never made with value metal or quality gems. They don't *have* them out there!"

Delbar sighed. "Yes, I know. They are troublemaking rubes and dreamers. You've studied their security forces and trade, but I have spent these years looking at their intellectual output, what of it we can obtain. I *know*–don't look at me like that. Their philosophers and scientists are not simpletons, Anibale. Some of their work is brilliant and they are researching areas that are foreign to us. They may have developed some advantages that we are simply not aware of."

"I think you give them far too much credit. Talkers and tale-spinners, the whole bunch of them!"

"It may be so, but I feel you should take a care and not assume they'll allow themselves to be easily run over."

"They won't be expecting it, Del. Surprise is always the most effective tactic. Even the primitive old First Domain armies knew this. Yes, I've read some of the old histories. Studied their armies and battles. I know this can work. It *will* work and I will take that momentum and use it to lever Harbor and Helm out of their centuries-old doldrums!" Anibale thumped his fist down on the table.

"Prepare a meeting for tomorrow mid-hour, midships staff suite."

Del looked at him with tired eyes for a minute, then nodded. "As you wish, Prime. I have advised as tasked. It is your hand that gives that small ball of ice a push at the top of a snowy hill. I hope it does not become a consuming white beast by the time we reach the bottom with it."

He rose and saluted, then exited the room. Anibale sat there and fought an inner battle between the crush of caution and the thrill of impending action.

He may be right. He may be, but I must keep going with what I've started. Marc is with that Teacher on Florinda or somewhere in their forsaken systems–I know it! Those fools will gain the knowledge and control of his new ship if I don't intervene. It's time to grip all the Systems in a strong hand. Mine! I will do this job and take my rightful reward after. But, it must start NOW.

Fifteen minutes later, Anibale sent a coded message to his BlueMil commanders to rejoin as a group at Hub System to prepare for an unprecedented and surprise invasion through the Gate at Farms, into the Eight Sisters of Frahma.

———

As their little podship approached the main Station in orbit around Florinda, Marc thought it was odd that Sil was not aiming them for the main docks. The native Florindan had insisted on taking the controls, but he steered them to a dark, seemingly little-used part of the docks–an archipelago of industrial-looking platforms, quite a distance from the main Station area.

"You know where you're headed there, Sil?"

"Yes. No need to worry. I have a place out here where I can come and go more discreetly."

"Is that why you didn't want to talk to your Station people?"

"Precisely. Just nav and security codes on approach. I would not wish to cause an unnecessary stir, at least not right now."

"Well, they didn't challenge your codes, so I guess they won't question this Rindd ship, but maybe that's not unusual for your people?"

Sil glanced back at Marc from the control seat. "Oh, it's quite unusual. That's one more reason to be discreet for now. I have a transport we can use to land on-planet. Then we can make ourselves more known."

It was clear that the dock they connected to was robotic. Some work lights came on and systems had to bring up temps and air supplies for the human areas. Paris looked nervous and apprehensive, but she helped them get their few things together to make the transfer to Sil's lander. She pulled out one of the energy pistols RR had left for them in the podship and expertly charged it for use.

"Let me go first, Sil, just in case," she said.

"There is no danger here, Paris, but yes, you can lead us into the dock."

As they entered the still-cold metal passageway, Marc let his hand linger for just a moment on the outer hull of the hatch frame to their podship–that little in-system bubble that had brought them so unbelievably far from Rindd to the Sisters System.

"Ahh, here she is," Sil said as they entered a small hangar dome. "It has been quite a while since I used the little Blue Swan."

Marc and Paris both stopped and stared. The ship was unlike any lander he'd ever seen. Unlike any ship of any kind, really. It was customized into a stylized shape, presumably that of the mythical creature for which Sil had named it. It appeared to be a functional lander with atmospheric wings and all, but the artwork and custom shaping were something he'd only heard rumored of in Harbor space.

"Sil? That's pretty fancy. Amazing, actually," Marc said. Paris had her mouth open.

He smiled gently as he turned to face them. "Isn't she lovely? Let's go on board."

Inside the Blue Swan, Marc started to wonder even more. The corridors were lined with expensive woods and trims of patterned metal. A stunning mural lined one side of the main passage to the bridge. It was the mythical swan of old Earth with long, flowing feathers done in some colorful style unfamiliar to Marc. When he and Paris were seated next to Sil in soft, true leather cushions, Marc just looked at him with a questioning expression. Sil smiled again but remained mum.

Once they were out of the dock and had descended through atmospheric braking, their energy shield faded out and the journey down to Florinda was smooth under Sil's expert piloting. The flight was especially striking because of the real windows in the Blue Swan–another extravagance he wasn't expecting. The greens and blues of the world slowly became a landscape as they settled down to meet it.

Paris nudged Marc and said, "Look over here." Out her side window, he saw some of the rivers and forest lands give way to a cityscape glinting in the morning sun. It looked very clean and organized.

"Our principal city, Analah," Sil said. "We're headed a bit east of there. We'll be landing soon."

The city passed below them as they turned to the right, and then a landing strip came into view. It was in a greensward area next to a very large building. As they approached and its apparent size increased, it appeared to be something other than a public or industrial building. It seemed to be some manner of a house–the largest single house Marc had ever seen.

It was like one of the castles from old Earth vids and stories. He never expected to see such an unlikely thing in real life! Several towers sprouted along the structure and a couple of domes glinted along its roof. Colorful flags flew from a cluster of poles near a pool and fountain.

Paris said, "This is your place?"

Sil still held the ship's controls for the landing, so he merely nodded as they touched down on the strip. When they had come to a stop, he turned and smiled at them.

"Welcome to my home."

Marc grinned back at him and said, "Damn, Sil. You didn't tell me you were the Emperor of Frahma!"

"Ha! Hardly an emperor. That would not sit well with Sisters folk, I'm afraid."

Paris said, "Well, what are you then? Some kind of President or something?"

"No, not that, either, Paris." Sil talked with them as they exited the Blue Swan and slowly walked across the field toward the grassy lawns and the fountain. The sudden rich smell of a natural environment full of living things was almost overwhelming. Paris sneezed. "I'm just a fortunate citizen of Florinda who has many interests and has become a focal point for others who share them. My home started as an artistic experiment with the landscaping and as a place for my rather extensive library. When others gathered here to share their interests and to peruse that library with me, it kind of grew on its own into a place of learning and science–an impromptu university of many subjects. I decided to formalize it as the SisterSon of Frahma Institute.

"That is my title, if there needs to be one. I am a SisterSon of Frahma–some would say *the* SisterSon, but I am a true citizen as are all others here."

Marc gestured at one of the huge fountains. Sunlight glinted through the white spray of the water. "You know, Sil, in Harbor we have the image of you Sisters folk as being kind of poor and backward. I'm astounded by the wealth and sophistication this represents. How do you fund it all without more robust trade with Harbor?"

"Yes, I know. Your Elite have you well trained to think of us as dreamy idealists who make impractical art and talk philosophy all day, dependent on the goods and materials from the Mother Culture of Harbor." Sil's eyes twinkled. "Well, we do make unusual artwork and enjoy talking philosophy a lot, but we are a practical people, as well."

Paris asked, "But, where does it come from?"

"Well, Frahma System is resource-rich. And don't forget, my dear, we have many worlds behind the Eight Sisters. Six known complete systems lie on the Lines behind Frahma and some of them have wonderful resources and interesting human populations. It has taken many centuries to come this far, but we sustain ourselves quite well now. Trade with Harbor is by choice but is also considered dangerous for obvious historical reasons. That's why we so carefully restrict and control both trade and our image in the minds of others."

They had reached the house that was a university and several groups of people had emerged and were approaching them, most waving and a few even giving out a cheer or two.

Sil tried to make some quick introductions amid many handholds and hugs, but Marc found it hard to focus properly on all the specific people here in the crowd as the group made their way into the front hall of the great building. Marc walked through the large open doors feeling like he was still in some dream.

Paris gawked and Marc realized he was doing the same. The carved wood entry hall led directly into a large library. No, a *huge* library, filled with what seemed to be antique true-books. *Layers* of shelves of them, stretching off into the distance on the floor level, and another sector of them on each side of a level above, surrounding an open space that rose to a shallow translucent green dome at the ceiling far above their heads. Rich, dark wooden arches stretched up to support that ceiling, and short, fluted columns stood in rows, one at the end of each shelf section, displaying a variety of glowing artwork objects.

"ZEK's Faces!" Paris muttered..

"Sil, this is all real? These are true-books, aren't they?" Marc said as soft laughter spread through the group.

Sil beamed at them. "Yes, a bit of an affectation, I'm afraid. All of our information is encoded and comp accessible of course, but I and many of my friends have a love for true-books, as you call them. I have had a representative collection printed on actual paper, crafted here, and bound to conform as well as possible to the original Earth books. There are several authentic old Earth books here, too. The library itself is inspired by images of one that existed in an ancient Earth country called Ireland."

He let them take it in for a few minutes, then said, "I will show you around the Institute later, but we are certainly all exhausted from these travels and events. Go with Jon, here, and he will provide rooms for you two. I need to arrange a few things upon my return, so let's meet in a couple of hours for a good Florindan meal in the dining hall."

On their third day on Florinda, Marc and Paris were meeting with some of the men and women from the Institute to discuss the implications of the actions taken by Anibale and the other strange events of their recent journey. Sil had stepped out for a while, but then returned and spoke softly to Marc.

"Would you mind taking a bit of a break and come with me? There's someone I'd like you to meet."

"Of course," Marc said.

He led the way back to the library and the front entrance, then outside onto the great lawn.

"She's just arriving, and I thought we'd meet her out here." Sil seemed energized and he was smiling. A landing craft had just settled down on the pad. This ship was another unlikely art piece, painted in polychrome swirls. It had an extender lift that lowered down now with a single person on it. She stepped off and began to walk toward them. A few meters away, she stopped and waited with her head tilted and holding an enigmatic smile.

Marc stopped short. "It's you! . . . You're the . . . you're the woman I saw in the Vision! I can't believe it!"

She smiled broadly then and walked forward extending her graceful hand.

"Marc, I'd like you to meet Leenah Bordu, my primary assistant here at the Institute. I believe you two have something in common that I was only recently made aware of."

Leenah took Marc's hand and said, "Hello Marc. I guess we have met before, sort of."

Marc felt like shaking his head to clear it, but he held her hand for a moment and said, "Hello, Leenah. Sorry for shouting out like that. I didn't know you were a real person! I thought she was a symbol in my vision. But, here you are! Wow!"

"Your vision may have been more real than you now imagine. I had a strong vision, too, and in it, I saw you floating out there in space." A faint shudder went through Leenah's body, and Marc released her hand. "We shall have some very interesting discussions about that and so much more, Marc. I am very pleased to meet you in person at last. After all, you are famous!"

"Famous? What do you mean? I'm just a cargo pilot from Farms."

Sil said, "Yes, but a cargo pilot who has had some strange and important adventures and who is even now the nexus of activity and attention of very powerful forces throughout all of the Second Domain."

"There are new developments that I can share with you," Leenah said. "Some that involve the Domain altogether and some that are specific to you, Marc. Let's go inside and get settled in and then we can talk."

"Of course. I'm intrigued to hear what you've found . . . and I have about a million or two questions."

"Me, too." Leenah smiled, and Marc felt like the sun just came out.

"So, what's all this about me being famous?" Marc asked, once they had eaten lunch and were sitting on some very soft skin-chairs on an airy porch overlooking the patterned blooms of the garden below. "That makes me a little uncomfortable."

Leenah wore a slim and smart-looking blue casual dress. "The events at Helm, when you activated the Star Artifact in the Great

Seat," she said. "We heard rumors of what happened, but then some specifics leaked. That was an official secured closed session for the Elites and Primes only, but someone managed to take vid of it. They also smuggled it out and published it domain-wide. We don't know who specifically was behind the leak. There are many factions in the Elites, vying for position and power as always.

"Marc, millions of people have seen you engage and empower the artifact and, more to the point, seem to overpower and intimidate ZEK himself–to his Faces! In particular, there is a still image taken from another angle. Here, let me show you." She brought up the image on a large screen. It was an impressive picture and Marc let out a breathy whistle. He saw himself from slightly behind, at an angle, but with his facial profile clearly in view. The photo showed him with a bright white and blue sphere of energy surrounding his hands as the Star redirected some of it out of its various arms, shooting blue and yellow sparks in a radial spray. In the background, the Golden Screen was entirely visible with ZEK's Faces all trained sharply on the Star and Marc. All five of the Faces exhibited an un-thinkable sight: the lips of ZEK's main Face were pulled back in a wild grimace. Abject fear showed in his yellow eyes. All four of the other Faces also exhibited expressions of shock and visceral horror. This unprecedented vision of ZEK as *weak and afraid* was plainly exposed and displayed, magnified on the immense Golden Screen inside the Great Seat Hall, the central nexus of ZEK's ultimate power.

Sil leaned in toward the other two. "And it is a *middie*, Marc, who is causing him that distress," he said. "That's what is important here."

Marc closed his mouth and looked from Leenah to Sil and back. "You mean, that image has been publicized and promoted across the worlds?"

Leenah nodded. "It has taken on a life of its own. I've seen it ev-erywhere from clandestine networks to hacked vidsigns, and even crude print posters that have been pasted up like old graffiti. In one incident on Farms, they even hung a huge twenty-meter print on the side of the space elevator admin building until the Purples pulled it down."

"You look a little purple yourself, Marc," Sil said, smiling.

"You have to be joking! This is amazing–and unsettling! I . . . I don't know what to think. I don't want to be some celebrity. Do they know it's me? . . . Marc, I mean?"

Leenah grinned at him. "Oh yes, indeed! You are 'Marc of the Star,' the cargo pilot who blasted ZEK out of his Faces! It's like I said, you're famous!" Both she and Sil laughed, and then Marc wagged his head and gave them a wan smile.

Sil said, "So, some of the *many* rumors that are going around are that you were killed by ZEK and his cronies for trying to assassinate him, or that you escaped to Rindd 1 and are being held in secret by the Rindders until they can help you make a military move against the Primes and ZEK, *or* that you are a completely insane wilder who tried and failed to kill ZEK and are now on the run to parts unknown.

"That last one is being circulated by some of the Harbor folk, of course, because too many people know that you were taken away alive. ZEK's office states only that, although startling, nothing of any consequence happened with the artifact and that you are being held for further evaluation."

"Yeah, they tried to evaluate me, all right."

Sil looked serious. "It is our great fortune that you were able to prevent them."

Marc said, "With your help, Sil. Only with your help. I couldn't have done that without your teaching, coaching, and support. Without your Song."

Marc was bursting to talk with Leenah, but Sil asked if they would like to see his garden, so all three went down the stone steps of the back portico and into the most beautiful flower display Marc had ever seen. Reds, yellows, purples, whites–flowers everywhere in coordinated clusters and rows that seemed to flow naturally from one rise or curve to another, while still exhibiting a pleasing design when viewed from above. It was simply amazing. The strong, sweet fragrances filled the air, and after a few minutes of showing them the main flower aisle, Sil said, "I have a few things I need to do in my offices, and I imagine you two have a great deal to talk about. I'll leave you here for now, if that's all right?"

Marc and Leenah both nodded and Leenah said, "Thank you, Sil. We'll catch up to you at dinner time."

"This garden seems like an impossible fantasy. I've never seen anything like it," Marc said once Sil had left.

"I know. This Institute is so special, but it is not unique by any means. I think of the Sisters, and Florinda in particular, as an oasis of human potential compared to Harbor's worlds. There is so much you have not seen yet, Marc."

"It can't be perfect, though. Leenah, there has to be strife and conflict and all the ills of people everywhere else?"

"No, it's not some utopia. There are problems, of course, but the culture is different from anything you've experienced. It's more co-operative and, well, *fair* I guess is the word. We have councils that have rotating memberships to run most of the everyday affairs and specialty groups to keep the peace and order when needed, but crime is extremely rare here and usually is caused by passions or illness. Some places in our systems are somewhat less 'wealthy' in terms of goods and infrastructure than others, but no one is truly hurting."

Marc shook his head. "How do you maintain that? Surely, it isn't as simple and miraculous as it looks."

"There are issues from time to time, but keep in mind that we have a smaller overall population here and many resources available to us coming from the many systems behind Frahma as well as the wonders of this amazing system itself. Every person is educated to the best level of their ability. That's extremely important. It's always been Sil's top priority. We are blessed here, Marc. Our natural wealth, well that *is* something of a miracle, I'd say."

"Well, it's a wonder to this Harbor boy, for sure. Let's sit over here for a bit. I want to hear your story and you would likely want to hear some of mine, yes?"

She smiled and they walked over to a curved wooden bench under a cascade of purple and white blossoms. A metal label said "Wisteria (Earth)".

Leenah told Marc enough about her work with the Gossamer people to orient him and then shared the details of the vision she experienced after taking the Kaaanlooo plant.

"After it was finished, Tonhaaa, the 'Doctor' as I knew him, told me that you and I would meet and that I must help you find the other path."

"What do you think he meant?"

Leenah stared at the flower petals on the ground at their feet. "I think he was talking about the other timeline, the other way that things could go instead of the devastation of war and the alien machine. The xenoplague again." She looked up at Marc and he saw both fear and determination on her face.

He said, "There may be war. I don't see how it can be avoided at this juncture, but we may be able to prevail over our enemies, you know. We might even be able to control that so-called plague ship if I can just get back to it."

"So-called? You believe it's something else?"

"Yes, I do. Leenah, I felt it as though I was a part of it." Marc described his own vision and how the Star acted as an energy link and a conduit to connect him to the ship. "It seemed like I merged into an intelligence that I could 'read' as benign. Ash Aliens? AI? I don't know. It did not mean harm to us. It resonated with all the life force and the singing of the plants that I saw in the vision space. It was as far away from a doomsday weapon as I could ever imagine. No one that I have told this to has had the slightest understanding of what I am telling you."

Leenah took his hand and said, "I believe it. I have been in that dimension, too, and I know what you felt. This is important, Marc. Part of the vision was a test to see which path I would take. There seem to be two ways we can go, a bright path like I took and as you naturally took, too, and then a dark path. I don't quite understand that, but I assume from what I've learned that it's based on *power*. Some of the early humans on Gossamer succumbed to that power and became evil, wild, and totally dangerous. There are still some like that on Gossamer today. I think I may have encountered one within the vision space, but I got away."

"One only wonders what ZEK or the Harbor Elites would do with that kind of power, eh?" Marc said.

"Exactly," she said. "This is more than a physical battle situation we are facing now. There are greater dangers and many unknowns in dealing with the SD, the spirit dimension, in conjunction with our everyday TD or tangible one."

Marc stared out at the green hedge across the pathway.

"I wonder if that spirit dimension has not been a part of us all along. I've had strange experiences all my life with this hand morph thing and even with voices and the feeling of the presence of others. I used to go out on the salt plains of Salina and into the low hills there sometimes, just for solitude and to think. Many times, as I was completely quiet out there, I would hear faint voices in my mind and feel my hands begin to change. It was very frightening at the time because I didn't know what it was about and Father had always warned me about such things.

"Now, I wonder if this is all a natural part of us, maybe a step in our evolution, as Sil once speculated."

Leenah said, "You should have seen the Gossamers! If you could watch them change their bodies and slip between the dimensions as I did . . . well, they can change their entire bodies enough to enter their stone temples even though there are no doors. I think Sil is right, but we are truly just at the start of a long process. You, though, seem to be especially talented. That may be why events have been drawn to you, or you to them, like some SD magnet pulling on the lives and events of our own worlds. The Doctor thought so. That's why he sent me back to meet you."

Leenah's eyes were on his and she smiled. He did, too.

"Remarkable. I guess you're right, but I wish someone had asked me first!"

"I don't think it works that way," she said.

"Pawns of the Universe, eh? Could be. Could be, indeed."

"We've been tracking some of the activities around Farms and in Prospect and Hub since you three made your astounding arrival. Gotta ask you about those Zips later, too! . . . but we have some intel on Anibale and his next moves. Sil will fill us all in on it shortly, but be prepared. It is going to shake everything up here and maybe everywhere. The storm is coming, Marc, and frankly, I'm afraid. Even with the help I've received and have been promised from the Gossamers and from you and the other middie groups. Nothing is assured here. We're going to need your help in all of this."

Marc paused to think about what he wanted to say next.

"Leenah, Anibale has taken everything from me that I ever had in life. My family, wealth, my ship and friends, and my freedom, but I've faced him many times now, and ZEK, too." He gazed up at the flowering vines where stars were peeking through, then he turned back to her.

"Look at this place! Sil, the Institute, your culture here, this beautiful world, and you–you, Leenah. You are all worth defending and sustaining, regardless of the risk. I just gained all this and now I feel that this is what I have to lose. Protect it? Of course. I will to the best of my ability, but I'm no military guy, Leenah. I'm just a cargo pilot like any other. I can fly and I can shoot, but to have a real chance to truly help everyone, I have to get back to that ship I found and see if I can activate it, maybe bond with it, and bring it to bear as a tool in our fight.

"There is everything to gain for all of us, middie and Elite, Sisters and Rindders alike. All of you want me to follow up on my newborn fame and be a leader. I'll play that role with your help and the help of Sil and all the others. I'm not looking for glory. You understand that? I'm practical and I just want this to be over and done to our advantage."

Leenah said, "I do understand it. That's what makes you the very face of leadership we all need, Marc. You aren't trying to be another Anibale or ZEK."

He swallowed hard and a half-smile came across his face.

"Let's just get this thing done, then," he said. "I'll do what I have to and I will live. It's clear to me that there must be an authentic middie uprising now to change the worlds for everyone. Anibale won't be deterred in his aggressions and ZEK won't just willingly step aside."

Marc gazed around the dark garden, pungent now with soft fragrances.

"And this place, this culture, this expression of humanity . . . *this must and will be protected*."

She beamed at him. "Now, that sounds like Marc of the Star, the most famous guy in the universe!"

Chapter Twenty-seven

Marc, Sil, and Leenah sat lightly on padded sofas in one of the private studies just off the main library. The .82 of Standard g here on Florinda felt great, especially after the time on Barrkon's, but Marc thought if he stayed here long, he'd eat too much, unconsciously trying to gain his Standard weight back.

Dark wood frames lining the study wall contained shelves of books and intricate paintings. One display had some primitive-looking items–tribal art from Gossamer, perhaps?–that Marc wanted to ask Sil about later. They were unlike anything he'd ever seen.

The door to their study opened and Paris came in, looking better these days in a comfortable outfit, but she still wore her gun on an intimidating black belt.

"Hey, Sweet Pea!" Marc called out.

"Gods, I hate that name. *Come on! . . .*" She pursed her lips, but he noticed she was trying to hide a smile. The other two were grinning broadly.

Sil said, "Please come join us, dear. Marc is trying to deal with the fact that he is worlds famous and probably the most important fugitive in history. How would you like to be his bodyguard?"

"Say what, Sil? His bodyguard? Who's trying to kill him now?"

"Everyone who isn't here, I think," Leenah said.

"Seriously, he is in danger and will be especially so when events proceed as expected very soon now," Sil said. "We can't keep Marc here in the Sisters indefinitely. He's going to become involved again in these new actions. I can't effectively protect him and neither can Leenah. He's a strong man with extraordinary abilities, but he will need a skilled and dedicated companion to protect him when things get tricky. We all think you would be the logical choice–if you'd be interested."

Paris sat on one of the benches and looked down. "Well, I was kind of thinking that I might find a place to settle in here on Florinda, Sil. I've never seen a place like this. Never dreamed it could exist. I don't need much and I don't mind working hard to earn my place. Don't mind that at all."

Sil nodded. "And we'd love to have you here, my dear, but there are things in motion right now that may very well affect this world and all the worlds. None of us can relax and settle until this works its way through. We will welcome you here if this is where you want to be, but I ask you to consider working with us for a while now in this crucial capacity."

Leenah said, "It is a dangerous role we ask you to play, Paris, but it's also one that may place you right in the center of history. By protecting Marc, you would be helping him and us bring about a major shift in the way things are. Plus," she smiled, "you'd be the personal bodyguard of 'Marc of the Star'–the most famous man of the millennium!"

Marc choked on his tea. "Now, don't believe all that, Paris," he said. "I think it's a great idea, and I would love to have your help if you're willing."

Paris looked up at him. "You mean that? You'd really trust me to protect you after all I've done?"

Marc paused and tilted his head. He said, "You know, Sil claims he's a pretty good judge of character, and I believe him. I happen to be a pretty good judge of it myself. I've seen you go through these experiences and change as you learned how things are. I *will* trust you because not only are you a very skilled and dedicated officer, but I think you've learned what you needed to." He held his gaze. "Does that sound like a correct assessment?"

"Yes. I did some foolish things on Barrkon's, but I just didn't know. Just a city girl who never got to see much of the worlds or learn much beyond police work and military. My eyes are wide open now and I'm learning so much every day here in the Sisters. What a library and staff you have here, Sil!"

He smiled at that and said, "Well, then. What do you say?"

"I'll do it, of course. I would be honored to earn your trust in me." She lifted herself up straight as the others beamed at her. "You said there were some events coming. What kind of events?"

"Ahh, that is the next thing we must discuss with the Senior Staff, and now that you are on board, so to speak, you may please join us in the meeting hall in the north wing in one hour."

Marc sipped down the last of his tea and they all went out of the study together as the day's last light from Frahma flowed in tones of gold and peach through the true-glass windows, casting rhombic reflections and patterns on the wood of the walls.

"Everyone uses the AA energy beams for ship's weapons because they seem to have been the Ash Alien's favorite tools, plus they are easy to come by on the old artifact ship remains, but I believe Harbor has become so dependent on them and have been so unchallenged for so long that they forget there are other ways to damage a ship."

As Sil spoke to the group of his closest military and civilian advisors in the wood-paneled room, Marc sat with Leenah and Paris at one of the tables up front. Sil pulled up an image on everyone's comm and also on a larger screen in the wall.

"Anibale and his band will come into the Sisters and threaten us with their energy beams. He'll surely demand the surrender of Florinda and all our ships, both commercial and military. I hope that he will so underestimate us that he doesn't expect any military at all. We'll see.

"What *he* shall discover is that we are well-prepared for him. We have our sentinel ships at our Gate mouth to Farms, of course, just as we do on the Farms side. These are fitted with nominal energy weapons at all times, but they have been upgraded, quite stealthily, over the last few decades. They are now full-on war-class beams equivalent to anything in ZEK's BlackMil armada.

One of the advisors said, "That's great, Sil, but that won't be enough to repel hundreds of their ships. I assume we have some more surprises for them?"

"Not sure how many ships he'll be able to bring, Julyan, but yes, indeed. Some surprises you all need to learn about so we can coordinate this defense action." Sil smiled at one of the military men and said, "We have slingshots!"

After a second, Marc said, "You're going to hit 'em with inerts?"

"Yes. Sometimes the simplest tools and techniques are the best, plus they are usually cheaper. We have ten small, very lava-black, planetoids that have been placed into an orbit that brings them sequentially into range of the Farms Gate. They have been altered to hold millions of equally dark rocks–projectiles, each a few meters wide. On the surface of each moonlet, there is a rail-gun mech that will act as a true kinetic gun and lob these rocks in clusters at any enemy coming through that zone. They will only fire out-system and with enough velocity to escape the system, so the projectiles will not threaten us here at home. Many, if not most, will not hit a target and will continue to fly, becoming astronomical objects. When they *do* intersect their intended Harborite target, they will be as devastating to the ship they hit as any energy weapon. They also have the advantage of being difficult to detect as the matte black of the material provides a very low albedo. Not impossible, of course, as they will carry detectible mass, but difficult. Also, hopefully, they will be unexpected.

He continued as a few heads were wagging. "Not to worry. We need to be smarter and more unpredictable than Anibale, but I know this is not enough on its own. We also, as most of you now know, have some four hundred conventional warships from our SeaRaptor class. Also, thirty-seven large system cargos have been refitted with full-strength AA energy beams along with some new stealth tech that our own engineers, with some recent and important help from Rindd, have developed. Anibale does *not* have that, giving us an advantage.

"Specifically, our team has revised the energy beam tech to be able to envelop our ships in a mirror-like shell that reflects not all but most of the energy from a weapon back out into space. Most of the residual energy that gets through, hopefully not so much as to cause damage, can be captured in a sublayer and used as a resource to charge up our own weapons. The remainder can be jettisoned. Energy is energy. It doesn't take sides."

Marc saw Doren, an advisor from Felice, raise a hand and start talking at the same time. "So, Sil, we know what Anibale is likely to do and we have these tools to hopefully turn his tail. Then what? What do we want to accomplish beyond kicking Harbor out of Sisters space? Do we close off trade with them? Blockade the Gate?"

Voices from the group blended in a soft murmur. They all seemed to be thinking the same thing.

Sil said, "That is the other reason we are here tonight. No, Doren, we are not going to be content with kicking Anibale out. We have been sending the Sisters Teachers into Harbor space, particularly to Farms, for many years now, preparing a movement toward change in Harbor. This is our opportunity to harvest that fruit.

"We do not wish to simply take their territory or resources just to take it. I'd rather we isolate ourselves from them and go about our own lives, but the middies in Harbor are finally waking up to their plight and if we can encourage and even participate in a revision–or a revolution–on their part, then we will all win greatly in the end. We will gain a much larger and more *humane* human domain that, working together, will far surpass what ZEK and the Council of Colors can offer us all in terms of productivity, fair treatment, open commerce, and quality of life.

"To that end, I have proposed that we do, in fact, *take Farms by force* and hold it against Harbor's efforts to reclaim."

The room was very quiet now as Sil continued. "This will do a couple of things. It will give us a tangible bargaining chip with ZEK–one that he cannot ignore. One that hurts them directly since the majority of their food comes from Farms. The second thing is that the majority of middies who we feel are ready to work actively against Harbor are located there and are already greatly stirred up by recent events, not the least being Marc's encounter with ZEK."

Murmurs of approval flowed toward Marc, and Leenah poked him lightly in the ribs.

Sil brought up a schematic chart of the Lines and Systems. "Once Farms is in our control, we'll need to blockade and guard not only our own Gate back to here but also the other Line Gates from Hub and Prospect. That's at least six ships at the three Gates. Once the BlackMils are routed out, of course."

Marc said, "Those warship upgrades sound good, Sil, but BlackMils are no easy pickings. How do you expect to be able to take Farms System and get them all out of there? They could take the planet hostage to you before you get them gone."

"That's where you and one other person come into the equation, Marc. You have to be the visible face of this–the emotional and inspirational leader of the middies. You already are from a distance, but now you must be the real, live thing for them. They will rally around you and do the work of driving out or capturing any BlackMils that land or try to occupy Farms."

Everyone started talking with and to one another again.

Leenah leaned over to Marc and said softly, "Sil has a surprise for you!" He raised an eyebrow to her big grin.

One of the other advisors asked Sil, "You mentioned another person?"

"Ahh, yes. Well, we have some more resources to consider. We might just have a trick or two under our hats, so to speak." Sil turned to one of the aides and motioned. The back door to the room opened and RR walked in.

———

Kera felt frustrated and tired. She sat at the room comp, absently flipping between each of the color Suite's signature screens, color after color, trying to think of a way to regain access to the Star. She almost believed she could feel it calling to her again, a faint weight, the attraction of some huge mass for which she stood just at the threshold of influence. She had to get closer. *Get to it, girl!*

She stopped on the screen with Jade's Suite Red logo emblazoned over an animated blood-red background showing slowly falling diamonds, glinting as they endlessly spun around and around. Her finger hesitated over the connect icon. Then, almost to her own surprise, she felt herself tap it.

A pale-looking woman's face appeared. "Welcome to Suite Red. How may I assist?"

Kera jerked her hand back. "Oh. . . I was . . . I was just trying to reach a woman named Valezah. I have some clothing that belongs to her."

The woman's face was unreadable. She looked down a moment then up again. "I'm checking. There is no one in our sector by that name."

"I suppose not. Well, take a message anyway. Tell her Kera called and would like to return her belongings."

The woman gave one nod and then she was gone, replaced by more diamonds, endlessly falling.

She killed the comp and stretched back in her reclining chair, trying to think. A half-hour later, just as the veils of sleepiness were about to close over her, the door chime sounded. She sat up with a jolt.

She activated the hatchway viewer and, with no real surprise, saw Valezah standing there.

"May I enter?"

After just a moment's hesitation, Kera opened the hatchway and motioned her in. "Yes, please."

Valezah had changed quite a lot. She had a visible scar on her face from the right eye socket down across her cheek. She had been shot, that was certain. Probably lucky to be alive. She was dressed in practical work clothing, better to infiltrate this sector, Kera presumed. An air of unintentional grimness had settled into her. Kera closed the door and they sat down at the little work table.

"Much has happened, Kera. To us and to you."

"Yes, but especially to you, it seems. Forgive me. I don't have access to all the information on current events."

"It's all right. No time or need to go into those details. You are having some thoughts about the future, yes? What is your intention?"

"My intention. Well. My intention is to live and to succeed. But I only have one real jewel to put down as a playing piece. My one lever to get out of this and gain something for myself."

"And that is?"

"My ability to control the Star and the ship that goes with it, of course." Valezah simply nodded.

Kera looked off toward the ceiling as she spoke, "I have been in its presence, Valezah. Just briefly and in the company of ZEK. He is very cautious. I could not be overt with it, but I could activate it enough to satisfy him. I don't like this. I don't like being under his thumb or Anibale's. I want to see the Star used for the good of all of us and for my own good, obviously." She gave Valezah a tight smile.

"I have to get back in its presence, but I thought it should be under the guidance and for the advantage of the one person who tried to help me here before I got sucked back deep into Suite Blue's grip.

That would be Jade, of course."

"A good intention, Kera. There is a problem, though. We do not know where the Star is kept, nor how to access it. ZEK surely has it tightly guarded."

"Yes, and not only ZEK, but the Council of Colors as well, but I do know where it is. It's in a special niche within the White Hall itself. I have been there."

Valezah's eyebrows went up at that, Kera noticed with some satisfaction.

That's right, queen bee, I've been places and seen things you have never dreamed of.

"That is . . . impressive. But, no one can simply walk into the White Hall."

"You can't, but *we* can if we have the right helper, and I know just who Jade can use to get us in there. She should have no problem gaining the cooperation of poor old Pas-Guin. ZEK and Anibale certainly didn't." Kera glanced up at her and smiled grimly.

From the control room of their observation craft, Marc and Leenah watched the monitors as five small Sisters ships maneuvered in a pentagonal formation. The space between them appeared to be empty. A test target ship, a derelict cargo, had been placed some distance away and positioned out-system from them.

On his way to his seat, Marc clapped RR's shoulder. "OK, RR. Let's see this thing. I still can't believe you guys are playing with Zip tech."

RR was at the monitoring center, watching the screens with help from Paris and guiding the group of pilots as they began to drift apart slightly. "Well, it's partly our engineering, too, but you are right. It does still seem weird." He looked up a moment at Marc and then over to Leenah, sitting in the pilot's seat. "Best take us back now. They will be firing the Gate weapon within one standard hour."

Leenah nodded and slowly guided their ship away from the

impending test zone.

Marc felt a combination of comfort and uncertainty with RR's arrival in the Sisters. Comfort to have this curious man around again who had helped so much and seemed to be so solidly on Marc's side of things, and yet uncertainty in what RR's and the other Rindders' deeper motives were. Plus, there was all this crazy connection to Zips and their outré tech.

"RR, you've never really explained how you Rindders were able to establish communication with the Zips."

He sat back in his flight chair as Leenah continued their retreat. She looked around and said, "Yes, RR, I'd really like to know how you managed that. My professional background is in xenobiology, and I've been dying to ask you about the Zips."

RR paused a moment as a soft smile played on his lips. "Well, a part of it was our doing, but it was mostly them. I guess you could say we were prepared enough to be lucky. One of our Suite Gray units was doing some preliminary tests on our FTL reconstruction and I suppose that's what caught the Zips' attention. They are very curious folk–that is to say, they are very curious about *everything*. Some of their ships appeared and made a colorful three-dimensional light display between them that we realized was a type of communication attempt toward us. It took a huge amount of processing and analysis, but over time, we managed to gain a very tentative understanding of their language system which consists of light and color matrixes mostly in the form of cubes with smaller extension cubes attached in various positions. It took them a while to understand that we use sound waves as our primary language medium. Seems that is profoundly primitive and unnatural to them, so they more easily connected to our visual imagery. Visuals for us, other than written language symbols, don't communicate much languaging detail. Once we could combine vid with our written words–quite another strange concept to the Zips–we began to establish some commonalities that bridged our differing systems."

Marc said, "So, you can talk with them now?"

"Not really–not flowing language yet, although it's getting closer. We can generally make them understand what we are doing and what we are requesting. Whether they truly understand those things the way we intend them is another matter. Many miscommunications have occurred, but we've reached a point now where they seem to get most things basically right.

"As you may have noticed on your jump here to Sisters, they have abilities that are beyond our current understanding. They don't seem to be able to explain them to us and this makes them think we are quite primitive, which I suppose we are. A typical exchange might be us asking how they cause their temporary Gates to open for them. They will say something that translates as "We use the Blue Tone." When we ask them to explain that term, they just repeat it as if we should know, like saying 'We use the wheel'. When we don't seem to get it, they laugh at us."

Leenah said, "They laugh at us? How do you know that?"

"Well, it wasn't clear at first, but their color matrix would go crazy for a while with all sorts of random color flashes all over the grids. It seems that the Zips are a merry bunch. The sense I get is that they probably otherwise wouldn't have bothered interacting with us humans, but they find us, well, amusing."

"Great," Marc said. "We're the play toys of a bunch of crazy Zips."

Paris, sitting next to Marc, snorted.

"Something like that, yes. But, I believe our relationship is stable enough for them to become our helpers in this military action. Once they understood what we were doing vis-a-vis the Harbor humans, they became completely fascinated and asked many questions. They can't conceive of same-species conflict and want to see how it goes. It would be something like one of us watching a single human to see his left arm do battle with his right leg.

"I requested some technical assistance in the form of these weapons, and they said, essentially, 'sure thing!'–and so, here we are."

"We're in our safe position now, RR."

"Thank you, Leenah. The five Sisters ships should be activating the temporary Gate shortly. Let's make dead certain they are aimed properly, yes? It could be a real problem if they are not."

Sil's voice came into their ear comms, "Yes, indeed, if you please. I'd rather not get a bad sunburn today."

Marc checked his visual comm, where Sil's image floated. He was monitoring the test from Florinda through a Zip micro-Gate relay for digital signals, arranged so he and the other Sisters elders could watch in real-time even at this considerable distance from the inner system. Another screen showed an onboard view from the target ship. Marc noticed that someone had attached a Harbor banner with ZEK's golden Faces onto its superstructure.

"Gate is in position and we're ready to power up, RR," one of the pilots said.

"Let's go, then. When you are ready there."

As they all watched the space between the pentagon of Sisters ships, Marc saw nothing at all for a minute, but then a toroid of deepest blue appeared, off the scale into the ultraviolet and rapidly sweeping into visible range. It was a thin donut shape made of light, larger than a ship, but far smaller than any regular Line Gate. As the color followed the spectrum through green and yellow, they could discern a dual rotation in its toroid form. It was altogether rotating slowly clockwise centered on its empty midpoint, and then the lighted tubular part of the toroid was also rotating extremely rapidly on its own internal circular axis, like a smoke ring made of light–a mad roller preparing to expel something from the black space within this newly opened Gate and into their own space, here above the Frahma system.

Suddenly, all the monitors dipped with auto-correction for extreme brightness. A column of blinding white with coruscated dark streaks was instantly *there*, screaming out of the new Gate like a monstrous torch–a perfect column of destructive force. It only lasted a fraction of a second and then it was gone, leaving afterimages in Marc's eyes. The vid feed from the target ship went dead. The ship had vanished.

The bridge was silent for a moment, then murmurs and a few cheers broke out. Paris croaked, "Golden Faces . . ."

Marc let out a soft whistle. "That was, . . . well . . .that was successful, I'd say, RR!"

Sil's voice hummed, "The telemetry confirms. The target has been vaporized. Wonderful cannon, RR, and damned scary, too."

RR looked relieved and pleased. He said, "Somewhere, in some other universe, a star has just lost a tiny bit of its guts."

Leenah asked, "That's the way this thing works, then? They can tap a Line into the heart of some random star in another galaxy and squirt it out here like a garden hose?"

RR said, "Well, yes. That's about right. They can even redistribute the kinetic reaction back through the same Line so the parts of the Gate mouth composed of actual matter here don't go flying off in the opposite direction or disturb our pentagon of control ships." He leaned over his portable Rindder comm and said something to the Rindd engineer back on Florinda.

"Just got a transmission from the Zips. Torry says their matrixes all went nuts–laughing, I presume. One-word translation after that: *Gone.*"

Marc leaned in close to RR. "That thing is probably too cumbersome to set up for ship-to-ship fights. Looks a hell of a lot like the xenoplague flare from the old Earth vids, too, eh?"

RR said, "You're right about the practicalities, but it may be useful as an intimidation weapon if not otherwise. I know what you are thinking, but that flare is no vector for molecular xenoplague virus, Marc. It's pure star fission–just a really big beam weapon with an admittedly crude aiming mech."

"We're still tracking the flare," Sil's voice came from the comm. "It's heading out-system in a hurry and will be beyond our farthest beacons in about twenty hours. I wonder what some alien astronomer will make of it some day a few million million years from now?"

Leenah said, "I just hope they know how to get out of its way."

Chapter Twenty-eight

Marc's warship was shaped like what he presumed was an aggressive Frahman deltoid sea creature with flat wing structures that rolled up on their outer edges. It had been painted mostly magenta with a large tooth-filled mouth and three blue-spotted eyes, each with a thin vertical streak of black giving it an intense look. The enemy would likely never actually see it in any detail, but that imagery might get transmitted to both foes and friends and Marc had to agree that somehow the artwork made him feel better about flying the sleek ship into trouble.

RR had provided some intelligence via the Zips that an abnormally large ship force was gathering in the far nadir reaches of the Farms System where the normal comm bots, cargo traffic, and military patrols don't usually go. Marc agreed with Sil and the others that Anibale was setting up his raid, but he couldn't quite believe that the Suite Blue Prime was so out of touch with reality that he would fail to anticipate their defenses at all.

Worse for him and better for us. Still . . .

He linked through on a secure channel to Leenah's ship, on the other side of their formation near the Gate to Farms. When her head bobbed up on screen from whatever task she'd been doing, she smiled at him.

"Ready there, Leenah?"

"We are set here. The rocks are loaded into Black Ball One and the beam and shield units are charged. He's really coming through, isn't he?"

"Yeah, it seems certain now. Just stay focused. I've seen how good a pilot you are. Which reminds me, how did a xenobiologist become such a capable ship pilot, eh?"

Leenah tilted her head over and said, "Well, I always had an interest in going to exotic places and it seemed logical to be able to fly myself when I needed to go–so I learned. Sil was helpful. He encouraged me to learn it well."

"Aha! He was grooming you for the air force!" Marc said. Leenah laughed.

"Well, he *can* be sneaky that way, but I'm just glad I can be here." Her face became serious.

Just then, an alert tone and light flashed on Marc's board. A sand grain-sized passive spybot had emerged from the Farms Gate, squirting its data in an instant to their comps before shutting off to become just another orbiting pebble in the Frahma System. Marc looked up at Leenah's image and their eyes locked for a moment. Then he hit the comm control.

"Stand by, everyone," Marc called out on all-hail. "Arm all systems and ordinance and keep off the comms now. This could be the big one."

On ship hail, he said, "Paris, take us dark now, then recheck the arms."

The Sister's warships were clustered in several groups behind-orbit from the Gate, which not-quite-object was itself orbiting around Frahma star. Gate-exiting ships normally emerged on a vector in line with that orbit, taking advantage of the velocity and direction of the

Gate. It was so second nature in Gate and Line piloting that Sil and the others predicted Anibale would do so without thinking. With all his Sisters ships now dark and trailing the Gate, Marc hoped that was true. Surprise is always best the first time. Not so good later on.

Marc's ship was one of fifty-four of the SeaRaptors positioned closest to the Gate, behind Black Ball One–a small lava-black asteroid that had been carved out and filled with inert kinetic ammunition: basically, big round rocks. Rail gun launchers and an automated feeding system had been installed so that the Ball was an orbiting robotic weapon system. It was big enough that the group's ships could coast behind its shadow in a more hidden and protected zone until needed.

Several dozen more of Sil's warships were in orbits around Florinda and the other main Sisters planets to protect the homeworlds and to help make the entire system appear as being with normal traffic. He ordered them lit up and with open comms to attract the enemy's attention. Some robotic decoy cargoes and other standard in-system ships had been placed in typical orbits as well, but no non-military ships were allowed near the Gate itself. They did not exactly expect Anibale to send normal pre-exit warning beacons. Anyone down-or-bit of the Gate could be run over.

Kind of like he did to me that first time on the other end of this Line. Crazy bastard.

For now, though, all they could do was watch the Gate and nervously wait.

When Anibale's ships emerged, they came through in a heedless dash. Marc heard Paris suck in her breath. "Twenty-three ships. Faces, Marc! They must be doing quad norm Gate speed."

"It won't take him long to establish demands." The moment he said that, the comms lit up. ". . . and, there he is."

Anibale's sigil appeared, quickly replaced with his stern face. He was dressed in his military fines of black carapace armor lined with blue cord and overlain with his shiny blue silk short-cape. His black eyes shot out from a silver filagreed battle helmet giving a look like a beam weapon as his voice boomed on all system-override channels.

"Florinda and Sisters System! I am Prime Blue acting on behalf of Harbor, Helm, and Humanity. You are holding and harboring a most dangerous escapee. I demand that you present and deliver the middie Marc 54Arons to my ship. Immediate and serious consequences will follow anything less than your *instant* cooperation."

Nothing happened for a moment as Anibale glared. Finally, he bellowed out again, "Florinda! Respond to Anibale, Prime Blue of Harbor! NOW."

A flicker on the response channel caused Anibale's eyes to twitch. The image cleared to show Sil sitting at a desk with a view of a greensward and trees behind him through a window. Sil looked very calm, Marc thought. Almost as if he were surprised to see Anibale's transmission. Sil cocked his head slightly and gave Anibale a quite pleasant look.

"Prime Blue. Your arrival is most surprising. I am Silveen, SisterSon of Frahma. I believe we have treaties with Harbor about mutual system infiltration. You surely know the rules."

"I have no time to bandy your rules. This is an emergency situation. You will hand the man, Marc, over to me now."

"The person you speak of is under our protection and service, having come to Frahma of his own will. You have no rights here, Anibale, Prime Blue. You are in extreme danger and you may cause a situation to occur that has not happened in many centuries. I strongly suggest that you turn your flotilla of ships back to the Gate and withdraw immediately from Sisters space."

Anibale sneered into the comm. "The man you have befriended and are protecting is a danger to all of humanity, fool Silveen. You keep him at your own peril and that of the rest of Harbor and Rindd. Or, perhaps, you are assisting him in his attempts to resurrect a xenoplague ship–that is what I said: a *xenoplague ship* that will destroy your worlds as well as our own!"

Sil remained calm but Marc thought he now looked like he was studying some unseemly insect through a magnifying glass. "Anibale.

Go home. No one will bring plague down upon us. You are here as Prime Blue. I do not see Prime Red, or Yellow, or any other color. You are acting alone. ZEK will strip you of your position and powers if you proceed. I say again, go home. You are in grave danger. I give you this warning."

Anibale had a different look on his face, a look of suspicion. He said, "You are the man who was with him on Barrkon's Oven. I remember your face from the vid feeds." Sil remained silent. "You are as crazy and dangerous as Marc is! This *entire system* is crazy and dangerous! Your adventurism will bring death down on everyone!

"Let it be known that the Sisters Systems, controlled here by Florinda and the people represented by this Silveen are renegade to Humanity and must be controlled for the sake of Humanity. I will take that control, Frahman! You have all languished here behind Farms for too long, spouting poems and grass. You should have been brought under ZEK's Face long ago.

Still, Sil said nothing and did not react. Marc whispered to Paris, "He knew Anibale would rationalize an attack any way he could."

Paris said, "Yeah. Let old Blue hang himself."

Anibale was visibly frustrated now. "There is an army above your heads, Silveen. You will submit to Prime Blue's immediate authority, the subjection of Florinda, and the commandeering of all vessels and industrial resources."

Sil stared calmly at him for a long while. An uncomfortably long while, Marc thought. Finally, he spoke one quiet word, "No."

The comms from Florinda went black.

Anibale's face turned bright red before he, too, disappeared off the screens.

"They're accelerating, Marc," Paris said.

"Yeah, I see it. He's heading for the trade Station." It was a logical first move, since the Station was kept out at Gate orbit, but in a fairly close trailing position. Sil had tried to empty the place, but there were still quite a few essential personnel on board. It seemed like yesterday that Marc had been right here, undocking from it with a load of intriguing and valuable Sisters merchandise, including a few crates of pimfruit. Now, the Station stared up the line at the approaching phalanx of Anibale's BlueMil ships.

Five Sisters warships had undocked from the trade Station and were turning now to face the threat while dozens of personnel escape pods popped off the back side of the Station wheel, each one firing its engines to drop orbit into the lower system.

An energy beam flashed from the lead BlueMil and a puff of debris scattered from the Station as a huge gap was ripped open.

———

Anibale watched the docking arm of the trade Station explode. Captain Bulo, at the helm, said, "Serves them right to keep this artificial border station out here. Damned isolationists!"

Anibale glanced at the man. "Keep your focus. Deflectors full. We're heading into their return fire."

The Florindan ships all fired at them, then immediately spread apart and dropped orbit.

Crazy Sisters ships. An older generation hybrid technology there. They are few, scattered, weak, and unprepared for us.

One of his BlueMil took a hit and fell back in the phalanx, hurt but not disabled. Anibale pressed for the kill here. "Beams?"

"Charged, Prime!" his weapons chief called over comm.

"Attack now," Anibale said, straining against his belts to instinctually sit on the edge of his chair.

The energy weapons cracked and the flash of light at the target caused the screens to dim. The trade Station was debris and dust. When they reached the spot, his ship shuddered with the impact of the pieces as the deflectors did their job.

Anibale got back on the system-wide comm and repeated his demands, but he received no further answer from Sil or anyone in Frahma System. Instead, an alarm sounded.

"Incoming! Prime, there are incoming masses behind us,

emerging from an asteroid trailing the Gate.

"How far . . . ?"

"Here, now, Sir." The young bridge tech looked up at him with a face of blank fear as a crash rang through the ship and the entire bridge shook them like a diredog with a mouthful of fish.

"Status!" Anibale yelled.

"Clipped us, Sir. Far edge of dorsal booms. We're functional so far."

Another voice said, "Those are inert kinetics! They're throwing rocks at us!"

"Might as well be nukes at this speed," Anibale said. "There will be another round. Lock on them this time and shoot them into dust. Report fleet damage!"

The reports came, but Anibale could see for himself that the rocks had done his fleet in. A chill went up his spine as he realized how specifically lucky his own ship had been. Sixteen of the BlueMil warships were either shards and grit clouds or were damaged so badly that they were tumbling wreckage. Hundreds of his officers and crew were certainly dead. Five other ships were seemingly intact, and the remaining ship was damaged but under power. That was Agar's ship, and he was dropping orbit toward Florinda.

Kresser looked up from the screen. "He's not responding, Prime."

Anibale watched as the ship receded in-system.

"Incoming!"

The second round of inert kinetics came in a more concentrated cluster, aimed at the larger group of four BlueMils trailing Anibale's ship. They fired at the rocks, eliminating most of them before they impacted, but then a halo of Sisters warships emerged from behind that small asteroid: the obvious source of the rock missiles. These vessels were different from other Sisters ships Anibale had seen.

"What is this?" he hissed.

"They're larger and coming fast, Sir! . . . Sir, there are several hundreds of them!"

"Deflect . . ." Anibale's command was cut short by the simultaneous burst of energy weapons from his own ships and the roar of the deflectors trying to repel the fire from the oncoming ships.

Another jolt rang through the ship as it took on a sudden spin. "We're hit. Only one engine functioning, Sir."

"Get us gone, Mister. Get us back through that Gate!"

"What about the others?"

"I will avenge them, but we must survive the day, Bulo. Do as I say and get us back through. We've lost this effort. Go NOW!"

As they altered delta-v and dropped orbit to realign with the Gate, several of the Sisters warships peeled off their formation to follow him.

I am still faster than your ridiculous boats. You can't keep up.

Indeed, his ship did outrun them, and as they approached the Gate zone, a systems-comm screen lit up with a familiar face. The grim visage belonged to the middie, Marc.

Anibale yelled, "YOU, you traitorous vermin! I should have known you'd be the instigator of this violence!"

Marc said sternly, "Anibale, Prime Blue. You have invaded and attacked the Sisters System with malice and criminal intent. You and your Mils have murdered thousands of innocent Sister's citizens. We will not allow you to prevail. We are all middies in the Sisters; there are no Elite here except for you and your combatants. There is no xenoplague here. We do not fear it. It is *you* who, without provocation, have attacked your fellow men, women, and children.

"Whether or not you answer to ZEK's Face for your unimaginable crimes, you *will* answer to us, middies one and all." Marc paused and raised his hand which glowed a dull, dangerous-looking red and seemed enlarged. "And, you will personally answer to me."

Marc was still staring at the blank screen. "I shouldn't have said that . . . showed my hand that way."

Paris said, "Why the hell not? Like you said, he's a criminal. Glad you said it." She was not looking up at Marc, but studying the data streams from all the in-system bots and cams. "That last ship of theirs is still heading toward Florinda, Marc. It's damaged, but he's under some power. Changing vector now and . . . he's making for a *target* on the planet!"

Marc called up the graphic plot, twirling the dimensional image so he could see the projected path. Sure enough, it intersected Florinda. He hit the link to the Institute, but Sil was already on screen.

"Sil! The Mil is headed your way–on purpose."

"Yes, we see him," Sil said. "An object his size could do grave damage at speed. I've already put RR on alert to try to eliminate him."

Paris looked back at Marc. "They're going to use that awful Gate weapon?"

"Might be the only way to protect Florinda. I just hope their aim and timing are good. Well, we can't help RR from here, so let's go see if we can rescue any of those poor Station folks who bailed out."

Three hours later, Marc and his other ship's captains, including Leenah, had rescued seventeen pods. Several more of the emergency vehicles had made it to lower orbits and would be intercepted by system craft or find emergency dock stations until they could be fetched. He sent his dock crew to secure one of the pods in their own tiny cargo hold and set up robotic nav on the other now empty pods to follow along with them in a train. The rescuees were all safely in the medlabs or the ship's mess.

The trade Station was history and the loss of the lives of those who had still been on board it weighed heavily on Marc's mind as they made the rounds. The other crew on his ship didn't disturb him except for business, but they kept looking over at him. All eyes and thoughts were otherwise on the BlueMil ship still plunging in its death drop to Florinda.

Paris was back at her screens after helping out below decks. She said, "It's almost time. We're getting a closer, hi-rez feed now. I'll put it up for everyone."

Once it was posted, the screens showed a clear view of the inbound ship from the point of view of one of the Gate weapon control ships. Paris made a little sound, waved to get Marc's attention, and pointed to the comm secondaries. A scratchy image came up, showing a very bedraggled and sweating bridge captain, obviously on board the plummeting ship. The auto-ident labeled him as Blue Senior Agar. Alarms flashed wildly and half of the equipment behind him was broken and smoking. He did not speak, but simply stared at them with haunted eyes for a moment until the feed broke up.

The pentagon of guide and control ships were in position and Marc heard RR's voice giving the command to fire. Once more, he had to wince from the instant brightness of the stellar material being ejected into the local space. The planet below glinted sharply in a momentary spectral highlight as the weapon belched its destruction at the in-falling ship. RR had only allowed a quarter-second blast, this close to the planet. After the flash, the scans showed only space where a fast-moving ship had just been.

Leenah's voice came over comms. "They got it! Wait . . . wait– there's a large piece of debris that must have ejected before the Gate beam hit."

Sil's voice came over the comm. "We're tracking it. It might be an AA engine pod or beam weapon that snapped off that ship, but it's coming in too fast and straight to get to it. Plot that, Sannie!" He turned away from the camera to watch the graphs. Marc had never seen him look so harried. "It's going to be a direct hit on Daroun. He must have aimed it that way. That's a hundred fifty thousand people. Impact in eight minutes." Sil's voice faded as he raced away from the comm, still relaying data and giving instructions. All Marc and his crew could do was watch and stay ready to help, should there be any way to do so.

The impact of the debris bomb was inevitable, a morbidly fascinating thing to witness. Marc felt totally helpless. Maddening. The blast was almost perfectly centered in the city of Daroun. Lives lost?

Too damn many. They didn't have any real warning. He slowly stood up from the chair he'd been wedged in for–how long? He didn't know and didn't care. His hips hurt and his legs cracked from being tensed and cramped for so long. He felt like an old man.

Chapter Twenty-nine

Leenah finally had time to return to the Institute following a week and a half of working with the recovery teams at Daroun. She was certainly tired, but she couldn't let that affect her. Over eight thousand died outright and many more were severely injured. It was so heartbreaking! So many families destroyed; so many survivors whose lives will never be the same.

Sil had called her back, though, to attend a meeting with Marc, RR, and the others. She had a fairly good idea what Sil was thinking and the prospect of it filled her with apprehension. In the meantime, she had some other work to do. Sil had asked her to continue their ongoing communications efforts toward the general middie population in Harbor Systems, primarily to Farms. Known internally as the MidSupport Program, it was how they coordinated the dispersion of Sisters Teachers into those systems and spread unbiased information from and about Sisters culture into what was otherwise a very controlled media environment in Harbor.

The Elites would certainly call it propaganda. She smiled to herself. I'm just a voice of the truth.

The first order of business was to package up that incredible vid of Marc addressing Anibale. It was so powerful! A piece perfectly suited to distribute into Farms System. Marc already held an almost mythical reputation as an opponent of ZEK and the Elites, a man who had actually shown some semblance of power over them. Leenah knew he would be naturally perceived as the leader of any organized resistance. This new recording would serve to solidify that role in a very powerful manner. Showing him alive and still giving the Elite hell, he would become much more real to them. As for Marc, now– she was certain *he* would take more convincing to truly own that role in his own mind, even though he really did have that kind of power.

It's hard to make a kind soul like Marc angry, she thought, but I sure wouldn't want to be the one who does.

Sil called her in the next day for the planning session.

"Thanks for coming on back, Leenah. I know it was hard to leave the rescue work. We all have to put our sorrows aside for a time and look to what happens next."

"I know," she said. "It is frustrating, but the cleanup and recovery efforts are well underway and in good hands out there."

"RR and Marc are here, along with the other ship captains. The Senior Advisors have all been briefed on our new plans for Farms. Now it's time to fill in the pilots and their support staff. Let's go in."

There were about thirty in the group, gathered in one of the larger meeting rooms in the Institute. Domain maps and System-specific maps were projected on large screens. A dim blue light filtered in from the outside sky through the semi-transparent dome above their heads as the men and women walked from map to map and talked with one another. Leenah found Marc and sat with him at the main table.

Everyone settled down and Sil spoke. "This is a critical tipping point, my friends. We knew this attack was coming. We prepared as best we could for it and we repelled Anibale and his troops. He will surely be punished and diminished for it, but I do not think he will be completely curtailed. What he certainly *will* do is become desperate. We must not let our guard down concerning him. We have suffered many losses. The trade Station is destroyed. Daroun is devastated. Many of you in this room have lost loved ones and friends, as have I.

"It has been our good fortune to have the help of our friends from Rindd and those formerly of Harbor itself." He nodded to Marc and RR and a soft huzzah sounded from everyone.

Sil continued, "We have marked the Gate to Harbor as closed. We sent the bots through to shout their screamer messages to anyone coming close to the other side, and there have been no traffic or message bots since Anibale fled the system. This is not a sustainable situation. My friends, we do not wish to be isolated from the other parts of humanity. That is not a good idea from any point of view. Also, with the possibility of non-Lines travel that has been so personally demonstrated to me via the Zips and RR here, I believe that such isolationism would not be physically possible to maintain indefinitely.

"We must re-engage with Harbor. The way I see it, we have a couple of choices. First, we can pretend that Anibale's actions were only those of a mad renegade, declare the considerable damages to ZEK and demand recompense for them, and then let the whole thing fade away over time."

Saul Tenns, a Friend of the Institute, spoke up. "That's how we ended the Old War. We've been in semi-isolation from Harbor and Rindd ever since. It's taken centuries to build up our own resources and our own cultural strengths, and yet, we cannot even now *freely* work within Harbor or help the middie populations to improve their lot."

"That's right, Saul," Sil said. "We've worked for more than a century now to send Teachers and information into the main middie populace–always secretly, always in danger–and doing so as the Elites have increased their control and abuses more and more."

"They're all egomaniacs!" Captain Colin lamented.

"Yes, that they are. Now, however, they are more. They are egomaniacs who have decided to go beyond the restraints that have held peace between them and the Sisters folk for hundreds of years. Anibale is a renegade, for certain, but he is not an anomaly. He is a harbinger! The first of many Elites to encroach and to impose on us and Rindd. Do I overstate this, RR?"

Leenah saw RR look slowly across the room, his vision mod unit glinting on his eye. He said, "No, not at all. The Rindd government, such as it is, is mainly betoken to ZEK and the Council of Colors on financial grounds, as you all know, but also, the Elites have already physically encroached on Rindd System.

A murmur went across the group and Leenah saw heads nodding. Many had just recently heard about Anibale's bold foray into Barrkon's Oven.

Sil said, "Exactly. This is the tipping point. This encroachment and abuse will not just go away. It will continue. That leads us to the second option."

"Stop them? You want to stop them, Sil?" Captain Lef said.

"We truly have only this choice, my friends. This is the time. We must take the new resources we have developed, the ones we have gained from our friends in Rindd–and, might I say hopefully, their Zip friends?–and, the new and remarkable resources represented by our association with the Gossamers through Leenah here. We must use the literal *and* symbolic power of Marc and the story of his journey and contesting of ZEK and the others. We must use our own technology and manufacturing works in the forms of our ships and weapons systems, and we must *bring* the changes we wish to see right into Harbor's own systems. Eventually to *all* of those systems. It is time for the Elite caste culture to change. It is ancient; it is decadent; it is abusive." Sil leaned forward.

"I propose that we begin by doing a thing that ZEK will not expect and that will shake him to his golden core. We take Farms."

Kera wore a red hood and servant's veil. She followed Valezah and Jade down the hallway leading to the Council's sector and, deeper within, the White Hall. Pas-Guin sweated under his sky-blue Suite Cyan fabric headpiece. It had a little round medallion on the back–a representation of a blue and green planet.

Oh, of course. Earth. Pretentious old fool.

He was muttering again as they walked briskly to the Council doors. "You can't just walk in there, Jade! Even with me, it's not allowed! I can't be responsible . . ."

"Now, Pas, you've shown it to others, you can show it to *me*, surely? I just need to see that it is there and being taken care of. It's not really the Council's property, now, is it?" she said.

She tried to walk as briskly as the others, but Kera noticed she had a slight limp.

"It's not yours either, Jade," he said.

"Pas, you hurt me! I'm looking out for all of us Primes. ZEK wants to keep things for himself, but that is not always for the best for all the rest of us, now is it? Someone else will be ZEK before too long, yes? Who has power right now?"

Pas-Guin gave a quick look back over his shoulder as they walked, then turned again. He did not look happy.

Kera wondered what else Jade had hanging over Pas-Guin's head to get him to do this, but she was happy to see her assumption confirmed that Jade would have *something*. After a few more tense minutes, they arrived at the same door Kera had entered before–the door into the darkened chamber of the White Hall itself.

When Valezah and Kera started to enter behind Jade, Pas-Guin bolted his arm out. "They cannot come in here! Only you, Jade! This is dangerous enough as it is!"

"They will come, Pas." She motioned to them and the two women dropped their veils. Pas-Guin jerked his head from one to the other, locking on Kera.

"YOU! What are you doing here? No, Jade! This is far too dangerous! ZEK will have us both vacuumed instantly!"

Jade's face went hard and her voice leathery, "MOVE ASIDE, Pas. She will come with me!" Jade pushed Pas-Guin back into the white chamber beyond and he stumbled as he made a croaking sound. Kera pointed to the correct wall niche and they headed toward it, Jade and Valezah each holding an arm of the still protesting Prime.

"Open it, Pas!"

"I shall not. I will not assist you further. I *can't*. The risk . . ."

Kera felt the Star. So close! She concentrated on it–pictured it behind that panel. It hummed in her mind. Then, of its own accord, the panel suddenly slid aside revealing the gray Star leaning on its tapered arms at a slight angle in the plain niche. Pas-Guin gasped. Jade and Valezah stared at it. Kera was just a few meters away from it.

Then, light blinded them as the white chandelier blazed above their heads.

ZEK and Bai rushed into the room from the Great Seat doorway, followed by a band of BlackMil guards, armed and visored, who rapidly took position. ZEK boomed, "You FOOLS!"

Bai, dressed in his long white robe with its rainbow corded belt, stopped short when he saw who was in his forbidden chamber. His face was whiter than usual.

"What is the meaning of this? How dare you enter this sacred space!"

Jade's face drained to a pasty yellow-white as Valezah stepped in front of her, hands splayed out in a warding posture toward the guns. Pas-Guin froze where he was and made mewling sounds.

In that instant of tableaux, Kera registered only a glimpse of all of it. Her mind was completely on the Star now and she reached out with all her energy and heart to it.

The Star Artifact suddenly glowed bright blue. Then green and red and yellow, then back to blue. It hummed loudly and everyone in the Hall heard it in their minds as well as their ears. It vibrated in its niche.

Kera heard ZEK's voice again, "Take her out, NOW!"

This is it. My only chance.

She lifted her head and stared at the Star, reaching out her arms in a final, desperate gesture of desire and control. The Star vibrated more violently, glowing so brightly now that it was difficult to keep looking at it. Then in an instant, it launched itself across the room and into Kera's arms, knocking her off her feet and onto the floor.

Everything in Kera's mind was locked and focused on the Star as it glowed there in her hands. It did not hurt. As she raised herself back up to her feet, she felt some tickles and scratches on her side and turned her eyes reluctantly away from the Star to see. The energy beams from the BlackMil's weapons were striking her, but there was shielding coming from the glow of the Star. It surrounded her as well as itself. Nothing would penetrate the glow, she realized. Nothing could hurt Kera when she was in the Star!

The Star was intimately connected to the great ship back on Marc's Pile and she saw it now in her mind: a multi-colored glowing craft floating so near her! It seemed so very close, she could reach out and touch it–did touch it with her mind. Then she saw it doubled and at a distance, as it lay now so far away on the black lava planetoid, and further, she saw more images of it in other places, like a mosaic of great ships reflected in glinting glass shards, cast out into unknown universes. All glowed in colored response to her.

A feeling of raw power and determination filled Kera's mind and heart and she looked back to the Star and focused inward as the buzzing and light surrounded her, blinding out ZEK's strained face, Bai's raised arm, the frozen forms of the others, and finally the very image of the White Hall of the Council of Colors.

Part Three

Xenoplague

Chapter Thirty

The lights from the White Hall of the Council of Colors were gone. In sudden, shocking silence, Kera started in alarm as she tried to see anything in front of her. Something had just happened, but she couldn't remember what it was. It was something important, though–something drastic–because she was breathing hard, sweating, and her heart was pounding like a mad drummer. Her eyes adjusted a little and she thought that this was a very odd place to be. There was the faintest haze of tawny light where she stood. Trees huddled in the edges of the darkness beyond. The air seemed heavy and hot.

What is this place? Where am I?

She looked down at the ground. It seemed like grass, but it undulated and waved around her feet like the patterns of water in a boil. She looked up again when a slight movement caught her eye. A creature stood there. It was much taller than herself: a lobed body with a rough texture looming in the dark. It was black and gray. With a rush of air, it unfolded a gigantic pair of broad wings that vibrated as they opened, sending a hot zephyr over her face. These wings were as tall as the body with subtle hints of dark red. A word formed in her mind: moth. Two half-globes lit up on each side of the thing's head. Eyes, she thought. Compound, gridded, alien eyes that shone with a sickening yellow inner light as, above them, two long coiled antennae made stiff little jerks as they slowly unfurled.

A voice sounded inside her head. Loud and startling. It made her jump.

"Who are you?"

Her gaze was locked on those eyes. She struggled to speak, and finally said, "I . . . I am . . . I . . ."

"I acknowledge you," it said. There was a long pause where she thought she should say more, but nothing came out of her mouth. At last, a coherent thought came, and she said, "I am myself. Who are you?"

The black moth stretched Its great wings and said, "I am the True One. I will devour you."

It began to move toward her with a crumbling sound. She felt her heart beat faster and she stepped back. Then another thought came and she said, "No! I am . . . I am . . . I . . . NO!"

The creature hesitated, then came forward again.

"I am . . . "

"*Who are you?*"

"I am . . . I am *KERA*." The thing hesitated again.

"What do you want?" The black and yellow eyes gleamed with iridescence.

"I am Kera. I want . . . I want . . . I want control! I want my power back! You can't take it from me!"

"I can. I will devour you. I will give you more power."

Kera felt her feet grasped by the ground, perhaps by the strange grass below. As the huge insect reached her, she cried out and beat against its hard, dusty body with her bare fists, but this made no impression on the creature. She began to wail but choked as it wrapped its dreadful wings around her. She was compressed in suffocating dirt as clouds of blackness poured over her. Kera fell into another space.

A cavern. She was in some great, dark cavern with huge black crystals depending from the coarse arches of the ceiling and up-thrusting from the rugged floor around her. Some were long enough to cross each other at strange angles. In that moment (or was it an hour?), more cogent memories of who she was began flowing back to her, but then she sensed something. A sound made her turn.

Another creature about the size of a man stood before her. It could have been a man except for the long black beak and feathers of a bird's head. It, too, spoke into her mind, but also into the space of the cavern.

"I am the True One. You are Kera. You have strength. You must choose your path."

One of the black crystals lit up with refracted images appearing deep below its surface. It showed two men walking in a field of grass in a beautiful green valley. Beyond them, she saw a large building with a bright dome and flags flying. The older man she did not know, but the other one was Marc. He walked steadily beside the other man who was speaking to him. She could not hear the words, but she could sense Marc's person in some direct way.

She knew he was elated yet tired, and she sensed that he was also angry, frightened, calculating, determined–oh, yes, determined–because of what he had been through. She thought she wanted to help him, but he was so far away. She reached out to him tentatively, but as she did so, he seemed to fade. He was fading into her past, she thought, and seemingly in response to that, his image became flat and uninteresting. She began to regard him like she would an exhibit in a museum–an insect in a collection. He was curious to her, but she could no longer touch his mind or his heart.

Her own thoughts drifted, and then she realized a new scene was before her in the murk of the crystal shard. Anibale sat at his bridge consoles, his face twisted into tense lines of anger and hatred. And of fear–very much of fear. As she watched him bark orders to his crew, she realized they were engaged in a battle. Anibale did not fade into flatness. Instead, as she focused more tightly on him, he became more present. She felt her anger and hatred growing stronger and stronger. Anibale! This man of such power–such stupidity and bravado! He controls by accident and raw intimidation. She had been forced to play along with him, submit to him, to get to this position! Anibale, the man who would be ZEK by being a fool! *He shall not win this power!*

She sensed the bird-man at her side, giving a flow of energy to her as she watched the crystal images.

Anibale suddenly turned to look straight at Kera's eyes and his mouth curled into a cruel smirk. He laughed at her. Laughed long and hard. *Laughed at HER!*

Without a thought, Kera held up her hands and felt a surge of energy pulse outward like a great black wind. It hit the crystal with a mighty crack. With a clinking hiss, the thing shattered into countless shards that flew in all directions across the cavern. She cringed involuntarily, but nothing pierced her or caused her any pain. Instead, she felt bold and very powerful. Yes, very powerful, indeed.

The bird-man stood still at her side. He did not speak but gestured to a place nearby where something was perched on a smaller crystal. Kera looked at him, then went to it. She found a beautiful small box with intricate carvings on all its surfaces.

"Attend. Learn. Use. You have chosen. *Power* is your path. You are responsible for it."

"Who *are* you? What is this?"

"I am the True One. I created all these things. I have devoured you."

Kera glanced at the box and then back at the creature, but he had vanished. She turned slowly back to the box again and lifted its ornate cover. A mew of surprise escaped her lips as she saw the intricate objects inside. They were made of many different types and colors of bright metals and crystals and had complex, impossible shapes. *Tools of Power*–this was what she had. The thought entered her mind from somewhere, but she knew it was correct. She took one of them out of its place and it began to move and change shapes. A few black metallic scales peeled themselves off of it, then hundreds. They flew up and onto her body as they increased in size, covering her in a plated armor that she could not materially feel as it had no weight.

When she looked at her reflection in one of the black crystal faces, she saw that every black scale had an eye on it. This would now be her protection in this realm and her ability to see and be aware. It gave her a feeling of such security within that it made her shudder with relief.

She replaced that tool and took out another. She winced when it flared into a golden light, but she held onto it with a firm grip as the rays surrounded her, amplified into her mind through the thousand separate eyes on her scaly armor. Through them, she saw the flow of energy refracted and perceived by one giant globe of eyes.

A wind rose up in the cavern. She felt herself being tugged by a gravity that pulled that air ever more rapidly past her. It was time, and so, she turned her inner strength toward the wind.

Kera took a deep breath.

Passing through the Line from Frahma to Farms and emerging once again from the very same Gate where he had been attacked by Anibale gave Marc a visceral perspective on the strangeness of his current situation. He had been at the mercy of Anibale then. Now, it seemed absurd that he was turning tables on the Elites like this and blasting into Farms space with an army and weapons of his own, but that was exactly what they were doing. As expected, a large group of about eighty BlackMil ships were in a tight sustaining orbit around the Gate. That was far more than normal for this zone, so ZEK was certainly prepared for some response from the Sisters.

Once the initial array of 50 Sisters warships appeared from their planned slow group exit of the Gate, the BlackMils maneuvered rapidly into a shielding mass guarding the direct approach orbits to

Farms itself. Anibale's ship, Marc noted, could not be ID'd anywhere within their group.

Marc lit up the broadcast comm and addressed the BlackMils.

"Harbor military ships. I am Marc, leading a mission of reparation and restitution to Zane's Ball System. Farms will be immediately surrendered to our complete control until proper recompense and justice is served to the citizens of the Frahma System who have been grievously harmed in an unprovoked attack by one of your Primes. Many thousands of our citizens have perished and grave damage has been done to our habitations and ecosystems. We are a peace loving people and we do not wish to engage with you or bring physical harm to you. You must, therefore, leave this system entirely, retreating immediately forward toward Harbor, and you must do so now. There will be no negotiations of this demand. Before any other considerations are made, Farms shall be under our complete control. I say again, you must begin your repositioning now. Any attempts to maneuver your ships toward Farms or to engage us in any way will result in an immediate and devastating response upon you."

Before any other communication could occur, a loud "ZZZIpppppp" "zzippppp . . . pppp" ripped through the comms as several Zip ships streaked by and disappeared in different directions.

When the comms cleared, an image was displayed from the BlackMil lead ship. A dark-eyed man with a yellow headpiece and black-lined yellow cowl stared at them for a second before speaking.

"I am Yon Bar, Master of Suite Black, whose ships are here before you. I serve Corrinda, Prime Yellow, and through her, all the Suites of the Elite. I and all of my Seniors, Pilots, and staff are dedicated to the preservation of Harbor and Humanity under the wise direction and commands of ZEK himself."

He paused as if not quite sure of his next words. "We find ourselves in an unprecedented situation, only now understanding what has taken place in Frahma. We sympathize with you and your losses. We will capture the ones who perpetrated this action upon you and we will deliver justice. There is no need for aggression toward us or the

Farms System. We ask you to remain here in front of your Gate and we shall confer through ZEK and the Council of Colors for proper relations and amends to you."

Marc's image was replaced with one of Sil, who met the BlackMil leader's stare.

"I am Silveen Don, SisterSon of Frahma and Senior of the Institute in Florinda. Master Bar, there was once an Old War between our peoples and yours. I'm sure you are familiar with the details of that conflict. We have been tolerant of Harbor and satisfied to remain separate and aloof from you for these eight centuries, but things have changed. Your pandering to the Primes and their increasing levels of interference and outright hostility have soured our relationship and have caused us to work, for many years now, to bring about a change in your system from within. The Midclass is no longer maintained in equanimity by Harbor but is used as a servile resource and persecuted as an inferior class of humanity. We of the Sisters have seen this and we have grieved for our brothers and sisters here in Harbor Systems. Our attempts to change this from within have not been fruitless. There is a movement and a consensus on Farms in particular that will bring change to the relationships in Harbor.

"We would wish to help and support from outside the System, but the recent unprovoked attack on our own lands and peoples has now brought us into a role of action that cannot and shall not be stopped. It is simply unacceptable to allow you to pursue control of the situation while we remain here at your pleasure.

"To be concise, we intend to take Farms today and we shall not accept any challenge to that act. We are prepared to back our claim with instant and devastating force in a manner unfamiliar to you. I give you this solemn warning now.

"There shall be no more discussion, Yon Bar. Withdraw now. From this moment, Farms is our system."

Sil motioned to Leenah who was operating the comms and his vid was replaced by a still image of Marc's hand, enlarged and glowing red hot. He nodded to her.

Xenoplague

"There," he said to Marc. "Let them look at that for a while."

Paris let out a muttered growl, and "Well, that was quick," when, in the next moment, the incoming comm lit up with the golden Face of ZEK. Connected through the Lines, his electronically enhanced voice seemed to vibrate in lower frequencies.

"I am ZEK. I have heard. I shall listen. Harbor respects its border agreements and I will restore order. Advance no further. Farms is not yours to take. We have not taken Frahma, though a rogue has caused you much harm."

Sil turned to Leenah. "Play the prepared program, my dear. Now."

She touched the control and a new video was beamed broadly to the ships in their path and on to the masses on Farms and to the worlds beyond. It showed Anibale's devastating attack on the Trade Station at Florinda, the debris flying off like broken ice crystals, the lifepods being towed, some broken and others empty of the bodies who took refuge in them. It showed the angry demands of Anibale and the calm resolve of Sil. It presented the images of the damaged BlueMil ship and its gaunt commander targeting and striking Daroun with his doomed craft and the chaos of the aftermath on the ground. It did not refrain from showing the graphic scenes of thousands of wounded and dead. Then, it showed a determined face–a face the Farms middies knew. It was the face of Marc of the Star, grim and focused as his voice boomed out with his excoriation of Anibale, Prime Blue, and his dire promises at the end.

". . . *It is you who, without provocation, have attacked your fellow men, women, and children. Whether or not you answer to ZEK's Face for your unimaginable crimes, you will answer to us, middies one and all. And, you will personally answer to me.*"

The video ended with the still image, once more, of Marc's hot-glowing and enlarged fist.

"Now, we advance," Sil quietly said.

He signaled a comm bot and, after a moment's pause, 359 more multi-hued Sisters warships began emerging through the Frahma Gate and into the slow-match orbit just in front of it, flowing through like words in a data stream, making a statement–changing the conversation. Also blinking into reality behind that phalanx came the special units serving as a guide for the Gate Beam Weapon. Those ships were bound each to the other in their rigid pentagonal grid by thin strands of sapphire blue light: the Zip-tech mechanism to precisely guide and maintain their relative positions.

Leenah quietly drew Sil and Marc's attention to an incoming feed from Tabletown on Farms. It had been showing news feeds of the events at the Gate but had switched to a still image: not the standard one of ZEK's Face and seal, but rather that now famous scene of Marc confronting ZEK in the Great Seat on Helm.

"The Gate Weapon is charging, Sil. All warships ready to fire now," Marc said.

"Do not fire. Let us continue to move toward Farms and toward our foes. They will fire first."

Yon Bar's grizzled face appeared again. Marc noticed he was sweating. "Stop your ships, Silveen Don! Invasion will result only in your destruction. Would you sacrifice your people? Withdraw, and I will allow you to return to Frahma safely."

"We will not respond. Show only the fist of Marc." Sil said. Leenah nodded.

Stretched minutes crawled as Marc thought about all their preparations for this moment. Would this guy actually fire at them now? Everything changes on this knife's edge, one way or the other.

The answer came in a coordinated fusillade of beam weapon energy columns aimed at the Sister's fleet. Twenty of the main grouping of BlackMil ships quickly advanced toward them as they fired.

Sil and Marc looked to the widescan of their own ships, where a series of spheres were now appearing. The schematic image of each Sisters ship struck with a BlackMil beam turned red, signaling the hit. An expanded shiny shell had instantly formed around each one.

Looks like a bunch of ball bearings out there.

Then, their ship lurched as an enemy weapon found them. A

high-pitched squeal made everyone instinctively grab their ears or headsets as their Zip design shielding came online. That sound was the overflow energy being directed to the storage units they had added to the ship. The majority of the blast had been redirected by the mirror-like energy shell out into local space, the beam greatly diffused by the shape of the reflective surface.

Sil punched his comm. "Gate Weapon maneuver! Go now, everyone."

Marc watched with concern and admiration as the collection of ball bearings moved in a pre-planned dance, flying themselves outward, forming into a giant ring and exposing the Gate Weapon that had been behind them. That strange construct was already in process, the roiling and rolling toroid within the space between the five anchor ships glowing purple and pinkish-rose. It was aimed at the BlackMil array, but with the greatest care not to target Farms itself behind them.

"We have to take this step while they are still grouped. Fire the damn thing," Sil said.

They had to shield their eyes as the fission column hard-cut into existence, roaring its white-yellow light in an inconceivably rapid cosmic retch. Just as suddenly, it was gone. As their eyes readjusted, it seemed deathly quiet to Marc, even though there had been no sound from the weapon.

The energy for their own shield systems had cycled back off. Sil called for scans and the screens revealed only a very few BlackMil ships. Those had been farther away and were now scattering back toward Farms. Three others were rotating and heading wildly system zenith or nadir, surely out of control. Of the great majority of the enemy's ships, including the larger one presumably holding Yon Bar, there was no sign at all.

"Marc, take us out front of our ring and lead us into Farms orbits slowly and carefully. Everyone regroup behind us. Watch out for any secondary actions." Sil sighed. "Thank you, Gate Weapon crew."

Marc led them out and confirmed that the others were complying with Sil's orders. It would take a while to get into Farms System proper. The bridge crew was busy tracking the surviving BlackMil ships that had retreated toward Farms Station. That was a little worrying since the current conditions or situation on Farms was still unknown.

"Look, Sil!" Leenah said.

A large number of ships had instantly appeared on scans emerging from the Station and its parking zone. Graphic symbols popped up indicating energy bursts and vid came online to confirm. Marc could see it now: the BlackMils were being attacked from the rear!

Hundreds of ships of all sizes and types were hurling everything they had at the Harbor military vessels. Cargo ships large and small, in-system transports, and even passenger vessels were in the fray and many were firing military-grade weapons.

Marc let out a whoop. "It's Farms! They're taking our side!"

Leenah said, "And, in a coordinated effort!"

Two of the BlackMils were destroyed and several more appeared to be newly damaged. They changed course away from the planet.

"A motley flotilla, perhaps, but a wonderfully welcome one," Sil said.

"Just a bunch of innocent cargo boats," Marc said, "but quite a few of our guys and gals have 'extra' weaponry and other surprises that *somehow* found their way on board."

He grinned at them. "Might have had a few of those myself."

Chapter Thirty-one

Marc guided the operation to gather all the Sisters ships into the vicinity of Farms Station. Even with this momentary victory, he felt the stress in his body and mind. Some of their ships had vectored off now to guard the Gates to Prospect and back to the Sisters. Only one Gate and Line were not covered: the one leading forward toward Harbor.

"The remaining BlackMils are backed up to the Gate to Hub," Marc reported.

"Thank you," Sil said. "Their options are limited. We shall see how long it takes for ZEK to respond, and the manner of it."

"Won't he throw everything he has at us now?" Leenah asked.

"Yes, but ZEK and the Elite have had an easy time for the last several hundred years. A surprise war leaves one at a loss. He has BlackMils all over the Harbor Systems, but not a war-ready army," Sil said. "He was certainly not expecting a large and contrary one to show up on his doorstep. He will respond, but ZEK is not impetuous.

He *is* without doubt a clever and resourceful fellow."

As they approached Farms Station docking zone, Leenah disconnected from her scans and went to Marc. "I know you're exhausted, but we have to deal with your arrival. You're more than one of the cargo pilots now."

He nodded. "We're all tired. Yes, I know. I'll do my best to be the figurehead, but after this part is done, I have to find a way to get myself back to my secret prospect and reconnect with that ship. With that tool, I can do more to help us all than with anything else. It's eating at me, Leenah."

"I know and I agree. We'll find a way. But be Marc of the Star for us now. We all need you in that role, in person, here at Farms."

At Farms invitation, they docked first, with the rare privilege of doing so right onto Station's wheel, with the other principal ships stabilizing just outside the safety zone. Marc and Sil led their small parade out onto the main floor of the oldest and largest of the Station's original docks. A large crowd had gathered–was still gathering–and a raucous huzzah and cheer went up as the two men emerged from the connecting tube passageway. The tubes were not often used directly these days and this one vented some freezing fog into the room from a couple of safety vents. It gave an extra and unintended flare of showmanship as RR, Paris, Leenah, and the other Sisters crew skittered through it quickly and jogged down the remaining ramp.

Marc recognized quite a few familiar faces among the crowd. Several nervous BlackMils were being contained by a serious-faced group of merchants on the far right side of the hanger. Someone had quickly hung up a "Marc of the Star" poster on the back wall, but it was drooping on one side. He knew he had to speak to them here and now. Sil and the others lined up behind him as he addressed the crowd.

"Thank you. No, no . . . that's good. Settle down my friends and hear what I have to say."

The hooting and clapping subsided, mostly, as he continued. "I am so proud of every one of you fine middies!" More cheering went up.

"Thank you for believing in our cause and for taking bold action that has saved many lives and set ZEK and the Elites right back on their rear ends. I'm here with all these amazing people from the Sisters and Rindd who have been working for so long on our behalf. Yes, on OUR behalf, middies, as well as for all of our long-term interests together. Listen to me. This fight is not over. It has just begun."

The hangar fell much quieter and Marc quailed somewhat inside as he looked at all the faces staring at him.

Damn it, I'm not cut out for this.

"We routed them, Marc!" a voice carried from the back.

One of Kera's old trader friends up in the front of the group said, "Let's barricade the Hub Gate and make ourselves into a company planet of our own!"

"We'll join the Sisters!" another voice called out.

Marc gestured them to be quiet. "Look. We can't stop here. We can't just become another Sisters or Rindd. We can't simply set up a new border and isolate Farms from Harbor. ZEK won't let it go and it wouldn't work for us either. Harbor Systems are dependent on Farms for about seventy-five percent of their food. How would you react if someone threatened that much of your critical resources? ZEK and the Primes will retaliate! If we all stay together in this effort, they cannot prevail. Barrkon's Oven isn't big enough to hold us all, and ZEK knows it. We have a solid grip on a vital resource." Marc leaned out, his face almost glowing with determination. "Let's keep twisting it tight until Harbor bows to the pressure."

There were some hoots and cheers, but many were thoughtful and more reserved.

"No, we have to finish what we started. I want to sweep the entire Elite system from power and truly liberate our middie populations once and for all. We must open up our many worlds to a fair and respectful economy, plus we need to reintegrate Rindd and the Sisters into a truly cohesive brotherhood of men and women. We'll do it the most peaceful way we can, but we are up against ancient and entrenched institutions."

"Shut 'em out and close the door, I say! Who cares what they do in Harbor?" an older balding man said. Marc recognized him.

"Frimm, I understand how you feel, but it's not like Sisters or Rindd. It's like I said, they will not simply back off now. We did not take these actions lightly. We've shocked Harbor by taking something precious and we've assaulted ZEK's own pride. To stop now would mean another drawn-out border war–a war of attrition between us and them. Millions could die and we could end up in a worse situation once it was over. No, for better or worse, we have stirred up the wasp's nest. We must take it on to the conclusion we seek while we have the momentum.

"ZEK, the other leaders, and those they empower will not change willingly. They will fight like demons. Don't let them intimidate you! They are men and women, just like us. Listen. We have advantages both technically and morally that they do not. We represent what is right for humanity! As you have witnessed today, we have new and unexpected weapons that give us great advantages. We have new advanced shield protection systems based on Zip technology. That's right, let me repeat that: ZIP technology!

A scattering of cheers and ahhs crossed the crowd. Marc heard the word "Zips?" several times.

"Do not fear this bold move we are making. It is the right move. It is an essential move now, and it is a plan and a move that is already in motion. Let's do what we have to do and put an end to our problems once and for all. Let's finish this together right now!"

Cheers went up and Marc saw that the majority of his fellow Farmers were with him. Some even began repetitively chanting his name and pumping their fists in the air, echoing the fist image still up on the screens. Marc slowly raised his own hand for them. He looked back at his own party and saw that Leenah and Paris were flanking him just behind, both of them beaming at him and the crowd, a tear shining in Leenah's eye.

After a few moments, Sil stepped up and said that a delegation from the official governmental body of Farms, Zane's Ball Authority, was coming up the elevator to meet with them.

"My friends," Sil said to the now muttering group, "We will await the ZBA's arrival and reconvene here shortly. All of us need to rest and recover a bit from our recent agitations and, perhaps, get something to eat here at Station while we can. Be back here in one hour and we will make assignments for the next part of our plan. Every single one of you will play an extremely important role."

Some cheers and the crowd noise followed them as they made their way to a Station food service center just off-corridor from the hangar. When they got there, Marc asked RR to sit with him.

"I have an idea, RR, but it will need your help," he said.

"Sure, what is it?"

"As fantastic as it is, we can't depend on the Gate Weapon to be as useful or reliable now that the BlackMils have seen it and felt its fury, but we still need to surprise them somehow once we get into our final situation with Harbor itself."

"You are very right, Marc. It was only meant to work well once or twice. It's too unwieldy for faster, closer battles and it is quite vulnerable once they analyze the recordings of it. What did you have in mind?"

"Well, I'm still amazed and intrigued by what the Zips did in placing that mini-Gate, or whatever you want to call it, inside the pentagonal structure they designed. If not exactly portable, it is *moveable* and can be accurately maintained in a specific place for some time, right?"

"That's right."

"If they can direct material from inside a star, they could place almost anything in there." He paused for a moment. "You remember that inflatable ship your team made for me?"

"Yes, twice I believe!" RR grinned.

"How fast could your engineers make a really big one? Big enough to contain a pentagonal guide structure inside of it and maybe a great deal larger than that?"

RR stared at him for a moment. Marc could almost see him

thinking about it.

"Could be done. It's a lot of material, but I have a manufacturing option that can speed things up dramatically."

"Really? Like what?"

"It's a quirk of our human FTL research. During our initial testings, we found a useful planet in a random system, definitely not on the AA Lines! Useful, except for one caveat. Like Earth, it runs at a different relative time velocity from Rindd and the rest of Harbor. We put robotic factories in place there so we don't have to spend much time on it in person."

"How much differential?"

"One to two hundred and seven. We can spend seven months manufacturing time and have the product back in one Rindd day."

Marc let out an airy whistle. "So that's how you guys can be so efficient."

"Yes, and it is one of Suite Gray's most valuable and protected secrets."

"No worries, RR. I'll never betray you or them. We're all in this together now anyway."

"That's why I am telling you about it." He gave Marc a tight smile. "So, yes, we could make such a thing, but what do you want it for and what goes inside, eh?"

"What I want it for is for sheer surprise and intimidation, RR. And, what goes inside? Mass."

RR's face lit up. "Ahh, mass. Just mass to make it seem more than it is. Am I right?"

"That's right. But it has to be a lot of mass. ZEK and his Elites have to believe completely that it is a real ship. Something quite alien. Something out of their very nightmares."

"A very tiny and carefully contained sample of neutron star, perhaps?"

Marc grinned at him.

"The Zips will love it," RR said.

When they reconvened, the huge hangar appeared to have about the same amount of happy people inside it. The elevator gondola carrying the ZBA delegation was just arriving at Station and Marc resumed his position with the others back at the ramp to their ship. It provided a slight elevation–a convenient makeshift stage where they could be seen and he could be heard. Leenah stood just at his back to his left and Paris and Sil on his right. The hatches opened to let the delegation into the hangar. Marc stretched to see them better and then several things happened very quickly.

He saw a glint of something metallic in the hand of one of the ZBA people and then two very sharp and loud explosions snapped and reverberated from the hangar walls. A hard hand landed on Marc's right shoulder and he had no choice but to collapse under its weight, kneeling on the ramp and losing sight of what was happening. A strange metallic singing sound swept around the room, followed by yells and voices all mixed up in an echoing acoustic mess. He immediately looked up just as Paris fired her energy pistol across the room toward where the ZBA people were. Her left hand was still on his shoulder. His ears rang.

After a long-stretched couple of seconds, time resumed its pace and he suddenly realized what had just happened. *A kinetic pistol–they're shooting bullets in here!*

That singing sound was one of the projectiles ricocheting off the hangar walls and beams.

Leenah kneeled at his side, looking frantically to see if he was hit, but then she jumped over to Sil who was holding his left arm. A red stain began to spread on his sleeve.

Paris had her arm around Marc now and yelled, "Up the ramp! Come on!"

He scrambled to his feet as he saw RR taking hold of Sil while Leenah held the wound closed as best she could. They all scampered up the ramp and into the tubeway as other Sisters crew fired into the back of the crowd where Paris had aimed her weapon. The main mass of the crowd had turned toward the initial shooters and were yelling and moving in that direction.

"Sil!" Marc caught up to them. "How bad is it, Leenah?"

She answered without taking her eyes off the temporary bandaging she was making. "OK, but not a nice wound. Still with us there, Sil?"

Sil's face was ashen but he managed to speak between clenched teeth. "Yes. I'll be all right. Looks like some of the Farms folk are not quite in favor of this revolution."

Leenah glanced over at Marc. "Good moves, Paris. They were trying to get Marc, too."

Paris was behind Marc, still guiding him as he walked. She gave Leenah a nod. "Saw that pistol glint just before they shot. They would have been glad to take any or all of us."

They all moved further back into one of the dock's auxiliary merchandising rooms where they could be secure and think about what to do next. A couple of Station medics took over from Leenah and transported Sil to the infirmary as RR came back in, red-faced and puffing, with word about what was happening in the hangar.

"Quite a melee out there. Six confirmed dead and a number of others wounded. Two of the dead are some of the perpetrators. Station crew have the others in custody."

Hours later, Marc led the Sisters group returning to their still-docked ships after meeting with those ZBA and Pilot's Association members who were not disposed to shoot bullets at them. Plans had been lined out for the next military moves and Marc was anxious to get them away from Farms Station. He was also angry that the Harbor loyalists had shot his friend. It didn't matter that they hadn't targeted Sil specifically. Like Paris said, they were trying for all of the leaders, especially himself. It still made him mad that Sil had been the one they actually shot. He was going to be all right, just sore for a while as the wound finished its healing routine from the medbots and nanos treatments. He was already on the comms again, negotiating logistical arrangements with the Farms pilots and their enhanced ships.

As Marc was going through the technicals, prepping the warship's systems for the battle to come, RR came to the bridge looking for him.

"Sil is back in his cabin now and wants a word with us before we set out."

"In person?"

"Says it's important. These guys can take over the checklists. Let's go before we get tied up in the launch-out."

They found Sil sitting at his cabin comm, his short-cropped white hair bobbing up and down as he leaned over the screens. His left arm was still somewhat constrained by the organic bandage.

"Can't use my manual interfaces, damn it all!" he said as they entered. He turned to look at them. "You know how I hate using verbals only. I need my hands!"

RR and Marc looked at each other and Marc couldn't help but smile. "You'll be good as new by the time we get into position out there, Sil. I'm just glad you're OK. What did you want to see us about?"

"Have a seat," he said, pointing to a couple of fold-out cabin chairs. "We need you to continue to lead our efforts here, Marc. You know how important and effective this is. . ." Sil gestured at him to hush as Marc started to say something in return. "But, I don't want you to be on this ship."

Marc stopped short at that and said, "You . . . OK. What ship, then, and why exactly?"

Sil turned his big skin chair on around and put his good right hand on Marc's shoulder for a moment. "I believe in your Vision, Marc. I know you are anxious to get to that Ash Alien ship on your little moon and bring it to our aid. That is not only an important task, but I believe it will become absolutely crucial when we get to the last stage of our venture–when we get to Harbor System itself. We'll need the impact of having a so-called xenoplague ship appearing in Harbor space to finally break ZEK's, the Primes', and the Council of Color's hold on power. You say it is a ship that can be controlled and is benign–even beneficent. I believe you and trust you in this. I have no doubts about it or about your ability to connect with it. Your talents, your instincts, and your powers have saved our lives more than once. I've seen them in action and I trust in them even more than *you* do right now.

"For the present moment, I need you to continue to be that excellent leader that you are and inspire this great middie band to do what must be done, but when the moment presents itself, I want you to break away and make a run for Salina and onward to your AA ship. To that end, RR here has something for you."

Marc glanced at RR, who had a funny look on his face. Sil continued.

"You'll need to be in a smaller ship, Marc. Take Paris with you, but you'll need to be able to make a black-arrow run through Harbor's blockade at the Hub Gate and on through Hub System to Salina and beyond. You'll need lots of power, a good AA gravity compensation system for the hard pull around Hub's star, and, of course, the Zip-tech shield system."

A black-arrow run. As hard and fast as one can go, diving into a Gate with no warning and no regard for or heeding of any other ships that may lie in one's path. Extremely dangerous and extremely illegal–and Sil was talking about two black-arrow runs in a row to get him to Salina. Marc let out a puff of held breath.

"I appreciate your trust in me, Sil, and especially your understanding of what the xenoplague ship could mean for us. I'm determined to get to it and fly it to our cause. It will change everything! But what ship do you want me to pilot to get there?"

"RR and Suite Gray have been working on something," Sil said. RR, smiling now, pulled up a portable screen and handed it to Marc. A very familiar ship form appeared.

"What? My cargo ship? Wait . . . is that an inflatable?"

Sil and RR both laughed. RR said, "No–no, it's not an inflatable this time, Marc. It's really your ship. Some of our Suite Gray operatives on Helm were able to simply purchase it outright from the Suite Blue docks. ZEK had commandeered it and Anibale had no further use for it. It was taking up room there and they were happy to offload it. Suite Blue just sold it to us right out from under ZEK's nose, tweaking it a bit in the process."

"That's astounding!" he laughed.

"We fixed it up a bit for you," he said, still smiling. "Popped it over to our secret factory world I mentioned for a faster retrofit. It has about twice the power it had before and we added the grav compensation Sil mentioned. Also, the Zip shielding and some other tweaks you'll like. There are a couple of BlackMil class AA beam weapons built into the front and rear superstructures. If you're fast enough, maybe you won't need to use them."

"What can I say? That is truly wonderful. So, how do we work this with the others?"

Sil said, "Just operate now from your Sisters ship as you normally would. We'll route the comm info from you into our lead warship and all the others in the flotilla will see you as if you were on board here like before."

Sil sighed and absently started to touch his wounded arm but then thought better of it. "We've both got jobs to do then. Lead the group into this next fight, Marc, and we will carry it forward. Use our activities and the distractions they cause to make your mad dash whenever you see the right opportunity to do so. No need to inform me or anyone. Go silently and quickly. Just go. I'll cover you for the rest of the battle on our end and then we can explain things as needed afterwards."

"All right, that sounds fine, but there's one other thing, Sil. Assuming all goes well and I get to Marc's Pile, I'm going to be attempting to connect with that AA ship–connecting like I did before."

"Yes?" Sil said.

"I had the Star that time. Now, I don't. I believe I can connect without the Star, but I won't know until I try. I need all the help I can get. Kera is confined on Helm under Anibale's thumb. There's only one other person I know who has experienced the visions like I did. If she would be willing to, I need Leenah to come with me."

Sil was still for a moment, then he said, "Yes, I see. Like yourself, she is a valuable team member here, but I see the need. It's her decision to take the risk, but I think she will. Take her with you if she agrees."

Marc thanked Sil and RR, then went to find Leenah.

Chapter Thirty-two

As his old cargo ship was not quite in proximity for them to transfer to it yet, Marc was in the Sisters warship's dining area with Leenah and Paris. Everyone was still in position at Farms Station, waiting for Marc's cue to set out for the Hub Gate blockade to begin the next phase of the conflict.

He guided the two women to a quieter corner table.

"You both know the risks of this black-arrow run and the nature of what we'll encounter attempting to engage my AA ship once we get to it. There's no shame in saying no to coming along."

"I know the risks, Marc, but this is too important." Leenah's eyes gleamed. "We're at very great risk out here now. Any of us could have been killed in the attack in the Station and we're all headed into battle. You have to get that AA ship and gain its control and both of us know that means more than just using the mechanical aspects of the Star controller. I was there in Vision space with you. The Spirit Dimension, I called it in my papers. We saw each other in our separate visions! I believe I can help you make the connection to that ship and I know deeply within me that it's important. I'm coming." She smiled and Marc felt his heart lighten.

"Paris?"

She turned from Leenah to look at him. "Hey, I'm your bodyguard. I'm going where you go, Mister! Like Leenah said, we're all in danger all the time anyway. Might as well go for a joyride."

Marc started to say something else when the bridge watch triggered an alert. The crewman's clipped voice popped through the wall comm and Marc's body comm simultaneously, causing the sound to double slightly. "Two BlackMil incoming at high speed. Not on our direct vector. . . They're onto the Gate Weapon." The five Sisters and Rindd ships still maintaining the Zip's pentagonal Gate structure had been parked at the farthest distance in case any unanticipated effects from the alien construct should disrupt the Station or its orbit.

Marc hit his body mic, "Get out of there now! Just cut it loose and run for it!"

"Too late," Paris grunted as she studied her hand comm showing the scan. "Those blackbirds are really moving!"

The real-time vids showed the results. The BlackMils hit the pentagonal Gate structure with beams but also with a scatter of kinetics. Their beams seemed to disappear into the blank space where the Gate itself would materialize if it were in action, but nothing happened for a moment. Then the purple glowing borders between the ships flared and seemed to fold inward, vanishing completely. The kinetics salvo took out three of the anchor ships completely and set the other two adrift. The BlackMils were moving so fast that they were beyond visuals by the time anyone could react.

"They stole our rock-tossing idea," Paris growled.

"BlackMils learn fast from costly mistakes," Marc said. He watched the debris clouds expanding where the three doomed ships had been. "Farms fleet! Can some of you go rescue our survivors? Everyone else: it's time to move. We can't let them take any more pot shots or surprise attacks. Get Sil on the comms and break docking now for Hub Gate." Privately to his companions, he said, "Come on, my friends, it's time to change horses."

"Change what?" Paris muttered as all three of them hurried toward the ship's main hatches.

The loss of the Gate Weapon was a blow, but Marc and RR had both agreed earlier that it was a likely target. The thing was too cumbersome and slow to set up and operate to be of continuing practical military use. It was a shame it had to happen so soon and here at the Station before they even got it into the next fight. The BlackMil leaders had learned the hard way and it was logical they would take chances to eliminate the most threatening weapon they had encountered.

They moved to Marc's old ship as the flotilla moved forward toward the Gate to Hub and Harbor.

Other than a few black pocket Lines, there were three useable Gates in the Farms system, one back to the Sisters, one to Prospect System, leading back toward the Rindd zone and with its own Lines forward to Hub, and finally, the one direct main Line leading forward to Hub System. Sil's own ships were still protecting the Gate back to the Sisters, but Marc had asked a contingent of the Farms flotilla to take control of the Gate to Prospect. The BlackMil ships had all retreated to the Gate to Hub, protecting the most direct route to that system and the farther main Line leading forward into Harbor itself.

Marc was thrilled to be back in his own ship. It felt like more of a homecoming than if he were back on Farms or Salina. Even the familiar smells of the corridors and cabins were a small joy. Paris seemed a bit unsure of herself at first but settled quickly into the scans and comms station. Leenah took the co-pilot chair. Marc settled into his seat and guided the cargo vessel away from Sil's main ship.

He considered the challenge coming so quickly now.

All this has to be put back in motion. So many people depending on me and the others to lead us into the next stage. The only way to Salina and the AA ship is through Hub. Just one big fat obstacle: the

BlackMil blockade at Hub Gate. I'll have to punch it hard with our black arrow and hope we make it through.

He shook his head to clear his thoughts, then put on his best face and voice for the main comm, routed now through Sil's lead ship.

"All right. You all know what is at stake, my friends. This effort represents our right and our duty to each other and to our families. What we do here will better all our lives going forward, for us and for all the generations to come. I am proud to take a lead in this and I'm humbled by your support. You know that I've encountered ZEK personally in his own profane hall. I've had numerous clashes with Prime Blue, Red, and some of the others, too. Now, *we* must all encounter ZEK and his Elites directly. Friends, this is going to be a hard purge of an old illness, one that has cost us much and one that has been too long delayed. Be strong and support your partners. Be aware of your circumstances and quick to respond. Do not be intimidated by our adversaries! We have great advantages and we will use them to our success!" Marc paused, looking into the comms camera. He nodded once. "Now, let us begin. Go ahead and split off the auxiliary group to reinforce our allies and friends at the Prospect Gate. Harbor will certainly try a back-door sortie through it at some point. Stay alert out there!"

Marc and Sil had agreed to put twenty five Sisters warships at that Gate to supplement the contingent of Farms ships. RR spoke in Marc's ear on a private channel, "Sil and I just arranged for a subgroup of ten of our ships to go on through to Prospect System to harass any BlackMils trying to attack through there and to forward a warning when they do."

Marc acknowledged that and triggered the comps sequences for the main Sisters and Farms armada to move out from Farms Station.

It was quite an impressive flotilla, he thought. They outnumbered the BlackMils at the Hub Gate by at least ten times if you included the many different Farms cargo and service ships. Not bad for a rapidly blended army.

As they vectored out toward the Hub Gate, all eyes were on the

BlackMils clustered there. They refused to communicate except to broadcast ZEK Faces imagery and recorded warnings. Leenah put up the Marc of the Star imagery through their own comms as a counterpoint and for the other middie fighters to see.

The BlackMils were a group of about fifty ships, a number slowly growing as ZEK pulled his resources in from other systems and passed them through the Hub Gate to reinforce the few warships that had survived the initial encounter.

Sil ordered all of their ships to activate the Zip-tech spherical shielding.

"Time to become shiny ball bearings again," Paris muttered. Then, "Hell, what's that?"

The screens showing the Hub Gate area suddenly lit up with a yellowish light. A vast and gigantic golden Face of ZEK appeared, superimposed in front of the Gate and glowering out at the Farms System.

Leenah said, "It's huge, Marc. That Face is the size of a small moon."

"Scans on it?" Marc called. There was a long pause as crew members rapidly requested and sorted data on the apparition. It was Sil who came back with an answer first.

"It seems to be a projection–only a projection. Immense indeed, but harmless. ZEK will know we can scan and dismiss it quickly. I think he's trying to intimidate us."

"Psych techniques," Paris said.

Marc got back on the general comm. "Nothing to fear, everyone. It is a gigantic projection meant to put us off balance. It is ZEK's Face all right, but it is a toothless face. I recommend we use it as a gigantic target instead." He heard a mix of cheers and excited comments of approval over the comm;

"Let's launch," he said. And, he thought, get this business over with while we still have some momentum.

The middie fleet started moving into a staggered formation toward the Hub Gate to allow each Sisters warship plenty of room to fire in sequence toward the BlackMil ships still clustered there. Marc knew the enemy ships would scatter like hornets once things began in earnest.

Their own initial attack moves appeared deliberate and slow when viewed from the back of the pack where his little cargo ship was stationed. As expected, most of the BlackMils broke out into maneuverable orbits around the Gate while a few remained clustered closely there to guard that important portal into Harbor's closer worlds. Once they began moving, the ridiculous Face projection quickly disappeared.

Marc glanced at his companions. Paris was calm and solid, and Leenah's hands were on her controls, but she was studying him.

"It irks me to be hiding back here behind the others," he said.

"I know. Just remember it's strategic. We'll be at greatest risk soon enough."

He sniffed and gave her a nod. "Yeah, I guess we will at that."

While they were still positioned at the rear, Marc tested the new engines on his ship, making a couple of short bursts to be sure they were ready to hit it with full power when the time came to make the black-arrow break for Hub and Salina.

The fight with the in-system BlackMils would be mostly carried out by the shielded Sisters warships using AA beam weapons. Their numbers, overwhelming the BlackMils for now, would allow them to advance as a mass to the Hub Gate, engaging ZEK's forces there and giving Marc, Leenah, and Paris a chance to bolt through the Gate.

Paris noted a couple of larger Sisters ships arriving on the other side of the Farms system out of the Frahma Gate containing and hauling a smallish rock, about the size of several of their big ships combined.

Sil called on the private comm. "That's a diversion, Marc. They have some engines installed on it. When you say go, I'll have them launch that baby right into the Hub Gate. They will probably have cleared out any traffic on the other side. When it goes, you can tuck in behind it to hopefully be less visible and less exposed."

"Could work. Can't hurt. Thanks, Sil. I don't know what will make the best moment to go, though. We may just have to do it cold."

"Patience. It will manifest."

It took only about ten more minutes, then RR broadcast an alert from Sil's ship.

"Bots inside Prospect System are reporting the flank attack through Prospect Gate. BlackMils are on the way from that side of the system." He triggered their planned counter maneuvers and a rearguard selection of the warships and some of the local fleet ships within their group changed course, positioning themselves to engage the new threat.

Marc watched the rearrangement begin and took a moment for a final assessment of his companions. Paris gave him a faint smile. She had been a great help on Sil's ship and she had learned much. She'd be OK, and he was truly happy to have her at his side in this.

Leenah concentrated on her screens now and she looked surprisingly calm and collected, but Marc knew she was as wired as he was. She glanced up at him again and the corners of her mouth curled up in a smile. Marc returned it. He could count on these two for anything that might happen.

"Some of those guys may make it through, Paris, and we're on the back side of our fleet—exposed."

"On scan. Let you know if they do." Her voice was tight and monotone.

"I have to rev this thing up now or we won't be in position to make the black-arrow run. It's going to make us really stand out." He tied in to Sil's comm. "They should launch that pebble, Sil. I think we have to make our move now, regardless."

"Done. Safe and fruitful journey to you all. Get word to us when you can."

Their counterforce fleet near the Prospect Gate took more damage from the BlackMils weapons than Marc had hoped. At least seven Farms ships and two Sisters were no more. Also, as he had feared, two BlackMils made it through and streamed in toward the back of the main group. Marc triggered the new engines and they all strained against the not-quite-perfect AA G-force compensation. His old cargo boat accelerated as if they had been shot from a beam weapon themselves. Leenah plotted a course to take them up behind the little asteroid Sil had provided but to get there, they had to pass through the rear of their own fleet and deal with these pursuing BlackMils on the way. The moment they began to move in such contrast to the others, the lead BlackMil ship targeted them and fired. The bolt found them and the cargo ship's Zip shield flared. For a moment, they vibrated like a Farms dog shaking a field pig. Marc locked the aiming comp on the attacker and fired his ship's new beam weapon for the first time.

"Faces!" Paris yelped. "That's really something to come out of this little boat!"

It hit the BlackMil on his aft section, their scan showing a puff of debris.

"That should stall him out at least," he yelled.

"Watch it! Here comes the other one," Leenah said, her voice terse.

"Get him!" Paris shouted as Marc fired again. This time, several of the Sisters ships in their receding line took hits and shone like little spheres as their shields took the energy. An assisting volley of shots from them was enough to take the second attacker out entirely.

Marc trimmed their ship's vector and speed to match the speed of the now-launched asteroid, positioning them as close behind the rock as possible. They carefully shot through the main cluster of their own group, passing Sil, RR, and all their other friends in a couple of moments. He gave them a mental salute and wished them to be safe. They were aiming straight for the Hub Gate now, directly into the hive of BlackMil ships guarding that passage. He hoped they were going fast enough to simply blow past them.

As they approached the Gate, trailing their stone shield, the BlackMil phalanx began to stir and expand.

"They're onto us for sure!" Leenah said.

The cargo's Zip shield flashed and rang again as Harbor shots hit their ship. Paris routed a scan image to him from their front camera, the one with the best view of the asteroid shield.

"The rock's beginning to break up on the edges. They must be bathing it in beam energy."

"At least it isn't rotating. We may be able to use it to our advantage," Marc said. Paris lifted an eyebrow. "Just an idea. We'll see. Sil will hit those guys with all the weapons they have. When he does, let's put a tight-focus low power beam on the rock's center."

Their view of the Gate bloomed fast now as they screamed toward it. The BlackMils went into an expanding toroidal formation leaving one ship behind, directly in line with their approach.

"Put the shield up to full power, Leenah." It was normally set to automatically react to incoming threats, but it could be manually set to full-on. She sent the command and the ship hummed and their lights dimmed a bit with the strain of the energy load.

"Here we go! I hope Sil and RR have the timing right!"

The closest approach would only take seconds and it was coming up fast. Marc intended to give the asteroid a hard push, but when he put his hand on the control for the focused beam weapon shot, he felt it merge into the mechanism. He let it happen without worry this time. The Sisters ships behind them started their massive beam weapon volley, lighting up the zone with hits on some of the BlackMils and a few strays that impacted the Gate itself, causing brightly glowing spots for a second before dissipating. The battle was on.

Just at their closest approach to the Gate and its single BlackMil guardian, Marc let his hand expand further into the mechanism of the ship's weapons control. He felt not only the beam weapon, but also the strangely different structure of the Zip tech shield, but he didn't seem to have any way to control them.

"He's coming up, Marc. You gotta do it now!" Leenah said.

Marc felt sweat on his nose. He was building up a lot of tension. He interrupted his own thoughts and made a decision to consciously relax. Instantly, his hand *flowed* into the rest of the machine and on into the ship itself. In that instant, he felt not only the controls but the sources of the energy for the weapons and the stored energy of the shield's collected bounty. He *grasped* that energy and flung it away with all his might.

A loud crack shook the ship and the lights went out for a moment. When they came back up, Leenah had a stunned look on her face as she held onto the console with one hand. Her other hand was on the piloting controller in case she needed to take over. Paris shook her head as if to clear it.

"Look at the scans!" Paris croaked.

Marc felt like he'd been slapped, but he looked. Their little asteroid had been obliterated and a visible, glowing shock wave propagated away from their ship in all directions. It seemed to have glitter in it–sparks of energy fluctuating and roiling as it expanded. It reached the one Gate-guarding BlackMil and either destroyed it or pushed it into the maw of the Gate itself. Marc couldn't tell which. It reached the Gate only to dissipate like the other beam shots did, lighting up the Gate aperture as a brightly glowing circle for a moment. Finally, on the rear scans, they saw it reach the BlackMil group who were now facing the Sisters armada. The Sisters ships all looked like silver bubbles with their Zip shields on full. Some of the BlackMils tried to reposition or scramble away from the oncoming energy and debris wave the cargo ship had produced. It was a chaotic scene, but in a play in which the cargo ship's occupants never saw the conclusion. Regardless of anything else in their way, their tiny ship bolted like a black arrow through the ancient Ash Alien Gateway, exiting out of Farms System entirely.

"Well, at least no sudden impacts on this side," he said. "Everyone OK?"

Emerging from the Gate into Hub System's space, Marc quick-scanned for enemy ships.

"There! Look, Paris. Several of them out here, standing off the Gate traffic lanes like I expected."

"Yeah, but they don't look so good."

"We didn't send beam shots through the Gate did we?" Leenah

asked.

"No, but maybe that shock wave got through somehow."

"What the hell was that, anyway?" Paris was trembling.

"Don't know what to tell you. It's part of my biomorph abilities, I guess. I'm learning to control and use them better."

"Remind me not to make you mad," Paris growled.

"I felt it, too, Marc. You connected with our ship," Leenah said.

"Hmm, one of those BlackMils is fragmenting in the same way Anibale's ships did back in Frahma," Paris said. "I wonder if some of our little asteroid rock might have been shot through the Gate like shrapnel?"

"That could be, Paris. Good analysis. A real surprise attack, then, even if not exactly intended on our part." Marc let out a lungful of air in a big sigh of relief. It felt like he'd been holding it for an hour.

"Our motion will be noticed for certain, but let's keep our profile as dark and mundane as we can. I need to check the shields again and make sure our gravity compensation is OK. We have a hard turn to make around Hub's star to aim ourselves toward the Salina Gate."

"Yeah, do check that, please," Paris groaned. "I don't want to be a stain on the wall after the U-turn."

He and Leenah smiled at each other and then they all got to work.

Marc could see the control readouts and also *feel* the grav unit and the shields. Those were now empty of excess energy, but the systems were fully functional, and so they aimed the cargo ship almost directly toward Hub's sun. It was a frightening-looking system dive, but they made the tight and fast, comet-like solar turn around it without problems. With the star's gravity assist, their trajectory gave them quite a speed boost as well. Hub frantically and repeatedly hailed them, but no one could intercept them at these speeds. Marc hoped they were wise enough to simply keep out of their way.

When they reached the Gate to Salina, it was empty of other vessels. Perhaps they had, indeed, all been cleared away to avoid being overrun, but there was no way to tell for sure. Marc trimmed their path to hit the Gate dead-center. With their unprecedented speed, they transpierced the Gate and emerged unscathed once again into Salina space. No ships on this side either.

"Ahh, good ole' home," he said.

"You're from here, Marc?" Leenah asked.

"Yep. I know dusty old Salina very well. Not a very attractive place to most people, but I like it for a lot of reasons." He looked away for a moment. "It's full of ghosts, though."

Marc pulled up his private maps for the zone they were targeting. "We have to be really efficient now to position ourselves for the Line I'm heading for. It's way off of the regular routes. In the past, Anibale and ZEK have tracked me that far, so they may have someone out there guarding the zone. They can't know exactly where to be, though. If I can get us close to my Line, we can get into it quickly and no one will be able to catch us, but finding my secret Line is our last barrier.

"I've only heard hints about this, Marc," Paris said. "You have a secret Line? That's something!" She had just returned from the small galley carrying some meals for them.

"Well, I can only say it's a Line I found that no one else seems to be able to locate. It is pretty subtle and I suppose I have my talents to blame for being able to detect it, but it is what it is."

"And this AA ship, the xenoplague ship, is there, in that new system?"

"It's there, Paris, but it's no plague ship. I know that because I've been able to connect to it, kind of like I connected to this little ship but on a very different scale."

Paris stared at him a moment, then nodded and turned back to the controls.

As he had anticipated, there was one non-military ship, skulking around their target zone. It was close to the mapped black pocket Line that Anibale sent his crew down when he thought it might be Marc's secret Line. When Marc used their nice, new AA engines to slow their ship into the actual spot, they were far enough from the monitor ship to relax.

"They can't get here for at least an hour," Paris said.

"More than enough time for us to make the dive. Once we are in, it won't matter if they come over here. They won't find my Line! Well done, everyone."

Leenah leaned her arm on the cushion between herself and Marc. "So, what do we do now?"

Marc smiled at her. "We do . . . nothing, my dears. I just have to sit here quietly for a while, but be ready for a slow Line transfer and Paris, please get a couple of beacon buoys ready to mark the other side."

Paris shook her head and muttered something as she watched Marc settle into his meditation-like trance, searching with his mind as well as his ship's sensors for a very faint presence—a long unused dent in the fabric of space here—his Line. Leenah reached over and put her hand on his. He squeezed her hand in return and he could feel her energy and her mind at the edges of his perceptions. It seemed that through her touch, she gently amplified his own efforts.

Paris looked up suddenly and said, "Oh, there really *is* one out here."

He smiled again as they felt the tug of the Line and then the drop-feel of going through the invisible Gate here. They were in Marc's Pile and the great AA ship was almost within his reach! He only wished he had the Star controller. It was time to see if he really needed it.

Chapter Thirty-three

ZEK huddled over the screens in his office. Sweat made his short head hairs feel itchy and greasy. Elder Bai had stepped out to confer with some of the other Council members. The comm was open to ZEK's MilLeader, Jorn Simm. Well, he mused, the *current* MilLeader, the highest ranking one left alive, damn the middies and meddling Sisters agitators.

"WAR, Jorn. This is called war. We haven't had one of these little get togethers in four hundred years and now, very suddenly, we do. Your BlackMil forces are inadequate to handle the numbers and strength of the Sisters fleet."

"Where did they all come from, ZEK? They couldn't have armed all those Farms cargoes without our knowledge!"

ZEK's face turned darker red. "The Farmers armed themselves, you fool. They've been doing it under your noses for years. Reckless ass that he is, Anibale was right to suspect them and keep prodding them about AA contraband. Now, we have an entire renegade fleet moving on us, backed by an unprecedented Sisters warship force and maybe some Rindder rebels as well. They all have big ships, big guns, some type of damnable unknown alien weaponry, and they are presently in control of OUR FOOD."

Jorn blanched and said nothing.

"At least you were able to take out that monstrous weapon. Who knows what other surprises they have. Remain in position and think how you can prevent them from entering the Hub Gate."

"We are circling the Gate and have a ship directly in front of it. We projected your Face image out into the system at its largest size. . ."

ZEK gave a guttural grunt. "Why are you wasting our precious time? They will laugh at it and decide to strike all the quicker. Start thinking strategically and come up with a plan–a *military* plan. Do it while you still have some time. We don't have much!"

He swiped the man off his screen, killing the connection. He paused a moment, breathing, then used a very private code to connect to another location. A strong and slightly bony woman's face came up. Her skin was of the most pure black tone he had ever seen. Stunningly beautiful. She looked up at his image.

"Well, I didn't believe you, ZEK," the woman said. "You said your FTL mine would likely never be needed, but now it is, yes?"

ZEK pursed his lips. "Yes, I did say that, Kaziet. I did. But I had you go ahead and construct it because contingency plans are just that–for the time when something happens that you don't imagine ever will, but *for* which you must make actual preparations."

"Yes. Because if you don't, you may lose everything, . . . I know, ZEK, and so, it seems you were wise. The mine is unique, if straightforward in design. Use it well, for there is only the one."

"And, our new disruptor?"

Her face became more thoughtful. "It is also ready, but it has been tricky working with the Zip schematic translations and that makes the process slow. For now, there is also only this one, ZEK. You'll have to choose which Gate you want to guard with it."

ZEK relished the fact that he had managed to steal Kaziet from

Rindd 1 where, as a top Rindd engineer, she had spent years infiltrating the odd Rindd splinter group that was so blatantly involved in the current uprising. Now, she was on ZELLINC, secretly working for him on some truly amazing technologies. She was the one who first alerted him about the Gray Rindders' unprecedented communications with the Zips. She and her team had managed to contact the damned aliens directly themselves and gain access to unique information about some of the AA derelict parts no one had ever understood before. This AA Gate controller had been sitting in protected storage for centuries, no one having the slightest clue what it was for. Now, it might just save Harbor, and ZEK himself.

At least the Zips seemed not to be partial to the Sisters and Farms middies.

He smiled at her. "How quickly can you deliver them all from ZELLINC to Harbor space?"

ZELLINC was only one Line back from Harbor itself, on its own Line that included Maiko's Mars far behind it, but it was a heavily trafficked route with all the industrial trade coming and going from that strong business and manufacturing system.

"They are shippable now. I'll have them there in one day, but with all the war uproar going on, you need to instruct your BlackMils to leave us alone. They'll want to inspect an unusual cargo moving toward the homeland." She stared at him without blinking.

"I'll do that, Kaziet, but most of them are too busy trying to save Hub right now. They probably won't even be around to see your little convoy. Do it now, do it fast, and keep it covered in every sense. We very well may have to depend on it for our survival soon."

"It will be done, ZEK."

Kaziet smiled and ZEK found he could not help but return it. He cut the connection as approaching boot steps made him turn from the screens. Bai was back escorting another man. The man's hands were bound behind him and a neural restraint web wrapped his torso. Bai's energy pistol was trained on him, but Anibale seemed to ignore that as he and Bai walked into the room.

"We have recovered your great war hero, ZEK. I present the wise and powerful Prime Blue to you." Anibale shot Bai a cruel look. ZEK felt his own face turn red again.

"*War instigator! Warmonger!* War *analyst* who thinks he knows his enemy without researching them! Prime though you are, I ought to execute you myself right out there in the Great Seat! But I don't have time to deal with you now. I have to clean up your mess and hope we all survive the outcome of the *war* you started!" ZEK's voice had started low and intense but was now roaring. Anibale started to speak.

"NO! You have no words that will alter your fate with me. You have no more business speaking, eating, or breathing here. We have lost FARMS thanks to your bungling, and the Mighty Middie Armada is threatening Hub next! Bai, get him out of here. I'm busy." He jerked around, back to his screens.

"Bai! I said, . . ." He glanced over at the Elder who was holding one finger to his ear and had a strange look on his face. It had turned almost as pale as his robe.

"The White Hall!" he hissed. "A break-in! Jade is there and the Star is in danger. NOW, ZEK! Let's go!"

Bai swiped his pistol at Anibale to indicate he was to go first. "I can't secure you quickly enough so you go with us. FAST. Move it, Prime!"

ZEK sputtered in frustration as all three of them ran into the corridor. A group of BlackMil and PurpleMil guards fell in behind them. The elaborate door to the White Hall was open and they rushed inside to find a dim and confused scene. Bai made a quick hand-sign that turned on the great chandelier's white light. Prime Red was indeed in the Hall along with Pas-Guin, another woman, and, ZEK was shocked to see, Kera.

"You FOOLS!" he yelled.

Bai screamed, "What is the meaning of this? How dare you enter this sacred space!"

The others cringed, but Kera reached out to the Star, exposed in its niche, and the Star responded with bright colors, rapidly changing and growing stronger.

ZEK had seen enough and felt his mental control return. "Take her out, NOW!"

As the guards raised their weapons to shoot, the Star suddenly flew across the room, striking Kera, who grabbed it and fell backward to the floor. They fired at her, but she seemed to be within some kind of shielding from the Star. As she lay there, she looked at them, looked straight at ZEK, and blinked once. Bai fired at her now, and ZEK had his own ornate pistol out, but it was no use. Kera was protected. He could see that. She seemed to fall asleep there on the floor, still holding the Star to her chest as if it were a precious child. Her skin turned a translucent white.

Elder Bai signaled a halt to the shooting and everyone took a breath. The guards took Jade and the others into custody and held them to one side of the Hall. More guards arrived, helmet visors down. ZEK still aimed his jewel-encrusted pistol at Kera, waiting nervously for any sign of life or motion.

***

"She's moving!" Kera heard someone yell. Her eyes flashed open. She was still in the White Hall. The tableaux of ZEK, Bai, Jade, Pas-Guin, and Valezah had not changed much. There were more BlackMils with guns in the room. They fired at her again, but she could hardly feel the beams. Instead, it almost felt like she could take in some of the weapon's energies and store it for her own use. The remainder simply reflected or disappeared into some other place, maybe into that other dimension of the Vision she had just emerged from. She still held the Star. She stood up.

There was one other addition to the scene: just inside the entrance to the Hall, Anibale stood like a stone figure, consternation and anger stricken across his face. He seemed to be bound.

Kera focused back on Elder Bai. His pale eyes were wide.

"Your belt," she said.

"What?" He unconsciously touched his multihued cord with his right hand.

"Give me your belt. Your *belt*, Elder. You have no more power here."

Bai's face darkened and he stood up straighter. "How dare you!"

Kera, still gripping the Star, smiled a grim smile and reached with her mind, out through the Star's still powerful field. The belt whipped off of Bai's cloak and flew to her like a multi-colored snake. It wrapped itself around the Star's arms, then as she shifted the artifact to her back, around Kera's body. She and the Star were now bound together, and Kera's hands were free.

Bai looked shocked as his robe loosened and hung like a tent on him, both of his hands frantically explored where the belt had been the moment before. Everyone began yelling, but Kera wasn't listening to the words. She flexed her now unencumbered hands. A huge BlackMil guard ran at her and tried to grab her arms. Anger lurched up in her in response. She shrugged him off and backhanded him across the face. The man fell back, stunned.

Power. That is what she felt now.

She turned on one foot and strode forcefully to the doorway of the White Hall where Anibale remained frozen.

"Do you want to live?" she snapped at him. "Come with me NOW."

Anibale did not move for a moment, then he nodded indicating his bindings. Kera touched the neural webbing and then the wrist shackle. Both dropped away. His face was dark red.

Kera strode out of the White Hall with Anibale trailing behind her. At their backs, the doorway closed. She did not look back but knew he was following as she marched toward the docking sector of Helm. He slowly came up beside her, huffing, with his blue shortcape swinging with his strides.

"You will not succeed with a coup, Kera. There are too many here who will come together to deny it, no matter what Ash Alien powers you've tapped into."

"I know that," she hissed. She did not slow her march down the corridor. "All the Primes desire what I could take today. I have to increase and secure my power. You will help me now and together we will do just that."

"Why should I help you? You are a renegade *witch* with a plague bomb strapped to your back. You don't know what you are doing!"

"You are the renegade, Anibale. The Star and I are one now. I've *seen* the recent conflicts. With your failed exploits in Sisters space, you've lost all power and all rights to any. I'm just an opportunist, but I'm not moving blindly. You will help me because you have no other choices, and because I offer you a way out of your situation."

"What do you mean?"

"We are almost at the docks. You will provide your lead ship–just yourself and me. I can pilot and navigate. I'll need you for all the other critical systems, including weaponry."

"It takes a seven crew minimum to pilot and navigate that size ship," he growled.

"Just you and me, Anibale! I'm an excellent pilot, and with the Star, I can do the other things."

He was silent for a while as they continued to fast-walk toward the docks. "Where are we going?"

"Get us on board and I will tell you more. Just do it, Anibale! You truly have no other choice except to submit yourself to ZEK again. You rather do that?"

"You'll help me, after?"

She turned and looked at him for the first time since they left the White Hall. "Yes, Anibale. You attach to me and the power here in the Star and you will be on the prevailing side. There will be power for you, too."

He grunted and fell back a half-step. "Dock 32. I will clear out the standby crew."

Kera looked again within herself and *felt* the Star's power: something like a comp info network, but with a different quality. More like tapping into someone's mind–a mind filled with capability, vast experience, and outright knowledge. She could feel how to work Anibale's AA hybrid ship–any Ash Alien ship, she suddenly realized. It was silly to think of his human crew trying to operate all the systems on manual like they do. They have no clue how to approach it!

True to his word, Anibale got on comm and disembarked his guards and crew people. As they approached the ship's portal, many of the crew stared in curiosity and with some concern at their Prime and his strangely encumbered companion. Kera had no time to think of them or anything else except getting on board and away from Helm. Another ship called to her from across the Lines and Systems.

———

"At least this is one place in the universe where no one will find us," Marc said into his suit comm. His boots transmitted crunching sounds up through the fabric and internal air of the suit as they left the cargo ship side-hatch and crossed onto the black lava plain. Each step kicked up volcanic grit that sparkled faintly in the dim sunlight before settling very slowly back down onto the blackened ground.

Leenah was next to him with Paris following just behind.

After a few minutes, he stopped as Paris caught up and raised one hand to shield her view. Her gun was in her other hand. She was trying to spot the alien ship embedded somewhere in the debris piles on the other side of the plain.

"I don't see it. Lots of junk over there, though."

"You're sure this is the right spot, Marc?" Leenah asked.

"It's rather camouflaged down inside that main pile. Let's pause here a moment. I want to try something before we get any closer."

Marc reached inside of himself, opening up to the power he had felt before from the Star. He touched his gloved hands together and stared at them as he tried to visualize the vibrant colors he'd seen here with Kera on that trip so long ago. At first, nothing seemed to happen, but then he lifted his head back up and saw the AA ship. The vessel emitted a subtle red glow, visually delineating it from its encasing webwork of debris.

"Oh. . . The Gods! The ship–there it is!" Paris said.

Leenah also had her hand up to shade her visor even though it wasn't necessary. There was an edge of excitement in her voice. "That's a big ship, all right! Much bigger than I imagined."

Marc concentrated. The ship brightened into a vibrant blue, then flared white once.

"Look. There's the hatchway Kera and I entered before. The ship is welcoming us."

He and Leenah started to walk toward the hatch but Paris hesitated. "You sure this is safe, Marc? We could be walking into a trap, intentional or accidental."

He glanced back at her, but her face was dark behind the visor. "I'm afraid you'll have to trust me on this one, Paris. I am already connecting to her and if there is anything to this at all, I am certain it is safe for us. Follow me."

They entered the AA ship without incident and carefully made their way into what Marc had called the bridge room when he and Kera were here before.

"This is where you found the Star?" Paris was looking around but seemed unnerved and tense. She still had her hand on her pistol.

"Yes, it was perched on that low pedestal. It wasn't bolted down or anything, just sitting there. It sang and called to me. The entire ship did. I wish it would sing to me again. I wish I had the Star."

"Maybe if you tried again, in here? It might be like a stronger signal or something," Paris said.

"She might have a point there, Marc."

"I'm not sure if it works quite that way, but yes, let's try here. This is the heart of the ship."

Marc leaned back against a low gray bench-like protrusion jutting from the wall and tried again to re-imagine the colors and the singing sound he had heard before. He relaxed, stilling his emotions and tried to picture the ship whole and free, flying through space. Nothing happened, but then–something. He felt an awareness–a watchfulness that seemed to be waiting. He remembered his Vision and pictured how it felt to fly over that green world below him with all the energies and instances of Life singing to him. It sent a thrill up his spine and he remembered the unexplainable joy he had felt.

Paris let out a little sound of surprise. The bridge glowed now in a pale blue. Marc opened his eyes. Leenah had stepped in front of him and had placed a hand on each of his arms. He could feel the physical pressure of them through his suit and also the energy flowing between them and the ship. The walls changed to greens and reds and increased in brightness. Then, hidden hatches closed, sealing them into the bridge area. Paris jumped and scanned the room with her pistol, crouching and sidestepping behind the pedestal. Marc checked his readouts and gave a soft laugh. She looked up at him.

"What's funny? What's going on?"

"It's all right, Paris. You can relax. I'm just connecting with Her. The Ship is providing us with a compatible atmosphere."

Sure enough, the room was rapidly filling with a very breathable mixture and pressure. When it finished, and despite an anxious look from Paris, Marc took off his helmet and gloves and breathed deeply, smiling at the two women. Then, they gladly joined him in the freedoms of a properly pressurized ship.

"Leenah, hold onto my arms again. I'm going to go all out this time. Let's see if we can connect more directly with Her."

Marc dipped his mind back into that space he had been in and, with renewed determination, reached out to the ship. With Leenah grasping him, the room and the present moment dissolved away and Marc entered a new Vision.

He was in his suit, floating in a black void with a planet below him. It was Harbor. Floating nearby was a female form. It looked a little bit like Leenah again, but it was not her. She was sans suit, and floating with her arms out beside her. Suddenly, she was next to him and smiling at him, but she looked indistinct, something more like a mechanical representation of a woman. As he tried to signal her with his hands, she began to change, morphing into a different shape. She grew and grew in size until she was a hundredfold larger. She seemed partly organic but also machine. Then Marc understood. She was this Ship.

He felt another energy like tendrils or webbing, bright yellow and strong, attaching to him. *Leenah.* Her strength combined with his and together they were both drawn toward the Ship. He reached his hands out toward her gray metallic skin and they began to expand rapidly and glow red, then yellow, then brightest white. He reached her and, beginning with his hands and then his entire body, he and Leenah flowed and merged into the ship's form completely.

Now, they were all three connected at their minds as well as bodies. He could see that the Ship was not a human person, nor an organic alien person. She was truly a construct, but one with a type of created intelligence that operated not only in physical quantum computer circuitry, but also in another realm of existence altogether. Here, while in this other realm himself, he understood it implicitly and could simply *be* with her as a composite, with the Ship available to him to control and operate as he needed. He felt a wave of joy and satisfaction waft over him and he laughed out loud, waking him from his Vision-only space and startling Paris. Leenah was smiling at him.

He started to say something to reassure Paris when he cut himself off and listened. There was a new presence. He felt it through the senses he had just awakened. Paris frowned.

"What is it, Marc?" Leenah asked. He raised a finger to have them wait a moment.

It felt very familiar and it was growing in energy. It attracted him like a gigantic magnet. As its force grew stronger, he tried to reach out and touch it. It felt like the Star.

"Someone found us after all," he said.

Chapter Thirty-four

Channeling her mind through the Star, Kera reached out to the AA ship she knew was now just below them. She and Anibale were in his small lander craft, on approach to the lava plain where she and Marc had fled with the artifact–so long ago, it seemed it was in some previous life.

They had encountered no resistance during their run through Hub and on to Salina. Kera's newly enhanced senses let her find Marc's very faint Line with relative ease. With Anibale's main ship in a secured parking orbit above, they were now in low approach over Marc's Pile.

She felt the Star, its branched form still bound to her back, brightening in its energy as it came closer to its original home. It was Anibale who spotted the *other* ship.

"That one is no derelict. Look." He hissed, "Wait . . . I know that ship!"

She glanced at his screen. She couldn't believe it! Marc's cargo ship was here, properly landed on the lava plain and showing no signs of damage. "Marc!" she said. "It's Marc down there."

"Not possible! I still have his ship! It's sitting in my docks. Marc is off leading the rebel forces in Farms right now. The scan confirms it's not one of his damned balloons. You think it is him in the ship?"

"Yes. I . . ." Just at that moment, she felt a strong tug at the Star. Not in its structure on her back, but in the energy of it that she was tapped into. It felt like someone tried to grab it and redirect the energy.

"He is here," she said flatly. "I feel him reaching for the Star. He is aware of us now."

"You can overcome him, yes?"

"I can control the Star and the Ash Alien ship. I've been through the Vision and received the power of it. There is no other possibility, but I must confront him. Marc has power, too. He has been through the Vision. He is in the alien ship now."

They landed near Marc's cargo ship. The huge and ancient Ash Alien ship that once housed the Star, the focus of so much effort and desire, was just across the plain, its dark hatchway appeared to be closed. The majority of its structure and shape was still hidden inside the gray detritus that had accumulated around and over portions of it. Kera remembered how it had glowed. She turned and looked at Anibale and saw a look of stark fear and distrust in his eyes. It's all of his nightmares come true.

They suited up. Kera wore the Star, re-bound securely over the suit and to her back with Bai's belt and some of her own energies. Anibale checked the gun he had brought from his main ship and held it at the ready. They exited their lander and strode with the long loping steps natural to this rock's gravity toward the alien hatchway across the plain, kicking up black grit as they went. As they neared it, the AA ship began to softly glow in the deepest of blues. The hatchway and its short ramp began to glow brighter, indicating the way to proceed. As they arrived, the hatch slid open for them.

"Wait, Kera! They could have set a trap for us."

"Come on, Anibale. I have the Star that controls this ship. I can already feel the connections. Marc and two others are inside, but they do not represent danger in the form of traps in the way you are thinking. There *are* traps here–far more subtle and deep ones that must be negotiated now. Follow me."

She strode forcefully up the ramp and into the open hatch and Anibale was obliged to follow.

Once they were inside, the hatch closed. Kera watched it with a kind of aloof curiosity. It looked like liquid metal blending where the edges touched. The airlock mech hissed an atmosphere into the chamber for them, and then the inner hatch moved silently out of the way, merging and morphing its gray substance into the bulkhead. She removed her helmet. Anibale waited a few moments, staring at her, then he very cautiously removed his own.

"They could shut off the air. . ."

"No, Anibale. You will have to trust me. There is no such danger here. You may continue to protect yourself and me with the weapon, but do *not* overreact. I am in control now and Marc *is* my friend."

They made their way toward the bridge, Kera recalling how she felt the first time she came this way and thinking again how incredibly things had changed. The ship looked the same, but everything else about herself and the overall situation was of another universe.

When they entered the bridge room, Marc and two women she did not know were waiting for them. The hard-looking woman on the left had an energy weapon pointed at them and Anibale aimed his in return. The other woman had a lean body with piercing blue eyes set in a delicate face. Marc was in the middle, suspicion creasing his expression. Then he recognized her. It gave her a moment of pride mixed with humor as she watched his reaction change to literal drop-jawed amazement.

"Kera!" His eyes jumped back and forth between her and Anibale. "And you, you ass! Turn her loose NOW or I'll kill you with my own hands!"

Kera couldn't keep from laughing, even knowing it was a bit cruel under the circumstances.

"I should rather turn loose of *him*, except that you'd do him harm and make a mess here on my bridge."

That put a stop to whatever Marc had planned to say or do next and she watched him try to process it as his flicking eyes landed on hers and stayed there.

"Anibale is working for me now. He owes me his future, you see."

"Kera? . . . What's happened to you?"

"Hello, Marc. It's simple. As you can see and sense, I have obtained the Star. Now, I control it. We are one. Nothing–not Anibale, not Elder Bai, not even ZEK himself can touch me!"

"But, . . . that's wonderful! You can help us finish things in Harbor!"

She stared at him without blinking. "Yes, there will soon be a power change in Harbor and Helm. I will be that power. The old ways are history now that I have control. You can call off your war, Marc. I've already won and I'll treat everyone fairly from this time on. It will be the start of a new era!"

The larger woman with the gun spoke, her voice almost a growl. "With you as ZEK? What makes you think you'll be any different?"

Kera switched her eyes to the woman as Marc turned his head and let out his breath. He nodded. "This is Paris, my friend and bodyguard. And, this is Leenah, my friend and colleague." He looked at her again. "Paris's question is a good one, Kera."

"All right. I'll explain it, but I suggest we stop pointing guns at each other. Relax, Anibale. And Paris? I ask you to also stand down. You cannot harm me in any case." She looked pointedly at Anibale.

He huffed, then slowly lowered his pistol. "It's true what she says," he rumbled. "I watched an entire squad of BlackMils fire at her repeatedly in the White Hall on Helm and she absorbed it all without harm."

The woman bodyguard, Paris, also lowered her aim but held her weapon as tightly as ever. She stared at them with an expression carved from stone. The other woman he had named Leenah was right next to Marc, holding onto his arm. It flashed across Kera's mind to consider her feelings for Marc after being so long apart and having gone through so many changes. She still liked him, but now she knew he was in a weakened position and her feelings were best described by one word: dispassionate. She was in control and there was room now for only that fact to manifest. She did not need Marc now and she could not waste time wondering about how they might have been able to live their old lives. That was all gone, cleaved away by stark chaos and fortuitous chance.

"You know that Vision you had out here on the lava plain, Marc? Well, I've had one, too. Through my Vision, I connected with the Star after it flew straight into my hands. I do control it and this ship. Once it is in motion, what others perceive to be an actual xenoplague ship will give me leverage and power to bring the old system down and replace it with something better, something more fair. I need to consolidate my power, using this ship to force the submission of ZEK along with the Primes and others of the Elite class and cause them to yield their rights and their deeply entrenched expectations without undue bloodshed. The old system has to end. I'm the only one now who can do it.

"The Star's Vision changed me, Marc, just as it did you. The True One gave me the power. I am *supposed* to have it and use it, and I *intend* to use it to correct many wrong things. No one can prevent that now. You want the middies to have power. I will give it to them."

Leenah said, "It's dangerous, Marc. She has taken the other way." Kera's eyes cut to her and then back to Marc.

He said, "I'm shocked, Kera. You are still a middie, too; it's who we are. You say you are in control, but if you follow this power path, you won't really be in control. It will control *you*, and, yes, things will change, but in the long run not for the better. We can't just replace one dictator for another, even if it is you, my friend." He glanced at Leenah. "I wish you could have visited the Sisters System with me, Kera. They have what we need in Harbor. I've never seen a more highly developed and humane culture. I would not have believed it possible until I saw Florinda." His eyes returned to Kera.

"I've connected with this Ship, too. I've internalized some of her

AI and other functions, even without the help of the Star. I believe I can fly her and bring the Ship to bear in our coming conflicts in Harbor. It's too important and too many lives are at stake for me to let you just take her."

"Spoken like a middie fool," Anibale hissed. "Power rules everything and always will."

Marc sneered at him. "You've proven that recently." Anibale growled and started to jerk toward him.

"Enough!" Kera held up a hand and he was pulled up short, struggling momentarily against an invisible restraint. Kera spat her words at Anibale. "You wear your power on your face like a rash!"

Leenah spoke. "Thousands of lives have already been lost. We have to complete the task before us. Your instincts have taken you into a Power approach, Kera, but it *will* lead to corruption. Paris is right. You'll only deceive yourself and become another kind of autocratic ruler. You are not the only one with a claim to the energies you've found in the Spirit Dimension. Marc has been a part of it all his life and has passed through the Vision that authenticated him. I, too, have been through just such a Vision. Did you know there is an entire planet of humans with this kind of skill and access? We all know that the current system must be dismantled for the safety and future of all people everywhere. The dangers of the xenoplague are not what we were taught, but the destructive power contained in this Ship is very real. It lies within the walls that surround us right now. We must not succumb to raw power."

Kera felt the power of the Star rising inside her mind along with another source, feeding an energetic determination to her intentions. "NO! No, I will use this and I will change things! I will *fix* our problems and no one will be able to control us, control me, ever again! This ship is *mine!*"

She reached out, channeling all her anger and her intentions through the space she could visualize as the Star. On her back, the physical Star began to glow in multiple hues and turn white along the tips of each branch, lighting up its small oval pods. The bridge room began to glow yellow in response. She closed her eyes and instantly perceived the physical structure of the ship around her–saw its many systems and could easily assess that they were all functional. The ship mechanics were sound and she knew she could fly it! But then, she reached a shape that resisted her. There was another person here! She flashed inquiry at it, but it only responded with enhanced impressions of the ship itself.

The ship AI! That's the intelligence Marc was talking about. It's the ship itself and he's already absorbed it. I have to have it!

She tried to focus on the AI form. It felt distinctly female and it was resisting her efforts to break the bond with Marc. Now, she could see that bond in her mind. It was like blue light intertwined with the body of the ship. Then she noticed another color: a golden yellow twining around his blues. It strengthened him and muted the ship, taking her farther from Kera's own energies. It was that woman, Leenah, helping him!

Marc spoke, wrenching her from the vision space.

"Stop this, Kera! You can't take Her from us. I won't let you!"

She opened her eyes.

Leenah gave out a tight cry of pain.

Anibale flicked his eyes back and forth, desperately trying to understand what was going on.

Marc leaned stiffly on the ledge behind him and Leenah held tightly onto his left arm with both of her hands. With their eyes still closed, both of them were in rigid concentration. Marc's hands had grown very large and were glowing blue. To her left, Paris had raised her gun again, as had Anibale, but neither of them had altered their positions.

Kera closed her eyes again, entering directly back into that other-dimensional space where she could perceive the ship and the color web that was Marc and Leenah. Then she remembered her tools–the special set of trans-dimensional Tools of Power she had been given in her Vision. As soon as the thought came, so did the tool case, appearing and opening its intricately carved cover to reveal whatever she might need.

"I need leverage. I need to pry them out of the way. Give me the right tool," she spoke into her Vision. The black metallic scales she had seen the first time now flowed out of the tool chest and multiplied as before, covering her and protecting her in that realm. The eyes on each scale opened and Kera could see even more clearly the structures of the Ship and the now vividly colored lines, cables, cords, and threads of Marc and Leenah, and of her own lines, like feelers, trying to make their way into the Ship's form.

"Good, but I need the best lever to gain control!" she called again into the Vision. Instantly, there was something in her hands. It was the Star Controller, shining in gold and white so brightly that it made her wince.

Of course, the only real controller is this one. The Star is the only way to dominate and replace the others. Must concentrate . . . on the Star!

She heard a scream. It was Leenah. Marc grunted and she could feel his strain, but he was not losing his intertwinement in the ship. She could see the ship's own structure fluctuating with conflict between responding to the Star and her, or to Marc and Leenah. A metallic groaning sound reverberated in her ears. Everything was bathed in red. She heard a ragged voice from her left side.

"Stop it! Whatever you are doing, stop it, Kera–or I *will* shoot you!"

Kera popped open her eyes. The walls of the bridge were deep red now, casting the room in an ominous pall. Paris had moved up a foot and was pointing her weapon at her. The Star, there in her hands, brightened and glowed just as in the vision space. Marc extended his expanded right hand out toward it.

"Let it go, Kera!" he yelled.

Leenah cried out, "You're tearing the Ship apart! She can't take this kind of conflict of control! Stop it!"

To Kera's dismay, the Star began to drift out of her hands and toward Marc's. It hovered, hesitating between the two poles of desire, moving in unstable increments, jerking in one direction and then back again. She howled in anger and frustration. Paris aimed her gun at Anibale, then back at her.

Anibale whipped around and fired one perfunctory blast at Paris, then swiftly fired a second shot directly at the hovering Star. As she spun, falling, Paris's return shot went wild, missing Anibale. She dropped clutching her legs. The Star sparked with furious, ragged lightning as it tried to absorb the energy from Anibale's blast.

"Foul plague! Kill it! Kill it now!" he yelled.

Kera screamed at him and her immediate burst of anger fed itself through the Star. An answering beam shot from it directly into Anibale and he fell to the floor of the bridge.

When she looked back, the Star had almost reached Marc. She closed her eyes and, within the vision space again, focused on it with all her mind. She could feel it returning to her! Her fingers touched the metal. It was hers again!

But, she still could not break Marc and Leenah's grip to disengage them from the ship's form and substance. They were at a stalemate.

"You can hold the Star, Kera," Marc said through gritted teeth, "but you can't fly this Ship without me. Think what you are doing! Let it go!"

"NO! I . . ." Kera stopped in the middle of what she was going to say because there was a new person suddenly present inside the vision space of the ship: a man, dressed in outlandish and primitive looking clothing, covered in feathers and leaves. He wore a large headdress of vines with strands of green leaves twined through them. His huge brown eyes stared starkly at her, startling her into silence.

She heard Leenah's voice saying, "The Doctor! The Doctor! I called him and he came!"

"What is this? What are you doing?" Kera yelled. "Stop trying to trick me and release this ship!"

Then, another voice: earthy, booming, and physical. A voice there in the room with them, not in vision space, shocked them.

"STOP THIS FOOLISHNESS NOW!" It came from Paris, alive

and still crumpled on the floor of the bridge.

"You are all destroying everything we worked so hard to achieve, everything we risked our lives for! Can't you see? Neither of you can grab total control here. This ship is more important than you, Kera! You're at your friend's throat. This thing has corrupted you already! We have to come to some kind of an agreement. Stop fighting over it before you destroy the very thing you're trying to win!"

There was a stunned pause before Marc said, "She's right. Paris is right. We have to stop this right now. The Star is under your control, Kera. Here, take it."

With the force that had been pulling it suddenly released, the Star recoiled in her hands, sparking a couple of colorful bolts before settling down again. She saw that his and Leenah's bonds to the ship remained strong and deeply enmeshed. Each, then, had a part of the great ship.

It was Leenah's forest man who compelled them to return their attention to vision space. He loomed beside them, seeming to drift in between herself and the ship. He spoke into their minds.

"Tonhaaa. I am Tonhaaa. I am the Doctor. People of Gossamer are my people. Leenah has called and I have come. I have seen this ship. I have seen this war. I see you, Kera, and the dark path you have taken. It is dangerous for us and it is dangerous for you. Your pain and fears drive you and they will eat you up."

She looked at this strange man from between the arms of the Star as she held it out in front of her in a warding posture. Her voice was venomous.

"What do you know about my pains, and who are you to interfere here?"

"I am the Doctor. I have the ability to change things that are misshapen. I can see how things may be and how they can be better. You are misshapen now. I will change you."

Kera felt her anger rising against this outrageous apparition. *"You leave me alone and get away from here!* This is my ship and my chance to be in control. My chance to be . . ."* Her mind faltered at his

404

direct stare. His eyes were immense and she felt like she was falling into them.

"What? Your chance to be what, Kera?" His voice reverberated. "Is it not your chance to be without fear and without shame and without anger against those who have hurt you for so long?"

"No! What do you know about who has hurt me? *Go away!*" She felt a chill of fear invade her heart.

Suddenly, the old man's face changed. She jerked back with the shock of it, then stared in true surprise. The face of her own mother now hovered in front of her perceptions. It was so real-looking and so detailed. She had almost forgotten! Mother was looking into her eyes with such an expression of love and wistfulness. At this prompting, she couldn't help herself. Kera cried.

"Mother! Oh, Mother! . . . *You, Doctor!*" she shouted at him. "How could you do this?"

She looked deeply into her mother's eyes. Her words caught in her throat. "Mother! Why did you have to leave me?"

Then the soft loving face of her mother changed again, morphing into a hard and rough one. It was the blotched red face of Gibb, her father, glaring at her in anger. He was yelling at her, but she couldn't understand him. He raised his fists to give her one of his 'lessons'. She flinched and screamed in frustration and pain, unable to escape him. It seemed to take forever, but when he finally struck her, flailing at her over and over again, there was no pain–no feeling at all. His face blurred then, and shattered like dust, floating away on an invisible wind.

Now, a rapid montage of imagery overwhelmed her. She was confronted with stark faces of low-life merchantmen who took advantage of her in Tabletown, exacting violence and sexual abuse as payment when she had no money; BlackMils who harassed her, tossing her into rough middie jails for days, suspecting her of trafficking illegal AA relics; the faces of four Elite artifact dealers from Prospect and their tough who raped her in the dirty dock of their systems cruiser, then dumped her, injured, in the Station hangar.

And Anibale, in his bejeweled Suites–his stark visage looming and laughing at her. He was laughing in her face! Then all the animated faces of all of her abusers came together, colliding into a swirling, gibbering mass that sped up into a streaked blur. Her own screams reverberated in her head and then slid quickly up in frequency until they disappeared into a resounding silence.

Kera gasped and tears streamed down her cheeks. She laid her head down on the central part of the Star, still humming there within her gripping white hands.

A cool and refreshing zephyr of air kissed her wet skin and she felt her tension release a little. Something else dawned into her perception. Someone was singing a low and strangely tuneful song in words she did not understand. There was another, repetitive sound along with the singing and she felt something rhythmically touching her hair.

She opened her eyes again within the vision space. It was the Doctor who was singing. Somehow, she knew he had always been singing. He was patting her lightly on the head with a gigantic leaf and was looking at her with sadness and an expression of open concern. Marc and Leenah were within her perceptions now, as well. They were quiet and attentive.

"What did you do? What just happened?" Kera asked him, her voice high-pitched and quivering.

He spoke into her mind without stopping his singing. "I changed your shape, Kera. You have sought so hard for control, for power over others, and for so long. It is no wonder to understand this. You have been like a cornered animal striking out instinctively. You have been blind to it for most of your life. It was hidden from your conscious mind, was it not? You thought you could overcome it with your own strength. Make everything be safe by taking control and having power over everything and everyone. Do you see it more clearly now, the origins of your struggle?"

She could only look at him and think about it. Could it be? Could all of her overdriven and focused efforts back on Farms and now in the greater doings of Harbor be attributed to the continual abuses she suffered as a child and young woman? Was she still running away from Gibb and making damn sure she could take care of herself? Making sure Gibb and no one else in the world could ever threaten her–strike her–again? Gibb was long dead now, and for all practical purposes, so were all her other abusers. Yet, they still haunted her, kept alive in her psyche by her own fears, and projected onto everyone else she came in contact with.

She let her head drop back down to the Star. She felt empty inside as the understanding slowly became certainty. She stayed silent for a while, eyes closed, drying tears still sticking to her face.

"I see it," she whispered. "I see it. That was hard, Doctor, but I see it now. I see it and I feel like–like all the air has been let out of me. I don't know if I can function in any other way."

The Doctor smiled at her. It was an amazing smile that felt like sunshine breaking. "I am Doctor. I have changed you, Kera, but I am also here to heal. It is all the same. Your ghosts cannot hurt you anymore. Listen. Listen now as I sing another song."

The tune he had been singing all along changed now to one sounding more hopeful. It took her mind onto another road leading somewhere else.

After a while, Leenah's soft voice brought Kera's thoughts back to the others. "Kera, I'm so sorry. We are here with you. Doctor will help all of us." As soon as she said that, the Doctor spoke again.

"There is one last step, Kera. You have been given the means to power and control. It is truly that, but it comes at great cost to yourself and others. I know. I have seen it on my own world. You can be free of it and make your own decisions and your own way. The power you desire can be truly and authentically yours: power *you* develop and create on your own. You must rid yourself of false and alien powers. Will you do that?"

"What about the Star?" she asked him, her voice almost cracking.

"You are bound to the Star and it is bound to you. You reached out to it, and it has responded. This is authentic and it is your own.

You will need this power to fly this ship in the final time–the time to come when many futures will be decided. There is, however, another set of power that you must let go of." In front of the Star, just in front of Kera, her tool chest appeared. Doctor raised his hands and then turned them, holding them out.

"My Tools! I hardly got to use them! No . . . This is what you want?"

"They represent the alien power given to you, Kera. It is corrupting. You cannot use it without changing your form into one of great danger to yourself and everyone around you. In the end, it is Death. Release them now. Release them and I can send them where they will not harm you or us ever again."

She hesitated, but then a new voice broke into her awareness. They were still in the vision space, but it was Paris now, there in the vision with them, who spoke.

"Let it go, Kera! It's evil. Let's work together and make things right. I have a plan I want you to hear. Just let the damn things go!" Paris was still sprawled on the other, mundane dimensional ground, her legs blackened by the blast from Anibale's weapon, but she was also here in the vision space with them. Marc and Leenah were gaping at her. Kera looked back at the Doctor who, silent now, smiled serenely at her. His hands still waited to receive her Tools of Power.

She made a decision and exhaled a long and warbling sigh.

The Tools floated away from her and sat gently down on Tonhaaa's hands. He dipped his leaf-corona head and brought his two hands together. There was a green flash of light and the Tools were gone.

The Doctor turned toward Paris and said, "Listen now, my strong one, and I will restore your vitality. Your losses are but little compared to your gains." He began a new song, a more powerful one, and Paris grunted and reached her arms down to her burnt legs. A pale white glow enveloped her as the Doctor's song grew louder. Kera heard the Doctor speak internally again, this time to Marc.

"Go to her now and place your hands on her legs."

Marc did this and his hands grew and blended with her for a long moment, then he released her.

Suddenly, the song stopped and all four of them were startled back into the tangible dimension of the Ship's bridge room. Kera still had her Star and Marc and Leenah were at the other wall. Anibale remained down on the floor, out but still breathing. Through the Star, Kera quickly produced a constraining force around him. There was no sign of the Doctor. They all looked at Paris who remained on the floor, her pants still black and smoking from the blast that took her down. She made a funny noise, then slowly got up and stood there for a moment. She looked up at them and grinned.

"Well. That's a whole lot better!" she said.

Marc and Leenah rushed over, talking to her and making sure she was truly OK. Then, they all turned their attention back to Kera.

"You found a way into the vision," she said to Paris. "I'm glad you did. Are you truly healed of that wound?"

"Looks like it," Paris said. "I guess that Doctor really is one."

Leenah said, "Looks like Marc is one now, too. How did you manage to enter the SD vision?"

"I just heard the panic and tension between you and I kind of followed it. I guess I needed to be there."

Kera walked slowly over to the others and they all sat down, thoroughly exhausted, on the floor together.

Marc said, "That took great courage, Kera." He gave out a great exhalation of breath and tension. "I'm here for you. I guess we're all in this together for sure now." She gave him a tired smile. "I'm glad you are a part of the Ship," he said.

"What in Faces do we do now?" she said. "Oh, wait . . . Paris, you said something about a plan. We could really use one right now."

Paris took a minute to look at each of them in turn. "Yeah, well, I've been thinking about it. You still have your Star thing. The Doctor said it was truly yours, so that's a good thing. Marc, you have the embedded connection to the Ship, with Leenah contributing to that. That's a good thing, too. Look, here's how I see it. We didn't come all the way out here to play games and maybe not be able to use this

Ship to help all of our friends who are fighting and probably dying right now. We gotta work together.

"I think we need to agree to some things. Here's what I'm proposing. We all group our efforts to fly this AA Ship to Harbor and use it in the fight. Once we are victorious and ZEK is overthrown, and notice I didn't say *if*, then we'll need to make a huge transition from the old government to something like what the Sisters are doing. That's not going to happen overnight. It might even take generations. People are stubborn and they won't want to change their ways, even if they think it's a good thing to do. We can't suddenly have a vacuum at the top where ZEK was. Most of Harbor will need a figure of authority to latch on to. I know a little about that, having been a prison guard and military policewoman for so long. I propose we set up Kera in that role since that's how her talents and interests run. *Not* as just another ZEK, though! She could be the 'Director of Harbor', or something. Let 'em focus on you while we all make the changes everyone needs and rebuild what's been destroyed. You can organize it from Helm.

"When it's all over, Marc and Leenah can take this Ship and maybe find us some more places to live and resources to use. If it is a terraform machine like you suppose, then that could be really useful, don't you think?"

Marc said, "Wow. I think that's the most I've ever heard you say at one time, Paris!" He grinned. "Yes, that's just what we should do. An excellent plan. What do you think, Kera? Leenah?"

Kera thought hard about it and tried to assess what the loss of her Tools meant. "It *is* what I was seeking in all this. I'm just unsure if I can control everything now without the power I had."

Leenah said, "Of course you can. Only it will be real now. It will be you yourself, using your own judgement and intelligence. People will respond to you with their hearts as well as minds if they sense that you *are* for real and not another ZEK making them bow down to her whims and appetites."

Kera remembered that there had actually been several female ZEKs in centuries past. All of them had been horrendous martinets, worse than the male ZEKs in terms of cruelty and manipulation of their subjects. No, she didn't want to be one of those.

She continued to examine herself in the light of what the Doctor had shown her.

I wanted to be in total control for my own reasons, to banish any who could hurt me. Now, I need to take control for the reason I thought I was doing it. To help make things right for everyone.

"So, yes. I agree. We will work together to fly the Ship into whatever the situation is at Harbor. Let's scare the hell out of ZEK and the others! It's not an empty threat, either. This may not be a xenoplague ship like they have claimed, but it can be a tremendously powerful weapon, a destroyer of worlds, as Earth found out. It might be a terraformer like you believe, Marc, but it can certainly be *used* as a weapon. Once all is done, I will be the leader you described. I can control the Primes and the others if I have your support and the support of the middies."

Marc smiled at her. "Thank you, Kera. I am so relieved and I also agree to this. We can only wield this Ship, either as a weapon or otherwise, if we work together. Leenah? You're an essential part of this, too. What do you say?"

"Of course! I will be right here, ready to help both of you work with her–the Ship, I mean. She is here, too, and I think there is enough of a human-like intelligence built into her that she can add to or hinder our efforts depending on how we work together. Being at odds like we were is very dangerous. Very dangerous, indeed." She shook her head slowly.

"That's settled, then." Marc took Leenah's hand and nodded as he reached out to take Kera's, who grasped Paris's sturdy hand, as well. They all felt a corresponding wave of something like comfort or satisfaction. The Ship.

"You know," he said suddenly, "this is a critical turning point. I think we should call this agreement something–for posterity, perhaps." He pondered a moment, then looked up at Paris. "I think it should be known as The Paris Pact, proposed and confirmed here on Marc's Pile. The beginning of desperately needed changes and the start of a new era for humanity!"

They laughed and Kera agreed with the notion.

"What about Blue Boy here?" Paris said. She was red-faced and Kera thought she was trying to change the subject. Anibale, still sprawled on the floor, moaned lightly.

"I have him restrained. He's not seriously injured. We should simply confine him for now. He may be useful in our negotiations and strategies later at Harbor."

Kera reached out through the Star and asked the Ship AI to form a restraining cell just off the main corridor, aft of the bridge. As they lifted him, Anibale regained consciousness. Sullen and bruised, he said nothing, but his bloodshot eyes glared with hatred as they worked in concert to remove him to the new brig.

Chapter Thirty-five

ZEK's main comm center was frothing with staff. He glanced up from his dimensional displays and watched the backs of heads in the room below moving and bobbing. BlackMil staffers and technicians were working intensely to keep his command comm to the military forces and the returning information flow functioning and up to date. His position in this raised control room at the back of the center let him command without being visible. He could address any or all of them as ZEK's Face on the giant screen at the front if he thought it necessary. For now, he was content to be an authoritative and potent voice in their ears.

"I want that Gate Disrupter in position now! That was a little probe bot that just got past your BlackMil wall, Jorn. It will be a warship next! You didn't hold the Sisters rabble to Farms. They fought right through you and took Hub! Your flank attack from Prospect failed, and your Farms blockade failed! You *will* secure the Harbor Gate!"

The ungainly disrupter device was being towed into place at

Xenoplague

Harbor's Gate leading back to Hub System. Kaziet and her crew
had done an amazing job to get the ancient Gate controller running
using her new connections with the Zips. They had worked several
large teams around the clock to get it ready in time. The only issue
now was: will it actually work at a real Gate?

It must! Only one way to find out.

He was happy that the Sisters and Farms rebels suffered substantial losses in the process, but they had simply overwhelmed his
BlackMil forces in Hub once they burst through from Farms. There
were so damnable many of them, and so strangely sophisticated
in their design and weaponry! How could he have foreseen such a
military buildup with the enemy hiding behind their opaque walls of
exclusion for centuries? They pretended to be peaceful artisans and
imponderable philosophers while secretly constructing entire fleets
of warships and covertly indoctrinating the Farms middies! It should
never have been allowed to happen, but there was no use whining
about that now.

With shocking swiftness, it had come down to just this one
weakest link: their own home Gate. Harbor was under a threat it
had never faced before. With the rebels in control back there, all
the worlds behind that Gate to Hub were cut off. There was no
precedent. During the Old War, there had been skirmishes back and
forth across the border Gates and within several of the Systems from
Hub to Frahma, but those old fighters did not have the numbers or
the technology to do what this strong armada now threatened to
do. They could burst down that main Line and attack through that
lone Hub Gate, suddenly gaining the entirety of Harbor's heartland
domains–taking the capital world and seat of government here at
Helm and the economic centers on ZELLINC. It would be a bloody
mess on a huge scale and mean the loss of the entire culture and
wealth of over a thousand years. ZEK knew he would not survive it.

The rebels were unbelievably bold but not reckless. The fact that
they had not yet made that final move showed that they understood
the cost of invading the Harbor System itself, but ZEK was certain

they were not having second thoughts, only planning and waiting for the right moment.

He must protect the Homeland. If he could not turn back the rebellion, but could somehow close them off behind the Gate, the Harbor Systems Group would instantly shrink from twelve to just four world systems, not including old Earth. That would preserve Harbor, but not be truly viable in the long term and it would certainly not be pleasant to live with that reality. Whatever the cost, he could not afford to lose this Gate and this battle. Harbor–Harbor at large–must survive.

"The Disruptor is in position, ZEK," a senior tech's voice came in his ear.

"All ships must stay back from the Gate at the limits we dictated. Kaziet, are you ready?"

The Rindd woman's face cut onto his side screen. "Yes, ZEK. On your command."

He turned his attention to the main screen showing the device. The great aperture of Hub Gate itself was outlined dimly behind it. He gave the signal and the Disrupter turned on for the first time. Almost instantly, in the mouth of the Gate, the stars that happened to be positioned behind it from the point of view of the camera seemed to ripple. Then a light red glow sheened over the space and remained there, glimmering almost beyond the visible spectrum. For the first time in perhaps millions of years, the great Ash Alien Gate had been closed. He, ZEK, had turned it off! It was a calculated, if drastic and dangerous risk, for it remained to be seen if the Gate would reopen when the Disrupter was deactivated.

ZEK got on the general comm. "I am ZEK. We have stopped the invaders at our door–for now. There is no reason to despair. Look! This is an accomplishment that has never before been achieved in the history of the Second Domain: I have closed a *Gate* and have it under my control. I am ZEK. I protect Humanity!"

Now, let them squirm in Hub System! Their plans depend on rushing that final Gate and now it is suddenly sealed in front of their noses.

ZEK smiled to himself, thinking now of how he could switch the Gate on and then back off again in the blink of an eye, allowing him to send very nasty things into the amassed ships on the other side and still prevent them from bursting through into Harbor. In fact, it was time to do that very thing and at the same time confirm it would reopen.

"Jorn! Are those swarmers ready?"

It took a moment for Jorn's haggard and ugly face to pop up on the BlackMil feed. "Yes, ZEK. The Gate is closed and we are in position to launch them straight through as soon as you open it."

"It will have to be fast, Jorn! Fast, as in you will have no more than ten seconds. Make sure your comps are calibrated and set those swarmers to disperse immediately on arrival in Hub."

The little swarmers were simple counter-measures. All human-made, with no AA construction in them, these thousand or so torpedo bots would arrive together in a cluster on the other side of the Gate, then rapidly disperse into a spherical region, looking for anything solid to home in on before exploding. Crude and effective, especially if the enemy ships were in close formations near the Hub-side Gate.

His new Kaziet-Zip-designed FTL mine was also being secretly prepped. Now *that*, unfortunately, was a single-shot weapon. He would hold that little surprise in reserve for the chance that the middie Marc's plague ship shows up, but he still worried at the level of trust he had been forced to place in Kaziet's charming hands.

After a few more minutes of prep, it was time to launch the swarmers. On his command, the Disrupter was cycled off, then back on again, just long enough for that launch window, and for the deadly assemblage to be shot through the Gate. It worked! As simple as flipping a dumb light switch off and on!

A comm bot had been cycled through with the swarmers and was auto-retrieved after an hour, back through the rapidly switched Gate, to report on damages.

"We graphed 359 warships and other support ships prior to the swarmers, ZEK," Jorn said, his face and voice terse through the combat comm. "A substantial troupe of ships were gathered close to the Gate on the other side and were impacted the most. They lost 39 ships and approximately 103 others appear to have been damaged but not destroyed. They are repositioning back from the Gate."

I'll bet they are. Knock on my door and you'll get bit, fools.

"Fine, Jorn. Stand by for a second round. They won't allow such a loss again, but we must remind them of our teeth from time to time."

"Yes, ZEK."

Something about their stalling nagged ZEK. He was still mulling over an incident that happened before the battles at Hub, while the rebels were still contained at Farms System. A small asteroid had blasted through the Gate from Farms to Hub. The rock had exploded just on the Farms side, but his trackers said there was a ship using the rock for a shield. ZEK became certain about it when a trackable object continued through the Gate at very high speed and made a hard turn around Hub's star, beelining for Salina. Someone was making a crazed black-arrow run. Middie Marc was out there, maybe trying to join up with Kera at their nasty plague ship. The man was a demon.

ZEK remembered that awful scene in the White Hall and how Kera was so untouchable while holding that Star controller. She had taken Anibale with her and commandeered his ship! He glowered.

Anibale is out there now with Kera. Maybe he will find some way to stop them. In any case, they won't make it through my Gate!

Thirty hours later, Jorn reported again. A probe bot was retrieved that showed a changed situation in Hub System. The rebel armada had been attacked by ships coming through the Beyond Gate. They were Rindder ships. Somehow, Kaziet had managed to get her Harbor-loyal Rindders to deliver a flank attack! Her Zip friends must be relaying comms signals–somehow bypassing the Lines and Gates.

The Sisters rabble suffered about ten more ship losses before repelling the Rindders back to Beyond and Golddust. Now, the middie herd had to protect their backs as well as their noses, but that still left over three hundred enemy warships gathered at his Gate. He could not let his guard down for an instant.

There was another aspect to the bot report, however. A different kind of ship had been tracked, coming in from the Salina Gate orbital zone. It was much larger and, in the last few seconds of data, appeared to be instrumental in running off the Rindd contingent. Was it the plague ship, with Marc, Kera, and her Star controller on board it? ZEK shook his head as this placed new and alarming weight behind his worst fears.

He wished he had higher resolution data, but it's hard to get the bots far enough in-system to acquire it and then get them back through the blocked Gate in time.

ZEK squirmed in his command chair and scratched his head.

Must talk to Kaziet and require her to put more leverage on the traitors. I want these vermin harried until they disperse out of Hub! Maybe we can take it back if there are enough Rindd loyalists. They know what's at stake here–their very livelihood! Cultivating dependency in one's subjects is always excellent governing policy.

Marc guided the immense Ash Alien terraform ship through the final Gate from Salina to Hub. It took their combined efforts to effect the proper movement of it. Kera was in charge of the technical guidance, "driving" the ship with the Star, since that was that controller's primary design function. He and Leenah were deeply tuned to SD vision space, merging in and out of the Ship's systems as the Artificial Intelligence parts of her needed this or that kind of input and guidance. It felt so strange, but at the same time, it was intuitive, especially if one simply relaxed into it.

He could *feel* the energy resources of the Ship and move them around as needed simply by reaching out with his hands and directly moving them. *Bi-modal,* Leenah had called it. It was being in one's physical tangible form in this regular space while also being in a symbolic yet empowered form in that other strange realm, the one he had thought of as vision space and Leenah had termed the Spiritual Dimension.

TD and SD merged! It sheds a lot of light on the nature of the ancient Ash Aliens and highlights why we've missed so many things about their technological remains. I wonder if that's why we've never been able to make a truly conscious robot or comp?

Paris was even helpful with her newfound awareness in the SD realm. He could feel her watchful presence there, ill-at-ease to be sure, but confident and ready to help if they ever needed it. As he continued to scan his Ship's systems, he also sensed a darkling depression in the aft crew area: Anibale in his cell. He could feel the brooding anger of the Prime's mind there. He shook his head and looked away from him, widening his inner view to sense the entire ship and crew. With the golden threads of Leenah's SD energy adding to his own, they considered their immanent passage through from Salina to Hub.

First, they modified the Ship's AA-style comms, creating virtual screens to accept Harbor technical standards in order to be able to connect with their comrades beyond Salina once they went through the Gate. That involved a bit of hard-wire work, but also a courtesy "ask" of the Ship AI within their SD vision space. She presented them with large view surfaces that also provided a touch of SD data flow. Marc could somehow feel the scene as well as see it visually.

So, 4-D comms are pretty great, he thought.

In their pass through Salina System, there had been no BlackMil ships at all. It seems ZEK's limited forces had been called in from the outer worlds leaving Salina abandoned. Marc was certain, though, that their emergence here would be tracked and rapidly bot-relayed to ZEK. That black-arrow run they had made earlier was not exactly subtle or concealed. ZEK would be watching for the plague ship to show up.

Leenah sent an expendable transmission bot ahead of them to

alert Sil and the Sisters fleet of their arrival. When they had emerged earlier out of Marc's Pile into Salina space, he had found a private bot near his faint Line, transmitting a low-energy repeating loop message from RR telling them the armada had taken Hub System with major losses but eventual success. He also relayed the amazing news that ZEK had found some unprecedented way to functionally *close* Hub's Gate to Harbor.

The normal trans-Gate comms lines from Hub to Salina were down, placing the entire Salina System incommunicado. They would not know the full extent of the situation or the current status until they passed through the Line and Gate to Hub themselves.

They made that Gate transit smoothly and the scans instantly lit up with Hub system's data. The main group of their friend's ships was arrayed around the now blocked Gate to Harbor and the rest were scattered in smaller clusters back from there for most of the distance to Hub's Heaven, the most exterior of this system's habitable worlds.

"They're under attack, Marc!" Kera's voice rang out. "Look at that group of ships coming out of the Beyond Gate."

Marc saw them immediately, a concentrated group moving in contrast to the Sisters fleet. Some of the ships were still emerging from the Gate leading back to the Beyond System and, eventually, to Rindd.

"Wait . . . ZEK's Harbor command is isolated now behind the blocked Gate. How's he coordinating that attack?"

Paris spoke up from her seat at the bridge scans. "Probably had it set ahead of time with instructions to go when some parameter was met."

Leenah started to say something then paused. "Marc, I think those are Rindd ships. It can't be RR's people!"

"Rindders? No, of course not. It has to be mainline Rindders, the ones in ZEK's pockets."

Marc coordinated with her and Kera to reach out in SD to see if they could learn anything about the attackers. Impressions of determination mixed with a kind of calm assurance and brilliance.

Leenah gained impressions of a small brown and green world and ships that felt of a certain kind of pattern.

"Rindd, all right," she said, "and not ours–that's certain."

Marc felt a surge of anger and impatience. "Let's go! They need us and this Ship is going to make a truly big impression." He sent an alert signal to Sil's ship, letting them know of their arrival and approach. He hoped it wouldn't take their friend's attention away from the battle, but in just a few seconds, Sil's haggard face came on screen and a smile broke across it.

"You made it! Wonderful timing, Marc, Leenah! We could certainly use your assistance!"

"Don't spend time on us right now, Sil. We're on our way." Marc closed their comm path.

It would have been humorous, Marc thought, if it weren't so serious. The sudden appearance of the "Plague Ship" caused an immediate reaction. Upon seeing their rapid approach–the huge ship closing on them at speeds much higher than any traditional hybrid AA/human warship–and appearing as an immense specter out of their nightmares, the Rindd ships making the flank attack from Beyond scattered, most of them running back into their Gate. Still, they had taken a toll on Sil's ships: seven more gone before Marc could get them in range. Aside from the unconscionable terror of the terraform beam, their own ship had an impressive array of powerful beam weapons and they used these to deadly effect to take out those Rindd attackers who did not make it back to their original Gate or who had attempted to bolt out through the other nearby Gates to Golddust or Prospect. None of them had headed to Hub's other Lines to Salina or Kayne, so Marc's earlier assumption still held. Those outlier systems had been abandoned by any BlackMils or Harbor-loyal Rindd troops in this fight. The only other Gate here at Hub, the critical one leading back to Farms, was heavily guarded by Sil's team.

As Sil's ships were regrouping from the Rindd attack, Marc re-connected with the armada's main comms and learned that the front sector of Sil's armada that had clustered around the Harbor Gate had been decimated by a kinetic weapon. They had lost close to forty ships. Having learned their costly lesson from the first surprise volley, they had backed off the Gate proper, depending on their Zip-tech shields to fend off any of ZEK's missiles that made it past their weapon sweeps.

When things settled again, Marc got Sil on a private line.

"So, ZEK has closed his Gate?" he asked. Sil looked older; tired. "That's amazing, but he's still lobbing those crude weapons through it. Damn. I just wish we could have made it sooner."

"I'm so glad you were able to retrieve your fabulous ship, Marc. We were worried for you because it was taking longer than we had hoped."

"Truly sorry, my friend, but we had company. My old friend Anibale and my old actual friend, Kera, joined us out there. It's a long story and I'll give you the details later, but here's the situation. This Ship is AA entirely and it is operational only by those who can work in our own physical, tangible dimension *and* in Leenah's spirit dimension at the same time. We went through some trying tests and almost came to blows, but now Kera rightfully has the Star Controller, Leenah and I have the integration and rapport with this amazing Ship AI, and Paris has authored a pact that binds us all in cooperation to help finish this middie effort to overthrow ZEK and the Elites."

Sil sat back and closed his mouth on whatever he was going to say.

Marc laughed. "Yeah, that's a lot to digest, but that's where we are. Oh, and Anibale is in the brig and probably not too happy." He grinned and Sil also smiled tentatively.

"You don't say. Well, you have had some adventures. I'll impose on you for all the details after this is over."

"You bet. Sil, where's RR? I can't find him on scans and haven't heard from him since we got into the system here."

"He's . . . not here right now. He said he had a special assignment critical to our endgame and he would not tell me what it is, although

I was quite insistent. He left just before that flank attack happened. I'm worried now that he might have run into those mainline Rindd ships on his way to wherever he was going."

Marc thought for a moment, then said, "I might have a clue to what he's up to."

He told Sil about his plan to have the Suite Gray Rindders make a huge fake alien ship to pull in as a surprise when they got into a final standoff situation in Harbor space. Sil was shaking his head and smiling by the time he was finished.

"Well, that might actually be quite useful. I wish he could have confided in me on it, though."

"I didn't tell him to keep it from you, Sil, so I don't know. Maybe he has something else planned. Something tells me there's more to it than my big alien balloon. I can almost sense it, but it's . . . I can't quite tell you in words."

"Well," Sil said, "we trusted him with our lives in Rindd System and he came up with the surprise of my life in that Zip ship transfer. I think I'll trust him now as well and see what happens. In any case, we have to continue our plans with or without him."

"Yeah, we sure do. So, what are your thoughts about the blockade of that Gate? How'd ZEK manage that?"

"Completely unknown and unexpected, Marc," he said. "We can't underestimate ZEK. He has many resources he can call on even if we did surprise him with our numbers and the quality of our warships. We can expect traps and ambushes to continue and to become the rule from here on into Harbor. However. . ." Sil paused and a small smile appeared on his face. "*I* am also surprisingly resourceful."

Marc cocked his head to one side. "OK, I've seen that look before. What have you been working on?" Sil broke into a full smile.

"Oh, just a way for us to bypass the Gate altogether. Everybody. All at once."

"What? You have a way to jump the entire armada past the Gate? That's unbelievable! It has to be the Zips, right?"

"Well, you and I know it can be done. We've watched Zips come and go without the convenience or inconvenience of Gates and Lines ever since we first encountered them over a thousand years ago, and we've gone along on one such ride, eh? But this actually has nothing to do with them. Is Leenah in our comm? It is all possible because of her."

Leenah had been in the next compartment over with Kera and Paris, but they were all so networked now within SD that she instinctively came to Marc, placed her hands around his shoulders, and then directly linked herself into the conversation.

"Dear, dear Sil! It's wonderful to see you," she said. "So, what are you guys plotting now?"

"Sil says he can transport our army to Harbor, en masse, literally bypassing the Gate. He says it's your doing."

"My doing? Sil?"

"Well, you have witnessed something like it before, my dear, on a much smaller scale, of course."

Leenah's nonplussed look blossomed into one of surprise. "You mean. . . Gossamer? The Doctor?"

"Gossamer. Yes. They are coming here to join our efforts and to do something only they can do. I expect them anytime now. Your Doctor, Tonhaaa, is determined to affect the outcome of this battle. He has seen variations–possible futures–in his Visions. Something I'm sure you both understand."

Yes, of course!" Leenah said. "But Sil, I saw them transporting or morphing themselves between TD and SD realms as individual people, dropping into their doorless stone temples. We're talking about entire warships here and an Ash Alien Gate! Did the Doctor say they could manage something this big?"

"He is worried about it. He believes that if we have one Gossamer citizen on board each ship, they can combine their efforts and take the entire fleet over to the other system in a single moment. He says it will be dangerous. I don't know how they will fare. I have my own worries for them, but he is certain they can make the jump with us."

Kera and Paris came in as Marc got up and began pacing the

bridge. "Sil, we all have to run this ship together as one team, so we all need to know what the strategy is. They're here now, so I'm bringing Kera and Paris into this discussion. " He took a moment to fill the other two in, then asked, "What about our Terraform Ship here, Sil?"

"You must certainly go in first. It's important that we ramp up the threats to ZEK one level at a time. If the threat of the so-called plague ship is enough to cause them to capitulate, then so much the better. I'd much rather not put more lives at risk. If not, then we intimidate them with the sudden, unanticipated appearance of the entire fleet. Beyond that, perhaps we'll have that special Rindd ship surprise you arranged, Marc. We just have to hope RR will be handling all that. In the end, if all else fails, well . . . there's your terraformer beam itself that could be, shall we say, *demonstrated* for effect upon an attacking fleet or a barren moon, perhaps. The people will remember the old vids and the stories. They will have to capitulate."

Kera leaned in. "Sil. I am Kera, and I am amazed and apprecia-tive of the leadership and sacrifices you and your people have made and are making. It is good to meet you and to work with you. Let me speak quickly so we can focus on what we have to do. You want us to jump the Gate first. That's certainly the right approach. In the short time we've had, we've become pretty good at operating this T-ship, but a Gate bypass is *way* beyond my abilities, or even all of us combined. We'd have to have one of these Gossamer people on board to facilitate it, then?"

"Yes, Kera. I was thinking of one person in particular. Leenah's on-world contact and friend, Brioleee."

Leenah's face lit up. "Brioleee! Oh, yes, Sil. She's ideal! Oh, I can't wait to see her again!"

Sil laughed along with the others. "I'm glad for you, my dear. She will be the first to test the technique with you and your. . . T-ship, did you call it? If she is successful, then we know the others can follow en masse when the time comes. The Doctor says they will know when that moment comes, so we will have to wait and trust them. This will be rather hard on my nerves, I think."

Marc said, "I believe and trust him, Sil. He paid us a visit back on Marc's Pile and solved a lot of serious problems for us."

"He paid you a visit? . . . Oh, goodness. I'd love to hear that story! But it will have to wait along with your others. I have to attend to some ship issues and I will alert you as soon as they arrive. We're going to have quite a lot of tales to tell after all this, aren't we?"

The Gossamers arrived in the Hub System in a Sisters transport ship the next work-day cycle. Hundreds of their citizens were on board, enough to assign at least one per ship, as promised. They watched their arrival on the vid feed from Sil's ship. The Doctor and several of the Elders of the Gossamer tribe emerged from the other ship all dressed in standard Harbor ship outfits but adorned with colorful accents of feathers, seed necklaces, twine wrist bands with embedded crystal stones, and other tribal decorations. Leenah, having worked with them for so long, knew most of this group of Gossamers personally. She was anxious to see Brioleee and laughed with joy when the lanky woman appeared through the portal following the Doctor.

"Oh, I can't wait to talk with her! Brioleee is a little different, but I know you'll all like her."

There were no further developments at the dangerous Harbor Gate other than the occasional ineffective follow-up to ZEK's initial swarm of little torpedoes. Marc felt tense but optimistic. The time was approaching to break the deadlock. A small shuttle came toward them from Sil's ship, bearing Brioleee.

"Leenahhhh, Leenahhhh, Leenahhh!" Brioleee squealed as she came through their portals. Marc was surprised at how tall and lanky the woman was. Leenah had tried to warn him, but the reality was fascinating. Her torso was about normal size, but her arms and legs were almost comical in their extra length, the combination giving her a spidery look. She seemed to be able to maneuver herself well, though loping a bit in the medium-low grav of the T-ship.

"Oh, it's so wonderful to see you!" Leenah said as they embraced one another. Once introductions were made, she asked, "How long before we need to make the special jump, Marc? Do we have time to visit a bit first?"

"Yes, you two go talk a while. I'll arrange things with Sil and the others so we can coordinate our efforts. Just remember that when we do go, we need to be ready not only to make this unique jump, but in the very instant we emerge over there to expect to confront ZEK, as if directly to his Faces."

Marc got Paris to help him prepare a meal from the supplies Brioleee had brought them. He made sure Anibale was fed and remained properly contained in his cell, then had the conference with Sil, Kera, and the other Sisters and Farms leaders. Several hours later, Leenah and Brioleee had rejoined them in the T-ship's bridge and it was time for the jump.

Leenah helped Brioleee into a low bench depression the Ship had produced for them at the back of the bridge room. She sat down beside the Gossamer woman and held her hand. Brioleee began to put her physical body into a meditative state as he and the others watched, then they all joined her in the vision space of the SD. Marc could still feel his hands, now fully morphed and integrated into the Ship's network of controls, but saw with his other vision. Within the SD realm, Brioleee was awake and energized, concentrating not on the closed Gate itself, but the *idea* of the space-time barrier between themselves and Harbor. He could see her own projected inner vision of Harbor System space, just beyond the Gate to Hub. The visual scene was *vivid*, much more so than his own simple memory of that place. He suddenly appreciated just how expert and attuned Brioleee was in this mode, and he felt much more confident about what was going to take place next.

The actual jump came with a sudden rushing sound that grew quickly to a seething howl like a vast windstorm, then rapidly dropped off again. They had arrived in Harbor System, bringing a very unwelcome gift to ZEK: an honest-to-middie, authentic, Ash Alien xenoplague ship.

Chapter Thirty-six

ZEK had hoped the secondary rounds of torpedoes would do more damage, but as he had anticipated, the Sisters rabble withdrew and shielded up until that second flanking attack came from Kaziet's Rindd ships. He was watching the Zip-tech data flow, trying to assess how much damage the Rindders had actually caused when Elder Bai came bursting into his control booth without any protocol or preamble.

"The latest comm bot data. Look, ZEK! It's true!"

"What are you talking about, Bai . . ." he began, feeling annoyed. Then he had turned enough to see the other screen that Bai was gesturing at. There, in Hub space, forming a new and dreadful presence amid all the Sisters and Farms ships, was one about five or six times larger than any other. It had a complex midsection surrounded by flat ribbon-like circular bands and there was a roughly spherical nose pod. The monstrous black orifice of a weapon snout loomed below. The thing was moving rapidly under its own power

Xenoplague

and was taking on the Rindd fleet.

"Yes, of course, Bai. That confirms my earlier suspicions. Marc and Kera have found their damnable plague ship and now it has been turned against our people."

Bai looked at him with weary eyes. "The Rindders are scattering. That xenoplague monster has active beam weaponry as well as its main doomsday vent. We may have lost Hub."

"And all the worlds behind it, Bai. All the worlds behind if I don't do something soon."

The Elder glanced again at the image of the huge plague ship, then back at ZEK.

"What can you do, ZEK? They can't make it through your blocked Gate, surely?"

"No, Bai. But I have the door key. I can sneak things through to them, eh? Just like I've been doing."

"You have something that can take out that ship? You smile. What is it, ZEK?"

"Oh, just a simple *human*-made FTL device. It won't destroy the ship. No, it won't! It will simply take it on a little unplanned trip. How fresh is that comm bot feed? We will need accurate target location specs."

"It is recent–within the hour, but you'll have to send several through in a sequence to know where the thing is in case they start moving again," Bai said, "unless your Zip comms can help us.

"Coming from that resource, we don't have that level of resolution or reliability yet–more's the pity. Frankly, it's amazing to have *any* comms connection to our Rindd fighters at this point."

An alarm buzzer started on Bai's and ZEK's comms at the same moment.

"ZEK," Bai said with a shocked voice. His face had dropped. "Never mind trying to track them in Hub System."

As ZEK looked at the in-system scanfeed, he felt his heart leap into his throat. The xenoplague ship was no longer in Hub System. It was in Harbor. Here. Now.

430

He hit the comm link to Jorn, who was responsible for getting his FTL device into position at the Gate. They almost had it in the right spot to be slipped through to Hub.

"Jorn! Abort that and bring it around to the new arrival!"

The man's face appeared. "What? What new arrival?" Voices mingled as Jorn looked back and forth and then someone handed him a viewpad. His face visibly drained to white.

"THAT new arrival," ZEK said. "Send it on its way, Jorn. Set the target seek controls and let it go. You truly don't want to have to go fetch it once it's active and gone from you." ZEK smiled grimly.

The plague ship had appeared not at the closed Gate itself, but quite some distance away in what appeared to be dark, open space somewhere between the Hub Gate and the one to Avalon.

What demon's conjuration is this? The damned Zips fly in and out of systems like that. Surely, they are behind Earth's plague ship like so many think. Well, this puts truth to Anibale's story of how the renegades at Barrkon's Oven got away. We have more to worry about than I had hoped. Must take them out now, quickly, with the device.

A man's voice cut into the comm system. A hail from the plague vessel.

"ZEK and the Council of Colors. I am Marc of the Star and your time has come to an end. You see what is before you. This ship has the capacity to destroy your world. There are no aliens here. We are all middies. We demand your unconditional surrender."

ZEK punched the comm control to appear online as his large Golden Face. He didn't have to force a glower on it. The one on his real face was enough.

"You vermin! You have no right to demand anything of ZEK or the worlds of true men and women. Put down your dangerous plague ship before you commit a horror upon your own people!"

Marc's reply came immediately, accompanied now by a visual. He looked out at ZEK from the ship's bridge with Kera at his side. She stared defiantly at the camera as Marc spoke. "Your hold on power for over a thousand years has been based on greed and inequality.

431

Xenoplague

The Midclass have been forced to tolerate your excesses, but now the Elite class has abused their privileges. You have all gone far too far, for far too long. It is time to change the system."

Kera spoke. "Power is only power, ZEK. It is always subject to overthrow by another, greater power. What you see before you in this special ship is great power, indeed, but it is not all that we have arrayed against you. There are secrets of the Ash Aliens that we now control–secrets you have never dreamed of. Your closed Gate will not protect you. This ship is your first and last chance to surrender and save yourself, your Elite comrades, and your very world."

She did not blink as Marc continued, "We do not wish to bring harm to anyone. Surrender now and we will not be forced to do so."

ZEK sneered at them. "You bluff. You think to intimidate me into fearful submission with your damnable *xenoplague* ship. I think your nasty Zip friends helped you leapfrog over the Lines and you are here in Harbor alone now, so terribly isolated from all your friends back in Hub. Where are *they*, eh? You are vulnerable, perhaps?" His mocking tone turned hard. "Vulnerable to a small but very dangerous object now tracking your demon ship and advancing relentlessly upon you."

"Your weapons cannot harm this kind of Ash Alien ship, ZEK," Marc said.

"You think your vessel is indestructible by our weapons? Well, perhaps so. Perhaps not. The small object heading toward you now is not a *weapon* at all, however.

"Your alien abomination is certainly a powerful weapon and your shielding, I'm sure, is equally strong, but you are not indestructible. You must stand down *now* and relinquish your ship to me and Elder Bai. You *do* see the small vessel approaching you now? Good. Scan it well. It is a simple thing really. A human-made answer to your alien plague ship.

"When humanity first leaped across space and time from Earth to Harbor, we used human-made faster-than-light technology. That is often forgotten, to our shame. The device approaching you now has no alien parts whatsoever. It is an FTL device that has been prepared especially for this encounter and without a care at all for the destination to which it is tuned. When it is close enough, it will *leap*, carrying itself and anything within a critical radius of it to . . . wherever it might go. Where is that destination? Who knows?

"Its settings have been randomized and there is no feedback loop. It and you will simply disappear from our present universe and either instantly disintegrate or, perhaps, end up in an unknown patch of space somewhere in a parallel universe or in the darks between galaxies. Perhaps–it is possible–that you will arrive in an alien system where you can live in peace until you die. However it works out for you, one crucial fact remains. *There will be no Xeno-plague ship threatening humanity here in the Second Domain!* You will never return to Harbor or see your home worlds again."

ZEK's voice boomed in his own ears. He held the glower firmly.

He could see Marc look down at their scans. Kera nodded to someone off-camera and a beam weapon fired from the plague ship. The FTL device was still a long way from them, but a strike like that should take it out in an instant. ZEK smiled broadly when the little craft suddenly turned into a metal sphere, something like a ball bearing in space. The Zip tech shield had worked perfectly. Yet another kudo to Kaziet and her team. The Zips may not be trust-worthy, but at least they seem not to have played any favorites.

"Surprise," he said smoothly. "We have a few Zip friends as well. That device will reach you in less than one hour. I have the only control that will abort its mission. I suggest you think about this and make the correct choice. I care not one grain of sand whether you cease to exist. In fact, it would make things much easier in the long run if you did." He paused and glared at them. "Shall we wait, then?"

Marc checked his scans off-screen again, then turned back to him. "Well, perhaps it's time for a little visit to Helm, don't you think? We'll be there pretty soon. You might want to call off your dog."

The pilot's face wore a worried look now, ZEK noted with some satisfaction. Kera's was still unreadable. He turned his voice and Face haughty and dismissive.

Xenoplague

"We tracked your acceleration in Hub. Even with your increased capacity, you will not reach us here in time, fool. The FTL mine is now active. I am ZEK, and you are dead."

It was hard to be a prisoner. Anibale had never been locked up before and he was frustrated, not so much at the physical restraint, but at the lack of access to information. He had tried everything he could think of to defeat the plague ship's containment, but it had sealed him into this small cell with an organic wall structure that flowed into shape at Kera's will or instructions. There was no door to test. He had been given food and water and there was a circulation of fresh air in here, plus, he had found that his intention to relieve himself caused an appropriate aperture to appear and then recede, morphing out of and back into the walls. There was no bed.

If I can intend for a toilet, why can't I intend for a door? Damn them all. I never thought I'd be locked up *inside* a plague ship. I just wish I knew what was going on.

He had felt a strange falling sensation not long ago, almost like a Gate transit, but different somehow.

I must know what is happening and I must get out of this place!

He let the thought sit in his mind as he curled up against the wall. After a while, drifting through a troubled sleep, he came back toward wakefulness. Within a dream, he felt a distinct impression that someone was watching him. It wasn't enough to pull him completely back to full alertness, but part of him thought enough of the anomaly to examine it more closely. He made himself relax his mind again and just listen and look within his dream state, trying to recall the impression. To his slight alarm, it returned.

It was female and it seemed to be looking and listening to him, waiting for something. He tried to gently rouse himself further without scaring her away. This was no dream fragment. The impression was quite strong now. She was truly there–somewhere. He cautiously reached out with his mind's eye and visualized a datascreen. His heart leaped when the female entity seemed to respond by turning her attention to his imagined screen. Then it lit up. He saw Harbor System displayed. There were BlackMil ships arrayed some distance away near the Gates and surrounding Harbor and Helm directly.

I'm in Harbor! Wait, is this real? Who is this woman?

A vision of a strange female face came to him. She was not quite human, but somehow mechanical as well as organic. She seemed to be studying him. In one flash of an instant, he saw her flicker into the shape of a ship: this ship. Then back again.

An AI! The ship . . . you are this ship? Yes?

Anibale was fully awake now. He felt more than saw or heard a simple affirmation from her. Carefully now, oh so carefully, he decided to try something. He made a picture in his mind of a shuttlecraft flying down to Harbor with himself inside. He visualized it as distinctly and clearly as he could imagine as if it were a dimensional video recording of an actual craft. He felt her watching him do this, but there was nothing more. A sharp pang of disappointment went through him. As he felt it, she seemed to become more intent! He kept his eyes closed and concentrated as hard as he could.

Yes! I will die here if I don't leave the ship on a shuttle. I am feeling very bad. Very bad. I must go now! I need your help, Ship! Help me out of here and into a shuttlecraft. I must go home! Must go to my own home right now!

He put as much emotion into his plea as he could muster, which then flowed a lot more than he had intended. Unexpectedly, the feelings he described truly poured out of him. He continued to visualize and make his plea to her until he was exhausted, mewling and still sprawled on the floor. A small sound made him open his eyes. The room's dim light became just a bit brighter as a small aperture opened up in the wall across from him. He sat up with a jerk.

The opening slowly increased in size until he was looking out into a darkened corridor. At that moment, he had a very strange sensation. It was a mental image of a small pod: a spacecraft of a design that one might expect from such a ship. Smooth and organic looking, powering up and ready to go. He knew how to move through the Ship to find it without a map. He did not know how he knew. It was just in his mind now. He did not hesitate.

He almost leaped out into the passageway, not taking any chances that the wall would close once more before he could escape. He immediately started down the corridor toward the pod ship that was still there, glowing, in his mind's eye. He turned around a curve and stuttered to a stop. A woman was coming toward him carrying a tray full of food items. It was that waif of a woman he had seen with Marc. Leenah, yes–that was the name.

The instant she saw him, she jerked and dropped the tray, spilling and breaking everything on it, the pieces scattering along the floor. She yelped and tried to turn back the way she came, but Anibale ran straight at her and landed a hard fist blow on the back side of her head. Leenah fell instantly into a limp pile of limbs on the floor.

Damn and damn. A new girlfriend, perhaps! Now, I have a hostage. Much better. Much better indeed.

He scooped her light form up and ran now, as fast as he could manage. The pod glowed brighter in his vision as he got closer to it. There! That wall was opening up for him! Sure enough, the gap increased until he could enter into a small flight-ready pod. He propped Leenah into one of the two seats it had extruded and sat down in the other one. He visualized some basic controls, but they did not appear for him. He visualized them more strongly and the Ship woman's face flickered for a moment. Then, the vision he had created of those controls glowed firmly in his mind. He realized then that he could fly this ship, but only with the imagined controls she had just provided. He was truly amazed by this, but there was no time now for such weak distractions, only for action. He was Anibale, Prime Blue, and this was war!

The pod closed behind him and extruded itself out of the side of the Ship like a small pellet. He was on his way back to Helm with a precious prize to guarantee his security!

———————✻———————

Kera looked back to the rear of the terraform ship's bridge where Leenah was caring for Brioleee.

"How is she, Leenah?"

Leenah smiled, but she looked worried. The lanky Gossamer woman had expended such a large amount of her SD energy in making the jump for them that afterward, she fell unconscious, incapacitated. Leenah held the strange woman's hands and hummed a tune to her that resonated in the room in both modalities. Paris sat next to them, looking tired.

Marc sat in the extruded seat beside Kera's own. He was piloting them toward Helm as fast as they could go but was visibly nervous and exhausted from their situation and his banter with ZEK. The FTL mine device was slowly gaining on them. ZEK claimed it was active, and Kera gingerly reached out to it with her enhanced senses. It seemed cold and metallic, and there was a kind of wind, sucking the space-time around it into its maw and sending it all down into a whirlpool that was every bit as deadly to them as a black hole.

Leenah had stopped humming and quietly said, "We can't fight ZEK without keeping up our own strength. Brioleee will need some liquids, too. I'm going down to the little galley the Ship produced. I'll bring something for us. Keep an eye on her, Paris."

"Don't worry, Leenah. I'll watch over her."

Marc nodded to them, and then he joined Kera's efforts to contact and manipulate the mine in SD, but the machine was a TD object made by human hands only. Reaching out through SD only, they couldn't get any kind of grip on it.

Marc sent a short blast of one of their T-ship's very tangible beam weapons at the thing. With the device turned on, the beam simply disappeared down the FTL path it had opened up. It slowed the mine's approach not one bit.

"Marc, we could try to power up the main terraform beam." Kera could hear the strain in her own voice. Her hands were white where she gripped the Star.

Marc shook his head as he studied the vector mapping screen displaying the path of the weapon.

"They launched it from the Hub Gate zone. Its position is too much in line now with Harbor in the background. Far too dangerous to fire the T-beam in that direction. It's like the Gate weapon–too powerful and unwieldy to use around inhabited worlds. And, it would involve a yet untested coordinated effort from all of us. Any mistake could be devastating."

"Then, maybe it's time to call in the armada. We're in this too far by ourselves."

Marc's face was red and his enlarged hands were glowing, enmeshed in the T-ship's control wall where Kera had shared part of the piloting interface with him. "They wouldn't be able to separate us from this damned mine," he said. "There's still a little time left. I don't want to pull the trigger on Sil's actions before the last moment and especially not while we are looking weak or threatened by ZEK. Let's try one more time to reach out in vision space and . . .Wait! What happened?"

The presence of Leenah, long a constant SD song in their minds, suddenly cut off, her absence there a stark silence. Kera searched with her vision and locked onto an anomaly within the Ship. There was a protrusion being formed on the outer hull, aft. It glowed in SD and she now felt the presence of someone on the Ship. Anibale. Not in his cell. He was running down-ship toward that protrusion.

"Anibale! He's escaped and heading for something. A pod maybe? Yes! A shuttle pod is forming. Ship, can you show me? What are you doing for that man?"

A virtual schematic showed up in her vision. It seemed the Ship was helping Anibale.

Paris spoke. "It's not Her fault, Kera. She is programmed to be support for the life forms on board, not to harm them. I can feel it from her. She doesn't understand why we had him confined."

Kera saw immediately that Paris was right.

"He's got Leenah!" Marc shouted. He had unfastened himself and jumped up. "I've got to get her! Kera, call the armada if you have to, but give me time to get away. I've got to catch them!"

"I'm going with you," Paris said.

"No, stay here and protect Kera."

"I'm supposed to be *your* bodyguard, Marc."

"I know, but I can move quicker on my own, and I have to go right now! Work with Kera to run the Ship! You can do it."

"It's launched. He's gone with her," Kera said. "I'm getting you another pod."

She was already asking the Ship AI to make a pod for Marc, and the Ship responded not only to the request but to the urgency she was projecting. A new pod formed just behind where the first one was.

Marc hesitated. "I have to go, but I can't leave you here with this . . ."

"Go get her, Marc." Kera's voice was tight as she cut him off. "We'll get you back or find you on Helm. We cannot lose this ship! But if it comes down to it, the mine is locked onto the main ship. I'll extrude more pods and abandon it to the wild portal. Now, go!"

He gave her a look filled with pain and panic. He nodded once, then bolted out of the bridge.

Kera and Paris looked at each other and both shook their heads. "Come on up here and help me out. We have to do something about this mine or we're dead in half an hour."

Paris came up and sat in Marc's chair. "Huh. Well, if we go, at least Marc and Leenah won't go with us," she said. Kera gave her a sharp look, then nodded. Paris rescanned the local zone. "Marc's pod is launched now. Both are headed straight for Harbor and Helm."

"I'll get us away one way or another, Paris. Marc is right. You have more sensitivity within SD than you think. Help me now and let's fight this thing." Kera turned her vision toward the FTL mine.

"I wish I could get a better grasp of it in the vision space. It's . . . slippery." She felt Paris's added energy to her own, but it wasn't enough for them to take hold. They tried over and over to touch it and Kera began to feel panic and dread rising in her. Then a new energy appeared with them.

"I cann helllp . . ." Brioleee said into their common vision space. "I am better now. I see it. The macheeene is strange and dangerousss."

Kera quickly glanced around and back, but Brioleee was still lying on the floor behind them with her eyes shut. "You were hurt, Brioleee. I don't want you to hurt yourself again."

"I will be better now and I can hellp. Loook . . ." Kera looked and saw a bubble of glowing color surround the FTL mine. It shimmered in blue and white. It did not slow the mine, but it seemed to give Kera and Paris a place to connect to in the alternate space they were now fully immersed in. She could feel how to attach herself to it, so she did.

Instantly, like opening up a sealed can of something under pressure, a blackness streamed out of the place where the mine was. It flowed rapidly and took shape in front of Kera. It was a creature with the head of a bird. She instinctively recoiled.

"I am the True One," it boomed. "You require Power to overcome it. I give it to you. You chose the path of Power. You are responsible for it. Follow it now." The voice thundered in her mind. She knew that Paris and Brioleee also reeled under it. The bird entity held a Golden Rod in its gnarled stick-like hands. It glowed with visceral power. He held it out to Kera. It would be so easy to take it and smash the mine–smash everything that threatened her or her friends! She should! The evil people deserve her wrath and her judgment! She felt her vision hands reaching out toward the Rod. She almost had it!

Then Kera felt the presence of the two others increasing until Paris and Brioleee were right next to her, floating above the image of the space-consuming mine and the black shrouds of the True One with his Golden offering.

Kera made a decision. "I will not. I will not become You. You represent the things I and my friends are fighting against. I gave up your Tools before and *I refuse your help.* Your price is too high."

She felt the other two women's hands on her arms, comforting her, encouraging her, feeding her their supporting energies. She gripped the Star again and the True One howled and he and his Orb flashed with a blinding crack and fell into the distorted mouth of the mine below them. A gigantic weight seemed to lift off of Kera and she felt good for a moment. Then she grew angry. Angrier than she had ever felt before. Angry at the temptation she had just had to deal with at such a moment, angry at the stupid mine that was even now sliding its doomsday toward herself and her friends, and angry at her entire life situation. It was time to fix this once and for all.

She felt Brioleee and Paris feeding her strength now in a powerful rush. Paris projected a memory vision and spoke to her of how Marc had gathered together the energy of the cargo ship in both the TD and SD modes when they made their black-arrow run. Kera sought the T-ship AI and asked for her help and acquiescence to do the same now. The Ship relaxed her internal controls to allow Kera in. Together, all four of them worked in concert as Kera gathered up the strands and cords and pools of the Ship's vital energies. She contained it, rolled it up, compressed it until it rippled, crackled, and glistened with kinetic potential. Finally, on a sharp intake of breath, she reached back in both dimensional modes simultaneously and threw it as hard as she could straight at the mine.

The huge and now hissing yellow ball of her energy projectile flew from her fingers, roaring out across the empty space between the T-ship and the pursuing mine, and crashed against the thing. It seemed to stall there for a moment, then it was drawn into the gullet of the mine's crude wormhole. Just before it disappeared completely to wherever the mine was randomly set to jump, it stalled again and brightened for a moment before it exploded in a massive eruption. The mine was physically close enough to them by now that the shock wave of matter being expelled crashed against the T-ship a few moments later, vibrating Kera and Paris out of their chairs and onto the floor with Brioleee.

Everything went still and all the lights were out. Kera opened her physical eyes and groped around. Her hand fell on Paris's arm. Paris grunted and shook herself.

"Well," she croaked, "that's that. Hell of a good job!"

Kera couldn't speak yet. She reached out to the Ship and saw a glimmer of her just as some lights began to flicker on one at a time within the bridge. She looked around. Paris was sprawled next to her, right where the chairs had been. Those had receded into the floor during the incident. The two of them remained there for a moment, catching their breath.

"Hey, where's Brioleee?" Paris said.

Kera looked behind them, but the Gossamer woman was gone.

"She may not have made it."

"Damn. She really strengthened that push at the end," Paris said. "The bridge is still sealed. I guess it took her physical body, too."

"I wonder. . ." Kera said and concentrated back into the vision dimension. Paris joined her and they held an open question in their minds with the shape of Brioleee. An impression of a smile came to them almost instantly. It never came into words for them, but Kera later claimed that Brioleee "told" them that she was fine now, but fully in the Spirit Dimension where she would remain. She was still able to help and to join forces with her other Gossamers and with all others who can tune to the vision space consciously along the Bright Path. Do not be concerned for her, she told them. Brioleee was happy.

They tried to raise Marc on comms without luck. The scans showed the two small pods arriving at Helm and beginning to dock.

"All right, Paris. Let's go help Marc and Leenah. We're going to take ZEK's nightmare right to his doorstep. That's where we have to be before we call in Sil's army for the final blow."

Paris said, "Yeah. Wait a sec. Keep looking into that scanner. There. Let's put *that* Face up on our outgoing feed for ZEK to see."

It was a freeze frame of Kera's countenance showing a stone-dead scowl and a fiery anger deep-seated in her eyes.

"Ha. Sure. Let him see that and we'll let the Ship do the talking. I need him to capitulate, though, not totally panic. We have to be ready to get Marc and Leenah out of there if things go badly."

Paris posted Kera's Face as a silent broadcast feed as Kera gripped the Star and slipped into full SD mode again to arrange an important plan with the Ship herself. The great terraforming beam that comprised the main function and purpose of the T-ship had remained dormant during all the proceedings so far. Kera needed it to appear as fully operational, displaying all of its color effects, to completely terrorize ZEK and the Elites of Harbor and Helm, but it was of the utmost importance that the Ship understood what this was for and that the beam itself never actually be turned on. The Ship AI was still weakened from the mine shock wave, but with Paris's help and, Kera thought, a vague sense of deep communications assist from Brioleee, the Ship confirmed that she understood their plan. There were many layers of safety protocols built into the terraform system. Those had to remain, and Kera had to require and gain assurance from the AI that they absolutely *must* remain.

Pulling her mind back out of the SD space, she gave Paris a strained glance. "We just want to light up the Ship so ZEK believes it's rigged and ready to fire an honest-to-goodness doomsday beam at them. We've destroyed his last toy. I need to goad him personally now. Shake him up by asserting absolute power delivered to his Faces by someone he knows as a mere middie girl from Farms." she said. "Now, let's go to Helm."

Chapter Thirty-seven

"Kera! You know me. I have treated you well. Speak to me now! You would not dare to use this terrible weapon against your own people. We are all human!" ZEK stared at the still image coming from the plague ship. He was sweating as he leaned forward in his chair in the control center suite behind the Great Screen.

"You will lose more than you will gain! You will never have support from survivors of it. You will be hunted down, not made into ZEK! Stop and stand down!"

The cursed plague ship had pulled into a matching orbit with Helm, its mouth glowing a deep reddish yellow and its metal hoop bands expanded and illuminated in flowing patterns of coruscating neon colors. It was aimed directly at them.

Bai was here, too. The old man was more agitated than ZEK had ever seen him.

"Genocidal maniacs! *Genocidal!*" Bai wailed.

That presumptuous image of Kera's face was all they had gotten from the ship since they had destroyed his FTL mine. It was impossible. How could they use enough energy to cause that level of explosion without harming their ship in the process? It had been so close to them!

The damned plagueship is truly alien and cursed, protected in some way we don't know yet. The middie fools have a lot to answer for, bringing such a monster into Harbor. There must be a way to contain them!

Bai said, "Look!"

The face image from the plague ship switched to a live feed of Kera. Her eyes were just as cold and angry as in the still photo, but now they flashed out at him.

"ZEK of Harbor. See what has come to you. Your pathetic attempts to harm me have failed. They served only to make me more angry and determined to see an end to your abuses."

"You are insane!" he growled.

"There is a difference between insanity and anger at injustice. I shall harm no world, harm no population on purpose, but I will take you and your Council out with one fell blast if you do not surrender to me personally. I represent the middies and *Helm* is forfeit to your excesses and abuses. You have very little time."

ZEK thought hard and fast. He was still projecting his Face and he steeled himself to make it look contemptuous.

"You have the plague weapon," he hissed. "You can kill me and everyone on Helm with it if you are so pathologically criminal to do so, but you are still isolated here, Kera. Your friends are all bottled up on the other side of the Gate to Hub. They have not come to rescue you! If you destroy Helm–if you destroy *me*–you will destroy the knowledge and control of the Gate lock. However you managed to jump the systems to get here in your ship of death, you'll have to jump back and take your xenoplague with you to Hub and Farms where you and your people will be isolated and abandoned behind an impenetrable wall."

Kera did not blink.

She said, "I give you one hour to gather up the Council Elder and members and present yourselves at the main dock."

The link went dead and the photo of the cold visage of the fool woman reappeared on all the screens in the control suite. He was certain it was being seen everywhere else in all the worlds, as well. He posted his own haughty Face, then turned to Bai who pointed at another scan screen.

"Look, ZEK. Two very odd-looking pods on close approach from the direction of the xenoplague ship."

"Weapons?" ZEK was shocked they could have come without being noticed.

"No. First one has just soft-docked." He studied the hangar camera's close-up and body scans. "Well. It's Prime Blue and someone else with him. A woman."

"Who is she?"

Bai did a couple of data scans, then spoke without turning to him.

"She is Leenah Bordu, a known Sisters operative and apparently a personal friend of Marc 54Arons . . . who just docked in the other pod." He finally turned and gave a tight smile. "He abandoned the xenoplague ship for her, ZEK! It looks like our Marc of the Star has lost his girlfriend, now in Anibale's clutches, and he's in hot pursuit!"

ZEK frowned at Bai's tone, but inside he felt a little thrill of anticipation. Perhaps the fanciful winds of fate were in his favor at last. "Which way, Bai?"

"No need to scurry. They are headed right for the Great Seat. They will all be next door to us here in just a few minutes."

Kera put up her still image, switched off the comm link to ZEK, and turned to Paris, who was sitting next to her with a grim look on her face.

"He hasn't made the connection. He thinks we were able to jump the Line because of something inherent in the Xenoplague Ship. It still hasn't occurred to him that the others might be able to jump, too."

She saw the corners of Paris's mouth tip up to make it a grim smile. "Yeah, you're right! It's just too far outside his way of thinking, I guess."

Kera said, "This gives us some time to try to reach Marc and Leenah–figure out what we can do to extract them safely. Let's try to reach them again in vision space, Paris. I don't know if Leenah is conscious, but Marc certainly is."

They closed their eyes to diminish the potentially confusing overlay of their physical surroundings and immediately, Kera felt the Ship around her. The AI seemed to be waiting for whatever was next. She tried to picture Marc and Leenah to the Ship as well, hoping she could somehow amplify their efforts, but the Ship seemed to be preoccupied. It felt like the Ship had seen the two of them but could not focus on them, glancing quickly, then looking away at something else. Kera felt another similar presence within the vision space, but it seemed far away and she couldn't identify it.

"Ship?" she projected, but there was no real response, so she took Paris's hand and they concentrated on Marc. They could feel something of his presence, far away now, approaching Helm. Kera could tell that he was angry, frustrated, and determined, but she couldn't make any more of a direct link. *Telepathy is not as straight-forward as I wish it was.*

No kidding, Paris responded.

At that moment, they both felt a draining power flow and a rushing sound changing from high pitch to low, steadily losing momentum and energy. Kera opened her eyes.

"Something's wrong with the Ship. We're losing the terraform weapon prep glow. She's shutting it down."

Kera tried to reach the Ship again, but this time, she would not acknowledge her presence and seemed to be fragmenting into and out of her human-style presentation and that of the larger machine she represented. She looked blocky and mechanical, then came a flash of smoother data flow, then stillness for a moment–jerking back and forth between states. Their ship began to drift slightly out of position relative to Helm.

She tried to control it more directly by grasping the Star. With great effort, she could recover their course, but the moment she relaxed, they began to drift again.

"What's wrong with her? I've lost control! It wasn't like this before! She must have been damaged in the blast more than I realized." Both of them were fully back in the TD mode in the bridge and Paris made a little sound.

"Huh. Probably so, but there's something else, Kera. It's like I said. We all have to work together to run this ship, and Marc and Leenah are not here anymore. You can't expect to continue to control it entirely by yourself, even with me helping a little."

Kera stared at her with her mouth open. "You're right, of course. I assumed I could still run things like I'd been doing. This could really put us in danger. It may be time to bring in the armada after all."

"That's your call, but I . . ." Paris dropped her eyes to a screen.

"What's wrong?"

"Zips on scan. Coming our way!"

In the next moment, the buzzing sounds of Zip ships came blasting into their speakers. It didn't diminish like it normally would, though. It seemed to increase as the Zip ships approached them.

"Four of 'em. That formation looks just like when they took Marc and Sil and me from Rindd to the Sisters. They're transporting a human ship!" Paris said.

Sure enough, there was a small vessel emerging from a network lattice of blue light strands stretched between the strange fuzzy-looking cocoons. It was on course to rendezvous with them. The Zip ships flashed white and withdrew with a rapidity that seemed comical. Gone, just like that, followed by the absence of the loud RF buzzing.

Paris poked at the comm. "Well, lookie who's hailing us. I should have guessed. It's RR."

A moment later, RR's smiling face appeared on screen. His eyes were dancing.

"Hi, Paris! You must be Kera. I'm pleased to meet you. I am Rass-Ruuk Biniun of the Suite Gray on Rindd, but everyone calls me RR. Mind if we board your rather daunting ship? I have someone very special with me who can help us win this conflict with ZEK and end all this hostility for good."

<hr />

Marc was surprised at the completeness of the SD vision control panel he was using to operate the podcraft the T-ship had produced for him. It even included functioning TD comms. Bi-modal. That was the right term. As he approached Helm, he could hear Anibale calling in to announce his presence and to avert being fired upon by the Helm Unit of the BlackMil Guards.

Fortunately, that also protects me. If he's hurt her in any way, . . .

It also surprised him that Anibale could use *his* controls within SD space. He had clearly developed some modicum of bi-modal capability or he would be as blind as ZEK to it. That could make him much more dangerous. *If Leenah regains consciousness, Marc might be able to connect with her and apply some type of surprise leverage to get her free, but Anibale might be able to detect SD communications now and interfere. He would have to be very careful in dealing with Prime Blue.*

The little pod followed a standard auto-docking routine, so Marc let it go without announcing his own presence in any way. He hoped if Anibale had noticed the second craft, he would think it was just an unmanned auxiliary that the T-ship had also produced, but there was no sign that he had taken such notice.

His pod secured itself in the main docks of Helm not more than three or four minutes after Anibale and Leenah's craft did. He had no idea what to expect on the platforms, so he prepared for the worst scenario: lots of suspicious and perhaps violent guards. He viewed his own hands in SD space and sent that special kind of energy that he had now become so familiar with. He did this with intention and a force of mental willpower. He felt the energies collecting and concentrating in his right hand, especially, waiting there to be unleashed when he needed it. He opened his physical eyes in the dark pod cabin. Multiple data lights flickered along the walls and his right hand was beginning to flood the entire cocoon in an ominous deep red glow.

When the hatch evolved out of the wall like an organic orifice opening up on some strange plant, Marc was ready. As it widened, he peeked out at the hangar platforms. Anibale's pod was right next to his, but the hatch on it was completely open and he knew they had departed it. In SD mode it felt *empty* and he could detect a faint hint of Anibale's essence receding. He also felt the first twinges of something from Leenah. She was regaining consciousness!

Marc held his hand in front of him as he exited the pod. It was glowing brightly and projecting a force field that he knew would repel attacks. The contingent of BlackMil on duty here saw him the moment he appeared and ran up with weapons pointed to stop him, but Marc sprinted past them and simply pushed them and their guns out of the way. He was encased in the white-yellow electric glow of the field now. It acted like a personal version of a Zip shield, but this tech was much older than the Zips, he felt, and a much more natural part of his own body and mind. He heard them yelling as he received several blasts from the BlackMil energy weapons, but he felt nothing. With the confidence that the shielding was protecting him, he ran after Anibale and Leenah, sensing them enough to guide his path.

He reached out to Leenah and felt her anxiety as Anibale led her farther into Helm's Suites and governmental zones. Alarms were sounding now and people were crowding into the corridors, not only BlackMils trying to stop him, but Suite staff and Elites caught by surprise and even some coming out of doorways and down other passages to see the spectacle of him running through Helm's hallways. His outstretched arm and fist formed a multi-hued glowing battering ram, its sparks drowning out the shouted words and angry demands of those he passed by. Only once did he lock on to anyone during his rush. One young middie man, serving some obscure government function surely, had the bravery to call out as he passed.

"Marc of the Star!" the proud voice shouted, but Marc had no time to turn and look back.

He felt an abrupt increase in his connection to Leenah, who was now aware of him. She was projecting a mixture of anguish for herself, fear for him, and anger at Anibale.

"Where are you?" he asked her.

"Great Seat. Great Seat–he says we're going right to it," came the faint reply.

"Stay strong! I'm coming!"

". . . shouldn't be here . . . you . . ."

"I have to be here, Leenah."

Another voice in his mind came haltingly as well. "Who? . . . talking . . ." Anibale. He was at least minimally tuned to the SD space. That was certain now.

He passed through and out of Suite controlled zones and into the main governmental sector now. The Great Seat was just ahead. Visions of his parents' bodies being burned by Anibale and his goons came into and out of his mind's eye as he ran. He would not let Anibale harm Leenah! His boots were pounding the richly polished wood floor. He was almost there, almost caught up with them. The entry doors and chamber to the Great Seat auditorium were crowded with a throng trying to get in, but there was still an indention left by Anibale and Leenah who had just pushed their way through. In the blur of his passage, as the press of Harborites fell back again at his approach, he saw a flickering of bright colors, men's and women's heads supporting intricate hats and fancy hair stylings, rich fabrics in jewel-tone colors draped over shoulders and arms, and expressions of one extreme or another: smiles, outrage, surprise, fear.

"He's going to confront ZEK directly. He's crazy angry," Leenah sent.

"Hold on. I'm here now!"

His fist clearing the way, knocking more than one slow-to-react Elite to his or her backside, Marc burst into the Great Seat itself. The spectacle of this place was overwhelming enough to penetrate even his own current concentration. The brilliance of the glittering walls and ceiling was enough to slow his run slightly. He shook his head and focused on his targets. The two of them were halfway across the great multicolored marble floor toward the Golden Screen at the opposite wall. The Faces were off and the hall's gallery seating was about half full but filling rapidly with Suite members and others, crowding in to witness this unprecedented commotion.

Another thought crossed his mind.

I've never actually seen this place from this angle before. Only from that spot below the Faces of ZEK.

He put that firmly aside and yelled out, "Anibale, Prime Blue!"

The man turned around with a snap of his now dirty cloak. He had Leenah by one arm and a pistol ready. It had been aimed at her, but now it's muzzle pointed straight at him. Marc still had his fist extended, glowing a hot red now.

The shock of surprise on Anibale's face was very gratifying. His cheeks turned bright red.

"YOU! How did you get here? . . . DEMON! . . . You'll die at my hands, and so will she!"

Marc stopped as Anibale fired one shot at him and then turned the gun back to Leenah, yanking her close to his left side. Shrieks came from the galleries. The shot's force dissipated at his fist shield with a crackling and popping that gave a smoky stench to the room. Some of its reflected energy rippled through the crowd, causing a few of the Elites to fall, injured, and the rest to scramble. Anibale was in a sorry state, his eyes wide and mouth open, almost drooling with his anger and confusion: exhausted and dangerously crazed.

"It's all over, Anibale. Let her go. You can't win anything here."

"I will take what is rightfully *mine!*" he screamed. "You have brought *plague* upon us! I have fought you all! I am ZEK! I AM ZEK! *I* protect!"

Xenoplague

"You protect your own fears and your own ambitions. Let her go!"

Anibale's head made tiny jerks every couple of seconds like someone was pulling a string. He couldn't let this go much longer, but Leenah's situation was precarious. Marc was at a loss for what he could immediately do next to fix things.

As he stared, Marc saw Leenah's foot reach out behind Anibale. She hooked it between his feet and yanked backward, pushed his torso, and ducked into a crouch, all in that same instant. Anibale's gun went off with a single blast, missing Leenah's head and hitting a massive blue jewel on the ceiling, causing it to fall and burst apart in the nearest audience stands. He flailed wildly, falling onto his right side while rotating around his displaced leg. He still had his hand on Leenah's arm and almost pulled her on top of him, but she wriggled free at the last moment and backed away from him.

Marc started forward toward her when more screams came from the galleries above. His heart leaped as two Helm Guard BlackMils jumped forward, blocking his way and aiming their weapons only a centimeter from his face. Leenah froze and then looked across the hall at Marc with a fierceness in her eyes he had never seen before. Anibale started to get up, then stopped, another guard's muzzle aimed at his face. Two more figures emerged from the door to the backstage area where Marc had been held before being presented to ZEK that first time, so long ago.

It was the Elder Bai and another swarthy balding man with rough features. It took another second for Marc to make the connection with the Faces he had seen so dramatically most of his life. This was ZEK himself, in human form: not a thing he had truly ever given any conscious thought about or ever expected to see.

ZEK pulled out his own weapon, a white, gem-encrusted energy pistol. He casually aimed it at Leenah and made motions with his other hand to quiet the crowd's murmurs and cries. His un-amplified voice still carried throughout the huge jeweled room.

"I AM ZEK! This disturbance ends now! You, Marc 54Arons, put down your weapon and your resistance immediately."

"Let her go first. Let her come to me."

"Ahh, is she special to you, then, middie Marc? Your girl, perhaps? You're finished! Your xenoplague ship is disabled and drifting. It will soon be destroyed! Your rebellious armada is stuck, blocked behind my own Gate forever unless you stand down!" He grabbed Leenah's arm and drew her in closer. She grunted in surprise and tried to pull away until he shoved the gun under her chin. Her dark eyes sought only Marc's.

"I'll kill her right here in front of you if you don't surrender yourself to ZEK now!"

Still stretching his biomorphed hand out like a molten threat, Marc did not answer him.

Bai stepped forward and said, "It seems you are here without your Star, *Marc of the Star.*" He pronounced that last phrase with a mocking sneer. "Well, I just happen to have one of my own."

The white-robed Elder brought his hands up from inside that robe to reveal a Star Controller. It startled Marc, who immediately tried to reach it with his mind. He felt Leenah join in, but there was almost no response from it, only a strange, indifferent kind of aware echo in return. It was there, but it did not seem to know him.

"Where did you find it?"

ZEK grinned a nasty grin. "Your options seem to be diminishing rapidly, pilot," he said. Bai stared at Marc and did not look at ZEK.

"Oh, it has been in our possession for well over a millennium, you see. It is an artifact from the first xenoplague ship, the very one that destroyed Earth all those centuries ago."

A sudden babble of human noise rose from the galleries. Bai looked up at the gathered Elites and held the old Star aloft. "Have no fear! Yes, this was the control unit for the terrible ship that we destroyed in the Earth's sun after our original home's demise. Without its ship, it cannot harm us now, but you have seen the other such ship lurking just outside of Helm at this very moment, threatening our very existence! And this man, here in the Great Seat, threaten-ing ZEK, the Council, and the People of Humanity–*he* is the one who started this rebellion against our culture, our livelihoods, our honored traditions–against our very lives!

"Who will stand by and let him succeed? Who will join together and attack him where he stands, alien-deformed and augmented as he is? Prime Blue here has fired a weapon in the Great Seat and even *he* has been rightly and properly subdued. Shall we stand here and let this *middie fool* fire his monstrous weapon at ZEK and the Council of Colors? They will destroy Helm! Kill us all! Who has the courage of the ancient ones to come down together to the floor of this hall right now and *take this monstrous plague threat down!*" He was yelling now, pointing at Marc with one hand, the old Star in his other. His voice echoed off the bright walls and mixed with the yells and clamor of the crowd, some of whom were rising and pushing one another, beginning to make their way to the floor.

Marc held his position as he saw them move. One younger Elite in a military uniform began to climb right over the tall railing to drop directly onto the floor where he was. Too far down. The idiot would probably break his leg. He also noticed that the Star Bai was holding was glowing a sallow yellow-green.

As Marc steeled himself for the energy he would need in the next few moments, an audible gasp rose from the collective audience in the Great Seat. The Faces of ZEK came to life behind ZEK himself. A different Face now projected from the giant golden star disc and its four attendant shield Faces. A lighter, yet still commanding voice boomed forth from the animated golden lips that now looked more real than animated.

"ZEK! Attend me now! You are deposed! I bring *truth* to Harbor and to Humanity."

Everything in the gigantic jeweled room came to an abrupt halt. The rail jumper hung with one leg over the wall. Someone's crying became loud in the absence of the cacophony of the previous moments. Every eye was on the Faces. ZEK had wrenched himself around to see, still holding Leenah and pointing his gun at her. Bai motioned to a guard who ran backstage. The pale Elder looked whiter than Marc thought possible.

And then, Marc shook his head in consternation and grinned, for looming there above him in filigreed splendor and in an overt expression of power was the mighty and golden Face of Kera.

Chapter Thirty-eight

The shocking sound of a female voice coming from the Golden Screen behind him caused ZEK to wrench his neck when he instinctively turned to see. He felt the woman tense as he pulled on her arm. His right arm crossed his chest, his right hand still pushing the pistol up under her chin. It had to be some alien trick! He saw Bai signal a guard to go check the shunts backstage and detain whoever was in there. Her words rang in his ears. He recognized her instantly. It was Kera.

He looked back at the scene in the Great Seat hall itself. Marc held his position, unmoving. His right arm and enlarged fist extended in challenge and himself still surrounded by that alien shield glow. A cluster of BlackMil guards surrounded him except in front of his great hand, but they could not penetrate the shielding around him. The crowd had frozen in place, all noise stopped by the unexpected turn of events.

ZEK yelled out but kept his eyes on the crowd. "Who are you and how dare you corrupt the Faces of the Golden Screen with your alien plague!" He noted with some satisfaction the moans and sounds of fear and anger coming from the audience, but Kera's implacable voice answered him immediately.

"You know me. You recently told me that we have no right to demand anything of ZEK. You are mistaken. I am here now to assert that right and to demand *everything* of you." She paused as something flickered in the room.

"I am overriding all transmissions. This is being broadcast into every human world, station, and ship throughout the Second Domain. From Rindd to the Sisters, this is being seen in real-time, now. Look to the Great Seat! Look and listen, for the worlds have changed!"

The flicker returned from somewhere in the center of the hall, in the large space between Marc and himself. ZEK turned, forcing Leenah's head around, too, so he could see. Instantly, a shockingly large three-dimensional human head appeared, hovering over the colorful swirls of the marble floor, obscuring Marc behind it. It was repeatedly segmented to show four faces, one toward himself and the Screen and the others to the audience galleries on each side and toward the rear of the hall. It was a monstrous projection and people in the galleries flinched back from it at first. The man's face looked calm and alert, his gray eyes piercing as he gazed down at them. Then he spoke, his male voice reverberating in the hall.

"I am Rass-Ruik Biniun of Rindd. ZEK–Elder Bai–the Council of Colors! You and your ancestors have kept great secrets over the many centuries of your existence. You have established the Elite class and have prospered at the expense of the Midclass who support you. For most of our history in the Second Domain, this has been relatively stable if unfair, but in our times, you and yours have become corrupt. You have used fear as a whip to slowly take increased advantages until today when your abuses are heaped upon us. We Middies have no authentic recourse in law or in practice against you–you who make up your own laws and fail to practice justice. Now, this will end.

"I said you have used fear as a whip–a tool to keep the status quo. You use fears that you have *devised*. It is rooted in the story of the xenoplague of old Earth, that story we all know so well, the story to which we have been indoctrinated since birth, as our ancestors were before us. As with most successful falsehoods, that story is partially true. There was a great Ash Alien ship. It did fire an energy beam at the Earth. Earth did suffer a horrific destruction. All living beings on Earth did die, leaving us as sole survivors: the Second Domain of Humanity. I am here today to tell you and to show you that almost everything else about that story . . . is false.

"THIS . . . is planet Earth. This is planet Earth as it exists today– *right now*, in a nearly live feed from our trans-FTL probe."

The face of Rass-Ruik disappeared, replaced with another projection.

ZEK flinched, causing Leenah to yelp in pain.

The globe of the Earth floated in the hall, larger than the man's projected head had been and nearly filling the entire Great Seat. It bulged out slightly over the edges of the gallery rails and almost reached the hanging chandeliers of gemstones above. The crowds gaped up at it as it slowly rotated, showing all the blue oceans and green landscapes of the continents, mostly recognizable in shape from the images and maps of old Earth. White ice caps accented the poles and massive dark green jungles swathed the tropics. The greens and yellows of forests and prairie lands lay unbroken across continents. Brilliant white clouds swirled around the globe forming storms over the night side and flickering with lightning. It appeared as a pristine world, fecund and promising, and it pulled at ZEK's own emotions as he was certain it did for all in this room and elsewhere. It was something visceral and unexplainable. It was deepest Home and it was stunningly beautiful.

Rass-Ruik's voice continued. "You have seen the ancient video images of the destruction of the old Earth, destroyed by an Ash Alien ship just like the one that is here and aimed at you right now.

Xenoplague

You will remember how one colony of humans was untouched by the destruction. They were stationed on the Earth's moon and it was they who provided some of the video that has been preserved in our traditions for so long."

ZEK felt himself sweating, trying to hold the gun firmly against the woman's chin and taking in this absurd display while staring through it at Marc, anticipating any false moves from either of them.

A piece of the ancient video played, superimposed over the planet. It showed the AA ship with its horrific beam blasting the Earth, then switching to the control room of that lunar station. A man sat at the console with a woman standing beside him. He bore an expression of awe and horror as he asked his staff to preserve their data. He was generally referred to as the "Man in the Moon" for some mythic reason lost to time. His image froze and scaled up to show his face more clearly.

The Rindder's voice said, "This man's name is Paul Bennett, he was the Director of the lunar station called Schwarzschild. He and his staff and crew were abandoned by the Harbor ships, left to die on the moon as those on more distant Mars surely did. Billions of people had just instantly perished on the Earth and the Harborites gave these few hundreds no thought at all.

"There is one thing you may have now noticed. The Earth did not remain destroyed. It was, in fact, regenerated *very* rapidly after the AA ship finished its beam. Paul saw it, too, and he realized what was happening. The Earth was being *terraformed*, not utterly destroyed. He realized there was a chance for them to survive."

"Shut it off!" Bai yelled to no one in particular. ZEK glared at him. The woman pulled hard, but he tightened his grip and prodded her small chin harder with the muzzle. She moaned and stopped fighting him.

"Paul and his people put together a makeshift flotilla of reentry-capable lifeboat ships and returned to the Earth once the great land and sea disturbances had settled down."

Now, scenes no one had ever seen before were projected over the

Earth, showing Paul and the others in their primitive craft.

"Many of those brave souls perished in that attempt, but Paul survived and his people established a colony on the New Earth where they still live today. It is called New Anchorage."

Images of the settlement showing its buildings and farms were displayed now in front of the entranced throng.

"People of Harbor! *There was no xenoplague on Earth!* There was never a xenoplague there, for it never existed. The plague was a myth, a story, and a *lie*, promoted to protect and serve those who created it."

A crackling sound emerged from Marc's gleaming energy shield and filled the quiet chamber for a second. Then, the overlay images faded out and the glorious image of the New Earth rotated sublimely in front of everyone again.

"Because knowledge of Earth has been actively suppressed for so long, there is something that a few may remember but that most have forgotten over the centuries. Earth does not lie on the Ash Alien Lines system. We humans originally made the jump to Harbor on our own merits, using our own, human-designed faster-than-light technology. This makes it easy for the Council of Colors to hide all current information about Earth since they also control the FTL knowledge. This also has hidden the fact that Earth and the universe in which it exists, do not run on an equal relative time basis with Harbor or any other Ash Alien system. This is an unexplained trans-dimensional effect that has now been observed with other non-AA systems. Earth time runs slow with a difference between us of almost precisely ten to one. We live now in H-1247, one-thousand two hundred and forty-seven years since the events of the destruction of Old Earth, but Earth itself and those who live there now are still recovering from those effects, for only 124 years have actually passed there!"

Gasps and muttering erupted from the audience in the Great Seat.

The guard Bai had sent behind the Golden Screen reappeared and ZEK heard him report that no one was in the Faces control room or anywhere in the backstage areas at all. ZEK glanced back up at the

Faces and saw that Kera was still there, gazing into the Great Seat, projecting a serene and knowing look from all five of the Golden Faces.

The image of the New Earth was replaced once more by the head of Rass-Ruik.

"The remainder of this story is best told by someone else. I have just returned from a challenging mission that took only one day for me but cost ten days of my time in Harbor space. It was a trip to Earth to request the help of this man." He paused as the image changed to a full-body projection of a much older man. "People of Harbor and the Second Domain, this is Paul Bennett. He is here with us right now."

"It can't be! This is an imposter . . . a fraud!" Bai yelled. ZEK started sidling away from Bai, forcing the woman to stumble along with him. She still looked away, out to Marc, who still held his huge red hand up like some alien statue.

"NO, Elder Bai. I am not an imposter," Paul said. His voice was strong: a deep baritone that carried a strange accent, apparent even in those few words. He was certainly a senior, but all who saw him could tell with a single look that this was the same Man in the Moon they had seen all their lives on the ancient videos and again, just now. The man's projected form, towering over the galleries, seemed to look around him at the gathered audience in the Great Seat. ZEK could see through it to Marc again, still holding his stance at the far end of the hall, seemingly at the feet of Paul. ZEK tightened his grip on the girl and tried to think of what to do.

"I do not know your history very well yet," Paul said, "but I do know that what Rass-Ruik has spoken of here about the destruction and terraforming of Earth is correct. I was there. I saw it. I lived it along with my colleagues, friends, and family. It was terrible and horrific and I did not think we would survive, but, as he told you, we found a way to return to the renewed Earth. We live and thrive there in our little colony, but there are not so many of us. I agreed to come here because I have long worked to uncover the truth of what happened that day and I have come to know that it has been repressed here in Harbor to your great detriment as well as to ours.

"I am a seasoned 156 years old now, and I have spent most of my life, aside from building the colony itself, in recovering and restoring the data we gathered on the Day of Destruction. I have been helped beyond my best imaginings in the last month or so by my new friend, RR, and his people from Rindd who call themselves Suite Gray, along with some incredible technology assists from their connections with the Zips. What I will now show you has never been seen."

His image was replaced by a new screen. As he spoke, images of the old Harbor ships and people were sequenced with scenes from Earth itself. It showed Earth global political authorities wearing their odd garb and displayed strangely compelling and realistic views of the lost ancient Earth cities.

"The Harbor leaders had come again and again into Earth System with new demands for resources, technology, and more colonists from Earth. The time offset worked against Earth. They could not respond fast enough to Harbor's needs. From the Harbor perspective, Earth remained plodding and slow to adapt to the changes, the new technologies, and the demands that they were constantly bringing for material support, more colonists, and eventually their call for independence. Earth's leaders were afraid of the rise of Harbor and all its worlds. They feared a reversal of fortunes with Earth becoming a sudden backwater and a dependent servant to the quick new worlds of Harbor. They declined Harbor's requests claiming it to be too costly and they kept tight controls on technology. They did establish the Executive Earth Authority in Harbor, which has evolved considerably into your Rindder people and culture. Along with it, they also sent a new, strong force of weaponized military ships into Harbor space, but Earth itself was struggling with a highly damaged environment and a burgeoning population."

Paul's voice softly flowed, mesmerizing in tone and accent, and there was silence for it within the hall.

"Commander Baldev Bhat was of the EEA group who developed Harborite warships, the first hybridized AA and human ships. He and his crews were the first to turn against Earth and support Harbor's Exec, Mansel Quinn. He presented Quinn with a major find."

The image changed to show the original AA terraform ship, first isolated and grounded on a barren planetoid surface, then restored to space as a functioning craft.

"The ship they found in the Prospect System was unique. It was intact and seemed to be a monstrous weapon ship. They discovered its star-shaped controller and learned how to fly it. They had no clue what the weapon was or how to operate it and they decided not to try. Rather, they decided to use it as an intimidation weapon by encasing it in a human FTL net and jumping it with them into Earth space and orbit. This they did, and made their demands again to an Earth who had now cut them off from further resources and flatly denied their bid for independence. Earth was perplexed by this strange weapon, however, and decided not to respond to Exec Quinn, who led the expedition, nor to his now military leader, Commander Bhat."

ZEK noticed Bai almost jumping from foot to foot now.

"This is a mockery! This man is trying to change history and fool you all!" Bai screamed.

"SILENCE!" came the booming voice of Kera, glaring down at him from the Faces. Her voice thundered, louder than any version of ZEK's Faces voice technology they had ever heard. Everyone jumped and held their hands over their ears except for ZEK, who winced as he gripped Leenah harder. Bai seemed stunned and remained silent.

In a more normal volume, Kera said, "You will listen and so shall we all. This man is not making up false history . . ." Her Faces looked intensely into the crowds on all sides. "He IS HISTORY!"

Paul continued as if nothing had happened. "With Earth's extended silence, Quinn became frantic. If they withdrew, they would lose all leverage, yet they could not stay in attack position indefinitely without actually attacking. After three days in position, Exec Quinn ordered Commander Bhat to take them into a closer, more threatening Earth orbit, but Bhat refused. He controlled the ship using the Star controller and said they should retreat. They had made a wild gamble and lost. In the end, the ship did rapidly retreat to a geosynchronous orbit, but it happened automatically as part of its programming to position the beam in one stationary place on the surface of the planet.

"Now, you must see for yourselves what actually occurred. This particular comms video has been the most difficult piece of the puzzle to recover and restore. It may be the most important recording in the history of the Second Domain. Its source was a human-tech monitor camera situated within the alien attack ship's bridge, feeding back to the other Harbor warships."

Bai was making little mewling sounds now.

ZEK glowered at him.

Doddering old fool. What a colossal mess he's made.

Paul's image was replaced by a set of new screens facing in all directions so everyone could see them. The view was of the inside of an AA-style bridge, as Paul had said. ZEK saw several crew people stationed at various comm controls along with Quinn, in his red cowl and ancient robe-like suit, and Commander Bhat, in a more military-looking outfit of silver with black boots. He was almost bald and had a severe look. No one had seen such clear images of these two before. ZEK recalled the secret vids Bai had shown him and the Council, and even those were taken from so far away that such detail was imperceptible.

The video showed Exec Quinn flying into a rage. He grabbed the Star controller, trying to pull it out of Bhat's hands and they went back and forth, fighting over the thing, each struggling to control it. Quinn was apoplectic.

"Let me have it! We can't leave here! You . . . let me . . . have it!"

Commander Bhat was turning red in his face trying to hold on. Each of them had their hands on two of the Star's arms when something new happened. It began to glow in rolling neon colors. Then the ship around them responded in more vivid colors, the hues chasing themselves around the room and visible on the screens as the entire ship's hull began to glow.

Bhat grunted and Quinn yelped.

"I can't turn loose! What's happening? I can't let go of it!"

"We are stuck to it, you fool. What have you done? You've killed us! It's alive!"

The AA ship began to respond to the conflicting Star Controller manipulations by skewing and turning around as the two men frantically flailed, trying to pull themselves away from the now orange-hot glowing object. The other crew members had backed themselves into the walls or escaped behind the camera's view. A single blinding flash illuminated the bridge, causing the camera to shut down for an instant. When the recording regained picture, Commander Bhat had been thrown free of the Star. The Star itself had gained a solid green color, then jerked from white to blue and back to green in a random, sharp, and unsettled pattern. Images of strange controls appeared on the bridge's walls now, seeming full of purpose, but seemingly completely unknown to Quinn and the others, since they stared at them in wonder. Quinn's hands were still stuck onto two of the Star's arms, and it jerked him bodily to face the front of the ship's bridge as the Star itself oriented into a new configuration. The remaining struts of the Star receded into the central pod, their end orbs glowing white. A screen image appeared in the front wall. Earth appeared. The ship was directly aimed at the planet below.

Then it happened. A view of the beam erupting from the AA ship: a bridge point-of-view unlike any other. The huge beam struck the Earth just above the tropical equator and the shock waves and initial debris cloud were very detailed and, although terrifying, also very impressive to watch. Commander Bhat tried to grab Exec Quinn, but he was repelled by the glowing Star and the glow around Quinn himself. Quinn was wailing in agony and Bhat was screaming at him again to let go.

"QUINN! You set the demon thing off! Give it to me! You've set it off! You have to let go of the Star! I don't care what you want any more, you have to stop the beam! STOP THE BEAM, you fool!"

The clamor from the video faded as Paul Bennett's voice came back into the tense silence of the Great Seat.

"There are two things you must all understand. The first is fairly obvious now. Although powerful in the extreme, the beam from the AA ship was not a doomsday weapon. It was not designed to harm worlds, but to *remake* them. This ship was a terraform ship used by the Ash Aliens to make marginal *lifeless* worlds habitable for themselves. There were multiple layers, multiple protocols in place, to prevent it from being used on any planet that had life already established.

Why then did this happen? You should see now that it happened due to the extremely foolish assumptions and misunderstandings of those who wielded such a tool without the most basic understanding of what it was supposed to be used for. They did this and then they fought over the controls. They fought with each other: two human men, fighting like two wretched little boys over the master control AI for the terraform ship! That is correct. The Star is the interface to a very sophisticated artificial intelligence that *is* the Ship itself. The Ash Aliens may never have anticipated that such wild and unwise animals might ever be in possession of their wonderful device. Quinn and Bhat confused the AI and caused conflicts in its programming that initiated the ship's terraform procedure by accident! *By accident, my friends.* The entire genocide, nearly *specie*-cide, of the human race and all the other animals and plants forever lost to us–billions upon billions lost to us–were the result of the most colossal and foolish mistake ever made by human beings."

There were gasps in the galleries and many were crying.

"The second thing you must understand," he said more softly, "is the perfidy and absolutely cunning conspiracy of deceptions that the first of whom would later become your Council of Colors Elders, Commander Bhat, devised in those hours that followed the terraform blast. It was he who came up with the plan to hide the truth of what happened behind a glorious and heroic constructed mythology declaring their own bravery in attacking the plague ship. They would return to Harbor with the news of the disaster but with the knowledge of their role in it completely contained. Earth was isolated by human FTL and the time shift anomaly. Bhat would say that the alien ship arrived on its own, attacked Earth on its own, and left the Earth with a horrific xenoplague: a *fictional* plague of radiation and bio-engineered viruses that would deconstruct all organic life down to radioactive atoms. Conveniently, this would make the Earth entirely uninhabitable and deadly forever. He could quarantine the Earth System and no one would ever know. That is, no one except the ship's crews who had accompanied them on this final foray to the doomed Earth.

"These, he took care of in a direct manner. Back in his own ship with the badly injured Exec Quinn on board and surrounded by his choice crew, he ordered the other Harbor warships to group together. Then Bhat took his ship's weapons controls."

The video now showed a recording from Bhat's ship cameras. The clustered group of his own unsuspecting Harbor ships was destroyed in cold blood with the energy beam weapon from Bhat's hybrid ship.

"Bhat and Quinn made a deal. Commander Bhat would return to his home on Rindd 1 and all of the Rindd Systems would become independent of Harbor. Exec Quinn would become the Power Seat of Harbor, in a newly arranged government based on a strong leader and a series of elite Suites that evolved from the color code assignments of the original Harbor discoverers' different administrative sections."

Paul's lanky form reappeared in the Great Seat. His leathery and lined face seemed to search the room and look into each person's eyes. It sent a shiver of dread up ZEK's spine.

"This is how your empires were born over twelve hundred years ago. I know. I was there. I am Paul Bennett and I am the true witness of your ancient history. It echoes to this very day and manifests its vile effects here within this very strange and obscene hall.

Aliens did not destroy Earth." Paul looked directly at ZEK and Bai now. "YOU did. You killed my family. You destroyed my home. You killed billions of your own kind out of stupidity and foolishness and covered it up for generations, taking the blame upon yourselves anew with each new Council Elder and Exec! You Harbor officials: YOU killed Earth!"

Suddenly, the Golden Screen lit up with a light that seemed to come from within the Faces themselves. Kera's voice thundered again.

"People of Harbor, Rindd, and Frahma, you have heard today. ZEK does not protect humanity. ZEK protects ZEK and all the privileges of the Primes and Elite class! Attend me now, Elder Bai and ZEK. You have seen the true beginning. Look now as your empire ends!"

In the center zone of the Great Seat, a new projection appeared. It was the Gate to Hub, still blocked by ZEK's machine. In a single instant, the scans and views were filled with several hundreds of warships already composed in a massive orbital sphere encompassing Harbor and Helm. Then, another ship blinked into existence. It was vast: larger than anything ever seen before. It was larger than Helm itself and exhibiting extreme mass. Zip ships appeared along with it, screaming their sawtooth buzz into everyone's ears. The largest Zip ship stopped in a stable orbit near the massive unknown vessel. No other ships dared get close to its planetoid-level mass.

ZEK growled in consternation as he saw his blockade annulled, the armada now magically on his doorstep, and this new alien threat. He glanced at Bai, but the Elder turned and ran, still carrying his Star Controller, into the doorway to backstage and his White Hall. Leenah started to yank harder at him and he turned back to her with panicked anger boiling and his gun newly focused on her. Marc! He'd almost forgotten Marc in all of this turmoil. He jerked around to see and the middie pilot was running straight toward him and Leenah, passing through the ghostly projection of Paul. He skidded to a stop a few feet from him.

ZEK yanked the woman around and held her like a shield, his gun to the back of her head. "I'll shoot her right now. I have little to lose."

"You may have your life, upon my word, if you surrender all to me right now. All controls, ships, and arms. All political power. Drop your weapon and let go of Leenah. Now."

"I'd rather cause you a lot of pain, traitor! I think I . . ."

ZEK felt something strike him in the back. It hurt like a bad puncture and he spun around with it, surprised to find that in that unconscious reaction, he had let go of Leenah and dropped his gun. As he twirled down to the marble floor and fell onto his side, he saw who was behind him. Her red cap framed a pasty white face that held a crazed set of features. Eyes wide and almost crossed, skin splotchy and creased, and a mewling wail that turned into a shriek of power emerging from her thin and strangely curled-up lips. Prime Red still held the simple dagger she had struck him with. She was cackling.

His body armor had kept her from succeeding in her fool task. He could feel the wound but knew it was not a fatal one. His anger at her, at the situation, at the betrayals and revelations of this day, rose in him like the damnable beam weapon itself. He slowly got to his knees, and as she shrieked one final, earsplitting laugh and her hand dropped the dagger, clattering to the floor beside him, he shot his right fist into her chin, delivering a solid blow that killed Jade, Prime Red, quite instantly.

Chapter Thirty-nine

Marc watched in amazement as Jade appeared from behind the Golden Screen and stabbed ZEK in the back. The instant ZEK released her, Leenah dipped down, then rushed to Marc's side, grabbing onto him for a moment, then turning back to the scene. It made him mad to see the angry red spots on the skin of her jaw where ZEK had prodded her. He noted with great satisfaction that Leenah now had ZEK's gun and was aiming it back at him.

Jade shrieked and giggled, plainly crazed. She dropped her knife. ZEK started to get up and then launched a shocking uppercut. The ancient woman flipped backward into a limp pile on the floor. ZEK picked up the dagger, turned, and threw it straight at Marc and Leenah. Marc flashed it aside with his hand.

ZEK hesitated, looking like he might charge them, but another disturbance made them all look to ZEK's right. Anibale was still standing where he had been held by a BlackMil Great Seat guard. During the confusion with ZEK and Jade, he had backhanded the distracted guard, sending the man to the floor. Now, with the guard's gun in his hand, he sprinted right in front of a surprised ZEK, not sparing him a glance, and headed for the doorway Bai had used. ZEK stood nonplussed for a beat, watching Prime Blue disappear, then faced Marc, his visage morphing from bewilderment and pain into a mask of visceral hatred. He glared, unable to decide his next move, and then he turned and broke for the door himself, following Anibale into the recesses of the Great Seat.

Leenah pulled on Marc's shoulder and he turned and looped his hand around her as they held onto each other.

"I'm so sorry, Leenah. I couldn't get here fast enough."

"Don't think about it. You held him off! Long enough for all this to happen. We should . . ."

The ground under their feet shifted with a massive jolt. Leenah yelped and fell backward, but Marc caught her as he flexed his knees to keep himself balanced.

Kera's Face above them became animated again and she spoke. "Something is happening to Helm, Marc. You and Leenah need to get out of there right now! Get to the podship and we'll pick you up!"

A large crystal gem fell from the upper recesses of the ceiling and shattered on the color-spiraled floor, directly between them and Kera's Face. Marc's hand shield instinctively flared to protect them from the shards.

"We're getting!" he yelped as another frightening jolt racked the Great Seat. He grasped Leenah's hand and turned with her to escape the hall. Most of the audience had remained in their galleries, spellbound during all the previous drama, but now, they were moving in a confused and panicked mass to escape the huge jeweled chamber. Screams rang out as more gems rained down on their heads and the quake continued to shake Helm.

Panicked Great Seat guards criss-crossed in front of them as Marc and Leenah ran to the main entry doorway, opposite the Faces. As they made the turn into the corridor, finely carved wooden mosaic panels were coming loose from the metal walls and falling to the floor and into the Suite's reserved boxes. Suite Elites and middie staffers were swarming out of the gallery exits into the passage and running in different directions, rushing into each other in massive knots. Marc flared his hand to a red glow and enlarged it into his shield again, but after maintaining it for so long, he could feel his energy for this running out. People howled and yelped as he moved forward, some panicked faces showing anger, some lighting up and shouting approvals. Leenah also had ZEK's fancy gun out, fanning it in front of them as they went. Having no alternative, the crowds gave way under their advance like water flowing to each side of a boat's prow.

The shaking had subsided as they ran, but now another jolt rocked them, almost causing Marc to falter. In between renewed shocks, the gravity of Helm also seemed to be shifting around, making them feel slightly drunk. He couldn't figure it out.

That's not Kera's doing. What's going on? The damned place is just coming apart! Gotta get us to that pod!

It seemed much longer than the minutes it actually took to reach the docks. Marc did a fast visual scan. The scene here was a mess. Everyone wanted to get off Helm and they were arriving at the docks demanding and pushing their way toward the various ships. BlackMils guarding one of the Suite's ships, Yellow's perhaps, actually fired their weapons at a nasty crowd rushing their portal.

"The pod ships are on the other side, Marc!" Leenah panted beside him. She looked exhausted and crestfallen. She was right. The pods were hidden behind far too many people, all crowding the docks now.

As they stood there at the threshold of the hangar bay, Marc heard a distinctive and loud clank. Another massive jolt shook the docks and a large crack appeared along the joint between the bay wall and the section of Suite offices just behind them. Their ears popped.

"It's coming apart on purpose!" he yelled. "That was some sort of latch. Helm is coming apart!"

"We're losing atmosphere," Leenah said.

"No time for pod ships. We gotta get to those power suits over there." The suits were lined up on the wall to their right, ready with power backpacks for maintenance crews to use outside when servicing the ships.

Just as they started to move that way, a guard with a crazy expression on his face jumped in front of them, screaming something. Leenah tried to fire ZEK's pistol, but nothing happened. Marc pushed at him with his weakening shield hand, but the guy slipped around and grabbed Leenah's pistol hand. She kneed the man in the groin and hit him on the back of his head with the pistol butt as he slumped down.

"Hell, Leenah! You OK?"

"Damn thing didn't fire!" she said.

"It's probably keyed to ZEK's biomarkers. Keep flashing it and looking mean!"

They reached the suits and Marc grabbed one for each of them. Fortunately, the crowds were thin here next to the wall and, as the air around them whistled and pulled at them, they were just able to get into the suits. As they finished the seals and pumped their suit air up, one truly massive floor jolt shook them, and the crack that had opened up before completed its run around them. The suit wall to which they were both still safety-tethered, silently floated away from the hangar section exposing them to raw vacuum and the black of space above. The air in the dock whipped away in a moment of wild flow, then stillness. The floor crack below them expanded and they could see lower sections of Helm below their boots. These sections were not exposed to space. All of them were completely sealed behind walls on each side of the gap. That expanding chasm now yawned below them like a vast metallic canyon.

"Oh, gods. They're all dead." Leenah cried.

Marc looked up. It was a terrible sight across the gap in the exposed hangar of the dock. All those who had thronged there, looking for an escape, were now floating in chaotic clusters, each one randomly rotating in the stiffness of death from vacuum exposure. It looked like a macabre slow-motion explosion of human sticks.

Flaccid paralysis. "Instant asphyxiation. They didn't have much time to suffer." Marc heard his own voice quivering.

"Listen, Leenah, this is no accident. Helm is separating–looks like into several parts. We have to get away from it and try to get ourselves out toward the T-ship where Kera can get to us. I think this section of Helm is going to rotate enough for us to launch right off of it, but we have to be ready when the right assist trajectory comes around." It was a risky if not unprecedented maneuver–one he had certainly never tried before.

He saw her nod within her helmet. "Yeah, I understand. Good idea. Better make sure our service pack rockets are ready for full thrust and have matching vector settings."

"Right. Let's not get too separated out there."

They disconnected from their tethers and watched the hangar-bearing portion of Helm drift ever farther away, its ghoulish human effluvium slowly spreading apart in a frost-glinted cloud. Several Suite ships that had sealed themselves up in time were backing off and changing course. Marc noticed another kind of exhaust cloud: trails emerging from below their part of the planetoid and now, some jets blasting out from their side of the structure with matching, opposing blasts from the dock section. The ejecta glinted like millions of fireflies. Helm was not only segmenting, but the parts were mobile, capable of changing their trajectories on purpose.

"Leenah, look at those jets. This is no self-destruct sequence. It's a controlled separation! Those have to be water jets from the big tanks down below."

"Yes, I see it, but why, Marc? What do they want to achieve? You think it's ZEK?"

"Maybe, but I'd put my money on Bai. Let's keep watching that upper edge of our piece. Be ready to go when we see the T-ship."

It didn't take very long for their Helm section to rotate into the proper position. It would be better to launch a little ahead of visual contact, but without a code to enter the data comps, they had to wait until it appeared over the limb of their wall. The power packs should get them gone and allow for enough course corrections along the way. The moment arrived, and Marc and Leenah leaped, launching themselves off the metal wall, taking advantage of the momentum from the rotation of their Helm segment, flying toward the T-ship with their propulsion packs blasting full power. Due to those dynamic exhausts, they had to stay slightly apart from one another, but Marc hoped their parallel actions would not cause too much drift.

He could see the T-ship off in the distance, holding its matching course to Helm's position. He was also surprised to see a few glints of the armada ships, those close enough to Kera to be visible. More impressive, though, was the far distant but looming apparition of his fake, small moon-sized Ash Alien ship. He grinned as he thought about RR and his crew constructing the thing and the bizarre Zips and their ability to Line-in and contain a few grams of neutron star or something to give it all that mass. It did the trick to intimidate ZEK and Bai.

Marc turned on his emergency comm within the suit now and made contact with Kera.

"Marc! We were afraid for you since the podship didn't launch!" she said.

"Yeah, sorry, but we didn't have time for it. Lots of folks didn't make it out of that dock alive. Can you ask our Ship if she can send us a shuttle or something?" He remembered to reach out directly to the Ship in vision space and he felt a tentative connection to the AI even from this distance.

"Will do. Keep together and we'll get you . . . What, Paris?" There was a moment of silence, and then Paris came on comm.

"Look at that. There's something else funny about Helm."

Leenah spoke from her suit comm, too. "Marc! Rotate enough to see Helm!"

"Damn. Just came from there. OK, I'm rotating."

As they left Helm below them, Marc saw that, as he suspected, it had split into several segments, not just two. Each slice was moving away from the others, spreading apart like a slowly opening pimfruit. There was something else there, being revealed now by the expanding segments.

"Leenah! The Visions! Yours and mine!"

"Oh, Marc! Yes!"

———————✳———————

Damned witch! Should have killed her years ago. Got to find Bai! Got to get off Helm right now!

ZEK ducked into the doorway leading behind the Great Screen, passing by the empty booth where he once connected to his Faces. There seemed to be no guards or anyone else backstage. A sudden, strong jolt almost knocked him to the floor. He looked around wide-eyed to see if he could tell what happened. Nothing. Then another, smaller bump caused a piece of equipment to fall from somewhere above him and crash into the floor a few feet away. He ran on, faster now, passing the closed entry to the White Hall. More jolts came, making it difficult to go as fast as he wanted.

He turned a corner and slid to a stop. Elder Bai sat on the floor of the corridor. The Star was at his side and he tapped furiously on a comp unit in his lap. He glanced up at ZEK, then back down.

"We can't defeat that thing, ZEK! I scanned it myself. It's truly massive and completely unknown to us. It could destroy us just by coming too close! Their own armada has to keep their distance from it."

"What are you doing, Bai? What's going on here?" ZEK felt his patience teetering like a glass-fragile pot, about to be smashed with the next fickle jolt.

Bai looked up at him again with his face tight in a grimace. "I'm saving our hides!"

He picked himself up off of the floor and slipped the comp unit into his robe somewhere. He grabbed the Old Star and started down the hallway.

Xenoplague

"Come on, ZEK! If you want to live today."

Bai did not wait to see if he followed. ZEK huffed to keep up with the older man. A new set of jolts rocked them as they reached a work portal. It opened at Bai's touch and he entered it quickly. ZEK hesitated a moment, then followed inside to find a utility area with steep stairs heading down. Bai was already on his way down, his head disappearing below the short and slightly rusty rail. ZEK followed.

They kept descending, passing one, then two more old-looking portals where Bai had to enter a code and insert his hand for a genescan. There was a strange musty smell in here. ZEK didn't like being down here, didn't like seeing the underbelly of his world. It was too depressing and seemed, well, unseemly to muck around in places like this. Bai, he had noticed, had no such scruples.

"Where are we going, Bai?" Another jolt shook them and ZEK grabbed the now slimy rail bar to keep from falling. "And, what in Ash Alien HELL is going on with Helm?"

Bai's voice, tight and determined, came floating up to him, reverberating a little off the metal pipes and tanks surrounding them.

"So many secrets the middie traitors have revealed. They are so full of themselves, so proud of ripping apart the fabric of Harbor. Well, there are more secrets than they know! I've triggered a failsafe sequence. It is for the protection of Helm, ZEK. There is no danger to you or me, but we must hurry!"

The gravity was failing down this far. The AA grav assists were not normally used toward the center of the planetoid and normal low-g conditions prevailed after a certain level. Made it easier to just skip and float down several steep metal steps at a time, though.

"These huge tanks are the water reservoirs, as you may have guessed," Bai said, still not looking back or up at him. "I doubt you've ever seen them before. They are used to redistribute and balance the mass for the smooth rotation of Helm, but they also serve another very reserved purpose. They also serve as a barrier and a camouflage for what lies here at the center of our little world. It is our most closely held secret, and the last one that has *remained* secret this terrible day.

480

This is the ultimate defense for Helm and Harbor, ZEK. No one has had to use it in over twelve hundred years."

ZEK wheezed now, even with the reduced gravity. They had entered a large open area surrounded with layered struts creating a self-contained inner shell of support, presumably to hold the shape of the cavity while the water tanks above them shifted mass around. At the center of the more open bay below them and therefore at the exact center of Helm itself, a gigantic object was gently contained by a webwork of smaller struts and pipes. It was an Ash Alien ship.

A shudder went down ZEK's spine as he realized what he was seeing.

"The *xenoplauge ship!* They kept it? It has been down here at Helm's heart all these centuries, Bai? What madness is this?" He felt a mixture of fear and rage boiling up in him.

"Yes, ZEK. It is the original ship. Settle yourself, man. This is our only hope now. I told you! The old Council decided to keep more than the Star control. It was First Elder Bhat who made that decision and who had the foresight to keep the ship well hidden in Prospect System until they could build Helm around it."

They were almost free of the steel stairs now, heading for a loose gangway made of tread rungs and several runs of roping to hold onto in the essentially zero-g bay. The gangway led straight to the main hatch area on the AA ship.

"Elder Bhat designed Helm himself. He wisely thought that we might need this ship someday and he wanted to study it further himself. He designed Helm to contain it and keep it secret. They constructed Helm mostly by bots out in the depths of the outer system here in Harbor. Then it was guided into its proper orbit once the ship was safely inside. Only a few humans knew. They were Bhat's select crew who had accompanied him to Earth on that last fateful mission. Those people became the original members of the first Council of Colors."

A massive sideways skew caused the shell struts above their heads to squawk and shudder. ZEK saw some seams opening up between parts of it.

"How do we get it out? Are you going to destroy Helm to do it?" he yelled.

"Come on, ZEK. Get in. Helm was designed to separate into multiple sealed sections to be flung apart quickly by reaction mass from the water tanks. The atmosphere in here will escape momentarily. Get in here now!"

ZEK followed Bai into the now-open hatchway. For an instant, it crossed his mind that he was entering the legendary plague ship that destroyed Earth–the very ship seen in the old vids–but his wits were so numb now with such revelations and shocks that he gave it no other thought.

Bai was into it ahead of him, scurrying like a fish down an organic-looking corridor. His long white robe trailing behind him made him look even more aquatic. ZEK followed as fast as he could, pulling himself along by whatever protrusions he could reach. Shortly, though, he reached the bridge room where Bai was already fiddling with the Star control and causing some lit-up readouts to be projected onto the inner wall.

"I'm closing the hatch and starting up the grav assist. Put your feet on this side or you'll fall. We'll have stable atmosphere, too." He pulled out his comp again and entered a command. "There! I've triggered the final Helm detach release."

"What about the people, Bai? They aren't prepared for this. Thousands could die!"

Bai turned on him, red-faced and angrier than he had ever seen him.

"They will die anyway!" he shouted. "We have to get this ship out and use it against our enemies! This is the most powerful weapon we have, ZEK! I have learned much about the Star Controller. It drives the ship some but mainly controls the weapon. The *weapon*, ZEK. I can make it glow a little, but I can't get through to the AI that runs the thing. We have to try, though! I can't fly the ship and deal with the weapon, too. I need you to control the ship's flight functions.

Look! There's a virtual display here that works just like a standard AA ship's control panel."

ZEK looked, and on the main forward wall, an eerie projection version of a control panel appeared. They heard a tremendous thump and hissing, but the ship did not move.

Must be the final separation of the sections. What a crazy mess.

"All right. All right, Bai. I'll fly the damned thing. Get me a screen and data scans to see what I'm doing."

The scans and main screen came to light showing their demon ship being uncovered and revealed by the receding segments of Helm, a slow and now silent explosion of metal, gemstones, and humans–alive and dead–unfolding into space like some blooming cosmic flower of death.

Chapter Forty

Anibale watched Elder Bai do something to a comp unit he held in his lap. The great leader of the Council of Colors, in Anibale's private opinion more powerful than ZEK in most ways, sat on the corridor floor like someone's lost child. Prime Blue felt some sympathy for him, for he was himself lost in all this chaos as well. After striking down that guard and grabbing his weapon, Anibale was literally on his own now, hiding in a utility niche with a view of the passageway, here in the strangely emptied operations zone behind the Great Seat and the Golden Screen. He heard weird noises and felt a huge jolt that seemed to shake the entire structure of Helm, but his mind was focused on only two things: escape detection and rearrest, and find ZEK and Elder Bai to complete his coup over them. Anything short of that meant death or worse.

If he could do that, he could address the problem of the middies and their horrors and lies as ZEK himself. If he could not, he would die in the attempt. He felt only grim determination and a strong undercurrent of rage.

Here was Bai, right in front of him, and he contemplated killing him or taking him hostage, but he hesitated, curious about what the old man was up to. The next jolt and tremor seemed to occur precisely as Bai made a final tap on his screen. Truly alarmed now, Anibale made up his mind, but just as he made the first leading motions to attack, he heard someone running toward them. He stopped himself and backed up a little further into the niche. It was ZEK! Perhaps he could take them both out at once!

ZEK stopped and talked to Bai and Anibale listened closely. When Bai got up and told ZEK to follow him if he wanted to live, Anibale decided to follow them both.

Maybe I can pick up something that will give me the final advantage, and just maybe, Bai will provide something that I can use to survive whatever is happening to Helm, whether they do or not!

It was not difficult to follow the two since they seemed to have no thought of being followed and Bai conveniently left every hatch they entered wide open.

It has to be something so terminal that he simply doesn't care. Helm is doomed, then. He must stay very close to them!

As Anibale paced them, heading ever deeper into the guts of Helm, he listened as Bai explained about the planetoid's history, its impending segmentation, and how he had another secret. As the gravity decreased, it was easier to simply slide down the rails behind and above them with his hands, remaining almost completely silent.

The next sight stunned him. The *original plague ship, here?* Here on purpose? Kept, apparently, by the Council? Did ZEK know about this? No! Apparently not, since he was exclaiming to Bai about it! He hid and listened, but there were more cracking sounds and jolts, and a fissure opened above them, air hissing now. He heard Bai say something about losing atmosphere. He moved quickly now. There was no time to waste. Helm was fragmenting into the segments Bai had spoken of! Amazing, but irrelevant to his immediate needs.

Anibale ran up behind the two men just as they entered the plague ship's open hatch. He feared mightily at that moment that they would close it immediately and shut him outside to face a terrible death, but it remained open!

He slipped inside as quietly as he could manage, hearing their voices fading as they receded down a rounded, organic-looking corridor. The hatch did not close for quite some time, and Anibale floated there against one of the inner walls, trying to catch his breath in the rapidly thinning air, his thoughts spinning in his head. Finally, the hatch hissed and closed and he slumped to the floor as the AA gravity assist came on. He remembered something. This was a plague ship, just like the other one Kera and Marc had found. He remembered how he had connected to the AI that seemed to form a fundamental part of the ship. It was so strange to think he could talk to it in his mind that way and have it respond to him. Maybe . . . maybe there is a similar AI on this ship! Perhaps, while still hidden here in the aft section of the ship, he could take control from those two up front who do not know about the AI. Perhaps it might give him the edge, and the power to prevail!

Before he got back up on his feet, he decided to try.

He closed his eyes and concentrated on an image of the ship itself. He tried to recall how that other AI felt in his mind. He projected a desire, an image, of control and power. *I need to control this ship! Show me how!*

A thrill of fear and anticipation ran through him as almost instantly, a response came. It felt like a set of eyes on him. He *intended* a stronger connection to it and it showed him an impression of the bridge with the two others inside it. They were not clearly defined, but Anibale could tell which one was which. Bai was holding the Star, and as soon as he noted that, the Star became the focus of the scene for him. The AI seemed to be emphasizing it.

I know. The Star controls the ship. You want me to take it and use it? Yes? These fools don't know about you, do they?

The AI stayed quiet but still showed him the Star. Just then, a new, hard jolt hit him. He had thought the Helm separation was over.

Perhaps the ship had been struck? He opened his eyes, but he was no longer in the ship corridor. He was in an entirely new place. It looked like a cavern, but it was so dark that he couldn't see very far into it. Huge crystal shafts, much larger than himself, criss-crossed in front of him. Strangely eroded columns of rock closed down from above and protruded from below like the teeth of a beast.

"You seek Power." The voice boomed in his mind and Anibale swung himself around to see who said it. There was no one behind him, but when he returned his gaze to the direction where he first looked, a large creature now stood there. He calmed his growing panic with his warrior training, casting his own harsh voice out, resonating with threat.

"Where is this place, and who are you?"

The thing looked like a man's body with a bird's long beak protruding from its black and leathery head.

"Are you an Ash Alien? A damnable ZIP?" he yelled.

Finally, the creature spoke into his mind. "I am the True One. I am the Path to Power. I can give it to you."

Anibale hesitated for a moment. "What kind of power? Can you help me take this ship? Overcome ZEK and Bai?"

"It is Power. You will use it."

"At what cost, eh? What is the price for this power?" Anibale sneered at him.

The bird thing regarded him by turning its beaked head around, one shiny black eye glinting at him.

"You will become me," it said. "I am Power. I do not die."

Anibale thought about this bizarre exchange. "What does this Power look like? How do I obtain it?"

The thing was suddenly in his face. It had shuffled so quickly, he didn't see the motion of it. It had a fetid odor. It extended a wrinkled claw from within its dust-black robe and held out a beautiful golden gemstone, as large as Anibale's hand.

"It is a Tool. It is yours to take. You must choose it," it hissed.

The golden stone glinted and gleamed there in the thing's claw, even though there was no light source to illuminate it. It drew Anibale's eyes and then his mind and heart. It sang to him of riches and respect and real power over others, over all the fools who don't understand and who will not cooperate with him. It flashed into his mind images of grandeur and closure and indestructibility: the satisfaction of empire, with himself the Emperor. It was so far beyond the concept of being ZEK that it made his imagination quail with the Power of it. The glints from the Golden Gemstone reminded him of where he was, and as he gazed anew at it, he found that his hand already held the Stone. It was his!

"You have chosen." The bird creature's voice reverberated, but he was no longer standing there in the cavern, where the giant crystal shards were reflecting now only the golden light from the Stone in Anibale's hand. "You are the True One. You are responsible."

Anibale closed his hand around the Golden Gemstone, feeling the energy surge into him, and jerked himself awake–suddenly back inside the other reality of the plague ship's aft corridor, his hand grasping empty, acrid air. He was still sitting on the floor, sweating and breathing rapidly.

It was a vision. He had had a Vision! This is what Marc and Kera talked about! He remembered Marc describing his Vision to him and later to ZEK in the Great Seat. He had not believed it.

The pilot's Vision was pathetic, though. This one was real! This one was about power! This one was about Anibale! He felt within himself for the Golden Gemstone and he could sense its presence. It had to be a non-physical thing, then, like the AI–ready to be used, but only by his intentions and mental energies, not a literal lever or weapon in his hand. He could use *this* kind of weapon to great advantage, though. He *knew* its power. It was potentially limitless!

Anibale got to his feet and began marching straight up the corridor and into the bridge. Out of the shadows, a man appeared ahead of him. His white hair was plastered to his head and he wore a tattered, old-style work suit. Both eyes were ancient bio-implants. His right hand was palm out, blocking his way.

Xenoplague

"Who in Ash Alien hell are you? Out of my way!" Anibale snarled. The man did not move.

"I am Old Jonas. I protect the Bottom and the Ship. I serve Elder Chau Bai. You may not pass here."

Anibale grunted and ran straight at him lowering his shoulder to push the old man over. When he contacted him, it was like running into a steel wall. Anibale bounced off the man's hand and landed back on the corridor walkway, hard on his seat. Old Jonas stood in the same spot as if nothing had happened. His hand, however, was about three times normal size and appeared to be shrinking back. Anibale realized that he had felt the collision in the vision realm as well as in his physical body. Tuning into that other mode, he could hear the ship AI chittering nervously, and a reverberation of energy that was rapidly dissipating. He could also sense the man's presence in that realm now: ghostly and cold, and full of what seemed a blue crystalline power source. He was in both worlds, just like Anibale.

He gathered himself, stood up, and reached out toward Old Jonas.

"I *will* pass you, Ghost. I *am* this ship now. I have the Power! Given to me by the True One! Stand aside or be destroyed!"

Anibale reached with his vision hand and grasped the Golden Gemstone. It surged and sparked to his touch. It was truly his to command! A feeling of pure potency rushed through him and he raised his hands, holding the Gemstone forward as it glowed with a yellow-white light. Both of Old Jonas's eyes whirred and contracted their mech-lenses. The man's hands were now outstretched in the vision world as well: enlarged and glowed white with a blue tint as they sparked and spit energy, making a loud electrical crackling sound.

"You may not pass here. I protect Chau Bai."

"Old Fool!" Anibale roared as he willed the Golden Gemstone to its maximum potency. He ran at the ancient man again and the two energy entities clashed with thunderous sounds that echoed up and down the ship's hall and cavities. In the edges of his awareness, he knew that those sounds existed only within the vision realm. With

490

his physical ears, he only heard the gruff thud of his contact and the creak and deep groans of what must be the old guard's metal bones, straining against him.

Anibale called upon the True One. "You gave me the Power! Let me overcome my enemies!"

The golden glow of his own hands, holding the Gemstone, darkened. A dramatic and alive "blackness" hovered where his hands were. It began to suck in the energy of the old man's hands, crumpling it and cracking it as it disappeared into his own Golden Darkness. He could feel it! Old Jonas also crumpled in the physical domain, his body folding and crumbling into smaller and smaller particles, the old uniform falling around the pieces until it was a heap on the walkway. An acrid smoke rose and filled the corridor.

Anibale kicked the detritus out of his way. Incredible confidence filled him now, and he straightened himself and walked briskly down the passageway toward the bridge.

"You will never control this ship, you fools!" He roared into the control room. Two shocked faces snapped around to see him. It was a most pleasurable sensation.

"Anibale! What? . . ." ZEK sputtered.

Bai stared, then yelled, "How can you be here? What did you do?"

"I am here because I have great Power. You do not understand this ship! There is an artificial intelligence that has to be engaged. You have not figured that out in twelve hundred years, Elder Bai, but I, Anibale, did! I can interface with it and control this ship."

Bai narrowed his eyes, drilling his stare into Anibale's face. "I know about the AI. I've tried to connect to it myself. Unsuccessfully, I'm afraid. You know how to connect to it? Great. Help us control it so we can fight the other plague ship and this monstrous new alien moon!"

Anibale glanced at the screens. The segments of Helm had already been ejected. They were in open space with the huge, massive alien moonlike ship or construct centered on their bow.

"Give me the Star, Bai!"

"I will not. You must work with the AI yourself. I have worked with the Star for most of my life. I can initiate the weapon and fire it! Just get us in the right position! There is no separate aiming for it. It uses the ship's attitude and shoots straight forward only. What are you staring at, ZEK? Get that propulsion restarted!" Bai shrieked.

ZEK glared at Anibale. "We don't have time for your spooky madness. We have to move this ship right now! Shut up and sit down, Anibale."

ZEK's words slapped him across the face.

Bai, staring forward again at the displays on the front wall, did not turn away as he rapidly spoke. "Don't even think about starting a fight here. We've all got a job to do. Help us do it, then we can figure the other things out."

Anibale huffed and thought about it. He wanted the Star! But he decided to reach out to the ship AI first. As he tried to calm his thoughts and felt for that presence, ZEK managed to fire the engines and get the ship moving. As their ship rotated, the incredible plane-toid-sized ship passed out of their frontal target center as the other xenoplague ship, the one with Kera still in it, he supposed, just began to slide into the edge of their view. It was not very far away. Bai held the Star with one hand while trying to operate a virtual control with the other. The Star was glowing dark red, now, and Bai yelped with excitement.

"It's on! I'm into the beam weapon protocols!"

A familiar face broke in on the comm screen. Kera looked angry and a little bit scared.

Anibale grinned. Out of your depth now, eh, middie Farms girl?

"Stop this madness, ZEK!" she said. "We have not used our terraform beam as a weapon. Do not be the first to do so! Stand down and surrender your ship to the people of Harbor!"

Off-comm, ZEK said, "Don't speak to her. Shoot her instead, Bai. Give her our answer."

Sweat gleamed on Bai's bald forehead. He squeaked with excitement as they all felt the terraform beam revving up its powers. The

Star glowed fiercely in vibrant reds and blues and the walls around them were sequencing through a complex series of animated color hues. Anibale could feel it directly through the energy of the Golden Gemstone and the feedback loops he could tentatively connect to from the AI. The damnable plague weapon–the original one!– was active. He tried to grab onto the control stream within the vision space and the weapon suddenly burst to life, shooting sputtering bits of white plasma-like energy into the space directly in front of the ship! They were staccato blips, not a steady stream, and they widely missed the monster ship target. By the time Kera's plague ship drifted on to become centered in their sites, the beam had failed.

Anibale was livid. "I knew it! Let me have the Star! I can fire the weapon if you let go!"

"NO. I can fire it again! Let me . . ."

"LOOK!" ZEK shouted. "The monster ship!"

The interruption was enough to make them stop and look at the monitor. The immense alien ship that had been lurking at the farther edges of their system was abruptly and instantly *here*. Close enough to dwarf everything else in their screens. It made the other plague ship look tiny! Kera's ship was under power now, trying to remove themselves from the axis of Anibale's ship, but the gigantic ship behind them was too big to maneuver like that. It was monstrously huge, but that also made it a large *target!*

Anibale had had enough of arguing. Who knew what weaponry that ship had or what it might do in the next moments! He put his hand around the Golden Gemstone in his vision world and tightened his grip, sending black and golden sparking energy from that place into this physical one as he reached for the Star controller. The ship AI jerked and stuttered, seeming to look at him with consternation and injury. The ship's engines failed. The Old Star, gripped by Bai's two hands and still glowing, vibrated and began to drift toward Anibale's outstretched hands here in the bridge, dragging the man bodily since he would not let go. Bai's face was strained as he desperately gripped the two horizontal struts. The silver pods on the ends of the struts had withdrawn and the Star continued to move across the few meters separating them. It moved slowly and under strain as if it were mired in muck. But it came.

Bai began to shriek again. "NO! Let go! The Star is *mine!* You can't take it from me!"

"Stop fighting over it! The power is out and we're drifting again!" ZEK yelled.

The Star reached him! Anibale grabbed it, trying to knock Bai's hands loose, but instead, they both became entangled in it. Their hands seemed magnetically bound and sank into the blinding white and red struts. Panic erupted on Bai's face.

"Bhat and Quinn! We are doomed!" he wailed.

Now that he held it, too, Anibale reached through the other-dimensional portal the Star had opened for him and he quickly envisioned the problem with the engines. They were confused by incomplete and competing commands. It would be complicated to straighten that out quickly, but he pushed at them with his mind and they sputtered into motion again. The AI was also much more clear to him now that he held the Star. It, too, was a mess, fractured and torn in many places. It was damage not only from today's foray, he realized, but also lingering scars from the original fiasco that ended with Earth's destruction, and probably a lot of amateur experimenting by Bai and his ilk over the centuries. This AI was a mental case.

He spoke through gritted teeth. "ZEK, use the side engine pods to put us back on target for the damned monster ship. I don't know how long I can keep them functioning."

ZEK had been entranced watching his and Bai's struggle. Now, he humphed and turned back to the controls. The ship had drifted on around in a stately circle and they could see the nine separated segments of Helm still drifting apart and receding rapidly in their slightly differing orbits. His home world of Harbor passed below them, beautiful in its patchwork of Suite designated zones and sporting light swirls of summer clouds. His own Suite Blue sector was just coming into the dawn. They needed to continue the ship

494

rotation to face the planetoid-sized AA ship again. He would deal with Kera and the other plague ship later.

Bai still struggled and Anibale wished he could just strike the old man with his fist, but he couldn't let go of the Star–and if he tried, he thought it might not let go of him.

"It's coming into range!" ZEK called. "Can you fire it? Can either of you fire our weapon? Here it comes now! FIRE it!" he screamed.

Bai sent some crude commands to the AI, all he had ever figured out how to do, Anibale supposed. It was worse than nothing. He must take control right this second.

I hold the Golden Gemstone and the Star. I am the Power. I am the True One! I shall prevail!

He felt the great stone in his hands, even though his physical ones were locked into the Star. It was his Tool! He compressed it with all his might and Bai yelped like he had been stuck with a knife.

"Fire it *now*, before we pass the target!" ZEK yelled.

Anibale felt for the beam weapon. The AI tried to throw up obstacles to him: pieces of programming that required top-level overrides and routines that were attempting to perform cross-check tasks that were damaged and fragmenting. He pushed harder, over-riding it all with brute, overwhelming force. The beam weapon–whether it was truly for terraforming or not–Anibale did not really care at this point–burst back into white, roaring life.

Their rotation brought the furious beam into contact with the edge of the looming, monstrous AA moonlet directly. As the beam struck and burned into the damned thing, the huge sphere suddenly and dramatically *burst*, causing millions of shreds to rapidly retreat and shrink away from the searing impact point. Gasses roiled where the immense rampart once stood, flaming out in bright yellows and blackish reds until it all went dark again. Billions of tiny glints flickered away from the area where the wall had just been. The terraform beam was still blasting through the remains, sweeping away toward its central point as their own ship rotated. ZEK added some thrust.

"Dead on it! We got them!" he hooted.

"No, ZEK. We achieved nothing at all," Anibale said, his voice dead with the realization of what just happened. ZEK snapped his head around.

"What do you mean? We destroyed them!"

"It was a ruse, ZEK. Same one I fell for before. Not once, but twice. Third time pays all. It was a fake ship, a damnable *balloon*, you idiot. We popped it with the damnable *plague weapon!*"

As the white-hot plague beam continued to spew its destruction, there was a true explosion deeper inside where the thing had been.

"But, it has mass! Look, there's a shock wave of debris coming."

Anibale looked through the Star. There was, indeed, some mass debris on the way. They had to have had some mass in that thing. That's what just went up, and now it was flying out in all directions. A quick analysis confirmed it wasn't enough to hole them or any of the other ships or Helm segments, so Anibale dismissed it from his mind.

"It's going to pass us without problems, ZEK. I can't stop the weapon beam now. We may never get it running again. We've stopped rotation again. Aim the ship toward Kera! We have to take out the queen bee! But, watch out for the sweep path of that beam! Keep it away from Harbor!" He watched as ZEK started to make the maneuver. Bai was limp, depending from the Star by his entrapped hands, but he was not unconscious. He was whimpering.

The roaring terraform beam continued to spew toward the now absent moonlet, but before ZEK could get them rotating once again, the ship's engines died. Anibale tried to restart them with another push, but it was hopeless. Bai woke up and began to pull at him and the Star again.

"It's coming! The debris wave!" he croaked.

"It won't harm us, fool. Stop flailing around."

"NO, you don't understand the danger. Turn off the beam!"

Just at that instant, the debris wave hit them. They couldn't physically hear anything inside their ship, but through the Star and the AI, Anibale felt like he was being pelted with hailstones. In a few moments, it was mostly over. The bow wave had passed them.

"See, Bai? I told you."

"Shut it off, Anibale, Prime Blue! Shut it off *now*," Bai cried.

ZEK said, "Shut it off, Anibale. Bai is right!"

He looked at ZEK and then at the screens. They were moving again. The debris! It was the pelting that gave them enough momentum to drift–to start rotating again, out of control. The engines still would not respond to him. The drift was slow but inexorable. Their massive, unleashed beam of destruction was still firing, belching its white death into space.

Harbor was coming into view.

Anibale frantically threw himself back into the vision space and tried to stop the beam. He squeezed the Golden Gemstone. He tried to interface with the AI. The beam did not stop. He could not stop it. The AI was spouting gibberish. With only part of his mind paying attention to the bridge reality, he heard but did not see Elder Bai screaming.

"No! Turn it off! Turn it off! ZEK! Anibale! . . . it is the PLAGUE . . ."

A strong tug on the Star made him refocus on the bridge. ZEK yanked on Bai's arms, yelling at him and slapping him hard across the face. He grabbed the old charlatan around his waist and with one final heave, Bai's connection to the Star broke with a snap. He and ZEK fell into a smoking jumble on the floor.

Anibale did not move. He still held the Star by its spars. It glowed brighter now that the obstruction of Bai's hands was cleared away. He heard a dark voice echoing deep in the alien distances of his mind. "*You are responsible.*"

"It is too late," he spoke into the room.

Anibale watched the forward screen as it revealed the unceasing, furious white eruption of the beam as it first touched the atmosphere of his own world and began its devastating slice across Suite Red, Suite Blue, and beyond.

"You fools," he said.

Chapter Forty-one

The bridge of his AA terraform ship seemed downright homey to Marc after their harrowing escape from Helm, but tensions had increased in the last few minutes as they watched ZEK and Bai's old T-ship sputter to life and succeed in emitting some burps of terraform beam from its now glowing maw. Those thankfully did not last and Marc hoped fervently that the Elite leaders were struggling unsuccessfully with the beam and the AI. Their ship rotated now in a way that looked uncontrolled to his experienced pilot's eye.

"Sil and RR are back in place with the armada," he said. "I sure hope I get to meet Paul before they take him home. Paris, check that feed. The BlackMils are still standing off. They don't want to get caught up in this battle of the Big Ships,"

He and Leenah had been intercepted by the bot pod Kera sent and they were returned to the T-ship without further problems. Since arriving, they had been sitting closely side by side, holding onto each other, watching the pimfruit sections of Helm float further apart

Xenoplague

and settle into safe orbits. He was certain they would never forget their strange flight in their power suits and the stunning sight of the other terraform ship revealed at what had been the center of Helm, appearing like some god child's gigantic surprise-box toy. It had taken a moment to register what he was seeing. A T-ship, just like theirs! But wait, no–it had to be, could only be, the *original* T-ship, the very one that destroyed Earth over a millennium ago!

And, I thought we had all the surprises in *our* pockets today.

"Leenah! The Visions! Yours and mine!" he had said over the suit comm.

"Oh, Marc! Yes!" Leenah had answered.

There, below them, they had seen Harbor, green and white and blue, filling much of their in-system view. Closer to them was the Terraform Ship–the very same one that destroyed Earth. Then a cloud of BlackMil warships and other Harbor ships. In the opposing direction, their own T-ship hovered close to them. Far beyond it, the huge fake AA ship remained in a more distant orbit, yet incredibly impressive and intimidating. Closer in, the huge armada of Sisters, Rindder, and Harbor warships faced the scene below them.

He and Leenah had floated there in space, each alone, isolated in their powered suits, centered directly between the two opposing jaws of the greatest conflict in the history of the Second Domain–perhaps in all of human history.

"At least we're wearing suits this time," Leenah had said.

Marc shook his head at these memories as he looked up from the control panel to the main screen here in their T-ship. It was filled with a view of his huge fake moonlike balloon. He was still kind of stunned at the psychologically affecting mini-jump RR had arranged for it. It was so close in now that it appeared to be an endless wall of metal. It leaped into this extremely close orbit after shedding most of its mass by closing the Gate Weapon-type device in its center. All the star mass, or whatever the Zips had brought in, disappeared back to whichever universe it came from. Now, the thing was instantly here, right in the face of ZEK and Bai. It looked daunting enough to

500

scare Marc.

And it was my idea and RR's design. I'd love to see ZEK's face right about now.

He noted a scan of a Zip ship sitting in Harbor System's outer zones. It wasn't doing anything out there, and he assumed they were the Zip audience for this crazy human drama.

Kera sat next to him, holding the Star. He saw her flinch. Behind him, Leenah let out a little yelp.

Paris, sitting at the scans to his left, said, "What's wrong? I felt something weird in the SD."

Leenah said, "It's the other T-ship. They are close enough now that we're able to pick up some of their AI's energy. It's hurting! It's really upset!"

"Yes, it is damaged," Kera said. "Quite severely and probably terminally. She is screaming."

"Look!" Paris said.

The terrible terraform beam had started again. This time, it was steady and did not falter or sputter. Somehow, they had gotten it to work. Kera had taken them out of the ecliptic the Old T-ship's rotation was presenting, so they were not in immediate danger of being hit by it. The other, more distant middie ships that happened to be in line were also scrambling to get off the projected sweep path. The white beam inexorably swept around until it approached the fake ship, then at the first touch, the massive balloon instantly disintegrated. A central bulk of leftover debris flew out of the thing in a spherical cloud. It would reach them in a few minutes.

Marc said, "I wish Anibale could have seen this. He'd be apoplectic!"

Kera turned to him with a strange look. "I think he just did, Marc. He's on that T-ship with ZEK and Elder Bai."

"What? You're sure? Take me to what you are sensing."

Marc closed his eyes and felt his way into his SD vision space. Leenah was here, too, and Kera's strong presence was easy to lock onto. They approached the other ship, reaching out feelers for the men on board. The SD roar of the beam and the raving chatter of the AI were hard to take and difficult to filter through, but he could distinctly sense the presence of all three of the Elites in the ship's bridge. Anibale was the strongest spot. He was holding their Star and had something else, some other power device. They quickly pulled back, but not before Marc knew that their engine had just quit.

"They're dead in space. No engine. Be alert now. Here comes the debris wave," Marc said, eyes open and watching on their screens. It hit and passed them with no problems. He watched as it struck the old T-ship.

"Look, they're rotating again–slowly but rotating," Leenah said.

Kera turned to her screen. "That beam is wild. They need to shut it down!"

"Maybe they can't," Marc said.

"Projection," Paris called out. "The terraform beam hits Harbor in less than a minute."

Kera pulled the Star close and it began to glow bright red. "Get us turned around, Marc! I may have to use ours to prevent another massive disaster!"

"Going! But I don't know if we can line ourselves up fast enough! We have to shoot outbound, too, so *we* don't hit the planet. These terraformers were never meant to be *weapons*, damn it. Everyone secure yourselves. This may get shaky."

The vector changes he put them through were severe and the g-forces made their heads hurt. He got the ship lower than ZEK's and turned so they could shoot it, but it was too late to prevent what they had feared the most. The awful white column touched the limb of Harbor and began its stroke of total destruction across the face of the planet.

Kera yelled. "Get me in position, Marc! Got to take them out before it goes any farther!"

Marc made a final adjustment and *willed* the ship to be still and steady for Kera. She wasted no time, calling up the same ancient Ash Alien technology–one designed to repair and enhance life–to obliterate its own twin. The insane roar of their own terraform beam ripped through the ship bi-modally, causing Leenah and Paris to instinctively cover their ears.

The Old Ship, carrying ZEK, Elder Bai, and Anibale, Prime Blue, ceased to exist and the beam from that ship stopped in that same instant, having at least partially done its lamentable work upon the planet full of Elites and middies below.

In the stunned quiet that followed the smooth shutdown of their own beam, everyone sat still for some time. Then, Sil's voice came softly over the comms.

"Repeating their original sin, but now upon themselves."

They gathered at Helm. Marc had been able to speak with RR and to meet Paul Bennett before he was returned to New Anchorage, but RR had to get busy with the job of organizing the Rindd engineering staff to retrieve the segments of Helm and re-assemble them. Fortunately, those were designed in a non-destructive modular way by the ancient Commander Bhat, so it was not as difficult a task as originally anticipated. They put the pieces back together and set Helm on a stable orbit again and left it to others to clean up the messes caused by the tremors and separation. He also worked with his Zip contacts to shut down the Hub Gate blocking device and open all trade lanes again. He said the Zips found the entire drama interesting and amusing.

Most of those who had remained in Helm's segments survived with surprisingly few serious injuries or deaths other than the horrific spacing of the crowd that was in the docks area when it was exposed. The Great Seat survived as well, although it was littered with gemstones and shattered pieces of carved paneling. Sil had some of his servicemen secure the huge hall until order could be restored.

Leenah had been crushed to learn of Brioleee's transition, but it came as a true shock to her, Marc, and the others when Sil informed them that nearly all the Gossamers who helped make the ship-jumps to Harbor from Hub were no longer in our tangible dimension. Even the Doctor, Tonhaaa, lived in SD modality only now, but as with Brioleee, all of them were happy and held no regrets for the help they gave to save not just Harbor's worlds, but also their own green paradise of Gossamer.

The world of Harbor was a great and costly loss. The terraform beam did not have time to complete its program, nor was it centered properly on its target world, but it still managed to rip the surface apart, the damage propagating around the planet and meeting itself on the other side. As with old Earth, there were no survivors. During the final days of the conflict, most of the Color Suite Elites had retreated to the seeming relative safety of their Harbor zones and lands. This had the effect, unintended as it certainly was, of eliminating most of the existing political structure that underpinned the old Harbor Elites system–the very ones who represented most of what had become corrupt. There were no more Primes, no more ZEK. A few of the Council of Colors Seniors survived, remaining on Helm as it flew apart, but the overall political structures were simply wiped clear.

Marc knew that this would not mean a simple transition for Harbor humanity away from their old and very traditionalized ways of thinking and acting. That's part of what they had discussed back on Marc's Pile when Paris outlined her Pact. It was time, now, to put that into place so order could be restored throughout the Second Domain.

Several Harbor standard days later, once all involved could reconvene on Helm, Sil called a governmental conference in the office areas that once belonged to ZEK and his Suite Green staff. Marc held Leenah's hand as they entered the large conference room. There was a good energy in the room, but the tone was somber. Some of the priceless artwork ZEK had enjoyed was propped casually on the floor or still hung askew on the leathered walls, but it didn't matter. Kera was already here, along with Paris, RR, and many others, most of whom Marc knew only by comm viewscreens or by name.

Marc stood before them all, grinning when they praised him for his leadership and strength in the events just concluded. He re-committed his coalition to the standards begun by their pact, leaving Kera in charge here at Helm to rebuild and reshape a new form of government, knowing it would take time and patience. The people would require, on many levels, a strong figurehead as well as a strong political operative to lead them now, and Kera was both. She had proven her strength and proven that it was, indeed, her own, earned with wisdom and heartbreak. Her role in the Great Seat incident, appearing in her own Golden Faces, was as famous now across the worlds as Marc's original showdown with ZEK.

Finally, they agreed to institute a new Council of Colors, but to rename it as the White Council. It would represent all the worlds of the Second Domain, and, most importantly, all the people of humanity instead of just a few with unearned privilege. The White Hall would no longer be a secretive enclave, but open to all for official use and just to enter and visit.

Sil made sure to emphasize the mandate from their alliance for Marc and Leenah to take on a program of exploration, once their duties in the restorations here at Harbor and Helm were complete. They would take the T-ship and explore the Lines and Gates system of the ancient Ash Aliens in detail and a depth never before accomplished or dreamed of because now they would be doing so bi-modally and with the willing help of the restored Ship AI. They would operate in both tangible and spirit dimensions, the way most of Sil's people believe the Ash Aliens themselves always did. Their research into SD itself would be a major component of this and would be made public through Sil's SisterSon of Frahma Institute.

RR expressed a desire to research human FTL in light of SD knowledge and the insights gained from working with the Zips. The Zips were another field of inquiry all in itself, of course, and Marc thought his friend had a lot of work cut out for himself.

Paris requested relief from her official role as Marc's bodyguard and was eager to travel back to Florinda where Sil said she would be welcomed with honors and open arms for all her service.

For all their satisfaction and organization efforts, though, Marc could tell that the people here in Helm, and surely also those on the scattered worlds of the Harbor Systems, were fundamentally upset, curious, and intrinsically wary of this massive change. They would have to proceed very carefully to try to reestablish trade, develop transitions for legal situations, and slowly institute the progressive ideas and life paradigms developed by the Sisters, supplemented and enhanced by Rindd's achievements and technical prowess, and with the heart and the robust energy of all the Harbor middies on all these many worlds from Gossamer to Farms to Maiko's Mars.

Kera would have the largest and most difficult oversight and planning job of all of them, but then, that's what she wanted and signed up for, Marc thought.

Seven days later, a ceremony to officially install Kera was held in the Great Seat. Some repairs had been made, but the huge hall was still a mess in many ways. The Golden Screen was mostly intact and the swirled marble floor where so much history had taken place was unbroken. People were milling around down there and also up in the galleries on each side when Marc and Leenah escorted Kera to the hall and on into the backstage area.

A young technician came nervously toward Kera as she stood outside the operations booth where ZEK would connect to his Faces on the Screen. He demurred, looking down at first, then tentatively spoke to her.

"The Main Face is operational, Commander, but the Auxiliary Faces are not. I'm afraid you will also need to be bio-engineered to be able to accept the shunts."

She looked him in the eye and smiled.

"Son, you weren't here the day Paul Bennett arrived and ZEK departed, were you?" she said. "I don't need the shunts, but I think I would like to sit here in the operations booth where I can see the comm screens until I'm on."

The young man was utterly nonplussed. He didn't know what else to say, so he nervously nodded and bowed at the same time, then turned and almost ran away, further backstage.

Leenah took Marc's hand and they went out into the main floor. The ceremony was starting and every seat in the galleries was now taken. Many more had crowded down onto the main floor until the guards had to limit the number. Most were middies, never having been allowed on this very privileged floor before unless they were in severe trouble, something Marc could attest to. Many of them recognized him and wanted to talk to him, but he gently rebuffed them, pointing to the Golden Screen of ZEK. A few Suite members, Elites, were here, too, and Leenah picked out some of the surviving Council members sitting in their accustomed boxes.

A gong sounded and the room hushed. Every eye here was on the Golden Screen, anticipating Kera's appearance, all hoping to witness again what they saw in those recent great events.

Suddenly, the Golden Screen came to life. Kera's resplendent Face appeared in the main center disc. When she last appeared here, it had looked more lifelike than the regular Face of ZEK and Marc had heard many people talking about it and hoping to see it for themselves. This time, it was far more impressive. Marc knew that Kera had reached into SD space to present something that did not rely on the shunt technology and could manifest in ways no 3D projection, bio-engineered or not, could ever do. It would serve to establish her image as a leader that surpassed all the previous ZEKs and symbolized a true change in things going forward.

Kera's Face projected out from the disc as a true person's face would. It just happened to be tens of meters high and fully golden. Not painted gold, but inherently golden from the inside out. It was as if Gold itself had come to life. She blazed a smile around the Great Seat and then the four smaller Faces came alive as well, exhibiting the same lifelike effect. She had them look in different directions across the crowd as she beamed that marvelous smile from each of them.

Cheers went up and the crowd rose to their feet with applause and shouts. It lasted long minutes and Kera simply waited patiently until it began to die down. She started to speak, but someone in the audience yelled, "ZEK!"

Others took up the traditional acclamation cry. "ZEK! ZEK! ZEK! ZEK!" The sound swirled around the great hall like the colors on the marble floor below Marc and Leenah's feet. Kera's smile did not stop, but it softened into a more serious look. Her eyes were bright and piercing, seeming to stab right through every single person in the Seat and across all the worlds where this was being broadcast.

Finally, the shouts of ZEK calmed down until there was silence again.

Kera looked out at her people and said in a booming voice, "I am not ZEK!"

The silence continued, but now there were murmurs and confused whispers. Heads turned to one another and back to the Golden Screen. When these things had settled back down, Kera spoke again. "ZEK is dead. I say again. I am not ZEK."

Her voice rang off the jeweled walls and the rich wooden panels.

"I am KERA."

Mankind, at last, raised the courage to
Penetrate Nature's remotest doors. Thus,
With energy and intelligence, he transpierced
The flaming limits of the Universe.
All its greatness, his open mind examined:
Finding what could be done and what could not.
Seeing that each finite thing has its form, nor can
Any thing alter from its natural form.
And so, Superstition, trampled, lies beneath us
As we rear our Trophies to the Skies.

DE RERUM NATURA (fragment), Lucretius. 75 BCE, Rome, Earth
– First Domain.

Far, far, O Earth, on distant paths
Your children sing and venture out
On myriad Ways built by Others.
A new Nature discovered with forms unseen.
Realms behind dreams await our desires.
To insight succumb our lulling beliefs,
A new vision and an endless fountain giving forth.
We Go.

Who shall speak for the ones who are silent?
We shall sing for them with our journeys.
Who shall sing for those who were lost?
We shall speak for them with our songs.
And with our songs, both heard and unheard,
We Create.

ArchSinger Nalaaan Deeev. 1,385 2D, Gossamer (Greater Sisters Systems)
– Second Domain.
Translation: Leenah Bordu, *Senior, SisterSon of Frahma Institute, Florinda.*

Acknowledgments:

My first and special thanks go to my talented sister, Judy K. C. Brown, for her excellent work and professional skills as my editor, but also for the happy encouragement over all these years for writing and reading, especially science fiction, of which, she is also a talented author. Any lingering mistakes, errors, or questionable judgements are strictly my own.

I'd like to thank the late, great L. Sprague de Camp and Catherine Crook de Camp for encouraging me in my dream to be a writer of science fiction when I had the opportunity to spend a few days with them in the 1980's. It finally took.

I would also like to express appreciation to the spirit and memory of another of my author idols, Roger Zelazny, for remembered kind personal words of encouragement. Also for similar kindness and encouragement from George R. R. Martin, with whom I spent a fascinating day back in the summer of 1982.

Thanks to my friend, Paul Greenway, for listening to me talk about my novel for years before getting to read it. Writing a novel is a solitary occupation, indeed, until the shipbuilding is done and the vessel sails from its haven port into the minds and hearts of others.

Many thanks also to my beta readers and online supporters.

Finally, muchas gracias to the great spirit plant, Mother Ayahuasca, for lovingly kicking me out of my old life-cocoon and providing me the impetus to overcome my fears and wake up and follow my dreams. To be truly fulfilling, life must be composed of both tangible and spiritual dimensions. Each of those, however, must be the real thing.

David P. Crews
Las Cruces, New Mexico
November, 2024

About the Author:

David P. Crews

David Crews has enjoyed a life-long love affair with science fiction. From gleeful immersion in children's SF and fantasy, to reading and collecting thousands of science fiction books throughout his life, one goal always beckoned: to write.

In his college years in the 1980s, he co-produced a nationally syndicated radio program about science fiction and its authors called "The Science Fiction Radio Show." David was able to interview and interact with most of the authors of the time including Ray Bradbury, Larry Niven, James Hogan, and in-person interviews and encounters with Roger Zelazny, Fred Saberhagen, L. Sprague de Camp, and George R. R. Martin. The interviews along with many others were published in two book volumes as "The Sound of Wonder" in 1985.

For over five decades, David has been an award-winning broadcast and cable commercial television director/editor, motion graphics artist, and animator. He runs his own post-production video and music company, CrewsCreative. He is also an award-winning independent filmmaker, having completed his first feature-length documentary, A Circle in the Desert (ACircleInTheDesert.com), which has garnered over 45 international film festival awards for Best Documentary, Nature Film, Inspirational Film, Cinematography, and more. He is also a composer of electronic music and with full virtual symphony orchestra. He has won a number of awards for Best Original Score or Best Composer, including ten for the feature film.

David has also been a national broadcast voice talent for over fifty years, including thousands of television commercials and programs, and has served as a long-time on-air radio host, including eleven years at KMFA-FM, the all-classical radio station in Austin, Texas. His voice has been heard worldwide through iHeart Radio and other streaming services.

David is also the author of nonfiction books, essays, and blogs on archaic religion, shamanistic practices, and entheogens. He has a serious interest in tribal shamanism and the use of ancient and sacred visionary plant medicines. He has traveled to the Amazon jungle three times over a twenty-year period to work with tribal and mestizo medicine men and women and the most potent whole-plant spirit medicines on the planet, particularly ayahuasca and huachuma. In his earlier life, David wrote and published an influential book on New Testament interpretation.

In 2020, he compiled a life collection of his poetry into a volume titled "A Path of Poems," which is forthcoming as a published book. His publishing imprint is JaguarFeather Publishing.

Originally from West Texas, David worked through his career in Odessa, Dallas, and primarily in Austin, Texas. He now lives, plays, and works, and creates his fiction, films, and music next to the ruggedly beautiful Organ Mountains of the high Chihuahuan Desert in Las Cruces, New Mexico.

Visit the Official Website for a Full Color MAP
to refer to while reading Xenoplague.
Also, lots of extras, exclusive graphics, and information!

Join our email list for updates, extra content, and information about
future stories.

www.DavidPCrews.com/author

As an independent publisher and author, your authentic personal
reviews are very important to our success! Please leave a review
wherever you purchased your copy of Xenoplague!

You can also send your review or comments directly to us at:

david@davidpcrews.com

www.ingramcontent.com/pod-product-compliance
Lightning Source LLC
Chambersburg PA
CBHW052348020726
47503CB00001B/161